Nicolaus Wecklein, Aeschylus, Frederic D. Allen

The Prometheus Bound of Aeschylus

and the fragments of the Prometheus unbound

Nicolaus Wecklein, Aeschylus, Frederic D. Allen

The Prometheus Bound of Aeschylus
and the fragments of the Prometheus unbound

ISBN/EAN: 9783337382957

Printed in Europe, USA, Canada, Australia, Japan

Cover: Foto ©Andreas Hilbeck / pixelio.de

More available books at **www.hansebooks.com**

COLLEGE SERIES OF GREEK AUTHORS

EDITED UNDER THE SUPERVISION OF

JOHN WILLIAMS WHITE AND THOMAS D. SEYMOUR.

THE

PROMETHEUS BOUND

OF AESCHYLUS

AND THE FRAGMENTS OF THE PROMETHEUS UNBOUND

WITH INTRODUCTION AND NOTES

BY

N. WECKLEIN

RECTOR OF THE MAXIMILIAN GYMNASIUM IN MUNICH

TRANSLATED BY

F. D. ALLEN

PROFESSOR IN HARVARD UNIVERSITY

BOSTON, U.S.A., AND LONDON
PUBLISHED BY GINN & COMPANY
1897

NOTE.

THIS book is a translation of Wecklein's second edition (1878), with such changes in text and commentary as were requested by Dr. Wecklein himself. The translator has allowed himself some freedom in the form of expression, but he has not knowingly departed from the substance of the original, and still less has he anywhere substituted his own views for those of the German editor. In the transcription of the metrical schemes into the notation commonly used in this country, his responsibility is somewhat greater than elsewhere, but here too he has endeavored to follow the editor's intentions. Two transpositions of parts of the Introduction and Appendix have been made, in conformity to the arrangement of other books of this Series. References to American grammatical works have been added, and in some cases these have replaced the original references to Krüger.

The thanks of the translator are due to Dr. Wecklein for his permission to make the translation and for his hearty co-operation in the work, and to the editors of this Series for efficient aid and timely corrections.

iii

INTRODUCTION.

I. The Myth of Prometheus before Aeschylus.

To the mind of the savage man, the generation of fire, when a tree is struck by lightning from the sky, or a spark elicited from a piece of wood by friction, is not simply a marvel, but a miracle. And the operation too of this same fire seems to him a miracle. Fire is the celestial agency which aids man in all the arts of life — in whatever he fashions and creates. The possession of fire, and the knowledge how to use it in the preparation of food and the practice of the mechanic arts, lift a community out of a condition of savagery and advance it to a life of culture and comfort. As man grows in independence, in self-consciousness, as he feels in himself the ability to guard against misfortune by his own prudence, as his standard of living and thinking is raised, he becomes aware of a distinct break with his past life — its uncertainties, its hampered conditions and its narrow horizon. What formerly he expected from the grace of the gods, and sought to obtain through sacrifices, he now believes that he can get by his own skill. Accordingly this transition from barbarism to civilization comes to be associated with the idea of a Titan-like struggle on the part of men to make themselves equal to God — with the notion of a curtailment of divine privileges for the advantage of the human race, and of defiance and revolt against the gods.

Out of these conceptions, the story of Prometheus, in its various shapes, has gradually grown. The origin of this myth is to be sought in the time when the Indo-European peoples still formed one community.[1] Fire comes in two ways. Either it descends from the sky as a flash of lightning and kindles a tree or shrub, or

[1] Compare Adalbert Kuhn's *The Descent of Fire* (*die Herabkunft des Feuers und des Göttertranks*), Berlin, 1859. See also Georg Curtius, *Greek Etymology*, p. 335 (5th edit.).

it is obtained by friction. The first is the older way and furnishes
the rudiments of the myth. In the ancient Hindu legend, Agni, the
divine impersonation of fire, is brought down to mortals from
the sky. In one account, having disappeared from the earth, he
is brought back from the abode of the gods by Mātariçvan, and
given to the Bhṛgus; in another the divine flame is brought to the
world from a cave among the Bhṛgus; in a third form of the story,
the Bhṛgus themselves fetch the fire-god and deliver him to mankind. The Bhṛgus are the lightning; the word means 'bright,'
'flashing,' from the root *bhrāǵ-*, akin to that of φλέγω and *fulgeo*.
Elsewhere Agni himself is called Mātariçvan; this rests on the
primitive conception that the fire itself, as lightning, descends of
its own accord upon the earth. A frequent surname of Agni is
Pramati, that is, 'Forethought,' 'Providence.'

But fire was obtained, in ancient times, by the twirling motion
of a wooden rod bearing upon the centre of a wheel or disk
of wood, — a method practised in India to the present day in
kindling the pure sacrificial fire. The twirling stick or drill was
called *pramanthas* (from *math-*, *manth-*, *mathāmi*, 'turn,' 'twirl');
and this word is the ultimate source of the name Προμηθεύς.[1]

These two conceptions of the origin of fire, became, in the course
of time, more or less combined and fused. The 'fire-drill'
προμηθεύς came to be identified with Agni Pramati and Mātariçvan; the fire-borer was metamorphosed into a provident fire-
bringer, who kindled an inflammable shrub at the fire of the sky
and brought it down to the earth. So arose the Greek notion
of a 'Forethinker' Prometheus, of vaguely defined nature, but
thought of rather as superhuman than divine, who steals fire from
the chariot of the Sun, from the hearth of Zeus, or from the forge
of Hephaestus, brings it to men in a tinder-stalk (νάρθηξ; see note
on verse 109 of the play), and so becomes the founder of human
civilization.

In the Attic religious system, Prometheus appears as simple
god of civilization, in intimate union with Hephaestus and Athena.
Just outside of Athens was the Κολωνὸς ἵππιος, a hill sacred to

---

[1] The Thurians venerated a Zeus Προμανθεύς. See Lycophr. 537, and
scholia.

Poseidon, which furnished the potters' quarter of the city, the Κεραμεικός, with admirable clay for the famous and much-sought Attic vases. Between this hill and the city lay the Academy, the sacred grove of the hero Academus. Here Prometheus was worshipped in conjunction with Hephaestus and Athena. In the space dedicated to the goddess Athena stood an old statue of Prometheus, with an altar. At the entrance was a pedestal with a relief representing Prometheus and Hephaestus. Prometheus was here figured as the more prominent and older god, with a sceptre in his hand; Hephaestus as younger and less important. On the same pedestal a common altar of the two deities was represented. In honor of Prometheus the festival called Προμήθεια was annually celebrated, with a torch-race (λαμπαδηφορία, λαμπαδηδρομία) from the Academy to the city. The torches were lighted at the altar of Prometheus, and the runners endeavored to outstrip each other without extinguishing their torches.[1] This solemnity is the remnant of an exceedingly ancient religious observance — the Renewal of Fire. The idea of a difference between pure, celestial fire and fire which has been defiled by human use is common to the Indo-European nations; and this notion led to the custom of replacing, from time to time, the polluted fire in house and workshop by the pure element, in the belief that this would bring renewed prosperity. How the torch-race arose from this usage, can best be seen from the following story, told by Plutarch in his life of Aristides, chapter 20. When the Greeks, after the battle of Plataea, consulted the Delphic oracle respecting the sacrifices they should make, the god gave directions that, as the fire in that region had been polluted by the barbarians, no sacrifices should be made until it had all been extinguished and fresh fire brought from the common hearth at Delphi. On this, the leaders of the Greeks ordered all fire throughout that country to be quenched, and the Plataean Euchidas proceeded to Delphi, promising to bring the new fire from the Delphic sanctuary with all possible despatch. He purified himself, sprinkled himself with holy water, and put a chaplet of laurel on his head.

---

[1] Schol. Soph. *Oed. Col.* 56; Pausanias i., 30. 2.

Taking the fire from the altar, he set out at full speed for Plataea, and arrived there the same day before sunset, having traversed a distance of a thousand stadia. He had only strength to greet his fellow-townsmen and give them the fire, when he fell to the ground and breathed his last. It was thought needful, we see, that the transportation of the fire should be as rapid as possible, so that its original purity might be preserved, and a continuity, as it were, established between the altar at Delphi and the new hearth at Plataea. In like manner at Athens the pure fire was taken from the altar of Prometheus and borne with the utmost despatch into the city to the quarter of the smiths and the potters. It is clear that at Athens Prometheus was a fire-god who stood in a very intimate relation to the handicrafts of the place.[1] He is mentioned with veneration by the citizen of Colonus in Sophocles's *Oedipus at Colonus*, verse 54 ff.:

χῶρος μὲν ἱερὸς πᾶς ὅδ᾽ ἐστ᾽· ἔχει δέ νιν
σεμνὸς Ποσειδῶν ἠδ᾽ ὁ πυρφόρος θεὸς
Τιτὰν Προμηθεύς.

Elsewhere a certain trait of insubordination and defiance attaches to Prometheus. Even in the Hindu legends we find the Bhṛgu characterized by this trait, and are reminded of the description in the *Homeric Hymns*[2] of the Greek Phlegyes, the counterpart of the Bhṛgus:

ἷξες δ᾽ ἐς Φλεγύων ἀνδρῶν πόλιν ὑβριστάων,
οἳ Διὸς οὐκ ἀλέγοντες ἐπὶ χθονὶ ναιετάασκον
ἐν καλῇ βήσσῃ Κηφισίδος ἐγγύθι λίμνης.

In the Hesiodic poetry (*Theogony*, 535 ff., *Works and Days*, 47 ff.) we find the myth of Prometheus detailed at length, but curiously interwoven with ethical ideas and overlaid with additions made with evident design. A naïve, peasant-like conception of civilization here finds expression, as something which has led men into resistance to the divine will, and so has brought evil into the world by way of retribution. In the *Theogony* the story runs thus:

[1] Compare Wecklein's essay on the torch-race, in *Hermes*, Vol. vii., pp. 437–452.

[2] ii., 100, ed. Baumeister.

'When gods and mortal men were divided[1] at Mecone, then the artful, crafty-souled Prometheus, son of the Titan Iapetus and of Clymene, brother of the sturdy Atlas, the high-souled Menoetius, and the blundering Epimetheus, sought, in the division of a sacrificial ox, to deceive the mind of Zeus. He laid on one side, as the portion of men, the flesh and the rich inner parts, wrapped them in the skin, and laid the ox's stomach upon them; on the other side he set apart for Zeus the white bones, artfully heaped up, and concealed by shining fat. Taken to task by Zeus for this unequal division, he smiled roguishly, and bade Zeus take his choice. Zeus perceived the trick, and foreboded evil in his heart to mortal men, — evil which was destined to be fulfilled. He raised with both hands the fat, and waxed mightily wroth as he beheld the white bones beneath.' In penalty, fire was withheld from mankind. 'But the son of Iapetus, friendly to man, outwitted Zeus, and stole the fire's far-flashing brightness in a hollow tinder-stalk. For this Zeus sent an evil on mankind. At his bidding, Hephaestus fashioned of clay a woman, whom Athena endowed with all charms. Then he gave to men the beautiful bane, and from her sprang the race of women, who dwell as a great plague among mortal men, like the drones of a bee-hive. But the kind-souled Prometheus, as a warning that Zeus's mind is not to be deceived, was bound to a pillar by chains riveted through its middle.[2] Then Zeus sent an eagle which devoured Prometheus's imperishable liver; there grew each night as much as the bird had consumed by day. The eagle was slain by Heracles,[3] and thus the son of

[1] That is, when, at the accession of Zeus to power, the separation of gods and men took place, and the patriarchal community in which the two races had lived together under Cronus had come to an end. Compare Schoemann, *die Hesiodische Theogonie*, p. 209.

[2] See note on verse 65 of the play.

[3] A painting, representing the chained Prometheus and his liberator Heracles, was seen by Pausanias the periegete (v., 11, 12) in the temple of Zeus at Olympia. In the vase-picture mentioned in the note on 65, Heracles, half-kneeling behind the impaled Prometheus, is just shooting an arrow at the eagle. The hook-beaked monster is flying toward Prometheus, whose pinioned hands are outstretched in an attitude of defence. Behind the eagle is a bearded bystander with a staff in his hand. Achilles Tatius iii., 8, describes a painting in which Prometheus was depicted with contracted

Iapetus was delivered from his pain, not against Zeus's will, to the end that Heracles's fame should increase upon the broad earth.'

According to the *Works and Days*, Zeus conceals the fire because Prometheus has deceived him, but Prometheus secretly purloins it again from Zeus. In retribution for this, Zeus sends to Epimetheus the woman Pandora, endowed by all the gods with manifold gifts.[1] Epimetheus receives her against the express warnings of his brother, and knows not the evil till it is upon him. For till then the generations of men upon earth had lived free from pain and heavy sorrow, and free from deadly disease. But the woman lifted the lid from the jar, and all sicknesses and sorrows flew forth and spread over land and sea. Only Hope remained

brows and lips and half-open mouth, his right thigh drawn up and his left leg extended in a spasm of anguish, his look directed partly toward Heracles, who, armed with bow and spear, was about to let fly his arrow, and partly toward the bird, which, perched on Prometheus's thigh, was burrowing into his vitals with its beak. This description nearly corresponds to a Pompeian wall-painting (Zahn, *Ornamente*, ii., Plate 30), in which Prometheus is fastened bolt upright to a lofty cliff; on his right foot, which projects a little, sits the eagle, its beak plunged into Prometheus's breast, while Heracles stands on the level ground below, aiming an arrow at the eagle. Similar representations of the liberation of Prometheus are found on a sarcophagus of the Capitoline Museum, and in a wall-painting in a columbarium (Jahn, *die Wandgemälde des Columbariums in der Villa Pamfili*, Plate I., 3). In the latter picture, Prometheus is suspended with extended arms on the face of a cliff, resting his left foot on a projecting rock. The eagle, at his side, grasping with one claw Prometheus's right foot, is tearing his breast, from which blood is trickling down. Behind Heracles, who is preparing for his shot, stands the goddess Athena, pointing at the mark, and so making it clear that the arrow is not to strike Prometheus, but the eagle.

[1] The myth of Pandora is represented on a cista of Praeneste (*Monumenti dell' Instituto arch.*, Vol. vi., Plate xxxix.; compare R. Garucci in *Annali dell' Inst.*, 1860, p. 99) in five scenes. In the first, Prometheus is exhibiting the stolen fire to a female figure (Themis?). In the second, he is giving the fire to a group of surprised and overjoyed men. In the third, Pandora is receiving from Zeus the fatal vessel, a two-handled jar with a tall cover. In the fourth, Pandora offers the jar to a man, who turns away in horror with a gesture of refusal. The fifth shows Prometheus nailed to a rock in an oblique posture, with outstretched hands and manacled feet; at his feet is the eagle, looking round in rage and alarm at Heracles, who has already raised his club to slay the monster.

within, for Pandora at the behest of Zeus had closed the lid before she could escape.

These two narratives seek to explain how evil came into the world. The first conception, that increased material comfort brought with it luxury and its evil consequences, appears to be more primitive and simpler than the other idea, that misery came into the world through womankind. Both conceptions are united in the account of the *Works and Days*, in which Pandora is no longer ancestress of the human race, but an independent personage. Prometheus is conceived as the genius of humanity. The human race, by a crime against Deity (for Prometheus fancies himself wiser than Zeus, see verse 62 and note), brings on itself divine retribution, and therewith all the pain and misery of life. Furthermore Prometheus, as giver of fire, was naturally thought of as the founder of burnt sacrifices. And since in sacrifices only a small part of each victim fell to the gods' share,[1] it might easily occur to the philosophizing poet to ascribe this fact to the presumptuous spirit of that founder, and to an intelligence which sought the advantage of mankind at the expense of the honors anciently accorded to the gods.

II. The Story of Prometheus in Aeschylus.

Prometheus is the son of the goddess Themis, — his father is nowhere mentioned. In the struggle between the Titans and Zeus he had at first sided with the Titans; afterwards — since he learned from his mother Themis that the victory would be decided, not by brute strength, but by craft and stratagem, and since the Titans rejected his counsels, — he forsook the losing cause, and ranged himself, with his mother, on the side of Zeus, to share in the fruits of victory. With his effective aid, Cronus and the Titans were hurled into the abyss of Tartarus. But in the adjustment and regulation of the new empire, a dispute arose between Zeus and Prometheus. It was Zeus's wish to destroy the old race of man-

---

[1] Hes. *Th.* 556:

ἐκ τοῦ δ' ἀθανάτοισιν ἐπὶ χθονὶ φῦλ' ἀνθρώπων καίουσ' ὀστέα λευκὰ θυηέντων ἐπὶ βωμῶν.

kind which had existed during the era of the Titans, and replace it by a new race adapted to the new order of things. But Prometheus came forward as the champion of the old generation of men, imbecile and insensate though they were. He awoke them to active exertion, he gave them fire stolen from the gods, he taught them all arts and handicrafts; in short, by developing in them thought and consciousness (444), he not only assured their existence, but made it nobler and happier.

But the day of license, of independent action, is past; every one has now his allotted post and his prescribed function. A universal regime, with Zeus at the head, has been established, to which the individual must conform, though conformity may seem, in contrast to the olden time, to involve suppression of personal freedom (compare 149 ff.). So Prometheus's wilful infringement of the new system (543), his revolt against the sovereign of the world, must needs be severely punished, — the more severely because Zeus's empire is new, and can be fortified only by prompt and vigorous measures against every act of insubordination.

Cratos and Bia, ministers of Zeus and personifications of his stern discipline, drag Prometheus to a wild region of Scythia, on the confines of the world; there Hephaestus nails him to a lofty cliff near the ocean. This severe punishment seems to Prometheus the height of ingratitude and cruelty on Zeus's part, — ingratitude toward one who has been his faithful ally in the stress of the conflict with the Titans, and cruelty toward a fellow-deity whose only offence lies in having done good to mankind. Such sufferings, borne with fortitude, may well awaken pity; and the daughters of Oceanus,[1] compassionate natures, startled by the resounding blows of the hammer, approach and utter bitter complaints against the cruelty of the new sovereign of Olympus.

But Prometheus is not bound down to passive endurance. He

---

[1] On a sarcophagus of the Blundell collection (*Engravings and Etchings of the principal statues, etc., in the collection of Henry Blundell*, Plate 108) is a relief representing five Oceanids, two of whom are kneeling, the foremost in suppliant attitude clasping the feet of Hephaestus. The latter sits, cap on head and hammer in hand, before the figure of Prometheus, who is already nailed to the rock.

has the means of active resistance, for he knows a secret, on the knowledge of which Zeus's future depends. He knows that Zeus will hereafter contemplate a marriage with Thetis, and that the son born from this union is destined to be mightier than his sire. With the aid of this secret, Prometheus thinks to take signal vengeance on his tormentor. Zeus must humble himself, or be hurled from his throne, like Cronus before him, and Uranus before Cronus. In the assurance that a day of reckoning will hereafter come, Prometheus receives with a scornful smile the offers of Oceanus, who now appears, ready to intercede with Zeus in the hope that by timely renunciation and submission, Prometheus may be admitted to pardon. These prudent counsels come prematurely. The authority of their propounder is insufficient, and Prometheus is himself in too passionate a frame of mind. Confident that the right is on his side, he treats Oceanus as a compliant weakling, caring only for his own case and safety. The offer of mediation fails of its intended effect; far from being moved to submission, Prometheus is only strengthened in his resistance.

From this sullen mood he is roused to violent passion by a visit of the frenzied Io,[1] the daughter of Inachus. Chosen by Zeus as

---

[1] The legend of Io demands a word. She was daughter of the Argive river-god Inachus, and a priestess of the Argive Hera. Beloved of Zeus, she was changed by the jealous Hera into a cow, and guarded by the hundred-eyed Argus. When Argus was slain, she was pursued by a gad-fly, and driven through the world, till at length in Egypt she was restored to her proper form and became the mother of Epaphus. This Argive legend, like the Corinthian myth of Medea, and the Attic myth of Iphigenia, seems to have originated under Phoenician influence, and afterwards to have had Egyptian elements engrafted upon it. Just as the wandering Heracles has arisen in large measure from the Phoenician Melkarth, so the wandering Io probably corresponds to the Phoenician Dido, likewise a wandering deity. In origin she is a moon-goddess (compare Suidas s.v. Ἰώ· Ἰοῦς· οὕτω γὰρ τὴν σελήνην ἐκάλουν Ἀργεῖοι), like Medea and Iphigenia. Later she was conceived of simply as priestess of Hera, as was Medea in Corinth. She was changed into a cow, just as Callisto (another name for the moon-goddess) was changed into a bear. The figure of a horned bull or cow belongs distinctly to the Phoenician moon-worship; in the Greek myths, it naturally suggested the notion of a metamorphosis. The paths of the moon were transferred from the sky to the earth, and these wanderings geographically defined in a variety of ways. — Argus Panoptes ('the all-seer') is explained by Macrobius (Sat. i., 19. 12) as the

his favorite, she is pursued by the jealous fury of Hera, driven
from land to land and sea to sea, through the abodes of many hor-
rible monsters. Although Prometheus knows, from the prophecies
of his mother Themis, that Zeus is to bring Io's sufferings to a
happy conclusion, and that from the progeny of Zeus and Io is to
come his own deliverer, nevertheless passion stifles in him all sober
thought; he sees in this act of Zeus nought but a wanton out-
rage, and his indignation and thirst for revenge pass all bounds.
The measure of his guilt is full; he utters a speech of defiance
and abuse, which Zeus can no longer overlook. Hermes, sent by
Zeus, appears and demands with dire threats the revelation of the
secret which Prometheus vaunts so loudly. The messenger is
dismissed with insult and mockery, and his threats are now fulfilled. In the midst of thunder, lightning, and a tumult of the
elements, Prometheus, together with the rock to which he is bound,
is hurled into the abysses of the earth, and his insolent speech is
stifled. So ends the Προμηθεὺς δεσμώτης.

Many ages elapse, and at length the rock to which Prometheus
is fastened emerges on the heights of Caucasus. The sullen wrath
of the Titan still remains. In punishment, an eagle is sent every
third day to devour his liver (the seat of passion); the liver,
however, immediately grows again. Prometheus had formerly
boasted that as an immortal he could not be killed by Zeus; now
he longs for death (see Fragment III. of the Προμηθεὺς λυόμενος).
Made pliant by suffering (see 512) he is now less averse to com-
promise than when he rejected the offer of Oceanus. Zeus, however, has meanwhile released the Titans from Tartarus and become
reconciled with Cronus. The curse of Cronus no longer rests
upon him, and the guilt is removed which formerly attached to his
dynasty and endangered its continuance. The Titans themselves

starry heaven. The name Epaphus
is simply a grecized form of the
Egyptian Apis; compare Hdt. ii.,
153: ὁ δὲ Ἆπις κατὰ τὴν Ἑλλήνων
γλῶσσάν ἐστι Ἔπαφος. When the
Greeks became acquainted with the
Egyptian goddess Isis, who was depicted as horned, they recognized in

her the Argive Io; compare Hdt.
ii., 41: τὸ γὰρ τῆς Ἴσιος ἄγαλμα ἐὸν
γυναικήῖον βούκερόν ἐστι κατά περ Ἑλ-
ληνες τὴν Ἰοῦν γράφουσι. See Preller,
Griech. Mythologie, 2d edit., ii., p. 38.
The suggestions of E. Plew in the
Jahrbücher für Philologie, 1870, p. 665,
are only in part probable.

come to visit Prometheus (Fragment I.) and give him tokens of reconciliation and peace. Zeus of his own accord has set them free; his dominion is assured; there is no longer fear of any insurrection. Now without detraction from his dignity he can offer the hand of reconciliation to Prometheus,[1] whose defiant spirit is at last broken. Zeus makes one condition — the revelation of the secret; but this is now a matter of mere form, because the reconciliation between Zeus and Cronus has done away with all actual danger to Zeus. So a compact is made. Prometheus divulges the secret, upon a promise from Zeus that he shall be freed from his fetters.[2]

Prometheus has carried his point; Zeus, in appearance, has made the first concession. But this concession is after all a formal one, and involves no humiliation of Zeus; the unbiassed observer cannot but feel the character of Zeus to be the higher and nobler.

In this way the first step towards a reconciliation is made. The part of mediator was taken, it would seem, by Gaea, the mother of the Titans. As in the *Prometheus Bound* an unsuccessful attempt at mediation intensifies the bitterness of Prometheus towards Zeus, so now a successful attempt heralds the return of friendlier feeling.[3] In like manner, as the height of Prometheus's fury was marked by the appearance of Io, so it is obviously suitable that Heracles, her descendant, should now complete the work

---

[1] σπεύδων σπεύδοντι, verse 192.

[2] In Philodemus περὶ εὐσεβείας (Gomperz, *Herkulanische Studien*, ii., p. 41) we read: καὶ τὸν Προμηθέα λύεσθαι ποιεῖ Αἰσχύλος ὅτι τὸ λόγιον ἐμήνυσεν τὸ περὶ Θέτιδος ὡς χρεὼν εἴη τὸν ἐξ αὐτῆς γεννηθέντα κρείττω κατασκευάσαι ἀρχήν. Cp. Hygin., *fab.* 54: *fide data* (by Jupiter) *monet* (Prometheus) *Iovem ne cum Thetide concumberet.*

[3] In the list of personages prefixed to the *Prometheus Bound* in the Medicean manuscript, the two names Γῆ, Ἡρακλῆς stand after Ὠκεανός. As we know that Heracles was one of the personages of the *Prometheus*

Unbound, it is probable, as Stanley first conjectured, that these two names come from the *dramatis personae* of that play, and that the two lists anciently stood side by side in the manuscripts. The confusion of the lists would be easy to account for if we suppose that Ἑρμῆς stood at the end of both (compare 950, διπλᾶς ὁδούς), and that the persons corresponded much as the respective scenes did:

Oceanids.	Titans.
Oceanus (father of Oceanids).	Ge (mother of Titans).
Io.	Heracles.
Hermes.	Hermes.

of reconciliation. Heracles is sent by Zeus [1] and slays the eagle (see Fragments V. and VI.). Nevertheless this is not done without an expiatory offering. The centaur Chiron had been accidentally wounded by Heracles with a poisoned arrow, and the only possible deliverance from the agony of the incurable wound is in death. The undeserved sufferings of Chiron Heracles offers to Zeus as an offset for Prometheus's merited sufferings, and the voluntary death of the centaur (for Chiron is by nature immortal) is to atone for the guilt of the chained Titan.[2]

By this act it is distinctly and solemnly proclaimed that Prometheus is in the wrong. Though formally the victor, he is in reality humiliated and brought to a tacit acknowledgment of guilt. All the circumstances show themselves now in a different light. How differently, for instance, appears the passion of Zeus for Io. From her is sprung Heracles, the benefactor of the human race, the pattern of heroic virtue. We can say of the union of Zeus and Io, what a poet (Hesiod, *Scut. Her.* 27) says of the love of Zeus to Alcmene, ' the father of gods and men bethought him of another plan, that to gods and busy men he might beget a defender against ruin (ἀρῆς ἀλκτῆρα).' Io suffered much, yet she could not finally regret her sufferings, since she was deemed worthy to be the ancestress of a noble race. ' Who was he,' sing the daughters of Danaus, in the *Supplices*,[3] ' who was he that at last brought rest to Io the wanderer, the unhappy one, persecuted by the gadfly? Zeus, whose reign is everlasting, he accomplished this. . . . For who else could have set bounds to Hera's insane plottings? This was the work of Zeus.' Heracles, as well as Io, has to undergo untold hardships before he enters into his rest in the abode of the blessed, and receives the blooming Hebe as his spouse.[4] Prometheus describes to him his wanderings, much as he had de-

---

[1] *Mittitur Hercules ut aquilam interficiat*, Hygin. *fab.* 54.

[2] Compare 1026–1029 with Apollodorus ii., 5. 4, 5: ἀνίατον δὲ ἔχων (Χείρων) τὸ ἕλκος εἰς τὸ σπήλαιον ἀναλλάσσεται κἀκεῖ τελευτῆσαι βουλόμενος καὶ μὴ δυνάμενος ἐπείπερ ἀθάνατος ἦν, ἀντιδοὺς δὲ Διὶ Προμηθέα τὸν ἀντ'

αὐτοῦ γενησόμενον ἀθάνατον (Welcker ἀντιδόντος Προμηθέως τὸν ἀντ' αὐτοῦ τεθνηξόμενον ἀθάνατον) οὕτως ἀπέθανεν. *Ibid.* 11, 10: παρέσχε ('Ηρακλῆς) τῷ Διὶ Χείρωνα θνήσκειν ἀθάνατον ἀντ' αὐτοῦ θέλοντα.

[3] Verse 571 ff.

[4] Pindar, *Nem.* i., 60.

scribed hers to Io, enumerating the dangers and toils which he must encounter on the journey to the Hesperides (Fragments VII.–IX.). He advises him, among other things, not to endeavor himself to obtain the golden apples, but to send Atlas for them, taking meanwhile the burden of the sky upon his own shoulders.[1]

Zeus therefore it is who ordains all things for good. Prometheus cannot but acknowledge this, and is obliged to admit that Oceanus's former advice was right, and to act accordingly. The acceptance of a vicarious punishment in atonement for his own guilt involves submission and humiliation, and his repentance is finally sealed by his liberation from bonds. Probably this was performed not by Heracles, but by Hermes, at Zeus's command. By way of voluntary penance Prometheus places on his head a wreath of *agnus castus* (λύγος), a sort of osier often used for fetters, and enjoins upon mankind, in whose behalf he had suffered, to wear this same wreath in remembrance of his bonds.[2] To the penance and humiliation which he once thought to force on Zeus (compare 176, ποινὰς τίνειν), Prometheus himself submits.

III. COMPOSITION OF THE TRILOGY.

So long as the *Prometheus Bound* was considered by itself, as a single play, and its inner connexion with the *Prometheus Unbound*

[1] Apollodorus ii., 5. 11, 11: ὡς δὲ ἧκεν ('Ηρακλῆς) εἰς 'Υπερβορέους πρὸς "Ατλαντα εἰπόντος Προμηθέως (unquestionably in Aeschylus's *Prometheus Unbound*) τῷ 'Ηρακλεῖ αὐτὸν ἐπὶ τὰ μῆλα μὴ πορεύεσθαι, διαδεξάμενον δὲ "Ατλαντος τὸν πόλον ἀποστέλλειν ἐκεῖνον. In this way the description of the pains of Atlas in *Prom.* 347 and 425 are seen to have reference to the following play.

[2] Athenaeus xv., p. 674 d: Αἰσχύλος δ' ἐν τῷ λυομένῳ Προμηθεῖ σαφῶς φησιν ὅτι ἐπὶ τῇ τιμῇ τοῦ Προμηθέως τὸν στέφανον περιτίθεμεν τῇ κεφαλῇ ἀντίποινα τοῦ ἐκείνου δεσμοῦ, καίτοι ἐν τῇ ἐπιγραφομένῃ Σφιγγὶ εἰπών ' τῷ δὲ ξένῳ γε λύγινον (so Weil, *Rev. Crit.* 1876,

p. 40, for στέφανον) ἀρχαῖον στέφος δεσμῶν ἄριστος ἐκ Προμηθέως λόγον.' *Ibid.* p. 672 e: ἱστορεῖται ... θεσπίσαι τὸν 'Απόλλωνα ποινὴν αὐτοὺς (τοὺς Κᾶρας) ἀποδοῦναι τῇ θεᾷ δι' ἑαυτῶν ἑκούσιον καὶ χωρὶς δυσχεροῦς συμφορᾶς, ἣν ἐν τοῖς ἔμπροσθεν χρόνοις ἀφώρισεν ὁ Ζεὺς τῷ Προμηθεῖ χάριν τῆς κλοπῆς τοῦ πυρός, λύσας αὐτὸν ἐκ τῶν χαλεπωτάτων δεσμῶν· καὶ τίσιν ἑκούσιον ἐν ἀλυπίᾳ κειμένην δοῦναι θελήσαντος ταύτην ἔχειν ἐπιτάξαι τὸν καθηγούμενον τῶν θεῶν, ὅθεν ἀπ' ἐκείνου τὸν δεδηλωμένον (τῆς λύγου) στέφανον τῷ Προμηθεῖ περιγενέσθαι καὶ μετ' οὐ πολὺ τοῖς εὐεργετηθεῖσιν ἀνθρώποις ὑπ' αὐτοῦ κατὰ τὴν τοῦ πυρὸς δωρεάν.

was disregarded, it was gravely misunderstood. The fact of
Zeus's justice and rectitude, placed by the poet far in the back-
ground, was easily overlooked; Prometheus's specious pleas,
readily awakening our sympathy and interest, obscured the real
and fundamental idea. It was believed that Aeschylus meant to
depict in Zeus the cruel, passionate, arbitrary tyrant; in Prometheus, the pattern of a true friend of humanity.[1] Or Prometheus
was taken as a type of the human race in its struggle with the
forces of nature, armed only with unshakable will and the consciousness of its lofty mission; and the central, ennobling idea of
the play was thought to be the triumph of submission.[2] Others,
again, imagined that the main purpose of the drama was the glori-
fication of Fate as the supreme, eternal power of the universe,
presiding over the conflict of a great intellect with the will of a
thankless tyrant, the conflict of humanity against the combined
force of hostile gods and hostile nature — 'of great gigantic Fate,
which lifts man up while it crushes him to earth.'[3] Finally it was
laid down that two conceptions of Zeus had to be distinguished in
Aeschylus's plays, — the Zeus of the current mythology and the
Zeus of the poet's own ideal; and that in the *Prometheus* the imperfect Zeus of the popular legends was represented.[4]

Welcker showed that the preserved play must be taken as part
of a larger whole — a trilogy,[5] and cannot be understood except in
connexion with the rest of the trilogy. Aeschylus was a deeply
religious man, and the belief, which pervades all his poetry, that
Zeus is an eternal, righteous, all-powerful ruler of the universe,
must surely have been dominant in this trilogy as elsewhere. If
anything seems to contradict this belief, it must have had its explanation and justification in the composition of the whole work.[6]

Aeschylus had before him a twofold conception of Prometheus.
The Attic mythology presented him as a pure divinity of nature,
as a benign and venerable object of worship. The rustic theology

---

[1] Schütz.
[2] A. W. von Schlegel.
[3] Blümner.
[4] Gottfried Hermann.
[5] The notion that the three Prome-
theus-plays formed a trilogy, was
first suggested by Siebelis, *de Aeschyli
Persis* (1794), p. 24.
[6] Schoemann.

of Hesiod, according to which all civilization was opposed to the divine will, gave to Prometheus, as the representative of the human race, the character of an impious rebel, seeking the aggrandizement of mankind at the expense of the gods, and bringing on men heavy punishment from the gods. Aeschylus undertook to combine the two myths. At the outset he makes Prometheus an enemy of the gods, rebelling against their authority in a spirit of self-will (αὐθα-δία) and defiance, and disturbing the order of the universe, to the advantage of mankind, it is true, but against divine right. At the end, the same Prometheus appears as a deity[1] of human culture, at peace with the other gods and much revered in his own province.[2]

Several traits of the Hesiodic narrative Aeschylus found unsuited to his use. The fraud in the apportionment of the sacrificial ox and the punishment of mankind by the gift of woman were omitted, and so was the fiction of a brother Epimetheus. Altogether, Aeschylus could not rest satisfied with Hesiod's explanation of the origin of evil. He adopted the Hesiodic tradition of a succession of different ages and races of mankind, but he thought out a theory which refused to ascribe the source of evil to Zeus and the other gods, and sought to reconcile the imperfection of human nature with the perfection of Zeus's government. Zeus, — so Aeschylus imagined, — on his accession to power, had intended, as part of his wise and perfect reorganization of the universe, to replace the existing race of men, which had survived from early times and still led the stupid unreasoning life of those times, by a new and more perfect race, endowed with qualities like his own. He did not wish to destroy humanity from jealousy or hate, but only to destroy the present human race in the interest of the general good. Prometheus, the short-sighted 'Forethinker' for the immediate and the individual, stepped forth in opposition to Zeus's far-reaching plan. He became the preserver of the

[1] It is to be remembered that Prometheus does not *become* a god; he is one from the beginning, according to Aeschylus's conception.

[2] Similarly in the *Eumenides*, the concluding play of the trilogy *Orestea*, the grosser conception of the Erinyes or Furies changes in the course of the play to the humaner and more refined ideal of the Attic Eumenides.

existing human race,[1] but at the same time the perpetuator of human imperfection, for all his services and benefits could not remove this imperfection. Furthermore, Prometheus's resistance has destroyed all claim of mankind on Zeus's beneficence. The old state of things remains; only Prometheus, who sought to remedy the deficiencies of men by interfering with the rights of the gods, is severely punished for his presumption and injustice. The poet has set two views over against one another, — a calm, steady judgment and an unreasoning sentiment. On one side stands Zeus, the powerful far-seeing ruler, who punishes sin relentlessly and imparts ' wisdom through woe' ($\pi\acute{a}\theta\epsilon\iota$ $\mu\acute{a}\theta\sigma$, *Agam.* 177), whose eye is bent on the whole and not on details; on the other side Prometheus, passionate and proud, with a Titan's vehemence and impatience of control, doing good from unreasoning impulse, winning affection by his kind offices, but failing to meet the demands of a rational judgment. Prometheus is therefore a truly tragic character: he is great and lofty in his love for mankind, his daring deeds, and his fortitude in suffering; he arouses our sympathy and interest, but by his one-sided zeal and reckless acts he merits and receives reprobation.

The poet has depicted Prometheus's revolt with admirable skill. His spectators believed as firmly as himself in the wisdom and justice of Zeus; he neither could nor would deceive them by letting these qualities be for the moment obscured; his aim was to interest them in the plot and awaken their curiosity. The momentary illusion is justified on artistic grounds, for a revolt against the divine government can spring only from short-sightedness. Nothing but short-sightedness can make it appear as if Zeus hated and envied mankind, — Zeus, who sent his son Heracles to be a champion of humanity. Short-sightedness it is which makes Zeus's treatment of Io seem wilful cruelty.

The inner history of the revolt, the thoughts and passions of the disputants, are not directly described, but according to ancient custom are allowed to show themselves in outward actions and the characters of the several personages. Prometheus's own atti-

---

[1] As in another form of the legend he was the maker of mankind.

tude appears in the tone in which he speaks of his secret, and
utters the hope that Zeus will be humbled (verses 167, 186, 520,
757, 907). In this way the dramatic effect of the play is enhanced.

The revolt is the subject of our drama. But an aimless action
is no fit dramatic subject. A revolt without inner meaning, a
mere bickering of one god with another, would produce no suspense, and would be simply an unpleasing spectacle, most of all
to the religious-minded spectator. That tension of interest which
is essential to a good tragedy, Aeschylus has produced by the
introduction of a myth, which originally had no relation to the
story of Prometheus. He used a story which we read in its older
form in Pindar (*Isthm.* vii., 60). Themis — so ran the legend —
when Zeus and Poseidon wooed Thetis, had pronounced the decree
of fate that the sea-goddess should bear a son mightier than his
sire ; should Zeus or Poseidon be united to her, this son would
wield a weapon more powerful than thunderbolt or trident (see
note on 924). Aeschylus omitted the reference to Poseidon,
made Prometheus participant in the fatal secret which properly
belonged to Themis,[1] and to this end made him a son of Themis
instead of a son of Clymene.[2] The knowledge of this secret
(for that which originally was an incidental revelation had for
dramatic purposes to be represented as a carefully guarded secret)
the poet makes the turning-point of the whole plot. The continued enmity between Zeus and Prometheus, and their final
reconciliation, both depend on it.

A danger threatening the sovereignty of Zeus, — this is the substance of the secret. This danger must have its cause. Now
Zeus's sovereignty was universally believed to be everlasting ;
accordingly this cause must needs be a temporary one, which shall
finally result in nothing. Such a cause the poet found in the
downfall of Cronus and the conflict of duties which beset Zeus at

---

[1] Apollodorus iii., 13. 6, 2: ἔνιοι
(that is, Aeschylus and others after
him) δέ φασι, Διὸς ὁρμῶντος ἐπὶ τὴν
ταύτης (Θέτιδος) συνουσίαν εἰρηκέναι
Προμηθέα τὸν ἐκ ταύτης αὐτῷ γεννηθέντα οὐρανοῦ δυναστεύσειν.

[2] The merging of Gaea and Themis
in a single goddess Gaea-Themis (see
note on 210) made it easy to represent the Τιτὰν Προμηθεύς as a son of
Themis, inasmuch as the Titans were
understood to be the children of
Gaea.

that time. It was right that brute force should be deposed by the
reign of intelligence; such is the law of the universe. In the
struggle with the Titans, Zeus was in the right, and Themis her-
self, the representative of sacred law and eternal order, stood on
his side in this struggle. As ruler of the universe, therefore, Zeus,
in overthrowing the Titan dynasty, simply fulfilled his higher duty ;
but in his personal capacity he violated filial piety by laying forci-
ble hands on his own father, and piety toward parents was one
of the most sacred laws, for the maintenance of which the Erinyes
kept strictest watch.[1] In the *Eumenides* (641) the Erinyes themselves speak of this offence: ' He (Zeus) has himself thrown
his aged sire Cronus into chains.' Zeus, then, was guilty, having
sinned against the Fates and the Furies, and whoever is guilty
must perish.

This guilt of Zeus was made by Aeschylus the cause of the
impending danger to Zeus. Yet his was after all an innocent sin
— more innocent, even, than Orestes's matricide, — and one easily
atoned for. As Apollo answers the Erinyes in the passage of the
Eumenides just quoted, ' Bonds can be loosed, therefor there is
remedy, and many a means of freedom ' (*Eum.* 645). Zeus undid
the bonds, made terms with Cronus, and so freed himself from all
taint of guilt. In this matter, too, Prometheus seems, at the
first hasty view, to have the right on his side, but in the end he is
obliged to admit his error.

It has been thought that the central idea of our drama was that
of a change in Zeus himself. According to Dissen and Caesar
this was the development and purification of Zeus's own character.
Keck conceived it as the cessation of a conflict between Zeus and
Fate (Moera),[2] and the perfecting of Zeus by a union with Moera,
the personification of eternal law. Welcker's view was that Zeus's
nature was changed, in that by making a compact with the son of
Themis, or Law, he united Law with himself ; and so, from an
irresponsible ruler who had attained to power through brute force,
he became a wise, just governor, versed in the decrees of eternal

---

[1] Compare *Supplices* 707: τὸ γὰρ   [2] Compare 515 ff.
τεκόντων σίβας τρίτον τόδ' ἐν θεσμίοις
Δίκας γέγραπται μεγιστοτίμου.

Fate, conforming his rule to moral order, and liable no longer to be overthrown. But this transformation of Zeus is an illusion. His milder sway and his more peaceable attitude are not the result of anything in the drama itself, but have their causes quite outside. There is no conflict between Zeus and Fate, only a conflict between a higher and a lower duty. The seeming guilt of Zeus is only a device of the poet, and serves in the end to convince Prometheus and the rest of the world that Zeus from the outset has been a wise and just, though a severe and high-handed ruler. The pious Aeschylus could not possibly have conceived of his supreme god as an originally imperfect being, transformed into a just and wise governor by some outside influence. Some of the gods, no doubt, were thought of as more perfect than others, but that the highest god could undergo discipline and training would have been inconceivable. The whole plot of the drama turns on the character of Prometheus. By his example it is shown that every revolt against Zeus must necessarily come from ignorance of his wise designs, that every fault imputed to him has its foundation in a purblind and malicious judgment, and that any seeming ground for insubordination, however specious and seductive, must in the end prove a snare and a delusion. In short, that holds true of Zeus which the daughters of Danaus, themselves the offspring of Io, sing of him in the *Supplices* (86) : 'Zeus's will is not easy to spy out and lay hold upon. Even from darkness of night and woe he bringeth forth clear light for mortal generations. That falls unerringly, not upon its back, whate'er in Zeus's head is destined to fulfilment. For darkly proceed and shadow-shrouded the paths of his thought, impenetrable to the searching glance. He hurls from the tower of their hopes guilty men, nor arms himself for the fray. All divine doing is effortless ; it thrones on high and maketh instantly thought to deed, without leaving its holy seat.'

This idea the poet has worked out in two connected plays, the Προμηθεὺς δεσμώτης and the Προμηθεὺς λυόμενος. The *Prometheus Unbound* followed immediately the *Prometheus Bound* in the order of the trilogy. This would be certain from internal evidence, even if it were not expressly attested by the scholiast on verse 511 :

οὔπω μοι λυθῆναι μεμοίραται· ἐν γὰρ τῷ ἑξῆς δράματι λύεται, ὅπερ
ἐμφαίνει Αἰσχύλος, and on verse 522 : τῷ ἑξῆς δράματι φυλάττει τοὺς
λόγους. The only question is, what was the remaining play of the
trilogy. The alphabetical list of Aeschylus's plays in the Medicean manuscript enumerates Προμηθεὺς δεσμώτης, Προμηθεὺς πυρφόρος, Προμηθεὺς λυόμενος. No one would doubt that these were the
three plays of the Prometheus-trilogy, if we did not know that
there was a satyr-play Προμηθεύς, which belonged with the trilogy
Φινεύς, Πέρσαι, Γλαῦκος, as after-piece. Two verses of this satyric
drama are preserved (Fragments 218 and 219 in Hermann, 189 and
190 in Dindorf) :

λινᾶ δὲ πίσσα κωμολίνου μακροὶ τόνοι,

and

τράγος γένειον ἆρα πενθήσεις σύ γε.

Now Julius Pollux in two places, ix. 156 and x. 64, mentions a
play Προμηθεὺς πυρκαεύς. The title πυρκαεύς ‘ fire-kindler’ suits
perfectly the satyr-play, in which, as Plutarch tells us (*Mor.* p.
86 f), a satyr was represented as running in joyful surprise to
kiss and embrace the newly kindled fire, and singeing his beard
thereby. But there is no good ground for supposing [1] that πυρκαεύς
is merely another designation for πυρφόρος, and that the Prometheus πυρφόρος was the satyr-play. Rather we must understand
that *Prometheus* πυρφόρος (the name of the Attic divinity) was the
original title of a tragedy, and distinguished that play from *Prometheus* δεσμώτης and λυόμενος ; while πυρκαεύς was a surname
added by the Alexandrine grammarians to designate the satyr-
drama originally called simply Προμηθεύς, and to distinguish it from
the tragedies of like name.[2] It can hardly be a mere chance that
the verse which is expressly cited from the πυρκαεύς (the above-
quoted fragment, 218 Herm. = 189 Dind.) obviously belongs to
a satyr-play, whereas the few hints we have of the contents of the

---

[1] With Canter, *Novae Lectiones* vii.,
21, Casaubon *de satyrica Graecorum
poesi*, p. 127, and others.

[2] The opinion that the Προμηθεὺς
πυρκαεύς was a different play from

the Προμηθεὺς πυρφόρος, and that the
former was a satyric play, the latter
a tragedy, was first brought forward
by Hemsterhuys on Pollux ix., 8,
p. 1140.

πυρφόρος (the passages will be given immediately) point rather to a tragedy.

Assuming that the trilogy of Prometheus consisted of the three plays Προμηθεὺς δεσμώτης, Προμηθεὺς λυόμενος, Προμηθεὺς πυρφόρος, we have then to inquire whether the *Prometheus* πυρφόρος was the first or the third of the trilogy. The common supposition, since Welcker, is that the πυρφόρος stood first, and that its subject was the ' furtum Lemnium,' as Cicero (*Tusc.* ii. 10) calls it, — that is, the stealing of fire from the volcano Mosychlus in Lemnos, the forge of Hephaestus. The three plays of the trilogy would then represent successively Crime, Punishment, and Atonement. But there are two objections to this view. In the first place, the *Prometheus Bound* presupposes no foregoing play; in its opening scenes the preceding events are narrated in such a way that it is impossible to suppose that these same events had just been represented on the stage. Secondly, the scholion on verse 94, ἐν γὰρ τῷ πυρφόρῳ τρεῖς μυριάδας φησὶ δεδίσθαι αὐτόν proves not only that the *Prometheus* πυρφόρος was a tragedy (for in the satyr-play *Prometheus*, as we have seen, the fire was represented as a novel phenomenon, so that the theft must have just taken place), but also that the punishment of Prometheus preceded the action of that piece, and was there spoken of as an affair of the past (δεδίσθαι).[1] Accordingly we must consider the Προμηθεὺς πυρφόρος as the final play of the trilogy.[2] Prometheus must have been celebrated in it as the Attic fire-divinity, the πυρφόρος θεὸς Τιτὰν Προμηθεύς of Sophocles (*Oed. Col.* 55), and the whole may well have closed with the institution of the Προμήθεια and the torch-race, just

---

[1] Unless indeed we evade this conclusion by questionable means. Welcker, for instance, conjectured ἐν τῷ λυομένῳ for ἐν τῷ πυρφόρῳ. L. Schiller (*Blätter für die bayer. Gymnasien* ix., p. 143) supposes that the words of the scholiast had reference to a threat ' δεδίσθαι σε χρή ' in the mouth of Zeus. Kviçala (*Zeitschrift für die öster. Gymnasien*, xxviii., p. 501) proposes to change δεδίσθαι into δεδήσεσθαι.

[2] This view was first advanced and urged by Rudolf Westphal, *Prolegomena zu Aeschylus Tragoedien* (1869) p. 207 fig. His only mistake is in believing that in the second play the liberation of Prometheus by Heracles took place against Zeus's will, and that the reconciliation was reserved for the third play. This conflicts with definite statements about the *Prometheus Unbound*, which we have enumerated above.

as the *Orestea* closes with the institution of the cult of the Eumenides.[1] We know nothing of the plot of the *Prometheus* πυρφόρος, and only a single verse of it,

σιγῶν θ' ὅπου δεῖ καὶ λέγων τὰ καίρια,

is preserved (in Gellius xiii. 19. 4).[2]

IV. PERSONAGES, PLACE, AND SCENERY.

The figures of Cratos and Bia were taken by Aeschylus from Hesiod's *Theogony*, 385 ff., where Κράτος and Βία, along with Ζῆλος and Νίκη, are said to be the children of Πάλλας ('Brandisher,' 'Shaker') and Στύξ ('Horror'). At the time of the conflict with the Titans, their mother Styx, with the advice of her consort, brought her children to fight on Zeus's side; henceforth the Styx, in recompense for their service, became the mighty witness of the gods' oaths (μέγας ὅρκος θεῶν), and her children became inseparable retainers and servants of Zeus. In the play Βία is only a κωφὸν πρόσωπον, a dumb personage. Her presence would be unnecessary, if Prometheus were not represented by a wooden figure (see 65).[3] This figure had to be brought upon the scene; and that

---

[1] The reconciliation of Zeus and Prometheus is depicted on a large drinking-cup of elaborate workmanship found at Vulci (see Braun in the *Bulletino Archeol.*, 1846, p. 114; Welcker, *Alte Denkmäler*, iii., p. 194). The painting on the inside of the patera shows Hera seated on a throne, with a sceptre and a flower in her left hand, offering with her right to Prometheus, who stands before her, a cup of nectar, as a token that he is thenceforth to share the banquets of the gods. Prometheus, full-bearded and with thick locks overhanging his forehead, wears the wreath of *lygos* on his head, and holds in his right hand a sceptre exactly like Hera's.

[2] The statement of the scholiast on Aristides, vol. iii., p. 501, 17, ed. Dindorf, Αἰσχύλος δὲ ἐν Προμηθεῖ δεσμώτῃ πολλοῖς γάρ ἐστι κέρδος ἡ σιγὴ βροτῶν, seems to be a mistake. Compare Carcinus, Frag. 7 (p. 800 Nauck):

πολλοῖς γὰρ ἀνθρώποισι φάρμακον κακῶν σιγή, μάλιστα δ' ἐστὶ σώφρονος τρόπου.

[3] In the Προμηθεὺς λυόμενος the use of a wooden dummy was impossible, because the liberation had to take place; besides, a new costume was required for Prometheus, which should exhibit the results of the new torture to which he was subjected. An actor accordingly must have taken the place of the wooden figure. That Prometheus in the Προμηθεὺς δεσμώτης was represented by a lay-figure, was observed by Welcker, *Aeschyleische Trilogie*, p. 30. Compare G. Hermann, *Opuscula* II, p. 146; C. F. Hermann, *de distribuendis personis*, p. 60.

this might be done in a manner suitable to the dignity of a god, the poet introduced two brawny forms for the purpose.

Two actors divided the parts between them. The first actor (πρωταγωνιστής) took the parts of Hephaestus (see note on 81) and Prometheus; the second (δευτεραγωνιστής), those of Cratos, Oceanus, Io, and Hermes. For Aeschylus at this time still worked under the limitation which was afterwards removed through the influence of Sophocles : only two actors were assigned by the state to each poet for the performance of his plays, and consequently only two speaking personages could be brought upon the stage at any one time. But the poet adapts himself to this restriction very skilfully. At the opening of the play Prometheus is silent until after the exit of Hephaestus. This silence is made necessary by the limitation to two actors ; at the same time it is highly characteristic and effective that Prometheus under extreme torture lets no sound of anguish escape him.[1] At 81 Hephaestus retires (see note), while Cratos remains to administer a parting rebuke. This allowed time for the actor of Hephaestus's part, for whom of course no change of dress was necessary, to take his position behind the figure of Prometheus, at the back of the wooden structure built up in front of the rear wall of the stage, to support the movable scenery. Between the several scenes in which Cratos, Oceanus, Io, and Hermes appear, passages of some length are interposed, so that the second actor had time for rest and the assumption of his different costumes.

A not unapt remark about the personages of Aeschylus's plays is found in the citation ' ἐκ τῆς μουσικῆς ἱστορίας,' contained in the Medicean manuscript. ' Aeschylus,' it is there said, ' has this claim to distinction in tragedy, that he introduces great and august persons. In some of his tragedies, indeed, the action is carried on entirely by gods, as in the plays called *Prometheus :* for these dramas are manned by the chiefest of the gods, and the characters upon the stage and the chorus in the orchestra are all divine per-

---

[1] Compare the scholiast on 436: σιωπῶσι γὰρ παρὰ ποιηταῖς τὰ πρόσωπα ἢ δι' αὐθαδίαν, ὡς 'Αχιλλεὺς ἐν τοῖς Φρυξὶ Σοφοκλέους [this should be Αἰ- σχύλου], ἢ διὰ συμφορὰν ὡς ἡ Νιόβη παρ' Αἰσχύλῳ, ἢ διὰ περίσκεψιν ὡς ὁ Ζεὺς παρὰ τῷ ποιητῇ [*Il.* A 511] πρὸς τὴν τῆς Θέτιδος αἴτησιν.

sonages.'[1] Of course these divine personages are represented as
acting in all respects according to the laws of human nature.

Upon the place where the scene of the play is laid, the scholiast
on verse 11 remarks correctly: ἰστέον ὅτι οὐ κατὰ τὸν κοινὸν λόγον ἐν
τῷ Καυκάσῳ φησὶ δεδίσθαι τὸν Προμηθέα, ἀλλὰ πρὸς τοῖς Εὐρωπαίοις
τέρμασι τοῦ Ὠκεανοῦ, ὡς ἀπὸ τῶν πρὸς τὴν Ἰὼ λεγομένων ἐστὶ συμβαλεῖν. From the narrative of Io's wanderings, especially from 719,
πρὶν ἂν πρὸς αὐτὸν Καύκασον μόλῃς, the scholiast has rightly con-
cluded that if Io, after leaving Prometheus, is to make a long and
devious journey and then arrive at the Caucasus, she cannot be
understood as starting from the Caucasus, consequently the Caucasus cannot be the scene of our play. Now the tragedians, at
the outset of a play, usually give some indication of the place, so
as to assist the imagination of the spectators. But in the Prometheus no mention is made of the Caucasus; only a dreary,
unpeopled region is described, lying at the outermost limit of
Scythia (see 117), and near the sea (573), so that Prometheus
from his cliff looks out upon the sparkling expanse of water (90,
1088). Scythia in Aeschylus's time was a generic term for the
northern part of the earth, from the Pontus to the Ocean.[2] At
the sound of the hammer, as Prometheus is nailed to the rock,
the daughters of Oceanus approach: consequently this sea is the
Ocean, not the Pontus nor the Maeotis. Furthermore, it is said
that Io, when she leaves Prometheus, is to take an easterly course
along the seashore (712), and much later after long wanderings,
is to go from the Caucasus southward and arrive at the Cimmerian Bosporus (729). The scene of the play is therefore a wild,
rocky, desolate region 'at the ends of the earth,' in the north
of Scythia close to the Ocean. As the poet departed from the
tradition in dividing the time of Prometheus's punishment into
two great periods, in order to get, as it were, the frames for
two pictures, — so too he has assumed two different places for the

---

[1] ταύτῃ καὶ ἄριστος εἰς τραγῳδίαν
Αἰσχύλος κρίνεται, ὅτι εἰσάγει πρόσωπα
μεγάλα καὶ ἀξιόχρεα. καί τινες ἤδη τῶν
τραγῳδιῶν αὐτῷ διὰ μόνων οἰκονομοῦνται
θεῶν, καθάπερ οἱ Προμηθεῖς· τὰ γὰρ δρά-
ματα συμπληροῦσιν οἱ πρεσβύτατοι · ὧν
θεῶν, καὶ ἔστι τὰ ἀπὸ τῆς σκηνῆς καὶ
τῆς ὀρχήστρας θεῖα πάντα πρόσωπα.

[2] See note on 807.

punishment,[1] to secure the desirable change of scenery for the second play. The punishment on the Caucasus is dramatically heightened by the appearance of the eagle; the earlier punishment is rendered more impressive by the loneliness of the spot and its remoteness from the civilized world.[2]

The scenery represents a rocky eminence with a cleft or gorge (φάραγξ). The right περίακτος shows the sea, the left. a barren mountainous region, intersected perhaps by torrents (89). The figure of Prometheus, after being nailed to the cliff in an upright posture, remains hanging there, rigid and motionless (see note on 87). The wild scenery, the costumes and masks of Cratos and Bia (ὅμοια μορφῇ γλῶσσά σου γηρύεται, 78), the smith's tools and the iron clamps and bands with which Hephaestus appears, the ring of the hammer, the extraordinary way in which several of the characters make their entrance, — the Oceanids in a winged chariot, Oceanus riding on a winged steed, and the horned Io suddenly rushing up the rocky slope, — all these worked together to heighten the weird effect of the play and to excite in the spectators mingled feelings of terror, suspense, and compassion.[3]

V. On the Date of the Play.

The sole hint afforded us for determining the time when the *Prometheus* was composed is the reference in 367–369 to the eruption of Aetna in Olympiad 75, 2 = 479–8 B.C. That the play is not one of the last works of the poet seems likely from the freshness of its diction, the simplicity of its structure, the limitation to two actors, and furthermore from the digressions and

---

[1] Compare Frag. III. of the Προμηθεὺς Λυόμενος, 28.

[2] If we compare the words ἄβροτον εἰς ἐρημίαν in 2 with the description in Soph. *Phil.*, 2, βροτοῖς ἄστικτος οὐδ' οἰκουμένη, it is easy to suspect that Sophocles, in laying stress on the loneliness and desolation of Philoctetes (a trait praised by Lessing for its effectiveness), borrowed

the idea from the *Prometheus* of Aeschylus. The scholiast also notices the resemblance of the two passages.

[3] Adding to this the recital of Io's adventures, we see why Aristotle (*Poet.* 18, p. 1456 a) cites the Προμηθεύς along with the Φορκίδες as an example of the τερατῶδες in dramatic art.

the descriptions of material phenomena which the poet has allowed himself in the passages relating to Atlas and Typhon, and in the scenes with Io and Heracles. On the other hand, several considerations are against the assumption of a very early date: the metrical structure of the lyric parts, the moderate length of the choral passages, and the proportion they bear to the dialogue parts, the occurrence of a solo for an actor (ἀπὸ σκηνῆς), the character of the metres, — all seem to point to a later period of tragic art.[1] From all this, however, it does not necessarily follow that the *Prometheus* is to be counted one of Aeschylus's latest plays. In fact, the evidence only amounts to this, that the *Prometheus*, in form and in substance, stands alone among the few preserved dramas of Aeschylus, and in this isolated position it may, so far as we can see, belong either to an earlier or to a very late part of the poet's career.

[1] Compare R. Westphal, *Griechische Metrik*, 1868, p. xlvii, and *Prolegomena zu Aeschylus*, pp. 8 and 191; R. Engelmann, *Philologus*, xxvii., p. 736. J. Oberdick, *Jenaer Litteraturzeitung*, 1876, Art. 380, assumes, following Westphal, that the play was revised and altered, for the purpose of a second performance, about the year 420, by Euphorion, the son of Aeschylus (Suidas s.v. Εὐφορίων; Quintil. x., 1, 66), basing this opinion especially upon the use of the word σοφιστής in 944. Compare H. Kramer, *Prometheum vinctum esse fabulam correctam*, Freiburg, 1878; A. Roehlecke, *Septem adv. Thebas et Prometheum vinctum esse fabulas post Aeschylum correctas*, Berlin, 1882; Theodor Heidler, *de compositione metrica Promethei fabulae Aeschyleae capita IV*, Breslau, 1884. — R. Förster, *de attractionis usu Aeschyleo* (Breslau, 1868), p. 44, urges the use of attraction in relative clauses, 446, 963, 984, as a proof of a late date. But this attraction must be recognized, in spite of Förster's objections (p. 17), in *Pers.* 342, χιλιὰς μὲν ἦν ὧν ἦγε πλῆθος, and in *Sept.*

310, ὅσων ἴησιν (compare p. 21). — As little weight have the arguments of E. Martin, *de responsionibus diverbii apud Aeschylum* (Berlin, 1867), p. 71; namely, the interposition of interjections (742) and of lyric metres (115, 117) between the trimeters, the occurrence of conjunctions at the end of a verse, closely joining one trimeter to another (for instance, 61, 104, 259, 341, *etc.*), the interruption of a dialogue between two persons by speeches of the chorus (see 631, 698, 745, 782, 810). — A. Schmidt, *de caesura media in Graec. trimetr. iamb.* (Bonn, 1865), p. 19, observes that the *Persians*, Aeschylus's earliest extant play, has the most verses which divide themselves into two equal parts (like 640 of our play), and makes this a criterion of the age of the *Prometheus*; he puts the play, with two such verses, on a line with the *Septem* (Olymp. 78, 1 = 467 B.C.), which has one. As a matter of fact, the *Prometheus* has only one, since in 770 Dindorf's correction cannot be regarded as right.

In the *Supplices*, *Persians*, and *Seven against Thebes*, the ratio of the choral parts to the dialogue is about 1 : 2 ; in the *Orestea* it is 1 : 3 ; in the *Prometheus*, on the contrary, it is 1 : 7. But long choral songs would have been out of place, since Prometheus remains on the stage during the whole play. In one place (436 ff.) the poet thinks it necessary to excuse his silence during a choral passage. The time needful for the second actor's changes of costume is secured, according to the ancient fashion, by long colloquies between Prometheus and the leader of the chorus (see 193, 436, 907).

Of all the plays of Aeschylus, the *Prometheus* has the greatest number of anapaests in the first foot of the trimeter, — 12 cases out of 30, not counting proper names (see note on verse 6). None of these anapaests, however, consist of a tribrachic word made anapaestic by position, like *Pers.* 343, ἑκατὸν δίς, κτέ. In general the structure of the trimeter is very careful (see notes on 2, 18, 116, 730) ; the tribrach in the fifth foot is found only once (52), whereas in the *Persians* (performed Olymp. 76, 4 = 472 B.C.) several cases of this occur (see *Pers.* 448, 492, and especially 501). Besides, a considerable number of the resolutions in the *Prometheus* must be laid to the charge of the unusual and peculiar subject-matter (see note on 715). We see, therefore, that the structure of the trimeter in our play shows only a single peculiarity, and on the whole favors the supposition of an earlier date.

Altogether, then, nothing stands in the way of the belief that the *Prometheus* was composed and performed at a time when the remembrance of the destructive eruption of Aetna was still fresh ; that is to say, not very long after Olymp. 75, 2 = 479–8 B.C.[1]

---

[1] W. Christ, *die Aetna in der griechischen Poesie* (*Sitzungsbericht der k. bayr. Akad. des Wiss., philos.-philol. Classe*, 1888, pp. 349 ff.), compares the description of the volcano, *Prom.* 351 ff. with that in Pindar, *Pyth.* I. He finds Pindar's description the more vivid ; and only in respect of the ποταμοὶ πυρός does he give the preference to Aeschylus, Pindar having conceived of the fiery streams as being inside the mountain. Christ prefers to put the eruption in 475, following Thuc. iii., 116, rather than in 479–8 with the Parian Marble ; but he concedes that the eruption may have lasted from 478 to 475, so that both dates would be right. He conjectures that the *Prometheus* was produced in Athens soon after Aeschylus's return from Sicily, somewhere about 468.

ΑΙΣΧΥΛΟΥ

ΠΡΟΜΗΘΕΥΣ

ΔΕΣΜΩΤΗΣ.

ΤΑ ΤΟΥ ΔΡΑΜΑΤΟΣ ΠΡΟΣΩΠΑ.

ΚΡΑΤΟΣ (ΚΑΙ ΒΙΑ).
ΉΦΑΙΣΤΟΣ.
ΠΡΟΜΗΘΕΥΣ.
ΧΟΡΟΣ ΩΚΕΑΝΙΔΩΝ.
ΩΚΕΑΝΟΣ.
ΙΩ Η ΙΝΑΧΟΥ.
ΕΡΜΗΣ.

ΥΠΟΘΕΣΙΣ.

Προμηθέως ἐν Σκυθίᾳ δεδεμένου διὰ τὸ κεκλοφέναι τὸ πῦρ πυνθάνεται
Ἰὼ πλανωμένη ὅτι κατ' Αἴγυπτον γενομένη ἐκ τῆς ἐπαφήσεως τοῦ Διὸς
τέξεται τὸν Ἔπαφον. Ἑρμῆς δὲ παράγεται ἀπειλῶν αὐτῷ κεραυνωθήσε-
σθαι, ἐὰν μὴ εἴπῃ τὰ μέλλοντα ἔσεσθαι τῷ Διί. προέλεγε γὰρ ὁ Προμηθεὺς ὡς ἐξωσθήσεται ὁ Ζεὺς τῆς ἀρχῆς ὑπό τινος οἰκείου υἱοῦ. τέλος δὲ
βροντῆς γενομένης ἀφανὴς ὁ Προμηθεὺς γίνεται.

Κεῖται δὲ ἡ μυθοποιία ἐν παρεκβάσει παρὰ Σοφοκλεῖ ἐν Κολχίσι, παρὰ
δὲ Εὐριπίδῃ ὅλως οὐ κεῖται. ἡ μὲν σκηνὴ τοῦ δράματος ὑπόκειται ἐν Σκυθίᾳ ἐπὶ τὸ Καυκάσιον ὄρος· ὁ δὲ χορὸς συνέστηκεν ἐξ Ὠκεανίδων νυμφῶν.
τὸ δὲ κεφάλαιον αὐτοῦ ἐστι Προμηθέως δέσις.

Ἰστέον δὲ ὅτι οὐ κατὰ τὸν κοινὸν λόγον ἐν Καυκάσῳ φησὶ δεδέσθαι τὸν
Προμηθέα, ἀλλὰ πρὸς τοῖς Εὐρωπαίοις μέρεσι τοῦ Ὠκεανοῦ, ὡς ἀπὸ τῶν
πρὸς τὴν Ἰὼ λεγομένων ἔξεστι συμβαλεῖν.

30

ΠΡΟΜΗΘΕΥΣ ΔΕΣΜΩΤΗΣ.

ΚΡΑΤΟΣ.

Χθονὸς μὲν εἰς τηλουρὰν ἥκομεν πέδον,
Σκύθην ἐς οἶμον, ἄβροτον εἰς ἐρημίαν.

1-127: Prologue (πρόλογος).
1-87: First Scene. Cratos and Bia, dragging the figure representing Prometheus, enter on the left; Hephaestus with smith's tools accompanies them.

1. χθονὸς πέδον: poetical periphrasis for χθόνα. Cp. Suppl. 260 χώρας 'Απίας πέδον, 662 πέδον γᾶς, Pers. 488 γῆς 'Αχαιΐδος πέδον. In such expressions, the adjective does not agree with the genitive, but with the substantive which makes the periphrasis, because this substantive forms one idea with the genitive. See below, 01, 110, 823; also Sept. 304 ποῖον δ' ἀμείψεσθε γαίας πέδον, Eum. 292 χώρας ἐν τόποις Λιβυστικοῖς, 320 ματρῷον ἄγνισμα κύριον φόνου, 718 πρωτοκτόνοισι προστροπαῖς 'Ιξίονος. — μέν: answered by σοὶ δέ in 3; the first part of the task (bringing Prometheus to the spot) is contrasted with the second part (nailing him to the rock). "We have done our duty, and here we are (ἥκομεν), now you must do yours." — τηλουρόν: this accent is expressly attested by the grammarian Arcadius περὶ τόνων, p. 73, 6. τηλουρός is formed from τηλοῦ as πονηρός from πόνος. Others derive the word from τῆλε and ὅρος (οὖρος) boun-

dary, so that it means cuius termini procul sunt; or from τῆλε and οὖρον space (cp. Curtius Etym.⁵ p. 340); but these derivations would require the accent τήλουρος.

2. Σκύθην: here used adjectively, as in 417. So Sept. 817 Σκύθη σιδήρῳ, Eur. Rhes. 426 Σκύθης λέως, Martial iv. 28, 4 Scythas zmaragdos. Cp. also 805; Ag. 100 'Ελλάδος ἥβας, Prom. Solut. Frg. X. 9 below Αἴγυν στρατόν, Frg. 322 Κουρῆτα λαόν. See also note on 701 below. — οἶμον: originally road, then strip, tract; cp. Il. xi. 24 τοῦ δ' (sc. θώρηκος) ἦτοι δέκα οἶμοι ἔσαν μέλανος κυάνοιο, ten stripes of blue steel. — ἄβροτον: ἀνάνθρωπον, Hesych. Hermann, following Buttmann Lexil. I. p. 136, thinks this use of ἄβροτος a blunder, due to a misinterpretation of the Homeric νὺξ ἀβρότη (Il. xiv. 78), which was wrongly explained by some of the ancients as the time "when mortals are not abroad," καθ' ἣν βροτοὶ οὐ φοιτῶσιν, whereas it is really an equivalent of νὺξ ἄμβροτος (Od. xi. 330), νὺξ ἀμβροσίη. But this is not necessary. As ἄνανδρος means both unmanly and destitute of men, ἀνάνθρωπος both inhuman and deserted of mankind, so ἄβροτος means immortal and void of mortals. — Similar resolu-

31

Ἥφαιστε, σοὶ δὲ χρὴ μέλειν ἐπιστολὰς
ἅς σοι πατὴρ ἐφεῖτο, τόνδε πρὸς πέτραις
5 ὑψηλοκρήμνοις τὸν λεωργὸν ὀχμάσαι
ἀδαμαντίνων δεσμῶν ἐν ἀρρήκτοις πέδαις.

tions in the third foot occur eight times in this play. The tribrach in the first foot always consists of a single word (see on 116); but in the second and fifth, and still more in the third and fourth feet, the first short of the tribrach is usually the final syllable of a word, or a monosyllabic particle closely connected with the preceding word (τί 351, γέ 740, δέ 993). In the third foot, the caesura thus made is followed, in six of the examples, by a word consisting of three short syllables; in the other two cases a proper name of four syllables follows (Κιλικίων 351, Ἰόνιος 840).—The repetition of the preposition gives to Σκύθην οἶμον and ἄβροτον ἐρημίαν, which otherwise would be close appositives, more the air of two separate statements. See Krüg. I. § 57, 10, 4.— The scholiast remarks on this verse: τοῦτο εἰς τὸ ἀπαραμύθητον τοῦ δεθησομένου· καὶ Σοφοκλῆς τὸ αὐτὸ περὶ Φιλοκτήτου λέγει. Cp. Introduction, p. 25, footnote 2, and verses 20, 270; also Ar. Ach. 704, ξυμπλακέντα τῇ Σκυθῶν ἐρημίᾳ.

3. Ἥφαιστε, σοὶ δέ: for σοὶ δέ, Ἥφαιστε. The vocative is often placed first in this way, to attract more promptly the attention of the person addressed. Cp. Od. xvi. 130 ἄττα, σὺ δ' ἔρχεο θᾶσσον, Il. i. 282 Ἀτρεΐδη, σὺ δὲ παῦε τεὸν μένος, vi. 429 Ἕκτορ, ἀτὰρ σύ μοί ἐσσι πατήρ. Frequent in Sophocles: cp. Ai. 1409, El. 150, O. T. 203, 1000, 1503, O. C. 237, 332, 507, 592, Ant. 1087, Phil. 700. Also [Plato] Theages 127 c ὦ Σώκρατες,

πρὸς σὲ δ' ἂν ἤδη εἴη ὁ μετὰ τοῦτο λόγος.—μέλειν: personal; ἐπιστολὰς is its subject. See Krüg. I. § 47, 11, 5 and II. § 47, 11, 2.—ἐπιστολὰς : = ἐντολὰς, commands. Cp. Suppl. 1012 φυλάξαι τάσθ' ἐπιστολὰς πατρός, Pers. 783 κοὐ μνημονεύει τὰς ἐμὰς ἐπιστολάς, Frg. 423 ἄκουε τὰς ἐμὰς ἐπιστολάς.

4. πατήρ: is said of Zeus not only by the menials, 40 and 53, and by Hermes, 947, 984, but even by Hephaestus, 17.

5. λεωργόν : κακοῦργον, πανοῦργον, ἀνδροφόνον, Hesych. Of these, the interpretation πανοῦργος agrees exactly with the derivation of the word from λέως, an adverb which the ancient lexicographers explain by τελέως, παντελῶς, ἅπαν. Cp. Archil. Frg. 112 Bergk λείως γὰρ οὐδὲν ἐφρόνεον = πάντως γὰρ οὐδὲν ἐφρόνεον, and the words λεώλης, λεώλεθρος = πανόλης, πανώλεθρος. Accordingly λεωργός signifies one who acts recklessly, in distinction from one whose conduct is regulated by principle. Cp. Archil. Frg. 88 πάτερ Ζεῦ, σὸν μὲν οὐρανοῦ κράτος, σὺ δ' ἔργ' ἐπ' ἀνθρώπων ὁρᾷς λεωργὰ καὶ θεμιστά, Xen. Mem. i. 3. 9 αὐτὸν θερμουργότατον εἶναι καὶ λεωργότατον. Hesychius gives also the form λαοργός (with the interpretation ἀνόσιος· Σικελοί). The adverb λέως is related to the intensive prefix λα- (λάμαχος, λακαταπύγων, λακατάρατος) as λεώς is to λαός, νεώς to ναός.

6. ἀδαμαντίνων: ἀδάμας· γένος σιδήρου, Hesych. Cp. 64; also Pind. Pyth. iv. 125 κρατεροῖς ἀδάμαντος δῆσεν ἄλοις, with iron nails, Pind. Frg. 88 ἐξ ἀδάμαν-

τὸ σὸν γὰρ ἄνθος, παντέχνου πυρὸς σέλας,
θνητοῖσι κλέψας ὤπασεν· τοιᾶσδέ τοι
ἁμαρτίας σφὲ δεῖ θεοῖς δοῦναι δίκην,
10 ὡς ἂν διδαχθῇ τὴν Διὸς τυραννίδα
στέργειν, φιλανθρώπου δὲ παύεσθαι τρόπου.

ΗΦΑΙΣΤΟΣ.

Κράτος Βία τε, σφῷν μὲν ἐντολὴ Διὸς
ἔχει τέλος δὴ κοὐδὲν ἐμποδὼν ἔτι·
ἐγὼ δ' ἄτολμός εἰμι συγγενῆ θεὸν

τος ἢ σιδάρου. The meaning diamond is not found before Theophrastus (Pindar, de adamante; Comm. Antiqu. p. 19).—ἀρρήκτοις πέδαις: cp. *Il.* xiii. 36 ἀμφὶ δὲ ποσσὶ πέδας ἔβαλε χρυσείας ἀρρήκτους ἀλύτους, 19 below δυσλύτοις χαλκεύμασι. πέδαι are *fetters*, δεσμά *bonds*, a more general term. The reverse combination in Eur. *Bacch.* 447 δεσμὰ διελύθη πεδῶν. Cp. *Ag.* 850 πῆμα νόσου, *Pers.* 543 λέκτρων εὐνάς.—Aeschylus admits an anapaest only in the first foot of the trimeter. The one exception is *Sept.* 569, where the proper name could hardly have been otherwise brought into the verse. (In 840 below there is no anapaest; see note.) This anapaest, like the tribrach and dactyl in the same place (see on 2 and 730), is never divided between two words: it generally consists of a trisyllabic word, but sometimes of the beginning of a longer word, as here and 64, 353, 796, 805, 811. There are thirteen such anapaests in the *Prometheus*.

7. τὸ σὸν ἄνθος: τὸν σὸν κόσμον, Schol. In Theognis 452, the 'clear lustre' of gold is called its καθαρὸν ἄνθος. — παντέχνου πυρός: cp. 110, and Xen. *Mem.* iv. 3. 7 τὸ δὲ καὶ τὸ πῦρ πορίσαι ἡμῖν, ἐπίκουρον μὲν ψύχους,

ἐπίκουρον δὲ σκότους, συνεργὸν δὲ πρὸς πᾶσαν τέχνην καὶ πάντα ὅσα ὠφελείας ἕνεκα ἄνθρωποι κατασκευάζονται, Plat. *Protag.* 321 c ὁ Προμηθεὺς ... κλέπτει Ἡφαίστου καὶ Ἀθηνᾶς τὴν ἔντεχνον σοφίαν σὺν πυρί. — πυρὸς σέλας: said by Homer *Il.* xix. 375. Cp. Hesiod *Theog.* 566 κλέψας ἀκαμάτοιο πυρὸς τηλέσκοπον αὐγήν.

9. σφέ: = αὐτόν, as *Sept.* 615, Soph. *Ai.* 51, *O. C.* 40, *Trach.* 234, Eur. *Ion* 54, 71, and often. The tragedians use σφέ for the accusative singular as well as plural, whereas in Homer it occurs only as plural. Krüg. II. § 51, 1, 14.

10. ἄν: in final clauses after ὡς and ὅπως, very common in Attic; cp. 654, 700, 824. Aristophanes always uses ὡς ἄν, and in Attic inscriptions ὅπως ἄν is frequent.

11. φιλανθρώπου κτέ.: that is, "turn his affections away from men to a worthier object."

13. ἔχει τέλος: = τετέλεσται. Cp. Soph. *O. C.* 1780 πάντως ἔχει τάδε κῦρος (= κεκύρωται). — οὐδὲν ἐμποδών: nihil vos detinet.

14. συγγενῆ: the scholiast explains, τὸν ἀπὸ μιᾶς ὁρμώμενον τέχνης, that is, "my fellow-craftsman." Rather we must understand the word of

15 δῆσαι βίᾳ φάραγγι πρὸς δυσχειμέρῳ.
πάντως δ' ἀνάγκη τῶνδέ μοι τόλμαν σχεθεῖν·
εὐωριάζειν γὰρ πατρὸς λόγους βαρύ.

τῆς ὀρθοβούλου Θέμιδος αἰπυμῆτα παῖ,
ἄκοντά σ' ἄκων δυσλύτοις χαλκεύμασι
20 προσπασσαλεύσω τῷδ' ἀπανθρώπῳ πάγῳ,
ἵν' οὔτε φωνὴν οὔτε του μορφὴν βροτῶν

blood-relationship; cp. 39, 289. He-
phaestus is the son of Zeus and Hera
(*Il.* i. 577 ff.), or according to Hesiod
Th. 927, the fatherless son of Hera;
Prometheus is the son of Themis.
Now Themis is the daughter of Ura-
nus, and Hera his grand-daughter.

17. εὐωριάζειν: ὀλιγωρεῖν, μὴ ἔχειν
φροντίδα, παρακούειν, Hesych. One
who is confident and unconcerned
(εὖωρος, s e c u r u s) in executing a
duty, is apt to take less pains. Cp.
our colloquial expression 'take it
easy.'

18. Θέμιδος: see Introduction, p. 17.
—αἰπυμῆτα: contrasted with ὀρθοβούλου. αἰπυμήτης, *of towering thoughts,*
is one who in his shrewdness and
sagacity aspires to too lofty things.
Cp. εὔβουλος Θέμις, Pind. *Isth.* vii. 32.
—The dactyl substituted for the
third iambus of the tragic trimeter is
very frequent; whereas in the first
foot Aeschylus uses it seldom, and
chiefly in proper names (730). In
this play the dactyl in the third foot
occurs eighteen times: it is always
divided in the middle by the caesura,
its long first syllable being either the
end of a polysyllabic word, or a word
of one syllable closely connected with
the foregoing (δέ 1009, τίς 1027). Cp.
note on 2.

19. ἄκοντα σ' ἄκων: cp. 671 ἄκουσαν ἄκων, 218 ἑκόντ' ἑκόντι, Eur. *Cycl.*

258 ἑκὼν ἑκοῦσι, *Hipp.* 319 οὐχ ἑκοῦσαν
οὐχ ἑκών. The poets are very fond
of repetitions like this, in which the
same word is twice used, referring to
different persons. Further instances
are *Od.* v. 155 παρ' οὐκ ἐθέλων ἐθελούσῃ = οὐκ ἐθέλων παρ' ἐθελούσῃ, iii.
272 τὴν δ' ἐθέλων ἐθέλουσαν ἀνήγαγεν,
v. 97 εἰρωτᾷς μ' ἐλθόντα θεὰ θεόν, Aesch.
Cho. 89 παρὰ φίλης φίλῳ φέρειν γυναι-
κὸς ἀνδρί, and below 20, 192, 276, 702,
921.

20. ἀπανθρώπῳ: see note on ἄβροτον, 2. The idea is further expanded
in the next verses. 'Eximia arte cu-
mulavit poeta infinitam mali magnitudinem' (Hermann). —πάγῳ: Hesychius has the gloss πάγοι· αἱ ἐξοχαὶ
τῶν πετρῶν καὶ τῶν ὁρῶν. Cp. *Od.*
v. 411 ἐκτοσθεν μὲν γὰρ πάγοι ὀξέες.

21. του: the pronoun τίς, like the
prepositions, is often, in poetical diction, placed in the second member of
a disjunctive sentence, when it really
belongs to both members. Cp. 156;
Soph. *Ant.* 257 οὔτε θηρὸς οὔτε του
κυνῶν, Eur. *Hec.* 370 οὔτ' ἐλπίδος γὰρ
οὔτε του δόξης, Soph. *Trach.* 3 οὔτ' εἰ
χρηστὸς οὔτ' εἴ τῳ κακός, 1254 σπαραγ-
μὸν ἤ τιν' οἶστρον, *O. T.* 810 ᾧ μὴ ξένων
ἔξεστι μηδ' ἀστῶν τινα δόμοις δέχεσθαι,
Od. iv. 87 οὔτε ἄναξ ἐπιδευὴς οὔτε τι
ποιμήν, Solon Frg. 4, 12 οὔθ' ἱερῶν κτεά-
νων οὔτε τι δημοσίων φειδόμενοι. See
on 458.

ὄψει, σταθευτὸς δ' ἡλίου φοίβῃ φλογὶ
χροιᾶς ἀμείψεις ἄνθος· ἀσμένῳ δέ σοι
ἡ ποικιλείμων νὺξ ἀποκρύψει φάος,

22. ὄψα: belongs by zeugma to φωνήν as well as μορφήν: *neither a voice* (shalt thou hear) *nor yet a form shalt thou see.* Cp. *Suppl.* 1006 πρὸς ταῦτα μὴ τάθωμεν ἐν πολὺς πόνος, πολὺς δὲ πόντος εἴνεκ' ἤρθη δορί. 'Frequentissime hoc fit ubi grammatici αἴσθησιν ἀντὶ αἰσθήσεως poni aiunt, quibus in locis cum nomine notio verbi congeneris tacite comprehenditur' (Lobeck). — σταθευτός: φλογιζόμενος· σταθεύειν γὰρ τὸ κατ' ὀλίγον ὀπτᾶν φασιν 'Αττικοί, Schol. σταθευτός· πεφλογισμένος ἠρέμα, Hesych. That is, *scorched.* From στατός and ἕω. — After 15 (δυσχειμέρῳ) we should expect rather the baleful effects of cold to be mentioned. But a Greek's imagination would be more vividly affected by a description of the sun's scorching heat; the allusion to cold follows later (25). — φοίβῃ: cp. φοῖβον ὕδωρ Hesiod *Frg.* 78. φοῖβον δὲ δήπου τὸ καθαρὸν καὶ ἁγνὸν οἱ παλαιοὶ πᾶν ὠνόμαζον Plut. *Mor.* 493 c. — Notice the alliteration φοίβῃ φλογί, and cp. *Sept.* 661 φλύοντα σὺν φοίτῳ φρενῶν, *Ag.* 492 φῶς ἐφήλωσεν φρένας. — This passage seems to be parodied in a fragment preserved in Eustath. *Comm. Od.* p. 1484, 27, χρόαν δὲ τὴν σὴν ἥλιος λάμπων φλογὶ αἰγυπτιώσει.

23. χροιᾶς: χροιά, corresponding to Ionic χροιή, is an older and less trite form for the common χρόα. Similarly we have ποία and πόα, ῥοιά and ῥόα, στοιά (Ar. *Eccl.* 676, 684, 686) and στοά. — ἄνθος: used as here of the color of the skin in Solon *Frg.* 27, 6 τῇ τριτάτῃ δὲ γένειον ἀεξομένων ἔτι γυίων λαχνοῦται χροιῆς ἄνθος ἀμειβομένης, Theodectes *Frg.* 17

ἧς ἀγχιτέρμων ἥλιος διφρηλατῶν σκοτεινὸν ἄνθος ἐξέχρωσε λιγνύος εἰς σῶματ' ἀνδρῶν (of the black color of the Ethiopians); of the color of the hair, Soph. *O. T.* 742 λευκανθὲς κάρα, Babr. 22. 8 τῶν τριχῶν ἔτιλλεν ἃς ηὕρισκε λευκανθιζούσας; of color generally, Hdt. i. 98 οὕτω πάντων τῶν κύκλων οἱ προμαχεῶνες ἠνθισμένοι εἰσὶ φαρμάκοισι (*colored with paints*). — ἀσμένῳ: *Il.* xiv. 108 ἐμοὶ δέ κεν ἀσμένῳ εἴη, Soph. *Trach.* 18 ἀσμένῃ δέ μοι ὁ κλεινὸς ἦλθε . . . παῖς, Eur. *Phoen.* 1043 χρόνῳ δ' ἔβα τότ' ἀσμένοις, Ar. *Pax* 582 ἀσμένοισιν ἦλθες ἡμῖν, φιλτάτη. On this dative of a participle of feeling, chiefly used with εἶναι and verbs of coming, see G. 184, 3, N. 5; H. 771 a. For the thought, cp. Deuteronomy xxviii. 67, 'In the morning thou shalt say, Would God it were even! and at even thou shalt say, Would God it were morning!'

24. ποικιλείμων: from ποικίλος and εἶμα. ποικίλον ἔνδυμα ἔχουσα, διὰ τὸ πεποικίλθαι τοῖς ἄστροις, Schol. For ποικίλος, cp. Soph. *Trach.* 94 αἰόλα νύξ, Eur. *Hel.* 1096 ἀστέρων ποικίλματα, *Frg.* 596 ὀρφναία νὺξ αἰολόχρως ἄκριτός τ' ἄστρων ὄχλος. For the second part, εἶμα, cp. Eur. *Ion* 1150 μελάμπεπλος νύξ, Orph. *Argonaut.* 1031 νὺξ ἀστροχίτων (511 μήνη ἀστροχίτων), Claudian *Rapt. Proserp.* ii. 363 nox picta sinus. — ἀποκρύψει: initial κρ, with the aid of the ictus, makes a long syllable; cp. 659 below θεσπρόπους, *Eum.* 403 ἄτρυτον, *Pers.* 217 ἀποτροπήν, 395 ἐπέφλεγεν. — ἀποκρύψει φάος: Archil. *Frg.* 74 Ζεὺς πατὴρ 'Ολυμπίων ἐκ μεσημβρίης ἔθηκε νύκτ' ἀποκρύψας φάος ἡλίου λάμποντος.

25 πάχνην θ' ἑῴαν ἥλιος σκεδᾷ πάλιν.
ἀεὶ δὲ τοῦ παρόντος ἀχθηδὼν κακοῦ
τρύσει σ'· ὁ λωφήσων γὰρ οὐ πέφυκέ πω.

τοιαῦτ' ἐπηύρου τοῦ φιλανθρώπου τρόπου.
θεὸς θεῶν γὰρ οὐχ ὑποπτήσσων χόλον
30 βροτοῖσι τιμὰς ὤπασας πέρα δίκης.
ἀνθ' ὧν ἀτερπῆ τήνδε φρουρήσεις πέτραν
ὀρθοστάδην ἄυπνος, οὐ κάμπτων γόνυ·
πολλοὺς δ' ὀδυρμοὺς καὶ γόους ἀνωφελεῖς
φθέγξει· Διὸς γὰρ δυσπαραίτητοι φρένες·
35 ἅπας δὲ τραχὺς ὅστις ἂν νέον κρατῇ.

26. ἀεὶ δὲ κτἑ. : the sense is, " ever will some evil be with thee, the pain of which shall make thee wretched," "one evil will ever be followed by another."

27. ὁ λωφήσων : cp. Soph. *Ant.* 261 οὐδ' ὁ κωλύσων παρῆν, *El.* 1197 οὐδ' οὑπαρήξων οὐδ' ὁ κωλύσων πάρα. See also 771 below; Soph. *Phil.* 1242 τίς ἔσται μ' οὑπικωλύσων τάδε. The scholiast wrongly understands a particular person (Heracles). λωφάω is here transitive, in 376 intransitive. In this use of the participle the object is commonly omitted.— οὐ πέφυκέ πω : οὔπω separated, as in 611, *Pers.* 179, *Cho.* 747, *Eum.* 590, Frg. 280, 5. In saying *thy deliverer has yet to be born*, Hephaestus means only, "no living soul can deliver thee."

28. ἐπηύρου: of the verb ἐπαυρίσκομαι only the second aorist ἐπηυρόμην is used by the tragic poets. ἐπηύρου is here ironical ; *such reward thou didst reap!* Cp. *Il.* i. 410; and xv. 16 οὐ μὰν οἶδ' εἰ αὖτε κακορραφίης ἀλεγεινῆς πρώτη ἐπαυρήαι, καί σε πληγῆσιν ἱμάσσω.

29. θεὸς θεῶν (see on 19) : said

with reference to βροτοῖσι. The gods have a common interest as opposed to mortals. θεῶν modifies τιμάς.— ὑποπτήσσων : cp. 174, 900.

30. τιμάς : *distinctive possessions, privileges, prerogatives*, like γέρα, 107. See on 229.— πέρα δίκης : this, in the mouth of the well-disposed Hephaestus, must be taken as expressing the poet's own sentiment.

31. φρουρήσεις : said in reference to the sleeplessness mentioned in the next verse. A φρουρός is forbidden to sleep.— ἀτερπῆ : cp. ἄζηλον 143 ; *Od.* xi. 94 ὄφρα ἴδῃς νέκυας καὶ ἀτερπέα χῶρον.

32. ὀρθοστάδην : see Introduction, p. 5, footnote 3.— κάμπτων γόνυ : of taking a posture of rest ; γόνυ κάμψαι· ἀναπαύεσθαι, Hesych. Cp. 396 ; *Il.* vii. 118 φημί μιν ἀσπασίως γόνυ κάμψειν, εἴ κε φύγησιν δηίου ἐκ πολέμοιο, Eur. *Hec.* 1080, 1150 ; Catull. lxiv. 303 n i v e o s flexerunt sedibus artus.

33. πολλοὺς δ' ὀδυρμούς : προαναφωνεῖ τὰς μονῳδίας αὐτοῦ, Schol.

35. νέον: adverbial. See Krüger II. § 46, 6, 7. The same thought recurs 96, 149, 310, 389, 942, 955.

ΚΡΑΤΟΣ.

εἶεν, τί μέλλεις καὶ κατοικτίζει μάτην;
τί τὸν θεοῖς ἔχθιστον οὐ στυγεῖς θεόν,
ὅστις τὸ σὸν θνητοῖσι προύδωκεν γέρας;

ΗΦΑΙΣΤΟΣ.

τὸ συγγενές τοι δεινὸν ἥ θ' ὁμιλία.

ΚΡΑΤΟΣ.

40   σύμφημ', ἀνηκουστεῖν δὲ τῶν πατρὸς λόγων
οἷόν τε; πῶς οὐ τοῦτο δειμαίνεις πλέον;

ΗΦΑΙΣΤΟΣ.

αἰεί γε δὴ νηλὴς σὺ καὶ θράσους πλέως.

ΚΡΑΤΟΣ.

ἄκος γὰρ οὐδὲν τόνδε θρηνεῖσθαι· σὺ δὲ
τὰ μηδὲν ὠφελοῦντα μὴ πόνει μάτην.

38. προύδωκεν: like κλέψας ἔπασεν, 8.—Cratos begins this angry colloquy with three verses (cp. 613), but afterwards speaks regularly two; Hephaestus speaks single verses throughout, in accordance with his gruff and blunt-spoken nature. — ὅστις: has a qualitative force, *one who betrayed* (was such as to betray) = *since he betrayed*. So 759; Pers. 744 ταῖς δ' ἐμὸς τάδ' οὐ κατειδὼς ἤνυσεν νέῳ θράσει, ὅστις . . . ἤλπισε.

39. δεινόν: *mighty, a mighty influence*. Cp. Sept. 1031 δεινὸν τὸ κοινὸν σπλάγχνον οὗ πεφύκαμεν, Soph. El. 770 δεινὸν τὸ τίκτειν ἐστίν, Eur. Andr. 985 τὸ συγγενὲς γὰρ δεινόν, Phoen. 355 δεινὸν γυναιξὶν αἱ δι' ὠδίνων γοναί, Iph. Δ. 917 δεινὸν τὸ τίκτειν καὶ φέρει φίλτρον μέγα. — ὁμιλία: Quint. Decl. 321 consuetudo alienos etiam ac nulla necessitudine inter se coniunctos componere et adstringere officiis potest.

41. οἷόν τε; licet? *is it allowable?* Cp. Ar. Thesm. 3 οἷόν τε . . . παρὰ σοῦ πυθέσθαι; *may a body ask?* — πῶς οὐ: cp. 580, 759; Soph. Ai. 677 ἡμεῖς δὲ πῶς οὐ γνωσόμεσθα σωφρονεῖν; Ar. Nub. 398 καὶ πῶς, εἴπερ βάλλει τοὺς ἐπιόρκους, δῆτ' οὐχὶ Σίμων' ἐνέπρησεν; Isocr. Paneg. 175 πῶς οὐ χρὴ διαλύειν ταύτας τὰς ὁμολογίας; — δειμαίνεις: refers to the foregoing δεινόν.

42. The first and second persons of εἰμί are less often omitted, yet see 178, 246, 320, 373, 987. Only with ἔτοιμος is the omission common; here it occurs even though ἐγώ is left out. Cp. Soph. Ai. 813 χωρεῖν ἔτοιμος (sc. εἰμί), O. T. 92, Eur. Med. 612. In 475 below, the missing σύ can be supplied from the preceding σεαυτόν. See Krüger I. § 62, 1, 5.

ρ´

ΗΦΑΙΣΤΟΣ.

45 ὦ πολλὰ μισηθεῖσα χειρωναξία.

ΚΡΑΤΟΣ.

τί νιν στυγεῖς; πόνων γὰρ ὡς ἁπλῷ λόγῳ
τῶν νῦν παρόντων οὐδὲν αἰτία τέχνη.

ΗΦΑΙΣΤΟΣ.

ἔμπας τις αὐτὴν ἄλλος ὤφελεν λαχεῖν.

ΚΡΑΤΟΣ.

ἅπαντ᾽ ἐπαχθῆ πλὴν θεοῖσι κοιρανεῖν.
50 ἐλεύθερος γὰρ οὔτις ἐστὶ πλὴν Διός.

ΗΦΑΙΣΤΟΣ.

ἔγνωκα τοῖσδε, κοὐδὲν ἀντειπεῖν ἔχω.

ΚΡΑΤΟΣ.

οὔκουν ἐπείξει τῷδε δεσμὰ περιβαλεῖν,
ὡς μή σ᾽ ἐλινύοντα προσδερχθῇ πατήρ;

ΗΦΑΙΣΤΟΣ.

καὶ δὴ πρόχειρα ψέλια δέρκεσθαι πάρα.

46. νιν : in tragedy this word stands for all genders, in singular and in plural. G. 70, 1, n. 4; 11. 201 D a. —ὡς ἁπλῷ λόγῳ : equivalent to ὡς ἁπλῶς εἰπεῖν, to speak plainly, bluntly. Cp. 975.

48. Cp. Eur. Iph. A. 86 τἀξίωμα δὲ ἄλλος τις ὤφελ᾽ ἀντ᾽ ἐμοῦ λαβεῖν τόδε.

49 f. The sense is, "another station would have another burden: every one is bound to service and obedience save Zeus, the sovereign ruler; he alone commands all and obeys none" (ὑπ᾽ ἀρχᾶς οὔτινος θοάζων, Suppl. 595). — ἐπαχθῆ : vexatious, disagreeable. — κοιρανεῖν : with dative, like ἄρχειν 940, ἐπιδεσπόζει στρατῷ Pers. 241. See Krüger II. § 47, 20, 3.

51. ἔγνωκα τοῖσδε : I recognize it (the

truth of what you say) by this (what is here going on). — οὐδὲν ἀντειπεῖν : sc. τὸ μὴ οὐ τὰ ἐπιτεταγμένα ποιεῖν.

52. δεσμὰ περιβαλεῖν : resolution in the fifth foot is very rare in tragedy. This is the only case in the Prometheus. See on 2.

53. ἐλινύοντα : ἐλινύω is absolute here, but is construed with a participle in 529.

54. ψέλια : the best manuscript has ψάλια, others ψέλια. Ammonius gives the distinction : ψάλια μὲν τὸ τοῦ ἵππου, ψέλιον δὲ τὸ ἄκροις βραχίοσι περιτιθέμενον κόσμιον. With such bracelet-like clamps Prometheus is fastened in the paintings described in the Introd., p. 5, footnote 3.—δέρκεσθαι : said with reference to προσδερχθῇ above.

ΚΡΑΤΟΣ.

55 βαλών νιν ἀμφὶ χερσὶν ἐγκρατεῖ σθένει
ῥαιστῆρι θεῖνε πασσάλευε πρὸς πέτραις.

ΗΦΑΙΣΤΟΣ.

περαίνεται δὴ κοὐ ματᾷ τοὔργον τόδε.

ΚΡΑΤΟΣ.

ἄρασσε μᾶλλον, σφίγγε, μηδαμῇ χάλα.
δεινὸς γὰρ εὑρεῖν κἀξ ἀμηχάνων πόρον.

ΗΦΑΙΣΤΟΣ.

60 ἄραρεν ἥδε γ' ὠλένη δυσεκλύτως.

ΚΡΑΤΟΣ.

καὶ τήνδε νῦν πόρπασον ἀσφαλῶς, ἵνα
μάθῃ σοφιστὴς ὢν Διὸς νωθέστερος.

55 f. **νιν**: τὰ ψέλια, Schol. ; see on 46.—**ἐγκρατεῖ σθένει, ῥαιστῆρι**: of these two datives the one denotes the inner power (dynamic dative), the other the external means (instrumental dative). *ἐγκρατεῖ σθένει* nearly = *ἐγκρατῶς*.—In *Il.* xviii. 477 Hephaestus wields a *ῥαιστὴρ κρατερή*.

56. **θεῖνε πασσάλευε**: the connective is omitted ('asyndeton') when a single idea is expressed by two or more verbs, the second being a stronger expression than the first. Cp. 58, 141, 302, 608, 698, 937; *Pers.* 426 *ἴπαιον ἐρράχιζον*, 463 *παίουσι κρεοκοποῦσι, Cho.* 280 *κινεῖ ταράσσει, Sept.* 60 *χωρεῖ κονίει*, 186 *ᾄδειν λακάζειν*, Soph. *Ai.* 60 *ὄτρυνον εἰσέβαλλον εἰς ἕρκη κακά*, 115, 811, 844, 988, *Ant.* 1037 *κερδαίνετ' ἐμπολᾶτε, El.* 719 *ἥφριζον εἰσέβαλλον ἱππικαὶ πνοαί, Trach.* 1255 *ἐγκονεῖτ' αἴρεσθε*, Eur. *Hec.* 507 *σπεύδωμεν ἐγκονῶμεν, Phoen.* 1434 *ἔκλαι' ἐθρήνει.*

57. **ματᾷ**: διατρίβει, χρονίζει, Hesych.

59. Cp. Ar. *Eq.* 758 ποικίλος γὰρ ἀνὴρ κἀκ τῶν ἀμηχάνων πόρους εὑμήχανος πορίζειν. .

61. **πόρπασον**: long ᾱ (not η), as in πόρπαμα Eur. *El.* 820. Cp. *ἐκθοινάσεται* 1025 (θοινατῆρος *Ag.* 1502, θοίναμα Eur. *Ion* 1495), and other tragic forms, as εὐνατήρ *Pers.* 137, εὐνάτειρα *Pers.* 157, ποινάτωρ *Ag.* 1281, ἱπποβάμων 805 below and *Supp.* 284, ἑκατογκάρανος 353 (καρανοῦται *Cho.* 628), κυναγός, βαλός, γάπεδον, γάμοροι, γάποτος, ἕκατι, δαρόν, δᾷος, and others.

62. **σοφιστής**: in Aeschylus's time this word had not acquired the meaning which Socrates and Plato afterwards gave it, and which through their influence passed into history. Cp. Athen. xiv. 632 c πάντας τοὺς χρωμένους τῇ τέχνῃ ταύτῃ (*i.e.* τῇ μουσικῇ) σοφιστὰς ἀπεκάλουν, ὥσπερ καὶ Αἰσχύλος ἐποίησεν 'εἶτ' οὖν σοφιστὴς κᾶλα παραπαίων χέλυν.' In this play, both here and 944, the word implies a crafty and unscrupulous cleverness.

ΗΦΑΙΣΤΟΣ.

πλὴν τοῦδ' ἂν οὐδεὶς ἐνδίκως μέμψαιτό μοι.

ΚΡΑΤΟΣ.

ἀδαμαντίνου νῦν σφηνὸς αὐθάδη γνάθον
65 στέρνων διαμπὰξ πασσάλευ' ἐρρωμένως.

ΗΦΑΙΣΤΟΣ.

αἰαῖ, Προμηθεῦ, σῶν ὑπὸ στένω πόνων.

ΚΡΑΤΟΣ.

σὺ δ' αὖ κατοκνεῖς τῶν Διός τ' ἐχθρῶν ὕπερ
στένεις; ὅπως μὴ σαυτὸν οἰκτιεῖς ποτε.

Cp. the sense of σοφίζομαι in Soph. *Phil.* 77 ἀλλ' αὐτὸ τοῦτο δεῖ σοφισθῆναι, κλοπεὺς ὅπως γένηται τῶν ἀνικήτων ὅπλων.— ἄν: the speaker does not mean that Zeus is a σοφιστής. Logically only Διὸς νωθέστερος belongs to μάθῃ ἄν. σοφιστής, though grammatically a predicate, refers only to Prometheus. The general sense is, "may learn that with all his artfulness he is slower-witted than Zeus."

64. αὐθάδη: with this epithet the Homeric νηλέϊ χαλκῷ, λᾶας ἀναιδής, and the Euripidean λάβρῳ μαχαίρᾳ, *Cycl.* 403, may be compared. — γνάθον: cp. γένυς used in the sense of πέλεκυς in Soph. *El.* 196 and 485, *Phil.* 1205, and πελέκεων γνάθοις in Eur. *Cycl.* 395.

65. στέρνων διαμπάξ: the passage of Hesiod, *Theog.* 521, δῆσε δ' ἀλυκτοπέδῃσι Προμηθέα ποικιλόβουλον δεσμοῖς ἀργαλέοισι μέσον διὰ κίον' ἐλάσσας, which should be construed ἐλάσσας (τὰ δεσμὰ) διὰ μέσον κίονα, *riveting the chains through the middle of the pillar*, was wrongly understood as ἐλάσσας κίονα διὰ μέσον (τὸν Προμηθέα). Accordingly, on an ancient black-figured vase, found at Chiusi and now in

the Berlin Museum (No. 1722; Jahn, *Archaeologische Beiträge*, Plate viii.; Baumeister, *Denkmäler* fig. 1568), we find Prometheus represented as actually impaled (on an upright stake passed lengthwise through the body). This revolting conception was modified by Aeschylus into one more endurable for the eye. Even in Hesiod's narrative the original notion is obscured: the older legend doubtless meant by the pillar a κίων οὐράνιος, that is, a sharp mountain-peak rearing itself to the sky. See on 349.

66. ὑπό: *because of, by reason of,* denoting the cause; as Thuc. ii. 85 ὑπὸ ἀνέμων καὶ ὑπὸ ἀπλοίας ἐνδιέτριψεν οὐκ ὀλίγον χρόνον, iv. 8 ὑλώδης τε καὶ ἀτριβὴς πᾶσα ὑπ' ἐρημίας ἦν (sc. ἡ νῆσος), Soph. *Ant.* 221 ὑπ' ἐλπίδων ἄνδρας τὸ κέρδος πολλάκις διώλεσεν, also *Ag.* 476 πυρὸς δ' ὑπ' εὐαγγέλου πόλιν διῆκει θοὰ βάξις.

67. αὖ κατοκνεῖς: see 30. — ἐχθρῶν ὕπερ: the tragedians often put the preposition after its noun when an attributive (as in 653 a genitive) follows both. Otherwise, the postponement of the preposition (with anastrophe of the accent) is per-

ΗΦΑΙΣΤΟΣ.

ὁρᾷς θέαμα δυσθέατον ὄμμασιν.

ΚΡΑΤΟΣ.

70 ὁρῶ κυροῦντα τόνδε τῶν ἐπαξίων.
ἀλλ' ἀμφὶ πλευραῖς μασχαλιστῆρας βάλε.

ΗΦΑΙΣΤΟΣ.

δρᾶν ταῦτ' ἀνάγκη, μηδὲν ἐγκέλευ' ἄγαν.

ΚΡΑΤΟΣ.

ἦ μὴν κελεύσω κἀπιθωύξω γε πρός·
χώρει κάτω, σκέλη δὲ κίρκωσον βίᾳ.

ΗΦΑΙΣΤΟΣ.

75 καὶ δὴ πέπρακται τοὔργον οὐ μακρῷ πόνῳ.

mitted in trimeter, as a rule, only when the preposition comes thereby to stand at the end of a verse. This occurs most frequently with περί, μετά, παρά, ὑπό, ὑπέρ, ἀπό, and ἐπί, in connexion with the genitive. The remaining cases in Aeschylus are: with the dative, ὑπό 365 below and *Pers.* 190, ἐπί *Suppl.* 1003, μετά *Pers.* 613; with the accusative, περί *Pers.* 61.

68. ὅπως μή κτλ.: for this form of warning see GMT. 272; G. 217, N. 4; H. 886.

70. ὁρῶ: said with emphasis after ὁρᾷς.

71. μασχαλιστῆρας: iron girths, passed round the body and nailed to the rock on either side.

72. The asyndeton of the two clauses (instead of μηδὲν ἐγκέλευ' ἄγαν, ἀνάγκη γὰρ ταῦτα δρᾶν: see on 373 f.) expresses irritation. Krüger I. § 59, 1, 8, and II. § 59, 1, 7. Impatience at the repeated admonitions is also implied in the compound ἐγκέλευε, command imperiously, urgently.

73. ἦ μὴν κελεύσω: defiant reply to Hephaestus's demand. — ἐπιθωύξω: cp. 277, 393, 1041; Eur. *Hipp.* 219 κυσὶ θωύξαι. The scholiast on 277 remarks, ἡ μεταφορὰ ἀπὸ τῶν κυνηγῶν: that is, the verb was properly used of a hunter's call to his dogs. — καὶ ... γέ: et quidem; γέ serves to emphasize the stronger statement. Cp. Eur. *Phoen.* 610 ΠΟ. ὃς μ' ἀμοιρον ἐξελαύνεις. ΕΤ. καὶ κατακτενῶ γε πρός. — πρός: adverbial. Cp. πρὸς δέ 929, καὶ πρός *Cho.* 209. G. 191, N. 2; H. 785.

74. χώρει κάτω: the scholiast understands this literally: διὰ τοῦ 'χώρει κάτω' τὸ μέγεθος ἐνέφηνε τοῦ δεσμευομένου θεοῦ. But it may mean simply, "proceed to the lower limbs." — κίρκωσον: ἀντὶ τοῦ κρίκωσον, Schol. κρίκος, ring, is read in *Il.* xxiv. 272. The older form κίρκος (circus) survived in the name of the bird (*Od.* xiii. 86 ἴρηξ κίρκος): see 857. Similar are the Attic forms φάρξαι for φράξαι, δαρχμή for δραχμή.

ΚΡΑΤΟΣ.

ἐρρωμένως νῦν θεῖνε διατόρους πέδας·
ὡς οὑπιτιμητής γε τῶν ἔργων βαρύς.

ΗΦΑΙΣΤΟΣ.

ὅμοια μορφῇ γλῶσσά σου γηρύεται.

ΚΡΑΤΟΣ.

σὺ μαλθακίζου, τὴν δ' ἐμὴν αὐθαδίαν
80   ὀργῆς τε τραχυτῆτα μὴ 'πίπλησσέ μοι.

ΗΦΑΙΣΤΟΣ.

στείχωμεν· ὡς κώλοισιν ἀμφίβληστρ' ἔχει.

ΚΡΑΤΟΣ.

ἐνταῦθα νῦν ὕβριζε καὶ θεῶν γέρα
συλῶν ἐφημέροισι προστίθει.   τί σοι

76. **διατόρους πέδας**: πέδας is generic, as in 6. διάτορος is here passive, *perforated;* the active sense (see 181) is more common. Schütz and Hermann understand it of holes originally made in the fetters for the reception of the nails. Rather it means "pierced by nails," "having nails driven through them," as in Soph. *O. T.* 1034 διατόρους ποδοῖν ἀκμάς means "feet pierced with needles." θεῖνε then refers to the nails. Hephaestus is bidden, before departing, to examine once more the different fastenings and drive the nails in each firmly home. — On the resolution, see note on 2. Three other resolutions of this foot occur (273, 680, 800). In 273 the second and third shorts of the tribrach are formed by a disyllable (διά); in 800 they begin a word of three syllables; in 680, as here, they begin a word of four syllables.

77. Cp. 53 and 68. — **ἐπιτιμητής**: cp. *Pers.* 827 Ζεύς τοι κολαστὴς τῶν ὑπερκόπων ἄγαν φρονημάτων ἔπεστιν, εὔθυνος βαρύς, Soph. Frg. 478 κολασταί

κἀπιτιμηταὶ κακῶν, Eur. *Suppl.* 255 τούτων κολαστὴν κἀπιτιμητήν, ἄναξ.

78. **ὅμοια μορφῇ**: ὡς ἐκτραπέλου (*grotesque*) πεποιημένου τοῦ προσώπου (*mask*) αὐτοῦ, Schol.

79. **μαλθακίζου**: on this use of the imperative to denote a permission, see Krüger I. § 54, 4, 2.

80. **ὀργῆς**: *violent nature.*

81. **κώλοισιν**: the dative depends on the notion of ἀμφιβάλλειν implied in ἀμφίβληστρ' ἔχει. — Hephaestus, with these words, quietly goes his way, while Cratos remains to give further vent to his scorn. In this way time was secured for the retiring actor to take his position for the part of Prometheus. See Introduction, p. 23.

82. Cp. *Il.* xxi. 120 τὸν δ' Ἀχιλεὺς ποταμόνδε λαβὼν ποδὸς ἧκε φέρεσθαι, καί οἱ ἐπευχόμενος ἔπεα πτερόεντ' ἀγόρευεν· ἐνταυθοῖ νῦν κεῖσο μετ' ἰχθύσιν κτἑ., *Od.* xviii. 105 ἐνταυθοῖ νῦν ἧσο σύας τε κύνας τ' ἀπερύκων κτἑ., Ar. *Thesm.* 1001 ἐνταῦθα νῦν οἴμωξι πρὸς τὴν αἰτίαν, also *Vesp.* 149, *Plut.* 724.

83. **ἐφημέροισι**: see on 546 f., and

οἷοί τε θνητοὶ τῶνδ' ἀπαντλῆσαι πόνων;
85 ψευδωνύμως σε δαίμονες Προμηθέα
καλοῦσιν· αὐτὸν γάρ σε δεῖ προμηθέως,
ὅτῳ τρόπῳ τῆσδ' ἐκκυλισθήσει τέχνης.

ΠΡΟΜΗΘΕΥΣ.

ὦ δῖος αἰθὴρ καὶ ταχύπτεροι πνοαὶ

cp. 253, 945, Eur. *Orest.* 976 ἰὼ ἰώ, πανδάκρυτ' ἐφαμέρων ἔθνη πολύπονα, Ar. *Nub.* 223 (Socrates speaks as a god) τί με καλεῖς, ὦ 'φήμερε, Cic. *Tusc.* i. 39, 94 apud Hypanim fluvium ... Aristoteles ait bestiolas quasdam nasci, quae unum diem vivant (Aristotle *H. An.* v. 19, calls these animals ἐφήμερα) ... Confer nostram longissimam aetatem cum aeternitate; in eadem propemodum brevitate qua illae bestiolae reperiemur.

86. The construction δεῖ τινά τινος is not elsewhere found in Aeschylus, but occurs several times in Euripides (*Hec.* 1021, *Phoen.* 470, *Hipp.* 23, *Ion* 1018, *H. F.* 1170, *Rhes.* 837). G. 172, 2, n. 2; H. 712 b.—προμηθέως: the proper name is here used as an appellative, *fore-thinker, counsellor.* Cp. Pind. *Ol.* vii. 79 ἐν δ' ἀρετὰν ἔβαλεν καὶ χάρματ' ἀνθρώποισι Προμαθέος αἰδώς. Etymological interpretations of proper names are frequent in Aeschylus. His view on the subject is expressed *Ag.* 681: τίς ποτ' ὠνόμαζεν ὧδ' ἐς τὸ πᾶν ἐτητύμως; μή τις ὅντιν' οὐχ ὁρῶμεν προνοίαισι τοῦ πεπρωμένου γλῶσσαν ἐν τύχᾳ νέμων; where Ἑλένα is explained as ἑλέναυς, ἕλανδρος, ἑλέπτολις. Cp. ibid. 1080 Ἀπόλλων ... ἀπόλλων ἐμός, and similar cases, *Sept.* 658, 829, 536; cp. also *Od.* i. 60 οὔ νύ τ' Ὀδυσσεὺς ... χαρίζετο ἱερὰ ῥέζων; τί νύ οἱ τόσον ὠδύ-

σαο, Ζεῦ; Eur. *Phoen.* 636 ἀληθῶς δ' ὄνομα Πολυνείκην πατὴρ ἔθετό σοι θείᾳ προνοίᾳ νεικέων ἐπώνυμον. On the thought, cp. 474 f. below, and the passage of Mark there quoted.

87. ὅτῳ τρόπῳ ἐκκυλισθήσει: cp. Eur. *Med.* 322 οὐκ ἔχεις τέχνην, ὅπως μενεῖς παρ' ἡμῖν, Thuc. i. 107 ἔδοξε δ' αὐτοῖς ... σκέψασθαι, ὅτῳ τρόπῳ ἀσφαλέστατα διαπορεύσονται. The clause depends on the verbal idea τοῦ προμηθουμένου implied in προμηθέως.— τέχνης: τῶν δεσμῶν, Schol.; another scholiast, τοῦ τεχνηέντως κατεσκευασμένου δεσμοῦ. Cp. Soph. *O. C.* 472 κρατῆρες εἰσίν, ἀνδρὸς εὔχειρος τέχνη, Frg. III. of the *Prom. Solutus* below, 8, qua miser sollertia transverberatus.—Prometheus is bound hand and foot, so that he cannot stir. This serves to excite the spectators' compassion (cp. 32), but it also affords a reason for the immobility, during the entire play, of the figure representing Prometheus. See Introduction, p. 22.

88–127. Second Scene. Prometheus alone.—With this invocation of the elements cp. *Il.* iii. 277 ἠέλιός θ' ὃς πάντ' ἐφορᾷς καὶ πάντ' ἐπακούεις, καὶ ποταμοὶ καὶ γαῖα, Soph. *Phil.* 936 ὦ λιμένες, ὦ προβλῆτες, ὦ ξυνουσίαι θηρῶν ὀρείων, ὦ καταρρῶγες πέτραι, ὑμῖν τάδ', οὐ γὰρ ἄλλον οἶδ' ὅτῳ λέγω, ἀνακλαίομαι. Apsines (*Rhet. Gr.* ed. Spengel I. p. 400) says: κινεῖ δὲ ἔλεον καὶ λόγος πρὸς τόπον τινὰ γινόμενος.

88. δῖος: *heavenly*, from the root

ποταμῶν τε πηγαὶ ποντίων τε κυμάτων
90   ἀνήριθμον γέλασμα παμμῆτόρ τε γῆ,
καὶ τὸν πανόπτην κύκλον ἡλίου καλῶ ·
ἴδεσθέ μ᾽ οἷα πρὸς θεῶν πάσχω θεός.

δέρχθηθ᾽ οἵαις αἰκίαισιν
διακναιόμενος τὸν μυριετῆ
95   χρόνον ἀθλεύσω. τοιόνδ᾽ ὁ νέος
ταγὸς μακάρων ἐξηῦρ᾽ ἐπ᾽ ἐμοὶ

δι-, διϝ- (Sanskrit di-, *shine*). Cp. *Il.* xvi. 365 αἰθέρος ἐκ δίης ὅτε τε Ζεὺς λαίλαπα τείνῃ. — ταχύπτεροι: said figuratively, with reference to the physical impression made by a passing breeze. Actual winged daemons — the guise in which the Winds and similar beings are depicted in ancient art — are not here to be understood.

90. ἀνήριθμον γέλασμα: of the slightly ruffled surface of the sea, lighted up by the sun. Cp. *Il.* xix. 362 γέλασσε δὲ πᾶσα περὶ χθὼν χαλκοῦ ὑπὸ στεροπῆς. The verb γελᾶν often denotes merriment or cheerfulness in a figurative sense ; thus Hesiod *Theog.* 40 γελᾷ δέ τε δώματα πατρὸς ... θεᾶν ὀπὶ λειριοέσσῃ σκιδναμένη. The scholiast on our passage renders γέλασμα by διάχυμα. In a different sense Catullus, lxiv. 273, says of the sea-waves leni resonant plangore cachinni. — παμμῆτορ γῆ: cp. Hom. *Hymn* xxx. 1 γαῖαν παμμήτειραν, *Cho.* 127 γαῖαν ἡ τὰ πάντα τίκτεται.

91. καὶ ... καλῶ: ἤλλαξε τὴν φράσιν, Schol. Cp. Soph. *Ai.* 859 ὦ φέγγος, ὦ γῆς ἱερὸν οἰκείας πέδον Σαλαμῖνος, ὦ πατρῷον ἑστίας βάθρον κλειναί τ᾽ Ἀθῆναι, καὶ τὸ σύντροφον γένος, κρῆναί τε ποταμοί θ᾽ οἵδε, καὶ τὰ Τρωικὰ πεδία προσαυδῶ, χαίρετ᾽, ὦ τροφῆς ἐμοί, also *O. C.* 1091. — κύκλον: cp. *Pers.* 504

λαμπρὸς ἡλίου κύκλος. This expression (like orbis solis) had its origin in ancient conceptions of the sun as a wheel of fire. In the Edda the sun is called *fagravhel*, that is, 'fair-wheel,' 'wheel of brightness.' See Grimm's *Deutsche Mythologie*, I. 586, II. 664.

92. πρὸς θεῶν: πρός τινος and ἐκ τινος, for ὑπό τινος, are common in Herodotus and the tragedians. Krüger II. § 52, 3, 1. πάσχειν ἐκ occurs 759, πάσχειν ὑπό 1041.

93 f. The transition from iambi to anapaests marks an outbreak of more violent passion. At 101, with a calmer mood, the quieter rhythm returns. — αἰκίαισιν (= ἀεικελίοις μόχθοις) διακναιόμενος: cp. 541. — τὸν μυριετῆ χρόνον: said like τὸν πλείω χρόνον (Ἀρ. *Ran.* 160, Thuc. iv. 117), τὸν πάντα χρόνον (Ar. *Nub.* 462). μυριετῆ πολυετῆ· ἐν γὰρ τῷ πυρφόρῳ τρεῖς μυριάδας φησὶ δεδέσθαι αὐτόν, Schol. (cp. Hygin. *Poet. astr.* ii. 15). Both numbers are merely hyperbolic expressions for a very long time. — ἀθλεύσω: absolute, *suffer*. Cp. *Il.* xxiv. 734 ἀθλεύων πρὸ ἄνακτος ἀμειλίχου. The word is Ionic.

96. ταγός: cp. *Pers.* 23 ταγοὶ Περσῶν, 323 νεῶν ταγός, Soph. *Ant.* 1057 ἆρ᾽ οἶσθα ταγοὺς (lords and masters) ὄντας ἂν λέγῃς λέγων ;

δεσμὸν ἀεικῆ.
φεῦ, φεῦ, τὸ παρὸν τό τ' ἐπερχόμενον
πῆμα στενάχω, πῆ πότε μόχθων
100 χρὴ τέρματα τῶνδ' ἐπιτεῖλαι.

καίτοι τί φημι; πάντα προυξεπίσταμαι
σκεθρῶς τὰ μέλλοντ' οὐδέ μοι ποταίνιον
πῆμ' οὐδὲν ἥξει. τὴν πεπρωμένην δὲ χρὴ
αἶσαν φέρειν ὡς ῥᾷστα, γιγνώσκονθ' ὅτι
105 τὸ τῆς ἀνάγκης ἔστ' ἀδήριτον σθένος.
ἀλλ' οὔτε σιγᾶν οὔτε μὴ σιγᾶν τύχας
οἷόν τε μοι τάσδ' ἐστί. θνητοῖς γὰρ γέρα

97. The anapaestic monometer forms a close, but a less emphatic one than the paroemiac.—δεσμόν: the singular as in 141. We have δεσμοὺς ἀεικεῖς 525.—ἀεικῆ: see on 113.

99. στενάχω, πῆ: as it were *I groan to think how*, etc. Cp. 182; Soph. *Ai.* 794 ὥστε μ' ὠδίνειν τί φῄς, Eur. *Hec.* 184 δειμαίνω τί ποτ' ἀναστένεις, Ar. *Nub.* 1391 οἶμαί γε τῶν νεωτέρων τὰς καρδίας πηδᾶν ὅ τι λέξει.—πῆ πότε: cp. 545; Eur. *Alc.* 213 ἰὼ Ζεῦ, τίς ἂν τῶς πᾶ πόρος κακῶν γένοιτο; Krüger I. § 51, 17, 10; II. 1013.

100. χρὴ: nearly = μέλλει.—ἐπιτεῖλαι: ἐπιτέλλεσθαι of the rising of heavenly bodies, Hom. *Hymn* iii. 371 ἠελίοιο νέον ἐπιτελλομένοιο, Hesiod *O. D.* 567 πρῶτον παμφαίνων ἐπιτέλλεται. The active in the 'Ιλιὰς μικρά (Tzetzes on Lycophr. 344) λαμπρὴ δ' ἐπέτελλε σελήνη. In a figurative sense, Theogn. 1275 ὡραῖος καὶ ἔρως ἐπιτέλλεται ἡνίκα περ γῆ ἄνθεσιν εἰαρινοῖς θάλλει ἀεξομένη.

101. καίτοι τί φημι: 'se ipsum obiurgat Prometheus; et paulisper ob malorum magnitudinem naturae suae oblitus iam ad se rediit' (Schütz).

—προυξεπίσταμαι: as son of Themis. Cp. 209, 873.

102. ποταίνιον: predicative; *shall not come unexpected.*

105. ἀδήριτον: *Il.* xvii. 41 ἀλλ' οὐ μὰν ἔτι δηρὸν ἀπείρητος πόνος ἔσται οὐδέ τ' ἀδήριτος. Here = ἄμαχος (ἀδήριτον· ἄμαχον, ἀκατάμαχον, Hesych.). Cp. ἀνίκητος, *invictus.* For the thought cp. Simon. Frg. 5, 21 (Plat. *Prot.* 345d) ἀνάγκᾳ δ' οὐδὲ θεοὶ μάχονται, Soph. *Ant.* 1106 ἀνάγκῃ δ' οὐχὶ δυσμαχητέον, *O. C.* 191 καὶ μὴ χρείᾳ πολεμῶμεν, Eur. *Iph. T.* 1486 τὸ γὰρ χρεὼν σοῦ τε καὶ θεῶν κρατεῖ.

106. οὔτε σιγᾶν οὔτε μὴ σιγᾶν: explained by 107, whence we see that the motive for silence is the pain of speaking (not caution as in *Ag.* 548, πάλαι τὸ σιγᾶν φάρμακον βλάβης ἔχω). The scholiast wrongly explains, ἀλλ' οὔτε σιγᾶν δύναμαι (ἀλγῶ γὰρ) οὔτε ἐλέγχειν· εὐλαβοῦμαι γὰρ τὸν Δία. Cp. Soph. *Phil.* 929 ὦ παῖ Ποίαντος, ἐξερῶ, μόλις δ' ἐρῶ, ἄγωγ' ὑπ' αὐτῶν ἐξελωβήθην μολών.

107. γέρα: see on τιμάς, 30.—Here and in 821 we find the thesis of the fifth foot formed by the long final syllable of a word of more than one

πορῶν ἀνάγκαις ταῖσδ' ἐνέζευγμαι τάλας ·
ναρθηκοπλήρωτον δὲ θηρῶμαι πυρὸς
110 πηγὴν κλοπαίαν, ἣ διδάσκαλος τέχνης
πάσης βροτοῖς πέφηνε καὶ μέγας πόρος.
τοιῶνδε ποινὰς ἀμπλακημάτων τίνω
ὑπαιθρίοις δεσμοῖσι προυσελούμενος.

syllable (θνη-τοῖς). This is very rare in tragedy (H. 1091, 5). It is excusable when, as here, a distinct pause, in connexion with the caesura of the fourth foot (hephthemimeris), immediately precedes. See also on 648.

108. ἀνάγκαις: said like αἰκίαι 93. — ἐνέζευγμαι: a favorite metaphor of Aeschylus. Cp. 578, 1000; *Ag.* 1639 τὸν δὲ μὴ πειθάνορα ζεύξω βαρείαις (sc. ζεύγλαις), 841 μόνος δ' Ὀδυσσεὺς . . . ζευχθεὶς ἕτοιμος ἦν ἐμοὶ σειραφόρος, *Cho.* 795 ζυγέντ' ἐν ἅρμασιν πημάτων, also *Ag.* 218 ἀνάγκας ἔδυ λέπαδνον. Figures and comparisons drawn from husbandry and rural life are frequent in the tragedians. With our passage cp. Eur. *Or.* 1330 ἀνάγκης εἰς ζυγὸν καθέσταμεν, *Hipp.* 1389 οἵαις συμφοραῖς συνεζύγης.

109. ναρθηκοπλήρωτον: τὴν ἐν νάρθηκι θησαυρισθεῖσαν, παρόσον τῷ νάρθηκι ἐχρῶντο πρὸς τὰς ἐκζωπυρώσεις τοῦ πυρός, Hesych. The νάρθηξ (*ferula communis*) is in modern Greek ἀνάρθηκας) is an umbelliferous reed-like plant, about four feet high; its stalk is filled with an acrid milky juice (habent fungosam intus medullam ut sambuci: Plin.). When dried it readily catches and preserves a spark of fire; the peasants of southern Italy use it as tinder. Cp. Phanias, *Anthol.* vi. 294 νάρθηξ πυρικοίτας, also Theophr. *Hist. Pl.* vi. 2, 7, Plin. *H. N.* xiii. 22. 42. On the mythical significance of the narthex, see Introduction, p. 2. — This clause

is properly explanatory of what goes before, nevertheless it is introduced by δέ as if it were a new and distinct statement. The scholiasts often render this δέ by γάρ; an example is *Cho.* 239 προσαυδᾶν δ' ἔστ' ἀναγκαίως ἔχον, which is explanatory of the foregoing words τέσσαρας μοίρας ἔχον ἐμοί. — θηρῶμαι: historical present. Krüger I. § 53, 1, 11; GMT. 33.

110 f. διδάσκαλος τέχνης πάσης: see on 7. — πόρος: absolute, as in 477.

112. τοιῶνδε ποινὰς ἀμπλακημάτων: cp. 564, 620.

113. ὑπαιθρίοις: explains προυσελούμενος; the insult of the punishment consists in its publicity. See also 158. Prometheus lays stress on the ignominious nature of his punishment, 97, 177, 195, 227, 256, 438, 525. For the connexion of ὑπαιθρίοις and δεσμοῖσι, see on ἀφεγγής 115. — προυσελούμενος: this word recurs 438; it is found elsewhere only in Ar. *Ran.* 730 (προυσελοῦμεν). Cp. *Etym. Mag.* p. 690, 11 προυσελεῖν λέγουσι τὸ ὑβρίζειν. It is therefore equivalent to αἰκίζομαι, the word employed in most of the similar passages of this play (cp. Hesych. προυγελεῖν· προσηλακίζειν, ὑβρίζειν). The etymology of the word is unknown: it has been proposed to derive it from προσφέλλειν, on the supposition that the digamma, falling out after σ, has lengthened the preceding syllable, as in θεουδής (θεοδϝής).

ἂ ἄ,

115 τίς ἀχώ, τίς ὀδμὰ προσέπτα μ' ἀφεγγής.
θεόσυτος ἢ βρότειος ἢ κεκραμένη ;⌣
ἵκετο τερμόνιον ἐπὶ πάγον
πόνων ἐμῶν θεωρός, ἢ τί δὴ θέλων ;
ὁρᾶτε δεσμώτην με δύσποτμον θεόν,

114-127 announce the approach of the chorus and accompany (from 120 on) the movements of the winged chariot. Similarly in the *Electra* of Sophocles anapaests of Electra accompany the entrance of the chorus.

114. A rush or whir is heard in the air.—ἂ ἄ: ἐκπλήξεως ἐπιφρήματα, Schol. 'Ce mélange de douleur et d'effroi, de faiblesse et de fermeté me paraît tout à fait admirable' (Patin).

115. The bacchic rhythms express surprise and amazement. — ὀδμά: an odor of the sea is supposed to precede the nymphs, in whose costume seaweed, shells, etc., may well have been prominent. Cp. Eur. *Hipp.* 1391 ἔα· ὦ θεῖον ὀδμῆς πνεῦμα ' . . . ἔστ' ἐν τόποισι τοισίδ' Ἄρτεμις θεά, Verg. *Aen.* i. 403 ambrosiaeque comae divinum vertice odorem spiravere.—προσέπτα: cp. Plaut. *Amphitr.* 325 vox mi ad auris advolavit. The verb, in a somewhat different sense, is joined with the dative in 555 and 644. — ἀφεγγής: (here nearly = ἀφανής) is, by a figure common in the poets, connected with ἀχώ and ὀδμά, whereas it is properly an epithet of the object from which they emanate. — For the situation cp. Soph. *Phil.* 203 προυφάνη κτύπος . . . βάλλει μ' ἐτύμα φθογγά του.

116. θεόσυτος: the tribrach in the first foot generally, in Aeschylus, consists of a single word of three syllables, as in 666. Here and 817 it is

the first part of a longer word : the remaining cases of this are *Sept.* 272 πεδιονόμοις, *Eum.* 806 λιπαροθρόνοισιν, Frg. 195, 2 βορεάδας. —Compounds in -συτος and in -ρυτος either double the medial σ or ρ, or do not double it, according to the requirements of the verse : cp. 643. With θεόσυτος ἢ βρότειος cp. 766. — κεκραμένη : ἡμιθέων, Schol. Demigods according to the later conception are not meant, but beings who, like the Oceanids, stand midway between the higher (celestial) gods and the human race : cp. 529 f., 902. For the expression cp. Eur. *Cycl.* 218 μήλειον ἢ βόειον ἢ μεμιγμένον ;

117. The rhythm (dochmius and cretic) indicates painful emotion. The question " Who can it be " (115, 116) is followed by the conjecture that the person in question comes as an unwelcome spectator of his sufferings. The reason of this conjecture is suggested by the opening words, ἵκετο τερμόνιον ἐπὶ πάγον ("a cliff at the end of the world"). — ἵκετο : *is he come* ; the subject is the unknown newcomer ; not θεωρός, which expresses the motive of the coming.—τερμόνιον : this adjective occurs only here : it is formed from τέρμων, while τέρμιος is from τέρμα.

118. ἢ τί δὴ θέλων : cp. Soph. *Trach.* 390 ἡμεῖς δὲ προσμένωμεν ; ἢ τί χρὴ ποιεῖν ;

119. ὁρᾶτε : said with reference to θεωρός. The imperative has the sense of ὁρᾶν πάρα.

120 τὸν Διὸς ἐχθρόν, τὸν πᾶσι θεοῖς
δι' ἀπεχθείας ἐλθόνθ' ὁπόσοι
τὴν Διὸς αὐλὴν εἰσοιχνεῦσιν,
διὰ τὴν λίαν φιλότητα βροτῶν.
φεῦ φεῦ, τί ποτ' αὖ κινάθισμα κλύω
125 πέλας οἰωνῶν; αἰθὴρ δ' ἐλαφραῖς
πτερύγων ῥιπαῖς ὑποσυρίζει.
πᾶν μοι φοβερὸν τὸ προσέρπον.

120 f. The iambi again give place to anapaests; see on 93. The speaker is outraged at the thought of becoming a spectacle for others; cp. 156. — πᾶσι θεοῖς δι' ἀπεχθείας ἐλθόντα: cp. Eur. *Hipp.* 1104 δι' ἔχθρας μῶν τις ἦν ἀφιγμένος, *Phoen.* 470 καὶ μὴ δι' ἔχθρας τῷδε καὶ φόνου μολών, *H. F.* 220 Μινύαισι πᾶσι διὰ μάχης μολών, *Iph. A.* 1392 similarly, *Androm.* 410 πατρὶ τῷ σῷ διὰ φιλημάτων ἰών, Soph. *Ant.* 742 διὰ δίκης ἰὼν πατρί, Ar. *Ran.* 1412 οὐ γὰρ δι' ἔχθρας οὐδετέρῳ γενήσομαι, [Plato] *Theag.* 130 b μοι δι' ἀπεχθείας ἐν λόγοις τισὶν ἐγεγόνει. These combinations of a verb of motion with διά arose from the local meaning of the preposition. Krüger I. § 68, 22, 2.

122. αὐλήν: cp. *Od.* iv. 74 Ζηνός που τοιήδε γ' Ὀλυμπίου ἔνδοθεν αὐλή. — εἰσοιχνεῦσιν: Ionic contraction, like πωλεύμεναι 645; used because οἰχνέω and πωλέομαι are epic words. Cp. Eur. *Med.* 422 ὑμνεῦσαι, *Hipp.* 167 ἀθτευν, *Iph. A.* 789 μυθεῦσαι. Cp. also *Ag.* 942 δῆριος (from the Ionic δῆρις).

124 ff. κινάθισμα: κίνημα πλήθους, Hesych. — οἰωνῶν: the chorus is now so near that Prometheus can distinguish the sound of wings. — ἐλαφραῖς πτερύγων ῥιπαῖς: cp. Eur. Frg. 597 ταῖς ὠκυπλάνοις πτερύγων ῥιπαῖς. — ὑποσυρίζα: this does not mean leniter stridet (Blomfield), but ὑπο- ex-

presses the idea of accompaniment, as in ὑπᾴδειν, ὑποστεναχίζειν, ὑπορχεῖσθαι, ὑπηχεῖν, succinere.

127. φοβερόν: see 156.

128–192. Parodos. It is commatic, that is, divided between actor and chorus. The chorus enter in a winged car (ὄχῳ πτερωτῷ 135, πτηνόσυτον θᾶκον 279), moved by theatrical machinery. The car, advancing from the right side, has gradually approached Prometheus. It is seen by the spectators while still invisible to Prometheus, who can only look straight before him. At 124 the chorus are already very near, and they hear the words of 127 (φοβερόν). — The Ὠκεανίδες are daughters of Oceanus and Tethys; see Hesiod *Theog.* 302. Hesiod (*ibid.* 346) enumerates forty-one by name, and adds πολλαὶ γε μέν εἰσι καὶ ἄλλαι, τρὶς γὰρ χίλιαι εἰσι τανύσφυροι Ὠκεανῖναι. Aeschylus's chorus consisted of twelve persons. — The first strophe gives the motive of the chorus for coming; this is what an unknown grammarian (in the hypothesis to the *Persians*) calls 'παροδικά, ὅτε λέγει (sc. ὁ χορός) δι' ἣν αἰτίαν πάρεστιν.' — The rhythms (ὁ ῥυθμὸς Ἀνακρεόντειός ἐστι κεκλασμένος πρὸς τὸ θρηνητικόν, Schol.) are in keeping with the sorrowful tone of the composition (see 144 ff.); they

ΧΟΡΟΣ.

στροφὴ α΄.

μηδὲν φοβηθῇς· φιλία γὰρ ἅδε τάξις
πτερύγων θοαῖς ἁμίλλαις
130　προσέβα τόνδε πάγον πατρῴας
μόγις παρειποῦσα φρένας.
κραιπνοφόροι δέ μ' ἔπεμψαν αὖραι·
κτύπου γὰρ ἀχὼ χάλυβος διῆξεν ἄντρων
μυχόν, ἐκ δ' ἔπληξέ μου
τὰν θεμερῶπιν αἰδῶ.
135　σύθην δ' ἀπέδιλος ὄχῳ πτερωτῷ.

are furthermore especially appropriate to a female chorus.

128. τάξις: said like στάσις Eum. 311 ὡς ἐπινωμᾷ στάσις ἁμά, Cho. 458 στάσις δὲ πάγκοινος ἅδ' ἐπιρροθεῖ.

129. πτερύγων ἁμίλλαις: = πτέρυξιν ἁμιλλωμέναις. Cp. 147. The emulation is between the wings of the right and left sides of the car, which are imagined as striving to outdo one another. Cp. Soph. Ant. 1065 τροχοὺς ἁμιλλητῆρας ἡλίου.

131. μόγις: 'Quod se patri aegre persuasisse dicunt, ut iis commeatum daret, id e vetere sexus muliebris, virginum inprimis disciplina iudicandum. Sic paedagogus Antigones apud Euripidem (Phoen. 89) viam circumspicit, verens ne quis in publicum prodeuntem regis filiam vituperet' (Schütz). Cp. Suppl. 996 ὑμᾶς δ' ἐπαινῶ μὴ καταισχύνειν ἐμὲ ὥραν ἐχούσας τήνδ' ἐπίστρεπτον βροτοῖς, κτέ. — παρειποῦσα: cp. Il. vi. 62; vii. 120 ὡς εἰπὼν παρέπεισεν ἀδελφειοῦ φρένας ἥρως αἴσιμα παρειπών. See also Il. i. 555, vi. 337, Hes. Theog. 90 μαλακοῖσι παραιφάμενοι ἐπέεσσιν. Grammatically παρειποῦσα can be taken with τάξις,

but in thought it stands as if ἐγὼ προσέβην had preceded. See on 201.

132. κραιπνοφόροι ... αὖραι : that is, "and I came with great haste."

133. ἐκ δ' ἔπληξε: δέ is often put between preposition and verb (tmesis). Krüger II. § 68, 48, 1. ἐξέπληξε, here and 360, is not wholly figurative, but is chosen with reference to the actual nature of the cause (here the blows). Cp. 370; Ag. 480 φλογὸς παραγγέλμασιν νέοις πυρωθέντα καρδίαν.

134. θεμερῶπιν : Empedocles 23 Δῆρις δ' αἱματόεσσα καὶ Ἁρμονίη θεμερῶπις. Hesychius interprets θεμερῶπις (αἰδώς)· ἐρασμία αἰσχύνη, but this is inexact, for θεμερός (from the root θε-) means settled, tranquil, sedate; cp. Hesych. θεμερή· βεβαία, σεμνή, εὐσταθής; also the words θέμα, θέμεθλον, θεμοῦν. Accordingly θεμερῶπις αἰδώς is the modesty which makes maidens quiet and sedate. Its opposite is implied in σύθην ἀπέδιλος.

135. σύθην: the tragedians omit the syllabic augment not infrequently in lyric passages and in the narratives of messengers. The temporal augment is much less often omitted; yet

ΠΡΟΜΗΘΕΥΣ.

αἰαῖ αἰαῖ,
τῆς πολυτέκνου Τηθύος ἔκγονα,
τοῦ περὶ πᾶσάν θ' εἰλισσομένου
χθόν' ἀκοιμήτῳ ῥεύματι παῖδες
140   πατρὸς Ὠκεανοῦ·
δέρχθητ', ἐσίδεσθ οἵῳ δεσμῷ
προσπορπατὸς τῆσδε φάραγγος
σκοπέλοις ἐν ἄκροις
φρουρὰν ἄζηλον ὀχήσω.

ΧΟΡΟΣ.
ἀντιστροφὴ α'.

λεύσσω, Προμηθεῦ· δνοφερὰ δ' ἐμοῖσιν ὄσσοις
145   ὀμίχλα προσῇξε πλήρης
δακρύων σὸν δέμας εἰσιδοῦσαν

see ἐρίθισι 181. — ἀπίδιλος: the scholiast cites Hesiod *O. D.* 345 γείτονες ἔζωστοι ἵκιον. Cp. Soph. *El.* 871 ὑφ' ἡδονῆς τοι, φιλτάτη, διάκομαι τὸ κόσμιον μεθεῖσα σὺν τάχει μολεῖν, Theocr. *Id.* xix. 30 ἄνοστα μηδὲ πόδεσσιν ἰοῖς ὑπὸ σάνδαλα θείης (Bion i. 19 ἁ δ' Ἀφροδίτα λυσαμένα πλοκαμίδας ἀνὰ δρυμὼς ἀλάληται πενθαλέα νήπαστος ἀσάνδαλος), Apoll. Rhod. iv. 43 γυμνοῖσιν δὲ πόδεσσιν ἀνὰ στεινοὺς θέεν οἵμους (said of Medea). — ὄχῳ πτερωτῷ: winged chariots are not rare in ancient art: cp. for instance Müller-Wieseler, *Denkmäler der alten Kunst*, Vol. II. Plate ix. n. 110, Plate x. n. 111, 112, where Triptolemus is seen mounted on a car furnished with swan's wings.

137. πολυτέκνου: see on 128. Cp. *Il.* xiv. 201 Ὠκεανόν τε, θεῶν γένεσιν, καὶ μητέρα Τηθύν.

138. περὶ πᾶσαν εἰλισσομένου χθόνα: cp. ἀψορρόου Ὠκεανοῖο *Il.* xviii. 399, *Od.* xx. 65. Cp. also

Ovid *Fast.* v. 81 duxerat Oceanus quondam Titanida Tethyn, qui terram liquidis qua patet ambit aquis. For the form εἰλισσομένου see on 345.

139. ἀκοιμήτῳ ῥεύματι: cp. *Il.* xiv. 244 ἄλλον μέν κεν ἔγωγε (the speaker is Sleep) θεῶν αἰειγενετάων ῥεῖα κατευνήσαιμι καὶ ἂν ποταμοῖο ῥέεθρα Ὠκεανοῦ, ὅς περ γένεσις πάντεσσι τέτυκται.

141 f. 'Synonyma haec vehementiam commoti animi produnt' (Schütz). — προσπορπατός: cp. 61.

143. φρουρὰν ὀχήσω: see on φρουρήσεις, 31. ὀχεῖν = sustinere, as in *Od.* vii. 211 ὀχέοντας ὀιζύν, xi. 618 κακὸν μόρον, ὃν περ ἐγὼν ὀχέεσκον ὑπ' αὐγὰς ἠελίοιο, xxi. 302 ἣν ἄτην ὀχέων ἀεσίφρονι θυμῷ. — ἄζηλον: cp. ἀτερπῆ 31, ἀμέγαρτα 402; and *Cho.* 1017 ἄζηλα νίκης τῆσδ' ἔχων μιάσματα.

145. πλήρης δακρύων: like a rain-cloud. Cp. *Sept.* 228 χαλεπᾶς δύας ὕπερθ' ὀμμάτων κρημναμενᾶν νεφελᾶν,

πέτρᾳ προσαυαινόμενον
τᾷδ' ἀδαμαντοδέτοισι λύμαις.
νέοι γὰρ οἰακονόμοι κρατοῦσ' Ὀλύμπου·
νεοχμοῖς δὲ δὴ νόμοις
150 Ζεὺς ἀθέτως κρατύνει,
τὰ πρὶν δὲ πελώρια νῦν ἀιστοῖ.

ΠΡΟΜΗΘΕΥΣ.

εἰ γάρ μ' ὑπὸ γῆν νέρθεν θ' Ἅιδου

Soph. *Ant.* 528 νεφέλη δ' ὀφρύων ὕπερ αἱματόεν ῥέθος αἰσχύνει τέγγουσ' εὐῶπα παρειάν, Eur. *Hipp.* 173 στυγνὸν δ' ὀφρύων νέφος αὐξάνεται, Antiphanes in Meineke *Com.* iii. p. 197 τὸ προσὸν νῦν νέφος ἐπὶ τοῦ μετώπου, Hor. *Epist.* i. 18, 94 deme supercilio nubem. The figure was used by Homer *Il.* xvii. 591 τὸν δ' (Hector) ἄχεος νεφέλη ἐκάλυψε μέλαινα. — εἰσιδοῦσαν: the accusative follows the dative ἐμοῖσιν ὄσσοις as *Cho.* 410 τέταλται δ' αὐτό μοι φίλον κέαρ τόνδε κλύουσαν οἶκτον, *Pers.* 913 λέλυται γὰρ ἐμῶν γυίων ῥώμη τῆνδ' ἡλικίαν ἐσιδόντα, Soph. *El.* 479 ὕπεστί μοι θράσος ἀδυπνόων κλύουσαν ἀρτίως ὀνειράτων, *Ai.* 1008 σοὶ γὰρ μολεῖν μοι δυνατὸν τοῖς σοῖς ἀρήξαντ' ἐν πόνοισι μηδαμοῦ. The reverse change (from acc. to dat.) in Eur. *Med.* 57 ὥσθ' ἵμερός μ' ὑπῆλθε . . . λέξαι μολούσῃ.

146. πέτρᾳ προσαυαινόμενον := πρὸς πέτρᾳ αὐαινόμενον. Cp. Soph. *Phil.* 954 αὐανοῦμαι τῷδ' ἐν αὐλίῳ μόνος, *El.* 819 ἀβανῶ βίον. — With αὐαινόμενον λύμαις cp. 93.

147. ἀδαμαντοδέτοισι λύμαις: nearly equivalent to ἀδαμαντίνοις δεσμοῖς λυμαντηρίοις (991). Cp. 580 οἰστρηλάτῳ δείματι, Theocr. *Epigr.* xiii. 4 κηροδέτῳ πνεύματι.

148. γάρ: the chorus explains to itself the reason of Prometheus's

maltreatment. — οἰακονόμοι: Zeus is meant. 'Sic et nos: *denn jetzt sitzen neue Herrn am Ruder*, quamvis de uno tantum sermo sit' (Schütz). For the figure cp. *Sept.* 2 ὅστις φυλάσσει πρᾶγος ἐν πρύμνῃ πόλεως οἴακα νωμῶν, ibid. 62, *Pers.* 767; also 515 below.

150. νόμοις: νόμοι are changeable laws, made by temporal authorities (cp. *Sept.* 1070 πόλις ἄλλως ἄλλοτ' ἐπαινεῖ τὰ δίκαια), in distinction to θεσμοί, immutable statutes, based upon eternal right. — ἀθέτως· ἀθέσμως, οὐ συγκατατεθειμένως, Hesych. That is, Zeus issues ordinances in his own right (186), without acknowledging the authority of a higher law. Cp. 324 οὐδ' ὑπεύθυνος κρατεῖ.

151. τὰ πρὶν πελώρια: in a general sense; *the former powers* (τοὺς Τιτᾶνας καὶ τοὺς τούτων νόμους, Schol.). The word πελώρια is appropriate in reference to the reign of the Titans. For the thought, cp. *Ag.* 108 οὐδ' ὅστις πάροιθεν ἦν μέγας, παμμάχῳ θράσει βρύων, οὐδὲ λέξεται πρὶν ὤν. — ἀιστοῖ: the verb denotes absolute annihilation, so that a thing is neither seen nor heard of more: from ἄιστος, *out of sight and mind.*

152. νέρθεν Ἅιδου: with emphasis, *nay, under very Hades.* That is, into

τοῦ νεκροδέγμονος
εἰς ἀπέραντον Τάρταρον ἧκεν,
155 δεσμοῖς ἀλύτοις ἀγρίως πελάσας,
ὡς μήτε θεὸς μήτε τις ἄλλος
τοῖσδ' ἐπεγήθει.
νῦν δ' αἰθέριον κίνυγμ' ὁ τάλας
ἐχθροῖς ἐπίχαρτα πέπονθα.

ΧΟΡΟΣ.

στροφὴ β'.

τίς ὧδε τλησικάρδιος
160 θεῶν, ὅτῳ τάδ' ἐπιχαρῆ;
τίς οὐ συνασχαλᾷ κακοῖς

Tartarus, following the conception of
Il. viii. 13 ἦ μιν ἑλὼν ῥίψω ἐς Τάρταρον ἠερόεντα, ... τόσσον ἔνερθ' Ἀΐδεω
ὅσον οὐρανός ἐστ' ἀπὸ γαίης (whereas
in *Eum.* 72 Τάρταρόν θ' ὑπὸ χθονός, Tartarus is equivalent to Hades). Into
Tartarus the other Titans had been
thrown: *Il.* viii. 481; Hesiod *Theog.*
719 τόσσον ἔνερθ' ὑπὸ γῆς ὅσον οὐρανός
ἐστ' ἀπὸ γαίης· ἶσον γάρ τ' ἀπὸ γῆς ἐς
Τάρταρον ἠερόεντα.
153 f. τοῦ νεκροδέγμονος: cp. *Sept.*
800 πάνδοκον εἰς ἀφανῆ τε χέρσον,
Suppl. 157 τὸν πολυξενώτατον Ζῆνα
τῶν κεκμηκότων. In Hom. *Hymn* v.
9, 17, 430, Hades is called Πολυδέκτης
and Πολυδέγμων. Cp. οἰστοδέγμονα
θησαυρόν *Pers.* 1020. — ἀπέραντον: see
1078. — δεσμοῖς ... πελάσας : "and
had put me in bonds there as here."
For the expression δεσμοῖς πελάσαι
cp. Eur. *Alc.* 229 βρόχῳ δέρην οὐρανίῳ
πελάσσαι, also *Il.* v. 766 κακῆς ὀδύνῃσι
πελάζειν.
156. μήτε τις ἄλλος : Prometheus
shrinks from the mention of mankind. For the position of τίς see on

21. — Nothing, to the unfortunate,
is so hard to bear as the malicious
exultation of their enemies. Cp.
Il. iii. 51; vi. 82; x. 103; Hesiod
O. D. 701, Aesch. *Pers.* 1034, Soph.
Ai. 382, *Ant.* 047, Eur. *Med.* 383.
157. δ' ... ἐπεγήθει: cp. 749; *Cho.*
195 εἴθ' εἶχε φωνὴν ... ὅπως διέφροντις
οὖσα μὴ 'κινυσσόμην. GMT. 333. ἐπιγηθεῖν, like ἐπιχαίρειν (cp. 158 ἐπίχαρτα, 160 ἐπιχαρῇ) signifies τὸ συν-
επιγελᾶν τοῖς ἀλλοτρίοις κακοῖς.
158. κίνυγμα: Eustathius on *Il.* iv.
281 says, τοῦ δὲ κινύω αὖθις παράγω-
γον τὸ κινύσσω· ἐξ οὗ παρ' Αἰσχύλῳ
αἰθέριον κίνυγμα, τὸ ἀέριον εἴδωλον. It
is formed like αἴθυγμα from αἴθυσσω,
αἴνιγμα from αἰνίττομαι. Cp. *Cho.* 196
ἐκινυσσόμην, *might be driven this way
and that, might waver.* αἰθέριον κίνυγμα
(oscillum) is a thing *waving in
mid-air.* It applies to Prometheus
in that he hangs in the open air with
nothing for his feet to rest on.
161. συνασχαλᾷ : from συνασχα-
λάω, whereas συνασχαλῶν 303 is future
of συνασχάλλω. Cp. Isocr. iv. 181
kind. For the position of τίς see on

τεοῖσι, δίχα γε Διός; ὁ δ' ἐπικότως ἀεὶ
θέμενος ἄγναμπτον νόον
δάμναται Οὐρανίαν
165 γένναν· οὐδὲ λήξει, πρὶν ἂν ἢ κορέσῃ κέαρ,
ἢ παλάμᾳ τινὶ τὰν δυσάλωτον ἕλῃ τις ἀρχάν.

ΠΡΟΜΗΘΕΥΣ.

ἦ μὴν ἔτ' ἐμοῦ, καίπερ κρατεραῖς
ἐν γυιοπέδαις αἰκιζομένου,
χρείαν ἕξει μακάρων πρύτανις,
170 δεῖξαι τὸ νέον βούλευμ' ἀφ' ὅτου

συοργισθῆναι τοῖς ἀδικηθεῖσιν, also συμ-
τονεῖν 274 below, and συγχαίρειν, συνή-
δεσθαι. In all these, συν- denotes
sympathy with grief or joy.

162. The ancient form τεός for σός
occurs now and then in the lyric portions of tragedy. In Aeschylus twice
besides this place, Sept. 105, Frg. 66.
— Only the melic trimeter (162 =
181) admits, in Aeschylus, three
resolutions in a single verse. Cp.
Suppl. 111 = 123, Ag. 485, Cho. 44 = 55.
A tribrach in the second foot is found
in only one other verse of this play
(715), and there in a proper name.

163. θέμενος: cp. Il. ix. 629 ἄγριον
ἐν στήθεσσι θέτο μεγαλήτορα θυμόν,
Tyrtaeus Frg. 11, 5 ἐχθρὰν μὲν ψυχὴν θέμενος, Theogn. 89 ἀλλὰ φίλει
καθαρὸν θέμενος νόον ἤ μ' ἀποειπὼν
ἔχθαιρε.—ἄγναμπτον: instead of this,
the metre demands a word which
shall form two iambi. Cp. the antistrophe 182. Probably H. L. Ahrens's
conjecture, ἀκνάμπετον, is to be
received (cp. ἄτευκτος and ἀπεύχετος,
καμψίπους and καμπεσίγουνος, παναρκής
and πανάρκετος). With ἄγναμπτον νόον
cp. Il. xxiv. 41 οὐδὲ νόημα γναμπτὸν
ἐνὶ στήθεσσι.

164 f. δάμναται: an epic word; active in sense here and Od. xiv. 487
ἀλλά με χεῖμα δάμναται, passive
Suppl. 904, as in the Iliad.—Οὐρανίαν γένναν: the race of Uranus. Cp.
205, and Frg. III. of the Προμηθεὺς
λυόμενος below, Titanum subolca
generata Caelo; also Il. v. 898
Οὐρανιώνων. Οὐρανίαν is said like Ag.
83 Τυνδαρέα θύγατερ, ibid. 1499 Ἀγα-
μεμνονίαν ἄλοχον, Il. xiv. 317 Ἰξιονίης
ἀλόχοιο. See also 599 below.

166. παλάμᾳ: coup de main, bold
or sudden stroke.— τινί: cp. Cho. 138
ἐλθεῖν δ' Ὀρέστην δεῦρο σὺν τύχῃ τινὶ
κατεύχομαι, Soph. Ai. 853 ἀρκτέον τὸ
πρᾶγμα σὺν τάχει τινί, Pind. Ol. ix. 30
σύν τινι μοιριδίῳ παλάμᾳ.

167. ἦ μὴν ἔτι: cp. 907 below.

168. ἐν: more vivid than the simple dative of instrument. Cp. 562,
6, and see on 426.—αἰκιζομένου: here
passive; in active sense 195, 227, 256.

170. νέον: new, and hence danger-
ous. So Suppl. 341 πόλεμον αἴρεσθαι
νέον.—βούλευμα: περὶ τοῦ ἔρωτος τῆς
Θέτιδός φησι, Schol. See Introduction, pp. 9 and 17.—'Id consilium
hic subobscure et ambigue Prometheus indicat; in quo magna cernitur

σκῆπτρον τιμάς τ' ἀποσυλᾶται.
καί μ' οὔτε μελιγλώσσοις πειθοῦς
ἐπαοιδαῖσιν θέλξει, στερεάς τ'
οὔποτ' ἀπειλὰς πήξας τόδ' ἐγὼ
175 καταμηνύσω, πρὶν ἂν ἐξ ἀγρίων
δεσμῶν χαλάσῃ ποινάς τε τίνειν
τῆσδ' αἰκίας ἐθελήσῃ.

ΧΟΡΟΣ.

ἀντιστροφὴ β'.

σὺ μὲν θρασύς τε καὶ πικραῖς
δύαισιν οὐδὲν ἐπιχαλᾶς,
180 ἄγαν δ' ἐλευθεροστομεῖς.
ἐμὰς δὲ φρένας ἐρέθισε διάτορος φόβος ·

ars poetae, qui sic et attentionem spectatorum acuit et actionis tragicae cursum, ne iusto citius ad finem perveniat, inhibet ac suspendit' (Schütz).

171. ἀποσυλᾶται: the present is here used, without reference to time, to express simply the working out of a result. Cp. 764, 048.

172 ff. οὔτε ... τ' οὔποτε: for οὔτε ... τε cp. 244, 260; and for οὔτε ... τ' οὔ(ποτε) Soph. *Ant.* 763 ἔμοιγε ... οὔθ' ἥδ' ὀλεῖται πλησία σύ τ' οὐδαμὰ τοὐμὸν προσόψει κρᾶτα, Eur. *Hipp.* 302 οὔτε γὰρ τότε λόγοις ἐτέγγεθ' ἥδε νῦν τ' οὐ πείθεται, *Heracl.* 605 οὔτε τούτοις ἥδομαι πεπραγμένοις χρησμοῦ τε μὴ κρανθέντος οὐ βιώσιμον, Thuc. i. 126 οὔτ' ἐκεῖνος ἔτι κατενόησε τό τε μαντεῖον οὐκ ἐδήλου. By οὔτε ... τε persuasion and force are contrasted. The change from οὔτε to τ' οὔποτε accompanies the change in structure from θέλξει to πήξας καταμηνύσω.

Similarly in the example from Soph. (*Ant.* 763) quoted above.— μελιγλώσσοις: recalls *Il.* i. 249 τοῦ καὶ ἀπὸ γλώσσης μέλιτος γλυκίων ῥέεν αὐδή. Cp. Eur. *Frg.* 891 εἴ μοι τὸ Νεστόρειον εὔγλωσσον στόμα ... δοίη θεός.—The caesura after the second foot of the anapaestic tetrapody (μελι-γλώσσοις) is not observed with absolute strictness before Euripides.

176. χαλάσῃ: sc. με. Here transitive, but intransitive in 58 and 179. Cp. λωφᾶν 27.

180. ἐλευθεροστομεῖς: cp. λαβροστομεῖν 327, θρασυστομεῖν *Suppl.* 203, χαριτογλωσσεῖν 294 below.

181. ἐρέθισε: see on 135. The tribrach in the third foot here consists of three syllables which belong in one word; this is admissible only in the melic trimeter. See on 162 and on 2. The aorist as in ἐγέλασα, ἥσθην, ἀπέπτυσα (1070 below). Krüger I. § 53, 6, 3; GMT. 60; H. 842.

δέδια γὰρ ἀμφὶ σαῖς τύχαις,
πᾶ ποτε τῶνδε πόνων
χρή σε τέρμα κέλσαντ᾽ ἐσιδεῖν· ἀκίχητα γὰρ
185   ἤθεα καὶ κέαρ ἀπαράμυθον ἔχει Κρόνου παῖς.

ΠΡΟΜΗΘΕΥΣ.

οἶδ᾽ ὅτι τραχὺς καὶ παρ᾽ ἑαυτῷ
τὸ δίκαιον ἔχων· ἔμπας, ὀίω,
μαλακογνώμων ἔσται ποθ᾽ ὅταν
ταύτῃ ῥαισθῇ·
190   τὴν δ᾽ ἀτέραμνον στορέσας ὀργὴν
εἰς ἀρθμὸν ἐμοὶ καὶ φιλότητα
σπεύδων σπεύδοντί ποθ᾽ ἥξει.

182 f. δέδια ... πᾶ ποτε: see on
99.
184. At 100 above, the figure is
that of daybreak after darkness; here
of reaching land after a stormy and
perilous voyage. — ἀκίχητα: an epic
word. Cp. *Il.* xvii. 75 ἀκίχητα διώκων.
185. ἀπαράμυθον: with long α- privative. So, in epic poetry, ἀθάνατος,
ἀκάματος, from the necessities of the
metre. ἀθάνατος kept this measure-
ment throughout, even in Attic poetry.
186–192. This fourth anapaestic
system does not correspond in length
to the third (167–177), as the second (152 ff.) does to the first (137 ff.).
Perhaps this is because it forms the
close. Cp. Soph. *Ai.* 257 ff. Possibly,
however, some verses have been lost.
Weil assumes a gap after ῥαισθῇ.
186 f. παρ᾽ ἑαυτῷ τὸ δίκαιον ἔχων:
cp. 403, 150; also Eur. *Suppl.* 429
οὐδὲν τυράννου δυσμενέστερον πόλει,
ὅπου τὸ μὲν πρώτιστον οὐκ εἰσὶν νόμοι
κοινοί, κρατεῖ δ᾽ εἷς τὸν νόμον κεκτημένος

αὐτὸς παρ᾽ αὑτῷ, Aesch. *Suppl.* 370
σύ τοι πόλις, σὺ δὲ τὸ δάμιον. For
δίκαιον see on 150.
187. ὀίω: = οἶμαι (758), o p i n o r, I
trow, I hope. Cp. *Il.* viii. 536 ἀλλ᾽
ἐν πρώτοισιν, ὀίω, κείσεται οὐτηθείς.
Here with short ι, as in Homer in
the middle of the hexameter, while
at the end ὀίω is used.
189. ταύτῃ ῥαισθῇ: said with reference to 160 f. See on 170. Prometheus speaks mysteriously and in a
tone of secret exultation over something not disclosed. With ταύτῃ cp.
τῶνδε 247.
190. ἀτέραμνον: cp. 1062. ἀτέραμ-
νος is an Homeric word. Cp. *Od.* xxiii.
167 κῆρ ἀτέραμνον. Hesych. defines
it, τὸ μὴ ἐνδιδοῦν, σκληρόν. Cp. ὀργὰς
ἀτενεῖς *Ag.* 71. — στορέσας: meta-
phorical; the figure is that of calm-
ing the waves after a storm.
191. εἰς ἀρθμὸν καὶ φιλότητα: so
Hom. *Hymn* iii. 524 κατένευσεν ἐπ᾽
ἀρθμῷ καὶ φιλότητι. Cp. *Il.* vii. 302
ἐν φιλότητι διέτμαγεν ἀρθμήσαντε.

ΧΟΡΟΣ. ·

πάντ' ἐκκάλυψον καὶ γέγων' ἡμῖν ·λόγον,
ποίῳ λαβών σε Ζεὺς ἐπ' αἰτιάματι
195 οὕτως ἀτίμως καὶ πικρῶς αἰκίζεται·
δίδαξον ἡμᾶς, εἴ τι μὴ βλάπτει λόγῳ.

ΠΡΟΜΗΘΕΥΣ.

ἀλγεινὰ μέν μοι καὶ λέγειν ἐστὶν τάδε,
ἄλγος δὲ σιγᾶν, πανταχῇ δὲ δύσποτμα.

ἐπεὶ τάχιστ' ἤρξαντο δαίμονες χόλου
200 στάσις τ' ἐν ἀλλήλοισιν ὡροθύνετο,
οἱ μὲν θέλοντες ἐκβαλεῖν ἕδρας Κρόνον,
ὡς Ζεὺς ἀνάσσοι δῆθεν, οἱ δὲ τοὔμπαλιν

193–396. **First Episode.** 193–283. **First Scene:** Prometheus and the Coryphaeus. The scholiast says: τὴν ὑπόθεσιν (that is, the exposition of the events supposed to precede the opening of the play) βουλόμενος διδάξαι, τὸ περίεργον (curiosity) τοῦ γυναικώδους ἤθους προσέλαβεν (availed himself of, as a motive). οὐκ ἂν γὰρ ὁ Ὠκεανὸς (who enters later) ἠξίωσεν ἐρωτῆσαι εἰδώς. The curiosity of the chorus is a natural consequence of their awakened sympathy. Still it is to be observed that Prometheus on his part is moved to tell his story by the longing to unburden his heart to sympathizing friends (see 198). He needs only the request in order to comply at once. — The Prologue and this first scene of the first episode constitute the first act of the drama, which expounds the situation and prepares the way for the following dramatic development.

196. εἴ τι μή: cp. Pers. 157 θεοῦ δὲ καὶ μήτηρ ἔφυς, εἴ τι μὴ δαίμων παλαιὸς νῦν μεθέστηκε στρατῷ, Suppl. 1016 εἰ

γάρ τι μὴ θεοῖς βεβούλευται νέον. Cp. 763. — It is noteworthy that all the speeches of the coryphaeus (which exceed a single verse) consist of four verses (see 242, 250, 472, 507, 631, 819, 1036) except 698 f. The same tendency in the speeches of other persons, 393, 511, 522, 589, 609.

197 f. ἀλγεινὰ μέν ... ἄλγος δέ: for the anaphora, cp. 238 and Pers. 27 φοβεροὶ μὲν ἰδεῖν, δεινοὶ δὲ μάχην.

200. ὡροθύνετο: an epic word.

201. οἱ μὲν θέλοντες: absolute nominative, used as if δαίμονες ἐν ἀλλήλοις ἐστασίαζον had preceded. Cp. Soph. Ant. 259 λόγοι δ' ἐν ἀλλήλοισιν ἐρρόθουν κακοί, φύλαξ ἐλέγχων φύλακα, Eur. Phoen. 1462 ἦν δ' ἔρις στρατηλάταις, οἱ μὲν πατάξαι πρόσθε Πολυνείκην δορί, οἱ δ' ὡς θανόντων οὐδαμοῦ νίκη πέλοι, Bacch. 1131 ἦν δὲ πᾶσ' ὁμοῦ βοή, ὁ μὲν στενάζων κτέ. Krüger I. § 56. 9, 4. See also on 569 below.

202. δῆθεν: scilicet; here without the usual tinge of irony (986), or notion of pretence. So Eur. Ion 831 Ἴων, ἰόντι δῆθεν ὅτι συνήπτετο.

σπεύδοντες, ὡς Ζεὺς μήποτ' ἄρξειεν θεῶν,
ἐνταῦθ' ἐγὼ τὰ λῷστα βουλεύων πιθεῖν
205 Τιτᾶνας, Οὐρανοῦ τε καὶ Χθονὸς τέκνα,
οὐκ ἠδυνήθην· αἱμύλας δὲ μηχανὰς
ἀτιμάσαντες καρτεροῖς φρονήμασιν
ᾤοντ' ἀμοχθὶ πρὸς βίαν τε δεσπόσειν.

ἐμοὶ δὲ μήτηρ οὐχ ἅπαξ μόνον Θέμις,
210 καὶ Γαῖα, πολλῶν ὀνομάτων μορφὴ μία,
τὸ μέλλον ᾗ κραίνοιτο προυτεθεσπίκει,
ὡς οὐ κατ' ἰσχὺν οὐδὲ πρὸς τὸ καρτερὸν
χρείη, δόλῳ δὲ τοὺς ὑπερσχόντας κρατεῖν.

203. ὡς Ζεὺς μήποτ' ἄρξειεν θεῶν: said instead of "that Cronus might remain in power," because the personality of Zeus is uppermost in the speaker's mind.

204. τὰ λῷστα πιθεῖν Τιτᾶνας: on the double accusative, see Krüger I. § 46, 11, 2. — The aorists ἔπιθον and ἐπιθόμην are very frequent in tragedy.

205. Cp. Hes. Theog. 644 Γαίης τε καὶ Οὐρανοῦ ἀγλαὰ τέκνα.

208. ἀμοχθί: the sense is, "in their pride of heart, they thought easily to master their foe by sheer brute force, without tedious manoeuvres." — πρὸς βίαν: opposed to αἱμύλας μηχανάς. Cp. Hor. Carm. iii. 4, 65 vis consili expers mole ruit sua.

210. πολλῶν ὀνομάτων μορφὴ μία: said in order to explain the identification of Gaea and Themis (cp. 1001), whom the common tradition distinguished as mother and daughter (so Hesiod Theog. 135, and Aeschylus himself in Eum. 2 Γαῖαν· ἐκ δὲ τῆς Θέμιν). In identifying the two, the poet seems to have followed a local Attic tradition, of which an Attic inscription, Ἱερίας Γῆς Θέμιδος, affords

a hint. In Arcadia, Demeter had the cognomen Themis; Paus. viii. 25, 4. Themis in 874 is called Τιτανίς, as being the mother of the Titans; the poet includes under the term Τιτάν all who belong to the Titan race. Similarly Prometheus, the son of a Titan, is spoken of as Τιτὰν Προμηθεύς, Soph. O. C. 56, Eur. Phoen. 1122, Ion 455. Aeschylus, having of his own invention made Prometheus a son of Themis, wished to guard against a possible feeling of bewilderment on the part of his spectators, that the functions given to Gaea in the cosmogonic accounts (see Hesiod Theog. 463, 470, 404, 626, 884) should be transferred outright to Themis.

211. κραίνοιτο: present tense, because the prophesier thinks of the future as already present. Cp. τίθησιν 848, τελεῖται 929.

212. Cp. Soph. Phil. 594 ἦ μὴν ἦ λόγῳ πείσαντες ἄξειν ἦ πρὸς ἰσχύος κράτος, and see Krüger I. § 68, 39, 8.

213. δόλῳ δὲ τοὺς ὑπερσχόντας: = τοὺς δὲ δόλῳ ὑπερσχόντας, subject accusative to κρατεῖν. A fuller and

τοιαῦτ' ἐμοῦ λόγοισιν ἐξηγουμένου
215 οὐκ ἠξίωσαν οὐδὲ προσβλέψαι τὸ πᾶν.
κράτιστα δή μοι τῶν παρεστώτων τότε
ἐφαίνετ' εἶναι προσλαβόντι μητέρα
ἑκόνθ' ἑκόντι Ζηνὶ συμπαραστατεῖν.
ἐμαῖς δὲ βουλαῖς Ταρτάρου μελαμβαθὴς
220 κευθμὼν καλύπτει τὸν παλαιγενῆ Κρόνον
αὐτοῖσι συμμάχοισι. τοιάδ' ἐξ ἐμοῦ
ὁ τῶν θεῶν τύραννος ὠφελημένος
κακαῖσι ποιναῖς ταῖσδέ μ' ἐξημείψατο.

more emphatic expression for simple δόλῳ. The position of δόλῳ is due to the antithesis. Cp. Eur. Andr. 215 Θρῇκην χιόνι τὴν κατάρρυτον, Soph. O. T. 139 ἐκεῖνον ὁ κτανών, Demosth. VIII. 28 ταῦτα τοὺς ἀδικοῦντας, XIV. 25 ταῦτα δ' οἱ κεκτημένοι. The aorist ὑπερσχόντας stands in connexion with χρείη κρατεῖν, "those were destined to be victors who *should have outdone* their adversaries in craft."

215. προσβλέψαι : προσβλέπειν is used in the sense in which ἀποβλέπειν is more commonly employed.

216. Cp. Ag. 1053 τὰ λῷστα τῶν παρεστώτων λέγει, Ar. Eq. 30 κράτιστα τοίνυν τῶν παρόντων ἐστὶ νῷν κτέ.

217. προσλαβόντι : συναιρομένῳ τῇ μητρί, Schol. The dative in agreement with μοί, whereas the following ἑκόντα (necessarily accusative on account of ἑκόντι) connects itself more closely with the infinitive. G. 138, N. 8 b ; H. 941. Observe that προλαβόντα μητέρα would have been an equivocal succession. In Soph. O. T. 353, after ἐννέπω σε ... προσαυδᾶν μήτε τούσδε μήτ' ἐμέ, comes the dative ὡς ὄντι γῆς τῆσδ' ἀνοσίῳ μιάστορι, because ὡς ὄντα ... μιάστορα might seem to refer to ἐμέ. Cp. also Soph. El.

959 ᾗ πάρεστι μὲν στένειν ... ἔστι ῥημένῃ, πάρεστι δ' ἀλγεῖν ... Ἠλέκτρα γηράσκουσαν, Eur. Med. 1237 δέδοκταί μοι παῖδας κτανούσῃ τῆσδ' ἀφορμᾶσθαι χθονός καὶ μὴ σχολὴν ἄγουσαν ἐκδοῦναι τέκνα (in both examples the accusative is used under influence of the metre).

219. Ταρτάρου : cp. passages quoted in note on 152 ; also Hesiod *Theog.* 851 Τιτῆνές θ' ὑποταρτάριοι Κρόνον ἀμφὶς ἰόντες. —μελαμβαθὴς : cp. 1029, 1050, *Il.* viii. 479 ἵν' Ἰαπετός τε Κρόνος τε ἥμενοι οὔτ' αὐγῇς Ὑπερίονος ἠελίοιο τέρπουντ' οὔτ' ἀνέμοισι, βαθὺς δέ τε Τάρταρος ἀμφίς.

221. αὐτοῖσι συμμάχοισι : cp. 1047. G. 188, 5, N.; H. 774 a. The article is generally omitted in this idiom.

223. κακαῖσι ποιναῖς : sometimes, it is true, ποινή (*indemnity, requital*) is used, like ἄποινα, in a good sense ; so *Suppl.* 625 λέξωμεν ἐπ' Ἀργείοις εὐχὰς ἀγαθὰς ἀγαθῶν ποινάς, *Cho.* 792 δίδυμα καὶ τριπλᾶ παλίμποινα θέλων ἀμείψει, Pind. *Pyth.* i. 113 ποινὰν τεθρίππων, *Nem.* i. 107 ἡσυχίαν καμάτων μεγάλων ποινάν. Here, however, κακαῖσι is added not simply to show that ποιναῖς has its bad meaning (*penalty*), for that is sufficiently indicated by ταῖσδε,

ἔνεστι γάρ πως τοῦτο τῇ τυραννίδι
225 νόσημα, τοῖς φίλοισι μὴ πεποιθέναι.

δ δ' οὖν ἐρωτᾶτ', αἰτίαν καθ' ἥντινα
αἰκίζεταί με, τοῦτο δὴ σαφηνιῶ.

ὅπως τάχιστα τὸν πατρῷον ἐς θρόνον
καθέζετ', εὐθὺς δαίμοσιν νέμει γέρα
230 ἄλλοισιν ἄλλα, καὶ διεστοιχίζετο
ἀρχήν, βροτῶν δὲ τῶν ταλαιπώρων λόγον
οὐκ ἔσχεν οὐδέν', ἀλλ' ἀιστώσας γένος
τὸ πᾶν ἔχρῃζεν ἄλλο φιτῦσαι νέον.
καὶ τοῖσιν οὐδεὶς ἀντέβαινε πλὴν ἐμοῦ.
235 ἐγὼ δ' ἐτόλμησ'· ἐξελυσάμην βροτοὺς
τὸ μὴ διαρραισθέντας εἰς Ἅιδου μολεῖν.

but rather to emphasize further the idea contained in ταῖσδε ποιναῖς, as it were ταῖσδε ποιναῖς, κακαῖς ποιναῖς. Cp. Soph. *Phil.* 477 σοὶ δ' ὄνειδος οὐ καλόν, Eur. *Phoen.* 94 φαῦλοι ψόγοι. — ἐξημείψατο: used in the sense in which ἀνταμείβομαι is commonly said. See on 215.

229. νέμει: see on 109, θηρῶμαι. — According to Hesiod *Theog.* 881, at the conclusion of the conflict with the Titans, the Olympian gods, following Gaea's suggestion, appoint Zeus as the sovereign of the gods: ὁ δὲ τοῖσιν ἐϋ διεδάσσατο τιμάς. Cp. ibid. 73 εὖ δὲ ἕκαστα ἀθανάτοις διέταξεν ὁμῶς καὶ ἐπέφραδε τιμάς.

230. διεστοιχίζετο: διῄρει, Schol. διετίθετο ἐν στοίχῳ καὶ τάξει, διῄρει· ἀπὸ τῶν εἰς τοὺς σηκοὺς εἰσαγόντων τὰ ποιμνία καὶ διακρινόντων ἐκ τῆς νομῆς ἑκάστῳ τὰ ἴδια, Hesych.

232 f. ἀιστώσας: see on 151 and 668. Aeschylus has taken the legend of a succession of ages and races of men, and modified it to suit his own conceptions. See Introduction, p. 15.

234. καὶ τοῖσιν: the article retains its pronominal force most frequently in connexion with καί, δέ (cp. 816), and γάρ. Krüger II. § 50, 1, 1–5.

235. On asyndeton in explanations see Krüger I. § 59, 1, 5. — ἐξελυσάμην: of deliverance from an impending disaster, not yet actually present. So *Od.* x. 286 ἀλλ' ἄγε δή σε κακῶν ἐκλύσομαι ἠδὲ σαώσω, Eur. *Andr.* 818 θανάτου νιν ἐκλύσασθε.

236. The infinitive with τὸ μή follows expressions signifying *prevention*, or any other action opposed to that expressed by the infinitive itself. Krüger I. § 67, 12, 2–4; GMT. 811. See also 865 below, *Ag.* 1170 ὅπως δ' οὐδὲν ἐπήρκεσαν τὸ μὴ (μὴ οὐ?) πόλιν μὲν ὥσπερ οὖν ἔχει παθεῖν, *Pers.* 291 ὑπερβάλλει γὰρ ἥδε συμφορὰ τὸ μήτε λέξαι μήτ' ἐρωτῆσαι πάθη.

τῷ τοι τοιαῖσδε πημοναῖσι κάμπτομαι,
πάσχειν μὲν ἀλγειναῖσιν, οἰκτραῖσιν δ' ἰδεῖν·
θνητοὺς δ' ἐν οἴκτῳ προθέμενος, τούτου τυχεῖν
240 οὐκ ἠξιώθην αὐτός, ἀλλὰ νηλεῶς
ὧδ' ἐρρύθμισμαι, Ζηνὶ δυσκλεὴς θέα.

ΧΟΡΟΣ.

σιδηρόφρων τε κἀκ πέτρας εἰργασμένος,
ὅστις, Προμηθεῦ, σοῖσιν οὐ συνασχαλᾷ
μόχθοις· ἐγὼ γὰρ οὔτ' ἂν εἰσιδεῖν τάδε
245 ἔχρῃζον εἰσιδοῦσά τ' ἠλγύνθην κέαρ.

237. τῷ : *therefore*, as in Homer. Cp. Soph. *O. T.* 511 τῷ ἀπ' ἐμᾶς φρενὸς οὔποτ' ὀφλήσει κακίαν. See on 234.
—τοιαῖσδε : in τοιοῦτος, τοιόσδε (see *Sept.* 27, *Ag.* 1075), οἷος, ποιῶ, the diphthong οι is often shortened. Krüger II. § 3, 3, 1; II. 02 D, d. In such cases ο was probably written; ποειν is often found in inscriptions.
239. ἐν οἴκτῳ προθέμενος : προ- has its temporal meaning, *though I begun by showing compassion.* Cp. *Ag.* 1008 καὶ τὸ μὲν πρὸ χρημάτων κτησίων ὄκνος βαλών, Eur. *Ion* 914 χάριν οὐ προλαβών. — τούτου : i.e. τοῦ ἐν οἴκτῳ τίθεσθαι.
241. ἐρρύθμισμαι : ironical, *have been disciplined, brought to order.* — Ζηνὶ ... θέα : appositional phrases like this, taking up the second half of a verse, are very effective; see 350, 461.
242. 'Iron' and 'stone' are, from Homer on, frequent designations of what is unfeeling or stubborn. In *Il.* xvi. 33 Patroclus says to Achilles, νηλεές, οὐκ ἄρα σοί γε πατὴρ ἦν ἱππότα Πηλεὺς οὐδὲ Θέτις μήτηρ· γλαυκὴ δέ σε τίκτε θάλασσα πέτραι τ' ἠλίβατοι, ὅτι τοι νόος ἐστὶν ἀπηνής, imitated by Verg. *Aen.* iv. 366 duris genuit te cautibus horrens Caucasus Hircanaeque admorunt ubera tigres; see also *Ecl.* viii. 43. Cp. *Il.* xxiv. 205 σιδήρειον νύ τοι ἦτορ, Hesiod *Theog.* 239 Εὐρυβίην τ' ἀδάμαντος ἐνὶ φρεσὶ θυμὸν ἔχουσαν, Pind. Frg. 88 ὃς μὴ πόθῳ κυμαίνεται, ἐξ ἀδάμαντος ἢ σιδάρου κεχάλκευται μέλαιναν καρδίαν, Aesch. *Sept.* 52 σιδηρόφρων γὰρ θυμὸς ἀνδρείᾳ φλέγων ἔπνει, Eur. *Med.* 1279 τάλαιν', ὡς ἄρ' ἦσθα πέτρος ἢ σίδαρος, ἅτις ... κτενεῖς, *Cycl.* 598 πέτρας τὸ λῆμα κἀδάμαντος ἕξομεν, Theocr. x. 7 Μίλων ὀψαμάτα, πέτρας ἀπόκομμ' ἀτεράμνω, Moschus iv. 44 μοχθίζει πέτρης δ γ' ἔχων νόον ἠὲ σιδήρου καρτερὸν ἐν στήθεσσι, Tibull. i. 1, 63 flebis: non tua sunt duro praecordia ferro vincta neque in tenero stat tibi corde silex, Ovid *Amor.* iii. 6, 59 ille habet et silices et vivum in pectore ferrum, Hor. *Carm.* i. 3, 9 illi robur et aes triplex circa pectus erat.

ΠΡΟΜΗΘΕΥΣ.

καὶ μὴν φίλοις ἐλεινὸς εἰσορᾶν ἐγώ.

ΧΟΡΟΣ.

μή πού τι προύβης τῶνδε καὶ περαιτέρω;

ΠΡΟΜΗΘΕΥΣ.

θνητοὺς ἔπαυσα μὴ προδέρκεσθαι μόρον.

ΧΟΡΟΣ.

τὸ ποῖον εὑρὼν τῆσδε φάρμακον νόσου;

ΠΡΟΜΗΘΕΥΣ.

250 τυφλὰς ἐν αὐτοῖς ἐλπίδας κατῴκισα.

246. 'καὶ μήν aut et vero, et sane aut atqui significat' (Hermann ad Vigerum, 332). Here it means et sane (with emphasis on φίλοις); in 459, 1080 it means et vero in 982, 985, atqui.—For the omission of εἰμί see on 42.

247. μή: cp. 959, Pers. 344 μή σοι δοκοῦμεν τῇδε λειφθῆναι μάχῃ; The chorus inclines to account for the severity of the punishment by supposing a more heinous crime.—τῶνδε: than what thou hast said; cp. ταύτῃ 189.

248. προδέρκεσθαι: foreseeing death is an evil, in that it benumbs man's energies and stupefies his faculties, since death is ever present before his eyes, and a fixed limit is set to his activity. By προδέρκεσθαι μόρον the poet means this anxious expectation of death. A somewhat different conception appears in Plato Gorg. 523 d, where Zeus says, πρῶτον μὲν οὖν παυστέον ἐστὶ προειδότας αὐτοὺς τὸν θάνατον. νῦν γὰρ προΐσασι. τοῦτο μὲν οὖν καὶ δὴ εἴρηται τῷ Προμηθεῖ ὅπως ἂν παύσῃ αὐτῶν. Here it is stated that men are not to know beforehand when they are to die, so that they may not try to deceive the judges of the lower world by premeditated artifices, and by providing witnesses to testify in their behalf. Cp. also Hor. Carm. iii. 29, 29 prudens futuri temporis exitum caliginosa nocte premit deus.

249. τὸ ποῖον κτέ. : = τὸ φάρμακον τῆσδε νόσου ποῖον εὑρών; remedium quod huic morbo adhibuisti quale fuit? 'Is qui interrogat, audiendi studio id, quod alterum dicere vult, occupaturus ipse orationem incohat, quam ab illo absolvi vult; ipse autem quia eam absolvere non potest, addit pronomen interrogativum' (Hermann ad Vigerum 25). — νόσου: cp. 384, 596, 606, 632, 977, 1069.

250. As in dealing with the myth of the golden and silver ages, 232, Aeschylus here uses great freedom in treating the myth of Pandora (Hesiod O. D. 94: see Introduction, p. 6), so that the original form of

ΧΟΡΟΣ.

μέγ᾽ ὠφέλημα τοῦτ᾽ ἐδωρήσω βροτοῖς.

ΠΡΟΜΗΘΕΥΣ.

πρὸς τοῖσδε μέντοι πῦρ ἐγώ σφιν ὤπασα.

ΧΟΡΟΣ.

καὶ νῦν φλογωπὸν πῦρ ἔχουσ᾽ ἐφήμεροι;

ΠΡΟΜΗΘΕΥΣ.

ἀφ᾽ οὗ γε πολλὰς ἐκμαθήσονται τέχνας.

ΧΟΡΟΣ.

255 τοιοῖσδε δή σε Ζεὺς ἐπ᾽ αἰτιάμασιν —

ΠΡΟΜΗΘΕΥΣ.

αἰκίζεταί τε κοὐδαμῇ χαλᾷ κακῶν.

the story is no longer recognizable, and only the deeper significance remains. Man, never deserted by Hope, strives ceaselessly for the attainment of his ends, unmindful of death and untroubled by the thought that he may be cut off before his goal is reached. Cp. Simonides Amorg. Frg. 1, 3 ἐφήμεροι ἃ δὴ βότ᾽ αἰεὶ ζῶμεν, οὐδὲν εἰδότες ὅπως ἕκαστον ἐκτελευτήσει θεός. ἐλπὶς δὲ πάντας κἀπιπειθείη τρέφει ἄπρηκτον ὁρμαίνοντας, Soph. Ant. 615 ἁ γὰρ δὴ πολύπλαγκτος ἐλπὶς πολλοῖς μὲν ὄνασις ἀνδρῶν, πολλοῖς δ᾽ ἀπάτα κουφονόων ἐρώτων.

252. σφίν : = αὐτοῖς, as in 457. Krüger II. § 51, 1, 10. σφιν in this sense is Homeric (Krüger II. § 51, 1, 17), but occurs in tragedy only in 481 below.

253. φλογωπόν: the brightness of the fire is put forward, as rendering it the more unfit for the ἐφήμεροι. The addition of this emphatic word justifies the repetition of πῦρ. Cp. Suppl. 508 ΒΑ. λευρὸν κατ᾽ ἄλσος νῦν ἐπιστρέφου τόδε. ΧΟ. καὶ πῶς βέβηλον ἄλσος ἂν ῥύοιτό με; — ἐφήμεροι: see on 83. Even the chorus feels it to be wrong that men should receive what properly belongs to the gods.

254. γέ: in answers, affirms by adding a further statement ("yes, and from it . . ."); cp. 258, 379, 746, 768, 774. — ἀφ᾽ οὗ: cp. 170.

255 f. Prometheus interrupts the question by his answer, and to the simple answer (αἰκίζεται) adds the significant statement οὐδαμῇ χαλᾷ κακῶν. By this addition the artifice for preserving the stichomythy is concealed, and the dialogue proceeds naturally. A more common device is the insertion of a question; this question is so connected in construction with the interrupted sentence which precedes, that in answering it the speaker simply takes up his unfinished speech where he left it off. Thus Pers. 734 ΑΤ. Ξέρξην φασὶν. ΔΑ. πῶς τελευτᾶν; ΑΤ. ἄσμενον μολεῖν.

ΧΟΡΟΣ.

οὐδ' ἔστιν ἆθλον τέρμα σοι προκείμενον;

ΠΡΟΜΗΘΕΥΣ.

οὐκ ἄλλο γ' οὐδὲν πλὴν ὅταν κείνῳ δοκῇ.

ΧΟΡΟΣ.

δόξει δὲ πῶς; τίς ἐλπίς; οὐχ ὁρᾷς ὅτι
260 ἥμαρτες; ὡς δ' ἥμαρτες οὔτ' ἐμοὶ λέγειν
καθ' ἡδονὴν σοί τ' ἄλγος. ἀλλὰ ταῦτα μὲν
μεθῶμεν, ἄθλου δ' ἔκλυσιν ζήτει τινά.

ΠΡΟΜΗΘΕΥΣ.

ἐλαφρὸν ὅστις πημάτων ἔξω πόδα
ἔχει παραινεῖν νουθετεῖν τε τὸν κακῶς
265 πράσσοντ'. ἐγὼ δὲ ταῦθ' ἅπαντ' ἠπιστάμην.
ἑκὼν ἑκὼν — ἥμαρτον, οὐκ ἀρνήσομαι·

257. οὐδί: cp. καί in 253.

258. Cp. 376. A different statement is made in 750.

259. δόξει δὲ πῶς: δόξει stands first because it takes up the thought of the preceding δοκῇ. Cp. Soph. *El.* 1429 ΧΟ. λεύσσω γὰρ Αἴγισθον. ΟΡ. εἰσοράτε ποῦ τὸν ἄνδρα;

260. ἥμαρτες: a moral wrong is not meant, but only an act of imprudence and mistaken judgment — rebellion, that is, against a superior adversary. This is clear from 266 and its explanation in 267.

262. ἔκλυσιν ζήτει τινά: that is, by submission. Cp. 316 with 315.

263. Cp. *Cho.* 697 ἔξω κομίζων ὀλεθρίου πηλοῦ πόδα (where the scholiast remarks, ἔξω πηλοῦ πόδα, παροιμία), Soph. *Phil.* 1260 ἴσως ἂν ἐκτὸς κλαυμάτων ἔχοις πόδα, Eur. *Heracl.* 100 καλὸν δέ γ' ἔξω πραγμάτων ἔχειν πόδα, εὐβουλίας τυχόντα τῆς ἀμείνονος.

264. Cp. Eur. *Alc.* 1078 ῥᾷον παραινεῖν ἢ παθόντα καρτερεῖν, *H. F.* 1249 σὺ δ' ἐκτὸς ὢν γε συμφορᾶς με νουθετεῖς, Terent. *Andr.* 309 facile omnes, quom valemus, recta consilia aegrotis damus.

265 f. With the words ἐγὼ δὲ ταῦθ' ἅπαντ' ἠπιστάμην and ἑκών Prometheus rejects the charge of imprudence, and restricts his ἁμάρτημα to the disregard of self-interest, as described in the next verse (267). So his 'error' is after all a noble action. — ἑκὼν ἑκών: repetition (ἀναδίπλωσις) emphasizes expressions of sorrow, entreaty, and asseveration. Cp. 274, 338, 688, 694, 887, 894, 999; also 577, 594, and 392, 937. — οὐκ ἀρνήσομαι: this refers only to the word ἥμαρτον. The sense is, "I will not object to your phrase ἥμαρτες" (260), "I will not insist on another word."

θνητοῖς ἀρήγων αὐτὸς ηὑρόμην πόνους.
οὐ μήν τι ποιναῖς γ᾽ ᾠόμην τοίαισί με
κατισχνανεῖσθαι πρὸς πέτραις πεδαρσίοις,
270 τυχόντ᾽ ἐρήμου τοῦδ᾽ ἀγείτονος πάγου.

καί μοι τὰ μὲν παρόντα μὴ δύρεσθ᾽ ἄχη,
πέδοι δὲ βᾶσαι τὰς προσερπούσας τύχας
ἀκούσαθ᾽, ὡς μάθητε διὰ τέλους τὸ πᾶν.
πίθεσθέ μοι πίθεσθε, συμπονήσατε
275 τῷ νῦν μογοῦντι. ταῦτά τοι πλανωμένη
πρὸς ἄλλοτ᾽ ἄλλον πημονὴ προσιζάνει.

267. **θνητοῖς ἀρήγων**: explanatory asyndeton. See on 235. — **ηὑρόμην**: cp. *Sept.* 878 μελέους θανάτους ηὕροντο, Soph. *Ai.* 1023 καὶ ταῦτα πάντα σοῦ θανόντος ηὑρόμην. 268 ff. **ᾠόμην ... με κατισχνανεῖσθαι ... τυχόντα**: instead of ᾠόμην κατισχνανεῖσθαι τυχών. Krüger I. § 55, 2, 3; H. 940 b. For Homeric examples see Krüger II. § 51, 2, 1 and § 55, 2, 2. Cp. also Soph. *Ai.* 606 κακὰν ἐλπίδ᾽ ἔχων ἔτι μέ ποτ᾽ ἀνύσειν, *El.* 65 κᾄμ᾽ ἐπαυχῶ ... λάμψειν ἔτι, 471 δοκῶ με πεῖραν τήνδε τολμήσειν ἔτι, Eur. *Alc.* 641 καί μ᾽ οὐ νομίζω παῖδα σὸν πεφυκέναι, Hdt. i. 34 ὅτι ἐνόμισε ἑωυτὸν (emphatic) εἶναι ἀνθρώπων ἁπάντων ὀλβιώτατον, Plat. *Rep.* iii. 400 b οἶμαι δέ με ἀκηκοέναι, Isocr. IV. 85 οὐκ ἐχθροὺς ἀλλ᾽ ἀνταγωνιστὰς σφᾶς αὐτοὺς εἶναι νομίζοντες. — **κατισχνανεῖσθαι**: cp. 147. Future middle used like αὐανοῦμαι, Soph. *Phil.* 954. Krüger I. § 39, 11. — **πεδαρσίοις**: see 710, 916; *Cho.* 846 λόγοι πεδάρσιοι θρώσκουσι. This Aeolic form (πεδά = μετά) Aeschylus uses in a few other words: πέδοικος Frg. 48, πεδαίχμιος and πέδωρος *Cho.* 589 f. — **ἐρήμου**: cp. Frg. 305, 10 δρυμοὺς ἐρήμους καὶ πά-

γους, Soph. *Phil.* 691 ἵν᾽ αὐτὸς ἦν πρόσουρος οὐκ ἔχων βάσιν οὐδέ τιν᾽ ἐγχώρων κακογείτονα. 271. **καί μοι κτέ.**: and so bewail my lot no more, presupposing the thought "your admonitions are unavailing." — **δύρεσθε**: δύρομαι = ὀδύρομαι belongs to tragic diction. 272. **πέδοι βᾶσαι**: i.e. so as to listen more conveniently to a long narration. A motive is thus provided for the descent of the chorus from its car into the orchestra. βούλεται γὰρ στῆσαι τὸν χορὸν ὅπως τὸ στάσιμον ᾄσῃ, Schol. 273. **διὰ τέλους**: cp. Soph. *Ai.* 685 διὰ τέλους εὔχου τελεῖσθαι. For the resolution see on 70. It is rendered easier by the fact that the chief caesura falls in the fourth foot (see on 2). 275. **νῦν**: said in reference to the thought which follows, "to-morrow your turn may come." — **ταῦτά**: adverbial, nearly = κατὰ κοινόν, *impartially, for all alike*. See on 398, and cp. Soph. *Ai.* 687 ταὐτὰ τῇδέ μοι τάδε τιμᾶτε. Properly it is the inner object (cognate accusative). 276. **πρὸς ἄλλοτ᾽ ἄλλον**: for the order, see on 702 and 19. —For the

ΧΟΡΟΣ.

οὐκ ἀκούσαις ἐπεθώυξας
τοῦτο, Προμηθεῦ.
καὶ νῦν ἐλαφρῷ ποδὶ κραιπνόσυτον
280 θᾶκον προλιποῦσ' αἰθέρα θ' ἁγνὸν
πόρον οἰωνῶν, ὀκριοέσσῃ
χθονὶ τῇδε πελῶ· τοὺς σοὺς δὲ πόνους
χρῄζω διὰ παντὸς ἀκοῦσαι.

ΩΚΕΑΝΟΣ.

ἥκω δολιχῆς τέρμα κελεύθου
285 διαμειψάμενος πρὸς σέ, Προμηθεῦ,

thought cp. Archil. Frg. 9, 7 ἄλλοτε δ' ἄλλος ἔχει τόδε· νῦν μὲν ἐς ἡμέας ἐτράπεθ', αἱματόεν δ' ἕλκος ἀναστένομεν, ἐξαῦτις δ' ἑτέρους ἐπαμείψεται, Pind. Ol. ii. 60 ῥοαὶ δ' ἄλλοτ' ἄλλαι εὐθυμιᾶν τε μέτα καὶ πόνων ἐς ἄνδρας ἔβαν.

277-283. The anapaests of the chorus accompany the action of the machinery by which Oceanus is brought on the scene. See on 114-127.

277. Cp. Soph. Phil. 1178 φίλα μοι, φίλα ταῦτα παρήγγειλας ἑκόντι τε πράσσειν, Homer Il. iv. 73 ὄτρυνε πάρος μεμανῖαν Ἀθήνην. — ἐπεθώυξας: see on 73.

279. καί: and so, accordingly.

282 f. πελῶ: future of πελάζω. — πόνους . . . διὰ παντὸς ἀκοῦσαι: as promised in 272. Compliance with this request follows much later, 755 ff. and in the speech beginning at 823. Curiosity and expectation are thus maintained.

284-396. Second Scene of the First Episode. Oceanus, father of the Oceanids, enters (from the right), mounted upon a winged steed (τετρασκελὴς οἰωνός 395) like

Pegasus. The scholiast understands a griffin, because of this word οἰωνός, but sea-gods, in older Greek art, are often seen riding on hippocamps or sea-horses. The machine here used was the αἰώρημα, a sort of crane with hanging ropes, by which persons could be swung aloft, moved through the air, and let down again. The scholiast remarks, καιρὸν δίδωσι τῷ χορῷ καθήκασθαι (καθιμᾶσθαι?) τῆς μηχανῆς Ὠκεανὸς ἐλθών· ὑπερβολῇ δὲ ἐχρήσατο, ὅπου γε Ὅμηρος οὐκ εἰσήγαγεν Ὠκεανὸν εἰς τὸν σύλλογον τῶν θεῶν (on this cp. Il. xx. 7 οὔτε τις οὖν Ποταμῶν ἀπέην νόσφ' Ὠκεανοῖο). The anapaests of Oceanus accompany the descent of the chorus from their chariot into the orchestra. — This scene and the second episode form the second act, the beginning of the action which leads to the catastrophe. See on 307 and 430.

284. δολιχῆς: an epic word. The way is long because Oceanus comes from the depths of the sea. Cp. 300 f.

285. διαμειψάμενος: cp. Sept. 334 διαμεῖψαι ὁδόν, 850 δι' Ἀχέροντ' ἀμείβεται

τὸν πτερυγωκῆ τόνδ' οἰωνὸν
γνώμῃ στομίων ἄτερ εὐθύνων·
ταῖς σαῖς δὲ τύχαις, ἴσθι, συναλγῶ.
τό τε γάρ με, δοκῶ, συγγενὲς οὕτως
290 ἐσαναγκάζει, χωρίς τε γένους
οὐκ ἔστιν ὅτῳ μείζονα μοῖραν
νείμαιμ' ἢ σοί.
γνώσει δὲ τάδ' ὡς ἔτυμ', οὐδὲ μάτην
χαριτογλωσσεῖν ἔνι μοι· φέρε γὰρ
295 σήμαιν' ὅ τι χρή σοι συμπράσσειν·
οὐ γάρ ποτ' ἐρεῖς ὡς Ὠκεανοῦ
φίλος ἐστὶ βεβαιότερός σοι.

τὰν ναύστολον θεωρίδα. 'Dicendum erat κέλευθον διαμείβεσθαι, pro quo τέρμα κελεύθου dixit ratione habita verbi ἥκω' (Dindorf). Cp. Eur. Phoen. 103 εἴθε δρόμον νεφέλας ποσὶν ἐξανύσαιμι· δι' αἰθέρος πρὸς ἐμὸν ὁμογενέτορα.

286. πτερυγωκῆ: formed like ποδάκης. Cp. ὠκύπτερος.

287. γνώμῃ: 'admirationis augendae causa non brutus, sed mente ac ratione praeditus esse fingitur' (Schütz). In Il. xviii. 419, the golden handmaids of Hephaestus are endowed with reason, speech, and power of action; in Od. viii. 556, the ships of the Phaeacians sail τιτυσκόμεναι φρεσί, and we are told that αὐταὶ ἴσασι νοήματα καὶ φρένας ἀνδρῶν. As these ships need neither helmsman nor rudder, so Oceanus's steed needs no bit, because of its own accord it obeys the will (γνώμῃ) of its rider.

289 f. τὸ συγγενὲς ἐσαναγκάζει: cp. 39. According to Hesiod Theog. 133, Oceanus is son of Uranus and

Gaea, and the oldest of the Titans. See on 14. — γένους: = τῆς συγγενείας.

291 f. ὅτῳ ... νείμαιμι: without ἄν, as Ag. 620 οὐκ ἔσθ' ὅπως λέξαιμι, Cho. 172 οὐκ ἔστιν ὅστις πλὴν ἐμοῦ κείραιτό νιν, Il. xxii. 348 ὣς οὐκ ἔσθ' ὃς σῆς γε κύνας κεφαλῆς ἀπαλάλκοι, Soph. Phil. 602 οὐκ ἔχων βάσιν οὐδέ τιν' ἐγχώρων κακογείτονα, παρ' ᾧ στόνον ἀποκλαύσειεν, Eur. Alc. 52 ἔστ' οὖν ὅπως Ἄλκηστις εἰς γῆρας μόλοι; 117 οὐδὲ ναυκληρίαν ἔσθ' ὅποι τις αἴας στείλας δυστάνου παραλύσαι ψυχάν. GMT. 241; Krüger II. § 54, 3, 8. — μοῖραν νείμαιμι: cp. Hdt. ii. 172 ἐν οὐδεμιῇ μοίρῃ μεγάλῃ ἦγον, Plat. Crat. 398 b μεγάλην μοῖραν καὶ τιμὴν ἔχει. This sense of dignity, station, rank was developed from the meaning due share, just due. Cp. Soph. Trach. 1238 ἀνὴρ ὅδ', ὡς ἔοικεν, οὐ νεμεῖν ἐμοὶ φθίνοντι μοῖραν.

294. χαριτογλωσσεῖν: see on 180. — ἔνι μοι: 'tis my nature; cp. 224.

296. Ὠκεανοῦ: instead of ἐμοῦ,

ΠΡΟΜΗΘΕΥΣ.

ἔα, τί χρῆμα; καὶ σὺ δὴ πόνων ἐμῶν
ἥκεις ἐπόπτης; πῶς ἐτόλμησας, λιπὼν
300   ἐπώνυμόν τε ῥεῦμα καὶ πετρηρεφῆ
αὐτόκτιτ' ἄντρα, τὴν σιδηρομήτορα
ἐλθεῖν ἐς αἶαν; ἢ θεωρήσων τύχας
ἐμὰς ἀφῖξαι καὶ συνασχαλῶν κακοῖς;
δέρκου θέαμα, τόνδε τὸν Διὸς φίλον,
305   τὸν συγκαταστήσαντα τὴν τυραννίδα,
οἵαις ὑπ' αὐτοῦ πημοναῖσι κάμπτομαι.

because the speaker is stating a future thought of Prometheus.   This
mention of his own name imparts
an air of assurance to his asser-
tion; cp. Soph. *O. C.* 626 κόμπον'
Οἰδίπουν ἐρεῖς ἀχρεῖον οἰκητῆρα δέξα-
σθαι.   At the same time it serves
the incidental purpose of inform-
ing the spectators who the newcomer is.
298. τί χρῆμα: cp. *Ag.* 1306, *Cho.*
885 τί δ' ἐστὶ χρῆμα; Eur. *Andr.* 896,
Suppl. 92, *Hipp.* 905, *H. F.* 525, *Or.*
1573 ἔα, τί χρῆμα;
299. πόνων ἐμῶν ἐποπτής: see
118. — ἐτόλμησας λιπὼν ἐπώνυμον
ῥεῦμα: cp. the scholion quoted on
284–396.
301. αὐτόκτιτα: cp. αὐτοφυής, αὐτό-
χυτος, αὐτόρριζος, αὐτόξυλος, *etc.* —
ἄντρα: cp. 133. — σιδηρομήτορα: cp.
Il. viii. 47 Ἴδην μητέρα θηρῶν, Asty-
damas Frg. 6 (p. 780, Nauck) οἰνομή-
τορ' ἄμπελον. Scythia is appropriately
called "mother of iron"; cp. *Sept.*
817 Σκύθῃ σιδήρῳ, Suid. Χάλυβεσ·
ἔθνος Σκυθίας, ἔνθεν ὁ σίδηρος τίκτεται.
According to Hesiod (Clem. Alex.
Strom. i. 307) and Aristotle (Plin.
H. N. vii. 57. 197) the art of casting

bronze was invented by the Scythians.
Cp. 714 below.
303. συνασχαλῶν κακοῖς: see on
161.
304. δέρκου: refers back to θεωρήσων. See on 119. — θέαμα: in the
sense of θέαμα δυσθέατον ὄμμασι (60).
Cp. Plut. *Ages.* 14 θέαμα τοῖς Ἕλλησιν ἦσαν. — τόνδε: of the speaker.
So ὅδε ὁ ἀνήρ = ἐγώ is frequent in
tragedy.
306. κάμπτομαι: first person, in
spite of τόνδε τὸν Διὸς φίλον above.
Cp. *Od.* ii. 40 οὐκ ἴκας οὗτος ἀνὴρ
ὃς λαὸν ἤγειρα, *Il.* x. 88 γνώσεαι
'Ατρείδην 'Αγαμέμνονα, τὸν περὶ πάντων Ζεὺς ἐνέηκε πόνοισι διαμπερές, εἰς
ὃ κ' ἀυτμὴ ἐν στήθεσσι μένῃ καί μοι
φίλα γούνατ' ὀρώρῃ, Soph. *O. C.* 1329
τῷδ' ἀνδρὶ τοὐμοῦ πρὸς κασιγνήτου
τίσιν, ibid. 284 ἀλλ' ὥσπερ ἔλαβες τὸν
ἱκέτην ἐχέγγυον, ῥύου με κἀκφύλασσε,
Trach. 1080 ὁρᾶτε τὸν δύστηνον ὡς
οἰκτρῶς ἔχω, Eur. *Cycl.* 290 νόμος
δὲ θνητοῖς ἱκέτας δέχεσθαι . . ., οὐκ
ἀμφὶ βουτόροισι τηχθέντας μέλη ὀβε-
λοῖσι νηδὺν καὶ γνάθον πλῆσαι σέθεν,
Dem. XVIII. 79 οὐδαμοῦ Δημοσθένη
γέγραφεν οὐδ' αἰτίαν οὐδεμίαν κατ'
ἐμοῦ.

ΩΚΕΑΝΟΣ.

ὁρῶ, Προμηθεῦ, καὶ παραινέσαι γέ σοι
θέλω τὰ λῷστα, καίπερ ὄντι ποικίλῳ.

γίγνωσκε σαυτὸν καὶ μεθάρμοσαι τρόπους
310 νέους· νέος γὰρ καὶ τύραννος ἐν θεοῖς.
εἰ δ' ὧδε τραχεῖς καὶ τεθηγμένους λόγους
ῥίψεις, τάχ' ἄν σου καὶ μακρὰν ἀνωτέρω
θακῶν κλύοι Ζεὺς, ὥστε σοι τὸν νῦν χόλου
παρόντα μόχθον παιδιὰν εἶναι δοκεῖν.
315 ἀλλ', ὦ ταλαίπωρ', ἃς ἔχεις ὀργὰς ἄφες,
ζήτει δὲ τῶνδε πημάτων ἀπαλλαγάς.
ἀρχαῖ' ἴσως σοι φαίνομαι λέγειν τάδε·
τοιαῦτα μέντοι τῆς ἄγαν ὑψηγόρου
γλώσσης, Προμηθεῦ, τἀπίχειρα γίγνεται.

307. Respecting this hortatory speech of Oceanus the scholiast remarks: σκόπησον τὰ τῶν ῥητόρων καλὰ παρὰ πρέποις εὐρεθέντα τοῖς τραγικοῖς. The speaker seeks to influence Prometheus by friendly warnings and advice, but his warnings are of such sort that a proud nature like Prometheus's can only be confirmed by them in its resistance.—ὁρῶ, Προμηθεῦ: cp. 144.

308. ποικίλῳ: συνετῷ, Schol. So Hesiod calls Prometheus ποικίλος, αἰολόμητις Theog. 510, ποικιλόβουλος ibid. 521, ἀγκυλομήτης ibid. 546, πάντων πέρι μήδεα εἰδώς ibid. 559, πολύιδρις ibid. 616.—With καίπερ ὄντι ποικίλῳ cp. Il. i. 577 μητρὶ δ' ἐγὼ παράφημι καὶ αὐτῇ περ νοεούσῃ πατρὶ φίλῳ ἐπίηρα φέρειν Διί.

309. γίγνωσκε σαυτόν: γνῶθι σαυτόν, ὡς ὁ ποιητὴς 'φράζεο, Τυδείδη καὶ χάζεο' (Il. v. 440), Schol. — μεθάρμοσαι: cp. Eur. Alc. 1157 νῦν γὰρ μεθηρμόσμεσθα βελτίω βίον τοῦ πρόσθεν.

310. νέους: proleptic, = ὥστε νέους εἶναι. Cp. Eur. Iph. A. 343 μεταβαλὼν ἄλλους τρόπους.

311. τεθηγμένους: for the metaphor cp. Sept. 715 τεθηγμένον τοί μ' οὐκ ἀπαμβλυνεῖς λόγῳ, Soph. Ai. 584 γλῶσσά σου τεθηγμένη.

312. ῥίψεις: hurl forth. Cp. 932, Ag. 1068 οὐ μὴν πλέω ῥίψασ' (flinging to waste) ἀτιμασθήσομαι, Eur. Alc. 679 νεανίας λόγους ῥίπτων ἐς ἡμᾶς.

314. παιδιάν: cp. Terent. Eun. 300 ludum iocumque dicet fuisse illum alterum, praeut huius rabies quae dabit.

317. ἀρχαῖα: old-fashioned; cp. Ar. Nub. 984 ἀρχαῖά γε καὶ Διπολιώδη καὶ τεττίγων ἀνάμεστα, Cic. Philipp. i. 10. 25 neglegimus ista et nimis antiqua et stulta ducimus.

319. τἀπίχειρα: properly "hand-money" (τὰ ὑπὲρ τὸν μισθὸν διδόμενα τοῖς χειροτέχναις, Hesych.). Here

320 σὺ δ' οὐδέπω ταπεινὸς οὐδ' εἴκεις κακοῖς,
πρὸς τοῖς παροῦσι δ' ἄλλα προσλαβεῖν θέλεις.
οὔκουν ἔμοιγε χρώμενος διδασκάλῳ
πρὸς κέντρα κῶλον ἐκτενεῖς, ὁρῶν ὅτι
τραχὺς μόναρχος οὐδ' ὑπεύθυνος κρατεῖ.

325 καὶ νῦν ἐγὼ μὲν εἰμι καὶ πειράσομαι
ἐὰν δύνωμαι τῶνδέ σ' ἐκλῦσαι πόνων·
σὺ δ' ἡσύχαζε μηδ' ἄγαν λαβροστόμει.
ἦ οὐκ οἶσθ', ἀκριβῶς ὢν περισσόφρων, ὅτι
γλώσσῃ ματαίᾳ ζημία προστρίβεται;

it means *wages*, as in Ar. *Vesp.* 581 ταύτης ἐπίχειρα, Plat. *Rep.* 608 c τὰ μέγιστα ἐπίχειρα ἀρετῆς καὶ προκείμενα ἆθλα. Cp. Soph. *Ant.* 820 οὔτε ξιφέων ἐπίχειρα λαχοῦσα. On the sentiment the scholiast remarks, γνωμικῶς δέ φησι. Cp. 320, Pind. *Ol.* i. 85 ἀκρίβεια λέλογχεν θαμινὰ κακαγόρους, Eur. *Bacch.* 385 ἀχαλίνων στομάτων ἀνόμου τ' ἀφροσύνας τὸ τέλος δυστυχία, Frg. 5 εἰ μὴ καθέξεις γλῶσσαν, ἔσται σοι κακά.
320. ταπεινός: *sc. εἰ.* See on 42.
—εἴκεις κακοῖς: cp. 179, Soph. *Ant.* 471 δηλοῖ τὸ γέννημ' ὠμὸν ἐξ ὠμοῦ πατρὸς τῆς παιδός· εἴκειν δ' οὐκ ἐπίσταται κακοῖς.
321. δ': can stand as fourth word when the three foregoing words form one idea, or belong very closely together (thus preposition, article, and noun, here and 381). For the thought cp. *Pers.* 531 μὴ καί τι πρὸς κακοῖσι προσθῆται κακόν, Soph. *Phil.* 1205 μῶν τί μοι νέα πάρεστε πρὸς κακοῖσι πέμποντες κακά, *O. T.* 667 εἰ κακοῖς κακὰ προσάψει τοῖς πάλαι τὰ πρόσφατα, Philemon, Meineke *Frag. Com.* IV. p. 34 κακὰ πρὸς τοῖς κακοῖσιν οὗτος ἕτερα συλλέγει.
323. πρὸς κέντρα κῶλον ἐκτενεῖς:

paraphrase of the proverb πρὸς κέντρα λακτίζειν (κέντρον = stimulus, *goad* for driving oxen and horses). Cp. *Ag.* 1624 πρὸς κέντρα μὴ λάκτιζε, μὴ πταίσας μογῇς, Pind. *Pyth.* ii. 173 ποτὶ κέντρον δέ τοι λακτιζέμεν τελέθει ὀλισθηρὸς οἶμος, Eur. *Bacch.* 795 θύοιμ' ἂν αὐτῷ μᾶλλον ἢ θυμούμενος πρὸς κέντρα λακτίζοιμι θνητὸς ὢν θεῷ, Frg. 607 πρὸς κέντρα μὴ λάκτιζε τοῖς κρατοῦσί σου.
324. Cp. 35, 150, 186.
325. πειράσομαι ἐάν δύνωμαι: cp. *Il.* xviii. 601 πειρήσεται, αἴκε θέησιν, xiii. 806 ἐπειρᾶτο, εἰ πώς οἱ εἴξειαν, Plat. *Leg.* 638 ε πειρώμενος, ἂν ἄρα δύνωμαι δηλοῦν. GMT. 489.
327. λαβροστόμει: cp. Soph. *Ai.* 1147 τὸ σὸν λάβρον στόμα, *Il.* xxiii. 474 λαβρεύεαι.
328. ἦ οὐκ: synizesis of these particles is especially frequent. See Krüger II. § 13, 6, 2. —ἀκριβῶς: here = *exceedingly*. Hesych. ἀκριβῶς· ἄκρως. For the characteristic pleonasm, cp. 944, *Pers.* 794 τοὺς ὑπερπόλλους ἄγαν, *Il.* vii. 39 οἰόθεν οἶος, 97 αἰνόθεν αἰνῶς. —περισσόφρων: see on 308.
329. προστρίβεται: a blunt metaphor. Cp. Ar. *Eq.* 5 πληγὰς ἀεὶ προστρίβεται τοῖς οἰκέταις.

ΠΡΟΜΗΘΕΥΣ.

330 ζηλῶ σ' ὁθούνεκ' ἐκτὸς αἰτίας κυρεῖς,
πάντων μετασχεῖν καὶ τετολμηκὼς ἐμοί.
καὶ νῦν ἔασον μηδέ σοι μελησάτω.
πάντως γὰρ οὐ πείσεις νιν· οὐ γὰρ εὐπιθής.
πάπταινε δ' αὐτὸς μή τι πημανθῇς ὁδῷ.

ΩΚΕΑΝΟΣ.

335 πολλῷ γ' ἀμείνων τοὺς πέλας φρενοῦν ἔφυς
ἢ σαυτόν· ἔργῳ κοὐ λόγῳ τεκμαίρομαι.
ὁρμώμενον δὲ μηδαμῶς ἀντισπάσῃς.
αὐχῶ γὰρ αὐχῶ τήνδε δωρεὰν ἐμοὶ
δώσειν Δί', ὥστε τῶνδέ σ' ἐκλῦσαι πόνων.

ΠΡΟΜΗΘΕΥΣ.

340 τὰ μέν σ' ἐπαινῶ κοὐδαμῇ λήξω ποτέ·
προθυμίας γὰρ οὐδὲν ἐλλείπεις. ἀτὰρ
μηδὲν πόνει· μάτην γὰρ οὐδὲν ὠφελῶν
ἐμοὶ πονήσεις, εἴ τι καὶ πονεῖν θέλοις.

330 ff. ζηλῶ σε: thou art to be envied, thou canst thank fortune. — καὶ
τετολμηκώς: having so much as offered. For καὶ cp. 197, for τετολμηκώς
381. Prometheus means, "one might
expect that the mere disposition to
show me sympathy would bring Zeus's
displeasure on you." πάντων gives no
good sense; Weil writes πόνων μετασχεῖν (cp. 274), following the scholion
ἐμοὶ συναλγῶν. The sense would be
best satisfied by τούτων μετασχεῖν.—
ἔασον: let it be, have done, as in Soph.
O. C. 593 ὅταν μάθῃς μου, νουθέτει, τὰ
νῦν δ' ἔα. Cp. the phrase ἔα τοῦτο.
333 f. πάντως ... οὐ: see 1053,
Eur. Hipp. 1002 πάντως οὐ πίθοιμ' ἄν.
— εὐπιθής: cp. 34. — ὁδῷ: errand.
See 325. For the dative cp. λόγῳ 196.
— The alliteration of π enhances the
force of these two verses.

336. On asyndeton in clauses that
state the reason, see Krüger II. § 59,
1, 7. — ἔργῳ κοὐ λόγῳ: cp. 1080.
337. ὁρμώμενον: sc. με. Cp. 176.
338. See on 266. — αὐχῶ: I flatter
myself. See on 688, and cp. Eur.
Med. 582 γλώσσῃ γὰρ αὐχῶν τἄδικ' εὖ
περιστελεῖν.
339. Cp. 326.
340 f. τὰ μέν: the sentence takes a
slight turn, and instead of τὰ δέ (on
the other hand), ἀτάρ follows.
342. μάτην οὐδὲν ὠφελῶν: cp. Cho.
881 καθεύδουσιν μάτην ἄκραντα βάζω. —
ὠφελεῖν often takes the dative, not
only in dramatic poetry (Krüger II.
§ 46, 8, 2), but even in prose; so IIdt.
ix. 103 προσωφελεῖν ἐθέλοντες τοῖς
Ἕλλησι.
343. καὶ ... θέλοις: there is a shade
of contemptuous doubt in these words.

ἀλλ' ἡσύχαζε σαυτὸν ἐκποδὼν ἔχων·
345 ἐγὼ γὰρ οὐκ εἰ δυστυχῶ, τοῦδ' εἵνεκα
θέλοιμ' ἂν ὡς πλείστοισι πημονὰς τυχεῖν.
οὐ δῆτ', ἐπεί με χαὶ κασιγνήτου τύχαι
τείρουσ' Ἄτλαντος, ὃς πρὸς ἑσπέρους τόπους
ἕστηκε κίον' οὐρανοῦ τε καὶ χθονὸς
350 ὤμοις ἐρείδων, ἄχθος οὐκ εὐάγκαλον.

344. σαυτὸν ἐκποδὼν ἔχων: and keep out of the matter. Cp. Xen. Cyr. vi. 1. 37 οἱ δὲ φίλοι προσιόντες συμβουλεύουσιν ἐκποδὼν ἔχειν ἐμαυτόν.

345. εἵνεκα: epic form of ἕνεκα, used by the tragedians for the sake of the metre, like ξεῖνος for ξένος, κεινός for κενός, κεῖνος for ἐκεῖνος, εἱλίσσειν (138, 1085) for ἑλίσσειν, μοῦνος (804, see on 543) for μόνος.

346. πλείστοισι πημονὰς τυχεῖν: cp. Pers. 706 ἀνθρώπεια δ' ἄν τοι πήματ' ἂν τύχοι βροτοῖς.—The scholiast says, Προμηθικῶς· οὐ γὰρ κατὰ τὸν ἀνθρώπινον λογισμὸν πολλοὺς αὑτῷ συνατυχεῖν βούλεται ὁ Προμηθεύς. (The commoner feeling is expressed by the proverb solamen miseris socios habuisse malorum.) The poet uses this thought to introduce a matter quite foreign to the play. From the mention of Atlas he passes to the description of Typhon, and this enables him to bring in the eruption of Aetna (367–369).

347. οὐ δῆτ', ἐπεί: cp. Soph. O. C. 431 εἴποις ἂν ὡς θέλοντι τοῦτ' ἐμοὶ τότε πόλις τὸ δῶρον εἰκότως κατήνεσεν. οὐ δῆτ', ἐπεί τοι τὴν μὲν αὐτίχ' ἡμέραν ... οὐδεὶς ἔρωτος τοῦδ' ἐφαίνετ' ὠφελῶν, Eur. Heracl. 505 αὐτοὶ δὲ προστιθέντες ἄλλοισιν πόνους, παρόν σφε σῶσαι, φευξόμεσθα μὴ θανεῖν; οὐ δῆτ', ἐπεί τοι καὶ γέλωτος ἄξια κτἑ., also Alc. 555.—The thought, which forms the transition to the following description, is

this: "I will not involve others in my misfortunes; the afflictions of my brother Atlas and of Typhon distress me sorely as it is."—For the following, cp. Hesiod Theog. 517 Ἄτλας δ' οὐρανὸν εὐρὺν ἔχει κρατερῆς ὑπ' ἀνάγκης, πείρασιν ἐν γαίης, πρόπαρ Ἑσπερίδων λιγυφώνων ἑστηώς, κεφαλῇ τε καὶ ἀκαμάτοισι χέρεσσιν· ταύτην γάρ οἱ μοῖραν ἐδάσσατο μητίετα Ζεύς.

348. πρὸς ἑσπέρους τόπους: that is, far toward the west. πρός with accusative, because the speaker thinks of the direction which one must take to reach the place. Cp. Frg. 327 Αἴγινα δ' αὕτη πρὸς νότου κεῖται πνοάς, Od. xiii. 240 ἣ μὲν ὅσοι ναίουσι πρὸς ἠῶ τ' ἠέλιόν τε ἠδ' ὅσσοι μετόπισθε ποτὶ ζόφον ἠερόεντα.

349. Pindar Pyth. i. 35 calls Aetna a κίων οὐρανία, and just so Hdt. iv. 184 says of Mount Atlas, ἔστι δὲ στεινὸν καὶ κυκλοτερὲς πάντῃ, ὑψηλὸν δὲ οὕτω δή τι λέγεται ὡς τὰς κορυφὰς αὐτοῦ οὐκ οἶά τε εἶναι ἰδέσθαι ... τοῦτον κίονα τοῦ οὐρανοῦ λέγουσι οἱ ἐπιχώριοι εἶναι. A mountain rising into the clouds seemed to the imagination a pillar supporting the vault of the sky. See Verg. Aen. iv. 247. This 'bearer' (ἄτλας) in the legend became a Titan, who as punishment for his sins had to carry the burden of the sky upon his shoulders (see the passage of Hesiod quoted just above). Conversely, colossal crea-

τὸν γηγενῆ τε Κιλικίων οἰκήτορα
ἄντρων ἰδὼν ᾤκτειρα, δάιον τέρας
ἑκατογκάρανον πρὸς βίαν χειρούμενον,
Τυφῶνα θοῦρον, πᾶσι δ' ἀντέστη θεοῖς,

tures are compared to mountain-peaks; thus in *Od.* x. 113 the queen of the Laestrygones is described, τὴν δὲ γυναῖκα εὗρον ὅσην τ' ὄρεος κορυφήν, and in *Od.* ix. 191 Polyphemus resembles ῥίῳ ὑλήεντι ὑψηλῶν ὀρέων.—In Homer, however, we read, *Od.* i. 53, ἔχει (*sc.* Ἄτλας) δέ τε κίονας αὐτὸς μακράς, αἳ γαῖάν τε καὶ οὐρανὸν ἀμφὶς ἔχουσιν. Here the original conception of supporting pillars still remains, and the pillars are not entirely replaced by a personal Atlas. The 'columns which keep earth and sky apart' still exist as such, and Atlas is only the person who 'holds' them. Aeschylus has followed Homer. In view of the familiar Homeric passage he says briefly κίον' οὐρανοῦ τε καὶ χθονός, leaving the office of the pillar, γαῖαν τε καὶ οὐρανὸν ἀμφὶς ἔχειν, to be understood; this office, indeed, is partly fulfilled by Atlas's own person standing on the earth.

351. τὸν γηγενῆ: cp. Hesiod *Theog.* 820 αὐτὰρ ἐπεὶ Τιτῆνας ἀπ' οὐρανοῦ ἐξέλασε Ζεύς, ὁπλότατον τέκε παῖδα Τυφωέα Γαῖα πελώρη, ... ἐκ δέ οἱ ὤμων ἦν ἑκατὸν κεφαλαὶ ὄφιος, δεινοῖο δράκοντος. Typhoeus is a personification of the subterranean vapors and gases which cause earthquakes and volcanic outbreaks. In the following description of Typhon (or Typhos) it is the poet rather than Prometheus who is speaking. The description itself is very like that of Pindar, *Pyth.* i. 30 ὅς τ' ἐν αἰνᾷ Ταρτάρῳ κεῖται, θεῶν πολέμιος Τυφὼς ἑκατοντακάρανος· τόν ποτε Κιλίκιον θρέψεν πολυώνυμον ἄντρον· νῦν γε

μὲν ταί θ' ὑπὲρ Κύμας ἁλιερκέες ὄχθαι Σικελία τ' αὐτοῦ πιέζει στέρνα λαχνάεντα· κίων δ' οὐρανία συνέχει, νιφόεσσ' Αἴτνα.—Κιλικίων οἰκήτορα ἄντρων: the scholiast remarks, οἰκήσαντα μὲν ἐν Κιλικίᾳ, κολασθέντα δὲ ἐν Σικελίᾳ (so in Pindar). In Homer *Il.* ii. 781 γαῖα δ' ὑπεστενάχιζε Διὶ ὣς τερπικεραύνῳ χωομένῳ ὅτε τ' ἀμφὶ Τυφωέι γαῖαν ἱμάσσῃ εἰν Ἀρίμοις, ὅθι φασὶ Τυφωέος ἔμμεναι εὐνάς, the story has another form. For the Homeric Τυφωέος εὐνάς Pindar, probably following Sicilian accounts, employs the very different phrase, τόν ποτε Κιλίκιον θρέψεν πολυώνυμον ἄντρον. In this way the name Typhon, which originally pertained to the volcano in Asia Minor, is brought into connexion with the Sicilian volcano Aetna. Aeschylus has used this form of the story.

352. ἰδὼν ᾤκτειρα: this reminds one of *Od.* xi. 582 καὶ μὴν Τάνταλον εἰσεῖδον χαλέπ' ἄλγε' ἔχοντα.—δάιον: applied to Typhon, this characterizes the destructive nature of the volcanic element. Cp. *Sept.* 222 πυρὶ δαΐῳ.

353. ἑκατογκάρανον: Typhon has this epithet in the above-cited passage of Pindar; cp. also *Ol.* iv. 11 ἑκατογκεφάλα Τυφῶνος ὀμβρίμου. The 'hundred heads' meant originally darting tongues of flame; this is more clearly brought out in Hesiod *Theog.* 825 ἑκατὸν κεφαλαὶ ὄφιος δεινοῖο δράκοντος, γλώσσῃσι δνοφερῇσι λελιχμότες.

354. πᾶσι δέ: δέ in transition to narrative, as in *Sept.* 568 ἕκτον λέγοιμ' ἂν ἄνδρα σωφρονέστατον ἀλκήν τ' ἄρι-

355 σμερδναῖσι γαμφηλαῖσι συρίζων φόβον·
ἐξ ὀμμάτων δ' ἤστραπτε γοργωπὸν σέλας,
ὡς τὴν Διὸς τυραννίδ' ἐκπέρσων βίᾳ·
ἀλλ' ἦλθεν αὐτῷ Ζηνὸς ἄγρυπνον βέλος,
καταιβάτης κεραυνὸς ἐκπνέων φλόγα,
360 ὃς αὐτὸν ἐξέπληξε τῶν ὑψηγόρων
κομπασμάτων. φρένας γὰρ εἰς αὐτὰς τυπεὶς
ἐφεψαλώθη κἀξεβροντήθη σθένος.
καὶ νῦν ἀχρεῖον καὶ παράορον δέμας

στον, μάντιν Ἀμφιάρεω βίαν· Ὁμολωΐσιν
δὲ πρὸς πύλαις τεταγμένος κακοῖσι βάζει
κτέ. Cp. 366.

355. συρίζων φόβον: metonymy. Cp. *Sept.* 385 ὑπ' ἀσπίδος δὲ τῷ χαλκήλατοι κλάζουσι κώδωνες φόβον.

356. ἤστραπτε: ἀστράπτω is transitive, as here, in later poets. — γοργωπὸν σέλας: cp. φλογωπὸν πῦρ 253, τυραπτὸν κεραυνόν 667. These compound adjectives in -ωπός are especially frequent in Euripides.

357 f. We are again reminded that Prometheus is the speaker. As formerly he looked with contempt on the rude and hopeless efforts of the Titans (πρὸς βίαν τε δεσπόσειν 208), so here he speaks with compassionate irony of Typhon's impotent rage. In this tone the following words ἀλλ' ἦλθεν κτέ. are said. Cp. furthermore Hesiod *Theog.* 837:

καί κεν ὅγε (Typhon) θνητοῖσι καὶ
ἀθανάτοισιν ἄναξεν,
εἰ μὴ ἄρ' ὀξὺ νόησε πατὴρ ἀνδρῶν τε
θεῶν τε.

— ἦλθεν: cp. 667, also *Sept.* 444 αὐτῷ . . . τὸν πυρφόρον ἥξειν κεραυνόν. — ἄγρυπνον: the epithet is transferred from the person to the thing. See on 115, and cp. Cleanthes *Hymn to Zeus* 10 πυρόεντα ἀεὶ ζώοντα κεραυνόν. The

sense is, "Zeus was not taken unawares" (ὀξὺ νόησε, Hesiod).

359. καταιβάτης: cp. Ar. *Pax* 42 Διὸς καταιβάτου (*Zeus descending in thunder and lightning*), Hor. *Carm.* iii. 4, 42 scimus, ut impios Titanas immanemque turmam fulmine sustulerit caduco.— ἐκπνέων φλόγα: cp. 917, Pind. *Frg.* 112 πῦρ πνέοντος κεραυνοῦ, Eur. *Suppl.* 640 κεραυνῷ πυρπόλῳ, Soph. *Ant.* 1146 πῦρ πνεόντων χοράγ' ἄστρων.

360. ἐξέπληξε: see on 133.

361. φρένας: praecordia. Cp. 881, *Eum.* 159 ὑπὸ φρένας, ὑπὸ λοβόν, *Od.* ix. 301 οὐτάμεναι πρὸς στῆθος, ὅθι φρένες ἧπαρ ἔχουσιν, Schol. on *Il.* xi. 579 φρένας ὁ ποιητὴς καὶ πάντες οἱ παλαιοὶ ἐκάλουν τὸ διάφραγμα, Arist. *H. A.* ii. 15 τὸ διάζωμα ὃ καλοῦνται φρένες. The bolt strikes Typhon in the midriff, the seat of his μέγα φρονεῖν.

362. ἐξεβροντήθη σθένος: passive of ἐξεβρόντησε σθένος αὐτῷ. G. 197, 1, N. 2; Krüger I. § 52, 4, 2.

363. παράορον: from *Il.* vii. 156 πολλὸς γάρ τις ἔκειτο παρήορος ἔνθα καὶ ἔνθα, the poet has taken the general meaning of παρήορος ἔνθα καὶ ἔνθα (*stretched out at length, in this direction and that*), without intending that παρα- shall have a definite application.

κεῖται στενωποῦ πλησίον θαλασσίου
365 ἱπούμενος ῥίζαισιν Αἰτναίαις ὕπο,
κορυφαῖς δ᾽ ἐν ἄκραις ἥμενος μυδροκτυπεῖ
Ἥφαιστος, ἔνθεν ἐκραγήσονταί ποτε
ποταμοὶ πυρὸς δάπτοντες ἀγρίαις γνάθοις
τῆς καλλικάρπου Σικελίας λευροὺς γύας·
370 τοιόνδε Τυφὼς ἐξαναζέσει χόλον
θερμοῖς ἀπλάτου βέλεσι πυρπνόου ζάλης,
καίπερ κεραυνῷ Ζηνὸς ἠνθρακωμένος.

σὺ δ᾽ οὐκ ἄπειρος, οὐδ᾽ ἐμοῦ διδασκάλου
χρήζεις· σεαυτὸν σῷζ᾽ ὅπως ἐπίστασαι·

364. στενωποῦ: defined more exactly by the next verse. Cp. 729.

365. ἱπούμενος: cp. Pind. *Ol.* iv. 10 Αἴτναν ἔχεις ἶπον ἀνεμόεσσαν ἑκατογκεφάλα Τυφῶνος, Frg. 93 κείνῳ μὲν Αἴτνα δεσμὸς ὑπερφίαλος ἀμφίκειται.

366. κορυφαῖς δέ: a sentence subordinate in thought is expressed as co-ordinate for greater vividness. κορυφαῖς stands in contrast to ῥίζαισιν. —μυδροκτυπεῖ: cp. Thuc. iii. 88 νομίζουσι δὲ οἱ ἐκείνῃ ἄνθρωποι ἐν τῇ Ἱερᾷ (one of the Liparaean islands) ὡς ὁ Ἥφαιστος χαλκεύει, ὅτι τὴν νύκτα φαίνεται πῦρ ἀναδιδοῦσα πολὺ καὶ τὴν ἡμέραν καπνόν. — Verses 366–372 are irrelevant to the play, but the poet wished to bring in this *vaticinium post eventum*, and the whole description of Atlas and Typhon is meant to lead up to it.

367. ἐκραγήσονταί ποτε: the spectators would think at once of the eruption of Ol. 76, 2 (479–478 B.C.) which the Parian Marble, line 68, mentions in the words καὶ τὸ πῦρ ἐρρύη κᾶον ἐν Σικελίᾳ περὶ τὴν Αἴτνην (as restored by Boeckh, *Corp. Inscr. Gr.*

II. p. 302). Another eruption, which took place Ol. 88, 2 (425 B.C.), is spoken of by Thuc. iii. 116 γῆν τινα ἔφθειρε (*sc.* ὁ ῥύαξ τοῦ πυρός) τῶν Καταναίων, οἳ ἐπὶ τῇ Αἴτνῃ τῷ ὄρει οἰκοῦσιν, ὅπερ μέγιστόν ἐστιν ὄρος ἐν τῇ Σικελίᾳ.

368. δάπτοντες ἀγρίαις γνάθοις: like a beast of prey. Cp. *Cho.* 325 πυρὸς μαλερὰ γνάθος, Phrynichus Frg. 5, (p. 721 Nauck) πεδία δὲ πάντα καὶ παράκτιον πλάκα ὠκεῖα μάργοις φλὸξ ἐδαίνυτο γνάθοις, Eur. *Med.* 1187 παμφάγου πυρός, Hdt. iii. 16 Αἰγυπτίοισι νενόμισται τὸ πῦρ θηρίον εἶναι ἔμψυχον, πάντα δὲ αὐτὸ κατεσθίειν τάπερ ἂν λάβῃ.

369. Cp. Eur. *H. F.* 464 τῆς καλλικάρπου Πελασγίας.

370. ἐξαναζέσει: see on 133.

371. ἀπλάτου: cp. Pind. *Pyth.* i. 30 τᾶς (*sc.* Αἴτνας) ἐρεύγονται μὲν ἀπλάτου πυρὸς ἁγνόταται ἐκ μυχῶν παγαί, Frg. 93 ἀλλ᾽ οἶος ἄπλατον κερδίζες θεῶν Τυφῶν᾽ ἑκατοντακάρανον ἀνάγκᾳ, Ζεῦ πάτερ, εἰν Ἀρίμοις ποτέ, *Eum.* 53 οὐ πλατοῖσι φυσιάμασιν. — βέλεσι: said of the streams of lava, which shoot forth like missiles.

373 f. Return to the subject, sug-

375 ἐγὼ δὲ τὴν παροῦσαν ἀντλήσω τύχην,
ἔς τ' ἂν Διὸς φρόνημα λωφήσῃ χόλου.

ΩΚΕΑΝΟΣ.

οὔκουν, Προμηθεῦ, τοῦτο γιγνώσκεις, ὅτι
ὀργῆς σφριγώσης εἰσὶν ἰατροὶ λόγοι;

ΠΡΟΜΗΘΕΥΣ.

ἐάν τις ἐν καιρῷ γε μαλθάσσῃ κέαρ
380 καὶ μὴ σφυδῶντα θυμὸν ἰσχναίνῃ βίᾳ.

ΩΚΕΑΝΟΣ.

ἐν τῷ προθυμεῖσθαι δὲ καὶ τολμᾶν τίνα
ὁρᾷς ἐνοῦσαν ζημίαν; δίδασκέ με.

gested by mention of the κεραυνὸς Ζηνός.—σὺ δέ: Prometheus recurs to the thought of 344. The sense is the same as if the words were σὺ δέ, οὐ γὰρ ἄπειρος εἰ οὐδ' ἐμοῦ διδασκάλου χρῄζεις, σεαυτὸν σῷζ', ὅπως ἐπίστασαι. Cp. 72 and Eur. *Iph. T.* 64 f. The expression οὐδ' ἐμοῦ διδασκάλου χρῄζεις recalls Oceanus's words 322 ἐμοί γε χρώμενος διδασκάλῳ.

376. ἔς τε (= ἔστε): used by Aeschylus five times in this play (457, 656, 697, 702) and once in *Eum.* (449).
—λωφήσῃ: see on 27.

377-380. Cic. *Tusc.* iii. 31 ut Prometheus ille Aeschyli, cui cum dictum esset

'Atqui, Prometheu, te hoc tenere existumo, mederi posse rationem iracundiae.'

respondit

'Siquidem qui tempestivam medicinam admovens non ad gravescens vulnus illidat manus.'

378. Cp. Menander fab. inc. 23

(Mein. IV. p. 240) λύπης ἰατρός ἐστιν ἀνθρώποις λόγος· ψυχῆς γὰρ οὗτος μόνος ἔχει θελκτήρια· λέγουσι δ' αὐτὸν οἱ πάλαι σοφώτατοι ἀστεῖον εἶναι φάρμακον.

379 f. ἐάν τις ἐν καιρῷ γε μαλθάσσῃ ... σφυδῶντα ... ἰσχναίνῃ βίᾳ: the foregoing word σφριγώσης, together with ἰατροί, has suggested the idea of an ulcer or tumor, and this metaphor is continued. The sense is, "wrath can be allayed when it has spent its force, and time has mitigated its hardness and crudity, but not while it is still turgid and malignant." μαλθάσσειν implies a gentle pressure, softening the ripened ulcer. σφυδῶν describes the fresh swelling, hard, full to bursting, and painful to touch (cp. Hesych. σφυδῶν· ἰσχυρός, εὔρωστος, σκληρός). ἰσχναίνειν is to 'reduce' the ulcer by pressure. Cp. Ar. *Ran.* 940 οἰδοῦσαν (τὴν τέχνην) ... ἴσχνανα. The scholiast quotes a maxim of the physician Hippocrates, πέπονα φαρμακεύειν, μὴ ὠμά. Figurative and literal expressions are mixed in these verses.

381. δέ: for the position of this word, see on 321.

ΠΡΟΜΗΘΕΥΣ.

μόχθον περισσὸν κουφόνουν τ' εὐηθίαν.

ΩΚΕΑΝΟΣ.

ἔα με τῇδε τῇ νόσῳ νοσεῖν, ἐπεὶ
385 κέρδιστον εὖ φρονοῦντα μὴ φρονεῖν δοκεῖν.

ΠΡΟΜΗΘΕΥΣ.

ἐμὸν δοκήσει τἀμπλάκημ' εἶναι τόδε.

ΩΚΕΑΝΟΣ.

σαφῶς μ' ἐς οἶκον σὸς λόγος στέλλει πάλιν.

ΠΡΟΜΗΘΕΥΣ.

μὴ γάρ σε θρῆνος οὑμὸς εἰς ἔχθραν βάλῃ.

ΩΚΕΑΝΟΣ.

ἦ τῷ νέον θακοῦντι παγκρατεῖς ἕδρας;

ΠΡΟΜΗΘΕΥΣ.

390 τούτου φυλάσσου μή ποτ' ἀχθεσθῇ κέαρ.

383. Prometheus grows impatient, and answers curtly, here and 386. At that point Oceanus loses temper, and the dialogue passes into a *stichomythy*. — εὐηθίαν: εὐηθία is a parallel form to εὐήθεια, as ὠφελία to ὠφέλεια. For the meaning of the word, cp. Thuc. iii. 83 οὕτω πᾶσα ἰδέα κατέστη κακοτροπίας διὰ τὰς στάσεις τῷ Ἑλληνικῷ, καὶ τὸ εὔηθες, οὗ τὸ γενναῖον πλεῖστον μετέχει, καταγελασθὲν ἠφανίσθη, Plat. Rep. iii. 400 e εὐηθείᾳ, οὐχ ἣν ἄνοιαν οὖσαν ὑποκοριζόμενοι καλοῦμεν ὡς εὐήθειαν, ἀλλὰ τὴν ὡς ἀληθῶς εὖ τε καὶ καλῶς τὸ ἦθος κατεσκευασμένην διάνοιαν, and the play on words in Dem. xviii. 11 κακοήθης δ' ὤν, Αἰσχίνη, τοῦτο παντελῶς εὐήθες ᾠήθης κτέ.

384. τῇδε τῇ νόσῳ νοσεῖν: cp. Soph. Trach. 544 νοσοῦντι κείνῳ πολλὰ

τῇδε τῇ νόσῳ, El. 650 ζῶσαν ἀβλαβεῖ βίῳ.

386. ἐμὸν δοκήσει: "it will be seen that this crime — of being right when one seems to be wrong — is *mine*, not *thine*." — ἀμπλάκημα: ironical, like νόσῳ above.

387. σὸς λόγος: not the last speech only, but the tenor of the whole colloquy.

388. γάρ: yes, for, implying assent to what precedes. — θρῆνος: ὁ οἶκτος, Schol. — οὑμός: possessive pronoun standing for the objective genitive (ἐμοῦ). Cp. Pers. 699 τὴν ἐμὴν αἰδῶ μεθείς. G. 147, N. 1; H. 604.

389. νέον: see on 35. — ἕδρας: on this use of the cognate accusative see Krüger II. § 46, 6, 2.

ΩΚΕΑΝΟΣ.

ἡ σή, Προμηθεῦ, ξυμφορὰ διδάσκαλος.

ΠΡΟΜΗΘΕΥΣ.

στέλλου, κομίζου, σῷζε τὸν παρόντα νοῦν.

ΩΚΕΑΝΟΣ.

ὁρμωμένῳ μοι τόνδ᾽ ἐθώυξας λόγον.
λευρὸν γὰρ οἶμον αἰθέρος ψαίρει πτεροῖς
395 τετρασκελὴς οἰωνός· ἄσμενος δέ τἂν
σταθμοῖς ἐν οἰκείοισι κάμψειεν γόνυ.

ΧΟΡΟΣ.

στροφὴ α΄.

στένω σε τᾶς οὐλομένας τύχας, Προμηθεῦ,
δακρυσίστακτα δ᾽ ἀπ᾽ ὄσσων ῥαδινὸν λει-
400 βομένα ῥέος παρειὰν

391 f. Oceanus betrays by this answer the hopeless difference of sentiment between him and Prometheus; hence the emphatic rejoinder στέλλου, κόμιζε, σῷζε. For the asyndeton see on 56, and cp. 937 below, and Soph. *El.* 632 ἰώ, κελεύω, θῦε.

393. ὁρμωμένῳ ... λόγον: equivalent in sense to ὁρμωμένῳ μοι ἐθώυξας ὁρμᾶσθαι, that is to say, "I needed not your bidding." Cp. 277. Oceanus speaks with ill-concealed vexation. These and the following words further hint at the mode of his departure.

394. ψαίρει: cp. Verg. *Aen.* v. 216 mox aëre lapsa (*sc.* columba) quieto radit iter liquidum, xi. 756 aethera verberat alis (*sc.* aquila). Here said of the movements of the animal's wings as he prepares for his flight. With this the stage machinery is set in motion.

397–435. First Stasimon. The Ionic rhythms accord with the sorrowful burden of the song, which calls to mind the words of Fr. v. Schlegel,

'Es geht ein allgemeines Weinen,
so weit die stillen Sterne scheinen,
durch alle Adern der Natur.'

397. οὐλομένας: the epic form οὐλόμενος occurs here and there in lyric passages of tragedy. ὀλόμενος = perditus, *accursed, baleful, unblest;* it corresponds, as participle, to the execration ὄλοιο, just as ὀνήμενος (*blessed*) corresponds to the benediction ὄναιο. On the genitive of relation see Krüger I. § 47, 21.

398 ff. δακρυσίστακτα: adverbial. Cp. Eur. *Or.* 410 εὐπαίδευτα δ᾽ ἀποτρέπει λέγειν, *Phoen.* 310 μόλις φανεὶς ἄελπτα κἀδόκητα, 1739 ἀπορθένευτ᾽ ἀλω-

νοτίοις ἔτεγξα παγαῖς.
ἀμέγαρτα γὰρ τάδε Ζεὺς
ἰδίοις νόμοις κρατύνων
ὑπερήφανον θεοῖς τοῖς
405   πάρος ἐνδείκνυσιν αἰχμάν.

ἀντιστροφὴ α'.

πρόπασα δ' ἤδη στονόεν λέλακε χώρα
μεγαλοσχήμονά τ' ἀρχαιοπρεπῆ (θ' ἑ-
σπέριοι) στένουσι τὰν σὰν
410   συνομαιμόνων τε τιμάν,
ὁπόσοι τ' ἔποικον ἁγνᾶς
Ἀσίας ἕδος νέμονται,
μεγαλοστόνοισι σοῖς πή-
μασι συγκάμνουσι θνατοί.

μένη, Soph. *Ant.* 527 φιλάδελφα κάτω δάκρυ λειβομένη, *El.* 962 ἄλεκτρα γηράσκουσαν ἀνυμέναιά τε. — ῥαδινόν: λεπτόν, ἰσχνόν, εὐκίνητον, ἁπαλόν, εὐδιάσειστον, Hesych. The phrase ῥαδινὸν ῥέος (alliterative) is an imitation of the Homeric τέρεν δάκρυ, *Il.* iii. 142, xix. 323.

401. νοτίοις ἔτεγξα παγαῖς: cp. Soph. *Ant.* 1123 ὑγρῶν Ἰσμηνοῦ ῥείθρων, Eur. *Ion* 105 ὑγραῖς ῥανίσιν νοτερόν, *H. F.* 98 δακρυρρόους πηγάς.

402 ff. ἀμέγαρτα τάδε: depends on κρατύνων. With ἀμέγαρτα cp. ἄζηλον 143. — ἰδίοις νόμοις: cp. 186. — θεοῖς τοῖς πάρος: cp. 151. — αἰχμή: 'spearpoint,' figurative for *rule of might.* Cp. *Cho.* 630 γυναικείαν ἄτολμον αἰχμάν.

406. στονόεν λέλακε: transitive, *sends forth a mournful cry.* Cp. *Ag.* 711 πολύθρηνον μέγα που στένει, *Pers.* 944 ἥσω τοι καὶ πάνδυρτον.

407 f. μεγαλοσχήμονα: cp. εὔμορφον κράτος, *Cho.* 400. — ἀρχαιοπρεπῆ:

in contrast to the recent dominion of Zeus. — ἑσπέριοι: the supplement is sugested by *Od.* viii. 29 ἠὲ πρὸς ἠοίων ἢ ἑσπερίων ἀνθρώπων. "West and East" carries out the idea of πρόπασα χώρα.

409. συναιμόνων: Atlas and Typhon. Both are undergoing punishment in the western world.

411 f. ἔποικον Ἀσίας ἕδος νέμονται: = Ἀσίαν ἐποικοῦσι. ἔποικος is here used in a general sense, conveying simply the idea of *dwelling*; so ἔποικον ἕδος = *seat of residence.* The scholiast, wrongly taking the word as *colonist*, imagines an anachronism (οὔτω γὰρ ἦν ἐποικισθεῖσα τοῖς Ἕλλησιν ἡ Ἀσία). With Ἀσίας ἕδος cp. Ἰθάκης ἕδος *Od.* xiii. 344, Θήβης ἕδος *Il.* iv. 406.

414. συγκάμνουσι: not = σὺν ἡμῖν κάμνουσι (Schol.), but like συνασχαλᾶν above (101, 243), συμπονεῖν (274). Cp. Eur. *Alc.* 614 ἥκω κακοῖσι σοῖσι συγκάμνων, τέκνον.

στροφὴ β'.

415 Κολχίδος τε γᾶς ἔνοικοι
παρθένοι μάχας ἄτρεστοι
καὶ Σκύθης ὅμιλος, οἳ γᾶς
ἔσχατον τόπον ἀμφὶ Μαι-
ῶτιν ἔχουσι λίμναν,

ἀντιστροφὴ β'.

420 'Αρίας τ' ἄρειον ἄνθος
ὑψίκρημνον οἳ πόλισμα
Καυκάσου πέλας νέμουσιν,
δάιος στρατός, ὀξυπρῴ-
ροισι βρέμων ἐν αἰχμαῖς.

416. παρθένοι: see on 723. — μάχας
ἄτρεστοι: cp. Soph. O. T. 885 Δίκας
ἀφόβητος, Sept. 875 κακῶν ἀτρύμονες,
Pers. 51 λόγχης ἄκμονες. Krüger II.
§ 47, 20, 9.

417 f. Σκύθης: see on 2. — οἴ:
σχῆμα πρὸς τὸ σημαινόμενον. Cp. 421,
805, 808. — γᾶς ἔσχατον τόπον: cp.
666; Soph. Trach. 1100 ἐπ' ἐσχάτοις
τόποις.

420. 'Αρίας: see App. In Cho.
423 "Αριον is explained by the Schol.
as Περσικόν. Cp. Hesych. 'Αρείας
πόλους· Περσικάς· "Αρειοι γὰρ ἔθνος
Περσικόν. · In 'Αρίας ἄρειον there is an
etymologizing play on words, as in
Frg. 305 τοῦτον ἐπόπτην ἴσως τὸν
αὐτοῦ κακῶν. Cp. Eum. 155 ὄνειδος ἐξ
ὀνειράτων, Pers. 995 ἄρειόν τ' 'Αγχάρην,
Il. vi. 201 ἤτοι ὁ κὰπ πεδίον τὸ 'Αλήιον
οἶος ἀλᾶτο. See also notes on 80 and
692. — ἄνθος: cp. Ag. 197 ἄνθος 'Αρ-
γείων, Pers. 59 ἄνθος Περσίδος αἴας
οἴχεται ἀνδρῶν, ibid. 252, 925, Suppl.
663 ἥβας δ' ἄνθος.

421. ὑψίκρημνον πόλισμα: probably the lofty Ecbatana ('Αγβάτανα

Pers. 961), the capital of the Medes,
is meant.

422. Καυκάσου πέλας: a geographical definition like ἀμφὶ Μαιῶτιν
λίμναν just above. — νέμουσιν: cp.
Eum. 1019 Παλλάδος πόλιν νέμοντες.

423. ὀξυπρῴροισι: cp. βούπρῳρος,
ἀνδρόπρῳρος. — βρέμων ἐν αἰχμαῖς: cp.
Eur. Phoen. 113 πολλοῖς μὲν ἵπποις,
μυρίοις δ' ὅπλοις βρέμων. With ἐν
αἰχμαῖς cp. Eur. El. 321 καὶ σκῆπτρ' ἐν
οἷς Ἕλλησιν ἐστρατηλάτει, Xen. Mem.
iii. 9. 2 ἐν πέλταις καὶ ἀκοντίοις διαγω-
νίζεσθαι.

425. The foregoing thought, "I
bewail thy sufferings in common
with all humanity," is followed in
the third strophe by the sole example of similar sufferings. This is then
described at length, after the manner
of the Homeric similes. The comparison of past instances is common
in tragedy; see Cho. 603 ff., Soph.
Ant. 944 ff., El. 837 ff., Phil. 676 ff.,
Eur. Med. 1282 μίαν δὴ κλύω μίαν τῶν
πάρος γυναῖκ' ἐν φίλοις χέρα βαλεῖν
τέκνοις κτλ., Hipp. 545 ff., H. F. 1017 ff.

στροφὴ γ'.

425 μόνον δὴ πρόσθεν ἄλλον ἐν πόνοις
δαμέντ' [ἀκαμαντοδέτοις]
Τιτᾶνα [λύμαις] εἰσιδόμαν θεὸν
Ἄτλανθ' ὃς αἰὲν ὑπείροχον σθένος κραταιὸν
430 ⟨γαίας⟩ οὐράνιόν τε πόλον νώτοις ὑποστενάζει.

ἀντιστροφὴ γ'.

βοᾷ δὲ πόντιος κλύδων συμπίτνων, στένει βυθός,
κελαινὸς Ἄϊδος ὑποβρέμει μυχὸς γᾶς,
435 παγαί θ' ἀγνορύτων ποταμῶν στένουσιν ἄλγος οἰκτρόν.

425–430. Responsion with the antistrophe has been disturbed by interpolation. See App.

426. ἐν πόνοις δαμέντα: ἐν is not
simply the equivalent of the instrumental dative, as often (for instance
Pers. 251 ἐν μιᾷ πληγῇ κατέφθαρται
πολὺς ὄλβος), but expresses the duration of the pain, as if it were πόνοις
ἐνεζευγμένον. See on 108. — ἀκαμαντοδέτοις λύμαις: interpolated from
148 (one manuscript has ἀδαμαντοδέτοις). — θεόν: like his brother Prometheus.

429 ff. For the thought cp. 348 ff.
In both passages Atlas is described
as 'upholding sky and earth,' but the
language is here even vaguer than in
the former place. The expression
σθένος γαίας affords a hint of the conception intended. While the heavens
press down from above, the earth
bears up against the pressure of Atlas's feet, and the *strength* with which
she resists this pressure is in the
poet's mind. — πόλον: cp. the scholiast on Ar. *Av.* 179 πόλον γὰρ οἱ παλαιοὶ
οὐχ ὡς οἱ νεώτεροι σημεῖόν τι (a point)
καὶ πέρας ἄξονος, ἀλλὰ τὸ περίεχον ἅπαν.
Εὐριπίδης Πειρίθῳ (Frg. 597) 'τὸν Ἄτ-

λάντειον τηροῦσι πόλον.' — νώτοις ὑποστενάζει: = νώτοις βαστάζων στενάζει.
But see App.

431 ff. Further description of Atlas's situation. 'Fluctus marinos quasi
misericordia Atlantis tangi fingit, quia
Atlas haud procul a mari in Maure-
tania stare ferebatur' (Schütz). —
συμπίτνων: sc. Ἄτλαντι στενάζοντι.
The wave which breaks at Atlas's feet
groans in sympathy with him, and
the lament is passed on to the depth
of the sea and finally to the dark re-
cesses of the lower world. So too the
rivers groan, whose sources are near
Atlas. With βοᾷ δὲ πόντιος κλύδων
συμπίτνων, cp. *Il.* xiv. 394 οὔτε θαλάσσης κῦμα τόσον βοάᾳ ποτὶ χέρσον, κτλ.

433. Ἄϊδος μυχὸς γᾶς: two geni-
tives, one of which (γᾶς) is more
closely connected with the govern-
ing substantive than the other. Cp.
Soph. *O. C.* 669 τᾶσδε χώρας ἵκου τὰ
κράτιστα γᾶς ἔπαυλα, Eur. *Suppl.* 53
τάφων χώματα γαίας, *Cycl.* 293 ἥ τε
Σουνίου δίας Ἀθάνας σῶς ὑπάργυρος πέ-
τρα. Ἄϊδος is here used in a broad
sense, of the gloomy nether world.
For the asyndeton στένει, ὑποβρέμει,
and for the whole description, cp.

ΠΡΟΜΗΘΕΥΣ.

μή τοι χλιδῇ δοκεῖτε μηδ' αὐθαδίᾳ
σιγᾶν με· συννοίᾳ δὲ δάπτομαι κέαρ,
ὁρῶν ἐμαυτὸν ὧδε προυσελούμενον.

καίτοι θεοῖσι τοῖς νέοις τούτοις γέρα
440 τίς ἄλλος ἢ 'γὼ παντελῶς διώρισεν;
ἀλλ' αὐτὰ σιγῶ. καὶ γὰρ εἰδυίαισιν ἂν
ὑμῖν λέγοιμι· τὰν βροτοῖς δὲ πήματα
ἀκούσαθ' ὡς σφᾶς νηπίους ὄντας τὸ πρὶν
ἔννους ἔθηκα καὶ φρενῶν ἐπηβόλους.

Sept. 900 διήκει δὲ καὶ πόλιν στόνος, στένουσι πύργοι, στένει πέδον φίλανδρον.

436–525. Second Episode. Prometheus and the Coryphaeus. Prometheus calls to mind the benefits he has conferred on gods and men, and his bitterness increases as he contrasts these with his present treatment.

436. μή τοι: see on 625.

437. σιγᾶν: see Introduction, pp. 23 and 27. — συννοίᾳ: cp. Soph. Ant. 278 ἐμοί τοι, μή τι καὶ θεήλατον τοὔργον τόδ', ἡ ξύννοια βουλεύει πάλαι, Hdt. i. 88 ὁ δὲ συννοίῃ ἐχόμενος ἥσυχος ἦν. The nature of the 'brooding thoughts' suggested by his pains is hinted at in the words καίτοι ... διώρισεν. — δάπτομαι κέαρ: cp. Od. i. 48 δαίεται ἦτορ, Il. vi. 202 ὃν θυμὸν κατέδων.

439. τούτοις: = istis, spoken with contempt.

440. τίς ἄλλος ἢ 'γώ: διὰ τὸ συμβαλέσθαι Διὶ κατὰ τῶν Τιτάνων, Schol. Cp. 219 with 229. Hence παντελῶς, finally, after all, if one goes to the bottom of the matter.

441 f. εἰδυίαισιν ἂν ὑμῖν λέγοιμι: cp. 1040, Suppl. 742 καὶ λέγω πρὸς εἰ-δότα, Ag. 1402 πρὸς εἰδότας λέγω, Il. x. 250 εἰδόσι γάρ τοι ταῦτα μετ' Ἀργείοις ἀγορεύεις, xxiii. 787 εἰδόσιν ὑμμ' ἐρέω πᾶσιν, Pind. Pyth. iv. 261 εἰδότι τοι ἐρέω, Soph. O. C. 1539 τὰ μὲν τοιαῦτ' οὖν εἰδότ' ἐκδιδάσκομεν, Eur. Hec. 670 οὐ καινὸν εἶπας, εἰδόσιν δ' ὠνείδισας, Or. 1183 εἰδότ' ἠρόμην, Hdt. iii. 103 ἐπιστα-μένοισι τοῖσι Ἕλλησι οὐ συγγράφω, vii. 8 ἐπισταμένοισι οὐ οὐκ ἂν τις λέγοι, Thuc. ii. 36 μακρηγορεῖν ἐν εἰδόσιν οὐ βουλόμενος ἐάσω, Plaut. Pseud. 996 novi: notis praedicas.

442. τὰν βροτοῖς δὴ πήματα: ἃ εἶ-χον πήματα πρώην, Schol. The present condition of mankind is known; but to put Prometheus's merit in a clear light, it is necessary to set forth their former wretched plight (447 ff.). In this sense Prometheus says below, λέξω δὲ μέμψιν οὔτιν' ἀνθρώποις ἔχων.

444. φρενῶν ἐπηβόλους: cp. Soph. Ant. 492 λυσσῶσαν αὐτὴν οὐδ' ἐπήβολον φρενῶν, Porphyr. Quaest. Homer. i. τὸ δὲ ἐπήβολος σημαίνει τὸν ἐπιτυχῆ καὶ ἐγκρατῆ ἀπὸ τῆς βολῆς καὶ τοῦ βάλλειν. Σοφοκλῆς Ἀλκμαίωνι 'εἴθ' εὖ φρονή-σαντ' εἰσίδοιμί πως φρενῶν ἐπήβολον καλῶν σε.'

445 λέξω δέ, μέμψιν οὔτιν' ἀνθρώποις ἔχων,
ἀλλ' ὧν δέδωκ' εὔνοιαν ἐξηγούμενος·

οἳ πρῶτα μὲν βλέποντες ἔβλεπον μάτην
κλύοντες οὐκ ἤκουον, ἀλλ' ὀνειράτων
ἀλίγκιοι μορφαῖσι τὸν μακρὸν βίον
450 ἔφυρον εἰκῇ πάντα, κοὔτε πλινθυφεῖς
δόμους προσείλους ᾖσαν, οὐ ξυλουργίαν
κατώρυχες δ' ἔναιον ὥστ' ἀήσυροι
μύρμηκες ἄντρων ἐν μυχοῖς ἀνηλίοις.

445. μέμψιν ἔχων: Soph. *Ai.* 179 σοί τινα μομφὰν ἔχων, Eur. *Phoen.* 773 ὥστε μοι μομφὰς ἔχειν, *Or.* 1069 ἐν μὲν πρῶτά σοι μομφὴν ἔχω. Cp. Soph. *Phil.* 322 ἔχεις ἔγκλημ' 'Ατρείδαις. In passive sense Thuc. ii. 41 τῷ ὑπηκόῳ κατάμεμψιν ἔχει (sc. ἡ πόλις) ὡς οὐχ ὑπ' ἀξίων ἄρχεται.

446. ὧν δέδωκ' εὔνοιαν: *the kindly feeling which prompted my gifts.* See Krüger I. § 47, 7, 6.

447. πρῶτα μέν: answered by ἦν δ' οὐδέν, 454 (cp. 707–700, 1016–1020). The third specification is introduced by καὶ μήν (459), the fourth by καὶ (462). — The scholiast remarks, τὸ παροιμιῶδες ἐξηγεῖται 'νοῦς ὁρῇ καὶ νοῦς ἀκούει.' A verse of Epicharmus ran νοῦς ὁρῇ καὶ νοῦς ἀκούει, τἄλλα κωφὰ καὶ τυφλά.

448 f. ὀνειράτων ἀλίγκιοι μορφαῖσι: see on 548, and cp. Ar. *Av.* 687 ἄνδρες εἰκελόνειροι. In a different sense *Ag.* 1218 ὀνείρων προσφερεῖς μορφώμασι. ἀλίγκιος is an Homeric word. — τὸν μακρὸν βίον: an expression for "the whole duration of life" (τὸ μῆκος τοῦ βίου), like our 'the live-long day.' Cp. Eur. *Hipp.* 374 νυκτὸς ἐν μακρῷ χρόνῳ, and 537 below.

450. ἔφυρον εἰκῇ: cp. Eur. *Suppl.* 201 αἰνῶ θ' ὃς ἡμῖν βίοτον ἐκ πεφυρμένου

καὶ θηριώδους θεῶν διεσταθμήσατο, and the passage of a tragedy preserved Stob. *Ecl. Phys.* i. 1 ἔπειτα πάσης 'Ελλάδος καὶ συμμάχων βίον διῴκησ' ὄντα πρὶν πεφυρμένον θηρσίν θ' ὅμοιον· πρῶτα μὲν τὸν πάνσοφον ἀριθμὸν ηὕρηκ' ἔξοχον σοφισμάτων (cp. 459), and finally the long description of the primitive condition of mankind in Lucret. v. 951 ff. — οὔτε ... οὐ: cp. 470; *Cho.* 291 οὔτε κρατῆρος μέρος εἶναι μετασχεῖν, οὐ φιλοσπόνδου λιβός, Soph. *Ant.* 249 οὔτε τοῦ γενῆθος ἦν πλῆγμ', οὐ δικέλλης ἐκβολή, *O. C.* 972 οὔτε βλάστας πω γενεθλίου πατρός, οὐ μητρὸς εἶχον, Eur. *Or.* 46 ἔδοξε δ' 'Αργει τῷδε μήθ' ἡμᾶς στέγαις, μὴ πυρὶ δέχεσθαι μήτε προσφωνεῖν τινα, *Tro.* 634, Frg. 326. — πλινθυφεῖς: lateribus contextos. The word is found only here.

451. προσείλους: compound of εἴλη, sun's warmth. Cp. προσήλιος, ἀντήλιος. — ᾖσαν: on the Attic form (from οἶδα) see G. 127 vii; H. 491.

452. ἀήσυροι: agiles, alacriter discurrentes (Schütz), that is, swarming. Root αε- (ἄημι), with added σ.

453. Cp. Hom. *Hymn* xx. 1 'Ηφαιστον ... ὃς μετ' 'Αθηναίης γλαυκώπιδος ἀγλαὰ ἔργα ἀνθρώπους ἐδίδαξεν ἐπὶ χθονός, οἳ τὸ πάρος περ ἄντροις ναιετάασκον

ἦν δ' οὐδὲν αὐτοῖς οὔτε χείματος τέκμαρ
455　οὔτ' ἀνθεμώδους ἦρος οὔτε καρπίμου
θέρους βέβαιον, ἀλλ' ἄτερ γνώμης τὸ πᾶν
ἔπρασσον, ἔς τε δή σφιν ἀντολὰς ἐγὼ
ἄστρων ἔδειξα τάς τε δυσκρίτους δύσεις.
καὶ μὴν ἀριθμόν, ἔξοχον σοφισμάτων,
460　ἐξηῦρον αὐτοῖς, γραμμάτων τε συνθέσεις,
μνήμην ἁπάντων, μουσομήτορ' ἐργάνην.
κἄζευξα πρῶτος ἐν ζυγοῖσι κνώδαλα,
ζεύγλαισι δουλεύοντα σάγμασίν θ' ὅπως
θνητοῖς μεγίστων διάδοχοι μοχθημάτων
465　γένοινθ', ὑφ' ἅρμα τ' ἤγαγον φιληνίους

ἐν οὔρεσιν ᾗτε θῆρες. νῦν δὲ ... εὐκη-
λοι διάγουσιν ἐνὶ σφετέροισι δόμοισιν.

457. σφίν: see on 252.

458. δυσκρίτους: belongs with ἀν-
τολάς as well as δύσεις. ' Words common to two members of a sentence,
the poets like to put in the second
member, to give it greater weight
and to bind the whole together. Cp.
El. 105 ἔστ' ἂν παμφεγγεῖς ἄστρων
ῥιπάς, λεύσσω δὲ τόδ' ἦμαρ, 920 ἡδὺς
οὐδὲ μητρὶ δυσχερής, *O. C.* 1399 οἴμοι
κελεύθου τῆς τ' ἐμῆς δυσπραξίας, Aesch.
Ag. 580 φράζων ἅλωσιν Ἰλίου τ' ἀνά-
στασιν, *Eum.* 9 λιπὼν δὲ λίμνην Δηλίαν
τε χοιράδα.' So Schneidewin on Soph.
O. T. 802 (κῆρύξ τε κἀπὶ πωλικῆς ἀνὴρ
ἀπήνης ἐμβεβώς). See on 21, and
1015 below; also *Cho.* 200 στίβοι ποδῶν
ὅμοιοι τοῖς τ' ἐμοῖσιν ἐμφερεῖς, Eur.
Heracl. 168 εἰς γόους τε καὶ τὰ τῶνδ'
οἰκτίσματα βλέψας, *Med.* 1366 ὕβρις οἱ
τε σοὶ νεοδμῆτες γάμοι.— As an example of a δύσκριτος δύσις the scholiast cites, οἷον Ὠρίων ὅτε δύων χειμῶνα
ποιεῖ.

459 f. καὶ μήν: nay even. See on
246.— ἀριθμὸν ... γραμμάτων τε συνθέ-

σεις: the invention of architecture,
astronomy, arithmetic, and letters is
elsewhere ascribed to Palamedes. Cp.
Soph. Frg. 379 οὗτος (Παλαμήδης) δ'
ἐφηῦρε τεῖχος Ἀργείων στρατῷ, σταθμῶν
τ' ἀριθμῶν καὶ μέτρων εὑρήματα ...,
ἐφηῦρε δ' ἄστρων μέτρα καὶ περιστροφάς,
Eur. Frg. 582 τὰ τῆς γε λήθης φάρμακ'
ὀρθώσας μόνος, ἄφωνα καὶ φωνοῦντα
συλλαβάς τε θεὶς ἐξηῦρον ἀνθρώποισι
γράμματ' εἰδέναι.

461. μουσομήτορα: cp. Hesiod *Theog.*
52 Μοῦσαι Ὀλυμπιάδες κοῦραι Διὸς αἰγιόχοιο, τὰς ἐν Πιερίῃ τέκε Μνημοσύνῃ.
Memory, instead of being called
simply ἐργάτις Μουσῶν, is more pic-
turesquely described as ἐργάνη μουσο-
μήτωρ. See also on 241.

463. ζεύγλαισι δουλεύοντα σάγμασίν τε: so in Latin *iugalia* and
clitellaria iumenta are distinguished. For ζεύγλαισι δουλεύοντα
cp. 908, Soph. *O. C.* 105 μόχθοις λα-
τρεύων τοῖς ὑπερτάτοις.

464. διάδοχοι: cp. 1027 and Frg.
IV. of the Προμηθεὺς λυόμενος below.

465. φιληνίους: cp. Pind. *Pyth.* ii. 21
ἅρματα πεισιχάλινα. Here proleptic.

ἵππους, ἄγαλμα τῆς ὑπερπλούτου χλιδῆς.
θαλασσόπλαγκτα δ᾽ οὔτις ἄλλος ἀντ᾽ ἐμοῦ
λινόπτερ᾽ ηὗρε ναυτίλων ὀχήματα.

τοιαῦτα μηχανήματ᾽ ἐξευρὼν τάλας
470 βροτοῖσιν αὐτὸς οὐκ ἔχω σόφισμ᾽ ὅτῳ
τῆς νῦν παρούσης πημονῆς ἀπαλλαγῶ.

ΧΟΡΟΣ.

πέπονθας αἰκὲς πῆμ᾽· ἀποσφαλεὶς φρενῶν
πλανᾷ, κακὸς δ᾽ ἰατρὸς ὥς τις ἐς νόσον

468. ἄγαλμα ... χλιδῆς: the passion for fine horses was very strong
at Athens, and led to much extrava-
gance. In Thuc. vi. 16, Alcibiades
takes credit for the splendor of the
Olympian θεωρία 'διότι ἅρματα μὲν ἑπτὰ
καθῆκα, ὅσα οὐδεὶς πω ἰδιώτης πρότερον.'
Cp. Hdt. vi. 35 Μιλτιάδης ἐὼν οἰκίης
τεθριπποτρόφου, [Dem.] XLII. 24 ἱππο-
τρόφος ἀγαθός ἐστι (sc. Φαίνιππος) καὶ
φιλότιμος ἅτε νέος καὶ πλούσιος καὶ
ἰσχυρὸς ὤν, and especially the beginning of Aristophanes's Clouds.
467. ἄλλος ἀντ᾽ ἐμοῦ: cp. Soph.
O. C. 488 κεἴ τις ἄλλος ἀντὶ σοῦ, Ai. 444
ἄλλος ἀντ᾽ ἐμοῦ, Eur. H. F. 510 ἄλλος
ἀντὶ σοῦ παιδός, Hel. 574 οὐκ ἔστιν ἄλλη
σή τις ἀντ᾽ ἐμοῦ γυνή. Also Eur. Suppl.
419 ὁ γὰρ χρόνος μάθησιν ἀντὶ τοῦ τά-
χους κρείσσω τίθησιν.
468. λινόπτερα: similarly Ennius
(quoted by Servius on Verg. Aen. i.
224), naves velivolae; Ovid
Pont. iv. 5, 42 velivolae rates;
cp. Suppl. 734 νῆες ὠκύπτεροι, Eur.
Hipp. 752 ὦ λευκόπτερε πορθμίς, Od.
vii. 36 νέες ὠκεῖαι ὡς εἰ πτερὸν ἠὲ
νόημα, xi. 125 εὐήρε᾽ ἐρετμά, τά τε
πτερὰ νηυσὶ πέλονται.—ὀχήματα: cp.
Suppl. 33 ξὺν ὄχῳ ταχυήρει, Od. iv.
708 νηῶν ὠκυπόρων ἐπιβαινέμεν, αἵ θ᾽

ἁλὸς ἵπποι ἀνδράσι γίγνονται, Soph.
Trach. 656 πολύκωπον ὄχημα ναός, Eur.
I. T. 410 νάϊον ὄχημα
469 f. Cp. Eur. Frg. 897 μισῶ σο-
φιστὴν ὅστις οὐχ αὑτῷ σοφός.
472 ff. μεσολαβοῦσαι αἱ τοῦ χοροῦ
τὴν ἔκθεσιν τῶν κατορθωμάτων διανα-
παύουσι τὸν ὑποκριτὴν [Αἰσχύλου],
Schol. That is, the object of the
interruption is simply to rest the actor. Accordingly, the coryphaeus re-
peats assentingly the sentiment which
Prometheus has last uttered. This
is often the case in such intermediate
speeches of the chorus. The words
πέπονθας αἰκὲς πῆμα, thou hast been
shamefully treated, voice the feeling
of indignation implied in Prometheus's speech. The chorus is amazed
at the unjust dispensation by which
Prometheus, who helped others, cannot help himself. — ἀποσφαλεὶς φρενῶν πλανᾷ: equivalent to οὐκ ἔχω
σόφισμα above. Cp. Pers. 392 φόβος
δὲ πᾶσι βαρβάροις παρῆν γνώμης ἀπο-
σφαλεῖσιν, Eur. Iph. A. 742 μάτην ἧξ,
ἐλπίδος δ᾽ ἀπεσφάλην, Ag. 1530 ἀμηχανῶ
φροντίδος στερηθεὶς εὐπάλαμον μέριμναν
ὅπα τράπωμαι. Asyndeton, because
the clause is explanatory of πέπονθας
αἰκὲς πῆμα. Krüger I. § 59, 1, 5.

πεσὼν ἀθυμεῖς καὶ σεαυτὸν οὐκ ἔχεις
475 εὑρεῖν ὁποίοις φαρμάκοις ἰάσιμος.

ΠΡΟΜΗΘΕΤΣ.

τὰ λοιπά μου κλύουσα θαυμάσει πλέον,
οἴας τέχνας τε καὶ πόρους ἐμησάμην.

τὸ μὲν μέγιστον, εἴ τις εἰς νόσον πέσοι,
οὐκ ἦν ἀλέξημ' οὐδέν, οὔτε βρώσιμον
480 οὐ χριστὸν οὔτε πιστόν, ἀλλὰ φαρμάκων
χρείᾳ κατεσκέλλοντο, πρίν γ' ἐγὼ σφίσιν
ἔδειξα κράσεις ἠπίων ἀκεσμάτων,
αἷς τὰς ἁπάσας ἐξαμύνονται νόσους.
τρόπους τε πολλοὺς μαντικῆς ἐστοίχισα,
485 κἄκρινα πρῶτος ἐξ ὀνειράτων ἃ χρὴ

474. ἀθυμεῖς: result of the helplessness just described.

475. ἰάσιμος: for the omission of εἰ and σύ, see on 42. The thought reminds one of Mark xv. 31 ἄλλους ἔσωσεν, ἑαυτὸν οὐ δύναται σῶσαι, only there is no derision in the words of the coryphaeus.

479 f. οὔτε ... οὐ ... οὔτε: instead of οὔτε ... οὔτε ... οὔτε (as in 454). See on 450. — βρώσιμον ... χριστὸν ... πιστόν: cp. Ag. 1407 ἐδανὸν ἢ ποτόν, Eur. Hipp. 516 πότερα δὲ χριστὸν ἢ ποτὸν τὸ φάρμακον; Schol. on Ar. Plut. 717 φάρμακον καταπλαστόν· τῶν φαρμάκων τὰ μέν ἐστι καταπλαστά, τὰ δὲ χριστά, τὰ δὲ ποτά. The form πιστός (for ποτός) occurs only here; but cp. πίστρα, πιστήρια. Not only the metre, but the assonance χριστὸν πιστόν, suggested the unusual form.

482. ἠπίων: cp. ἤπια φάρμακα Il. iv. 218, xi. 830; ἠπίοισι φύλλοις Soph. Phil. 697.

484. τρόπους τε πολλοὺς μαντικῆς: on these means of prophecy (dreams, voices, omens, birds, sacrifices) cp. Xen. Mem. i. 1, 3 ὅσοι μαντικὴν νομίζοντες οἰωνοῖς τε χρῶνται καὶ φήμαις καὶ συμβόλοις καὶ θυσίαις, Ar. Av. 720 φήμη γ' ὑμῖν ὄρνις ἐστίν, πταρμόν τ' ὄρνιθα καλεῖτε, ξύμβολον ὄρνιν, φωνὴν ὄρνιν, θεράποντ' ὄρνιν, ὄνον ὄρνιν, Eur. Suppl. 211 ἃ δ' ἔστ' ἄσημα κοὐ σαφῆ, γιγνώσκομεν εἰς πῦρ βλέποντες, καὶ κατὰ σπλάγχνων πτυχὰς μάντεις προσημαίνουσιν οἰωνῶν τ' ἄπο. — Prophecy is reckoned among the instrumentalities of human progress.

485. ἔκρινα: κρίνω is the regular word for the interpretation of dreams. Cp. ὀνειροκρίτης, and Cho. 37 κριταὶ τε τῶνδ' ὀνειράτων. — For the thought cp. Pind. Frg. 96 εὕδει δὲ (sc. ζῷον, the soul) πρασσόντων μελέων, ἀτὰρ εὑδόντεσσιν ἐν πολλοῖς ὀνείροις δείκνυσι τερπνῶν ἐφέρποισαν χαλεπῶν τε κρίσιν.

ὕπαρ γενέσθαι, κληδόνας τε δυσκρίτους
ἐγνώρισ' αὐτοῖς ἐνοδίους τε συμβόλους·
γαμψωνύχων τε πτῆσιν οἰωνῶν σκεθρῶς
διώρισ', οἵτινές τε δεξιοὶ φύσιν
490 εὐωνύμους τε, καὶ δίαιταν ἥντινα
ἔχουσ' ἕκαστοι, καὶ πρὸς ἀλλήλους τίνες
ἔχθραι τε καὶ στέργηθρα καὶ συνεδρίαι·
σπλάγχνων τε λειότητα, καὶ χροιὰν τίνα
ἔχουσ' ἂν εἴη δαίμοσιν πρὸς ἡδονὴν
495 χολή, λοβοῦ τε ποικίλην εὐμορφίαν·

486 f. ὕπαρ: cp. *Od.* xix. 547 οὐκ
ὄναρ, ἀλλ' ὕπαρ ἐσθλόν, ὅ τοι τετε-
λεσμένον ἔσται. — κληδόνας κτἰ.: κλη-
δόνες (or φῆμαι) are foreboding voices,
ἐνόδιοι σύμβολοι signs which befall us
on leaving home or on journeys. Cp.
Cramer *Anecd. Ox.* IV. p. 241 ἐνόδιον,
ὅταν ἐξηγήσηταί τις τὰ ἐν ὁδῷ ἀπαν-
τῶντα λέγων· ἐάν σοι ὑπαντήσῃ τοιοῦτος ἄνθρωπος ἢ τόδε βαστάζων ἢ τόδε,
συμβήσεταί σοι τόδε, Chrysost. on
Paul. *Ephes.* 4, *Homil.* 12 πολλῶν
δειμάτων αὐτοῖς (the Greeks) ἡ ψυχὴ
μεστή, οἶον· 'ὁ δεῖνά μοι πρῶτος ἐνέ-
τυχεν ἐξιόντι τῆς οἰκίας· πάντως μυ-
ριάδει κακὰ συμπεσεῖν.' 'ἔξω δὲ ἐξελ-
θόντι ὁ ὀφθαλμός μοι ὁ δεξιὸς κάτω-
θεν ἀναπηδᾷ· δακρύων τοῦτο τεκμήριον,' Hor. *Carm.* iii. 27, 1 impios
parrae recinentis omen du-
cat et praegnans canis aut
ab agro rava decurrens lupa
Lanuvino fetaque vulpes.
Rumpit et serpens iter in-
stitutum, si per obliquum
similis sagittae terruit man-
nos.

488. γαμψωνύχων: cp. *Il.* xvi. 428
αἰγυπιοὶ γαμψώνυχες. The large, soar-
ing birds of prey (eagles, hawks,

ravens) served for augury. — σκεθρῶς:
cp. 102.

490 ff. εὐωνύμους τε: cp. on 91;
also *Ag.* 444 στένουσι δ' εὖ λέγοντες
τὸν μὲν ὡς μάχης ἴδρις, τὸν δ' ἐν φοναῖς
καλῶς πεσόντα, *Pers.* 76 τεζονόμοις ἔκ
τε θαλάσσας. — δίαιταν... συνεδρίαι:
this, too, was a part of augural sci-
ence, as affording prognostications of
human conditions. Cp. Aristot. *Hist.
An.* ix. 1 τοῖς ὠμοφάγοις ἅπαντα πολε-
μεῖ, καὶ ταῦτα τοῖς ἄλλοις· ὅθεν καὶ
τὰς διεδρίας καὶ τὰς συνεδρίας οἱ
μάντεις λαμβάνουσι· διεδρα μὲν τὰ
πολέμια τιθέντες, σύνεδρα δὲ τὰ εἰρη-
νεύοντα πρὸς ἄλληλα. Accordingly
στέργηθρα is the untechnical, συνεδρίαι
the technical term.

493 ff. Examination of sacrificial
victims (extispicina) had to do
with shape, position, and color of the
inner organs. This was especially
the office of the ἱεροσκόποι or θυοσκό-
ποι. — καὶ χροιὰν... χολή: and what
color the gall must have, to be agreeable
to the gods. Cp. Eur. *El.* 826 ἱερὰ δ'
εἰς χεῖρας λαβὼν Αἴγισθος ἤθρει· καὶ
λόβος μὲν οὐ προσῆν σπλάγχνοις, πύλαι
δὲ καὶ δοχαὶ χολῆς πέλας κακὰς ἐφαι-
νον τῷ σκοποῦντι προσβολάς.

κνίσῃ τε κῶλα συγκαλυπτὰ καὶ μακρὰν
ὀσφῦν πυρώσας δυστέκμαρτον ἐς τέχνην
ὥδωσα θνητούς, καὶ φλογωπὰ σήματα
ἐξωμμάτωσα, πρόσθεν ὄντ᾽ ἐπάργεμα.
500 τοιαῦτα μὲν δὴ ταῦτ᾽· ἔνερθε δὲ χθονὸς
κεκρυμμέν᾽ ἀνθρώποισιν ὠφελήματα,
χαλκὸν, σίδηρον, ἄργυρον χρυσόν τε τίς
φήσειεν ἂν πάροιθεν ἐξευρεῖν ἐμοῦ;
οὐδείς, σάφ᾽ οἶδα, μὴ μάτην φλύσαι θέλων.

496 ff. κνίσῃ ... τέχνην: this τέχνη is the ἐμπυρομαντεία, which derived signs (σήματα) from the form, brightness and power of the sacrificial flames. Cp. Apoll. Rh. i. 144 αὐτὸς δὲ θεοπροπίας ἐδίδαξεν οἰωνούς τ᾽ ἀλέγειν ἠδ᾽ ἔμπυρα σήματ᾽ ἰδέσθαι. Such ἔμπυρα (= φλογωπὰ) σήματα, of evil portent, are described Soph. *Ant.* 1006 ἐκ δὲ θυμάτων Ἥφαιστος οὐκ ἔλαμπεν, ἀλλ᾽ ἐπὶ σποδῷ μυδῶσα κηκὶς μηρίων ἐτήκετο κάτυφε κἀνέπτυε καὶ μετάρσιοι χολαὶ διεσπείροντο, καὶ καταρρυεῖς μηροὶ καλυπτῆς ἐξέκειντο πιμελῆς. — Incidentally, in κνίσῃ ... ὀσφῦν, the poet refers to the doctrines as to what part of the victims should be offered to the gods, and in what way. There is here a vague allusion to the story in Hesiod (see Introd. p. 5). Cp. also *Il.* i. 460 μηρούς τ᾽ ἐξέταμον κατά τε κνίσῃ ἐκάλυψαν, δίπτυχα ποιήσαντες, ἐπ᾽ αὐτῶν δ᾽ ὠμοθέτησαν. — μακρὰν ὀσφῦν: = μεγάλην ὀσφῦν. Cp. *Eum.* 75 δι᾽ ἠπείρου μακρᾶς. The so-called ἱερὸν ὀστοῦν, os sacrum, is meant. Cp. Etym. Magn. p. 468, 28 ἱερὸν ὀστοῦν, τὸ ἄκρον τῆς ὀσφύος· οὕτω γὰρ κέκληται ὅτι μέγα ἐστίν (hence the epithet μακρὰν), ἢ ὅτι ἱερουργεῖται τοῖς θεοῖς.

499. ἐξωμμάτωσα, ἐπάργεμα: these correspond in their proper significations. ἄργεμος, νόσος ὀμμάτων (cataract), ἀφ᾽ οὗ ἄργεμα κατὰ Δίδυμον τὰ ἐπὶ ὀφθαλμῶν λευκώματα (albugo), Eustath. p. 1430, 60; ἐπάργεμα λέγεται τὰ ὄμματα, ὅταν ᾖ τετυφλωμένα ὑπὸ λευκωμάτων, Hesych. On ἐξομματοῦν, *take scales from the eyes*, cp. the verse from Sophocles's *Phineus* in Ar. *Plut.* 635 (ἀντὶ γὰρ τυφλοῦ) ἐξωμμάτωται καὶ λελάμπρυνται κόρας. Here "open the eyes" is said for "make plain." What we perceive, seems to us, as it were, to have eyes. So τυφλός means *invisible* as well as *not seeing*.

501. ἀνθρώποισιν: to be joined with the verbal substantive ὠφελήματα. Cp. 612; Ar. *Nub.* 305 οὐρανίοις τε θεοῖς δωρήματα, Plat. *Apol.* 30 a τὴν ἐμὴν τῷ θεῷ ὑπηρεσίαν, Eur. *Iph. T.* 387 τὰ Ταντάλου τε θεοῖσιν ἑστιάματα. Krüger I. § 48, 12, 4; G. 185; H. 765 a. For the dative with ὠφελεῖν see on 342 above.

502. ἄργυρον χρυσόν τε: the last two objects, united by τέ, form together the third member of the series. Cp. Cic. *Div.* 1. 51 aurum et argentum, aes, ferrum.

504. φλύσαι: cp. Cic. *de Fin.* v. 27 dixerit hoc quidem Epicurus, semper beatum esse sapientem, quod quidem solet ebullire nonnunquam.

505 βραχεῖ δὲ μύθῳ πάντα συλλήβδην μάθε,
    πᾶσαι τέχναι βροτοῖσιν ἐκ Προμηθέως.

ΧΟΡΟΣ.

    μή νυν βροτοὺς μὲν ὠφέλει καιροῦ πέρα,
    σαυτοῦ δ' ἀκήδει δυστυχοῦντος· ὡς ἐγὼ
    εὔελπίς εἰμι τῶνδέ σ' ἐκ δεσμῶν ἔτι
510 λυθέντα μηδὲν μεῖον ἰσχύσειν Διός.

ΠΡΟΜΗΘΕΥΣ.

    οὐ ταῦτα ταύτῃ μοῖρά πω τελεσφόρος
    κρᾶναι πέπρωται, μυρίαις δὲ πημοναῖς

505. Cp. Eur. Frg. 364, 5 βραχει δὲ μύθῳ πολλὰ συλλαβὼν ἐρῶ, Lucret. vi. 1083 sed breviter paucis praestat comprendere multa.

507 f. Paratactic for μή νυν βροτοὺς ὠφελῶν σαυτοῦ ἀκήδει, according to a favorite Greek mode of expression. Cp. Dem. ix. 27 καὶ οὐ γράφει μὲν ταῦτα, τοῖς δ' ἔργοις οὐ ποιεῖ. In ὠφέλει the time of the action is not thought of, only its sense as opposed to ἀκήδει. Observe that ἀκηδεῖν is an epic word.

509 f. The prediction of Prometheus in 476 is fulfilled; the account of his achievements has brought the chorus to enthusiastic admiration. He has only, they think, to exert his inventive genius in his own behalf, to become as powerful as Zeus himself. To the enlightened spectator this utterance, in a certain sense, is true, since at the end of the trilogy Prometheus is to take his place at the side of the other gods, and so of Zeus, as an object of worship. The thought serves furthermore as transition to the mention of the secret and the revelation of Prometheus's designs.

511 f. Prometheus tacitly accepts the words ἐκ δεσμῶν λυθέντα μηδὲν μεῖον ἰσχύσειν Διός, but as to time (οὕτω) and manner (ταύτῃ, as you suppose; cp. on 247) of his release the chorus, he asserts, is wrong. — μοῖρα πέπρωται: cp. τὴν πεπρωμένην μοῖραν, Hdt. i. 91. This general statement leads to a discussion of the nature of Destiny. — τελεσφόρος: Eur. Heracl. 899, μοῖρα τελεσσιδώτειρα. — κρᾶναι: here intransitive, go into fulfilment (οὕτω μοῖρα πέπρωται ταῦτα ταύτῃ κρᾶναι). Cp. Cho. 1075 ποῖ δῆτα κρανεῖ, ποῖ καταλήξει μετακοιμισθὲν μένος ἄτης; — The scholiast remarks, οὕτω μοι λυθῆναι μεμοίραται· ἐν γὰρ τῷ ἑξῆς δράματι λύεται, ὅπερ ἐμφαίνει Αἰσχύλος. — Eur. Med. 365 ἀλλ' οὔτι ταῦτα ταύτῃ, μὴ δοκεῖτέ πω, seems an imitation of this passage. Cp. Ar. Eq. 843 οὐκ ἀγαθοὶ ταῦτ' ἐστί πω ταύτῃ μὰ τὸν Ποσειδῶ.

δύαις τε καμφθεὶς ὧδε δεσμὰ φυγγάνω·
τέχνη δ' ἀνάγκης ἀσθενεστέρα μακρῷ.

XOPOΣ.

515 τίς οὖν ἀνάγκης ἐστὶν οἰακοστρόφος;

ΠΡΟΜΗΘΕΤΣ.

Μοῖραι τρίμορφοι μνήμονές τ' Ἐρινύες.

XOPOΣ.

τούτων ἄρα Ζεύς ἐστιν ἀσθενέστερος;

ΠΡΟΜΗΘΕΤΣ.

ουκουν ἂν ἐκφύγοι γε τὴν πεπρωμένην.

XOPOΣ.

τί γὰρ πέπρωται Ζηνὶ πλὴν ἀεὶ κρατεῖν;

---

513. φυγγάνω: the meaning of the present is, *I am to escape;* so 525 ἐκφυγγάνω, *I have the means of escaping.* Cp. Soph. *Phil.* 113 αἱρεῖ τὰ τόξα ταῦτα τὴν Τροίαν μόνα.

514. τέχνη: sollertia. "Skill avails nought against Necessity" is a general sentiment. Prometheus hints that the time of his release is fixed by Fate; he cannot change it, nor can Zeus himself. This last idea is taken up by the chorus in 517.

515. οἰακοστρόφος (cp. 148): that is, "in whose hands lies the execution of the law of the universe?"

516. τρίμορφοι: as it were, ἑνὸς ὀνόματος (Μοίρας) τρεῖς μορφαί. Reversed in 210 Γαῖα πολλῶν ὀνομάτων μορφὴ μία.—μνήμονες: cp. *Ag.* 155 παλίνορτος οἰκονόμος δολία μνάμων μῆνις. In *Eum.* 382 the Erinyes call themselves κακῶν μνήμονες, σεμναὶ καὶ δυσπαρήγοροι βροτοῖς. The Μοῖραι are the representatives of eternal law, the Erinyes carry out this law by punishing all who violate it. Cp. *Eum.* 334, where the Erinyes say, τοῦτο γὰρ λάχος Μοῖρ' ἐπέκλωσεν ἐμπέδως ἔχειν, θνατῶν τοῖσιν αὐτουργίαι ξυμπέσωσιν μάταιοι, τοῖς ὁμαρτεῖν ὄφρ' ἂν γᾶν ὑπέλθῃ, and Hesiod *Theog.* 217 καὶ Μοίρας καὶ Κῆρας ἐγείνατο (sc. Νὺξ) νηλεοποίνους (where Κῆρες = Ἐρινύες, cp. *Sept.* 1054 φθερσιγενεῖς Κῆρες Ἐρινύες, and *Eum.* 321, where the Erinyes are said to be daughters of Night). — This verse taken together with 010 f. shows why Zeus is still subject to Fate. Prometheus has in mind the danger of loss of sovereignty. See Introduction, p. 17 f.

518. οὐκουν ... γε: the power of Fate over Zeus is limited to the infliction of penalties for his transgressions of universal law. Cp. the words of the Pythian priestess, Hdt. i. 91 τὴν πεπρωμένην μοῖραν ἀδύνατά ἐστι ἀποφυγεῖν καὶ θεῷ.

519. Cp. *Eum.* 125 τί σοι πέπρακται πρᾶγμα πλὴν τεύχειν κακά;

ΠΡΟΜΗΘΕΥΣ.

520　τοῦτ᾽ οὐκ ἂν ἐκπύθοιο μηδὲ λιπάρει.

ΧΟΡΟΣ.

ἦ πού τι σεμνόν ἐστιν ὃ ξυναμπέχεις.

ΠΡΟΜΗΘΕΥΣ.

ἄλλου λόγου μέμνησθε, τόνδε δ᾽ οὐδαμῶς
καιρὸς γεγωνεῖν, ἀλλὰ συγκαλυπτέος
ὅσον μάλιστα· τόνδε γὰρ σῴζων ἐγὼ
525　δεσμοὺς ἀεικεῖς καὶ δύας ἐκφυγγάνω.

ΧΟΡΟΣ.

στροφὴ αʹ.

μηδάμ᾽ ὁ πάντα νέμων
θεῖτ᾽ ἐμᾷ γνώμᾳ κράτος ἀντίπαλον Ζεύς,
530　μηδ᾽ ἐλινύσαιμι θεοὺς ὁσίαις θοίναις ποτινισσομένα
βουφόνοις, παρ᾽ Ὠκεανοῦ πατρὸς ἄσβεστον πόρον,

522. The scholiast remarks, τῷ ἑξῆς δράματι φυλάττει τοὺς λόγους. — λόγου: λόγος (like ἔπος) is often used of the subject-matter of a discourse. Cp. Eur. *Hel.* 120 ἄλλου λόγου μέμνησο, μὴ κείνης ἔτι.

524. ὅσον μάλιστα: like ὅσον τάχιστα. Krüger II. § 49, 10, 2; II. 651.

526-560. Second Stasimon. The subject — praise of peace with Heaven and a tranquil life — is suggested by the words of the coryphaeus 519 τί γὰρ πέπρωται Ζηνὶ πλὴν ἀεὶ κρατεῖν; The dactylo-epitritic rhythm corresponds with this sentiment, and 'affords, in the midst of the heat of tragic pathos, a moment of refreshing coolness and cheerful calm' (Westphal).

526 ff. ὁ πάντα διοικῶν Ζεὺς μηδέ-

ποτε ἀντίπαλον κράτος ποιοῖτο τῇ ἐμῇ γνώμῃ, ἀντὶ τοῦ μηδέποτε ἐναντίος μοι γένοιτο, Schol. — θεῖτο κράτος ἀντίπαλον: see on 163.

529 f. ὁσίαις θοίναις: the sacrificial feasts which the Oceanid maidens set for the gods on the shore of Ocean, remind one of the banquets of the Aethiopians in Homer (*Il.* i. 423 Ζεὺς γὰρ ἐς Ὠκεανὸν μετ᾽ ἀμύμονας Αἰθιοπῆας χθιζὸς ἔβη κατὰ δαῖτα, θεοὶ δ᾽ ἅμα πάντες ἕποντο). The gods visit the banquets of the Oceanids, as in Ovid, *Fast.* iv. 423, frigida caelestum matres Arethusa vocarat; venerat ad sacras et dea flava dapes. — βουφόνοις: cp. *Eum.* 283 καθαρμοῖς χοιροκτόνοις, *Ag.* 209 παρθενοσφάγοισι ῥείθροις.

532. ἄσβεστον πόρον: cp. 139. Hesych. explains, ἄσβεστον· ἀκατά-

μηδ' ἀλίτοιμι λόγοις·

535 ἀλλά μοι τόδ' ἐμμένοι καὶ μήποτ' ἐκτακείη·

ἀντιστροφὴ α'.

ἁδύ τι θαρσαλέαις

τὸν μακρὸν τείνειν βίον ἐλπίσι, φαναῖς

540 θυμὸν ἀλδαίνουσαν ἐν εὐφροσύναις. φρίσσω δέ σε
        δερκομένα

μυρίοις μόχθοις διακναιόμενον _ _ ‿ _.

Ζῆνα γὰρ οὐ τρομέων

ἰδίᾳ γνώμᾳ σέβει θνατοὺς ἄγαν, Προμηθεῦ.

στροφὴ β'.

545 φέρ' ὅπως ἄχαρις χάρις, ὦ φίλος, εἰπὲ ποῦ τίς ἀλκά;

ταυστον. Cp. also *Ag.* 058 ἐστιν θάλασσα, τίς δέ νιν κατασβέσει; For
πόρον, see 806; *Cho.* 366 παρὰ Σκα-
μάνδρου πόρον, *Pers.* 493 ἐπ' Ἀξίου
πόρον.

534 f. τόδε: "the following rule
of life." — ἐκτακείη: ' videtur a scrip-
tura in tabulis cereis petitum esse,
quae igni admoto aut solis radiis
colliquescit ideoque deletur' (Schütz).
Cp. 789, and Critias Frg. 2, 12 λήστις
δ' ἐκτήκει μνημοσύνην πραπίδων.

536. Cp. Theogn. 765 ὥδ' εἴη κεν
ἄμεινον· εὔφρονα θυμὸν ἔχοντας νόσφι
μεριμνάων εὐφροσύνως διάγειν τερπομέ-
νους.

537. τὸν μακρὸν βίον: all the days
of one's life. See on 449. — τείνειν:
Pers. 708 ὁ μάσσων βίοτος ἢν ταθῇ
πρόσω, *Ag.* 1362 ἢ καὶ βίον τείνοντες
ὥδ' ὑπείξομεν, Eur. *Ion* 624 βίου αἰῶνα
τείνει, *Med.* 670 ἄπαις γὰρ δεῦρ' ἀεὶ
τείνεις βίον;

538. φαναῖς ἐν εὐφροσύναις: cp.
Plat. *Phaedr.* 256 d εἰς γὰρ σκότον οὐ
νόμος ἐστὶν ἔτι ἐλθεῖν τοῖς κατηργμένοις

ἤδη τῆς ἐπουρανίου πορείας, ἀλλὰ φανὸν
βίον διάγοντας εὐδαιμονεῖν. — ἀλδαίνουσαν: ἀλδαίνειν, like ἀλιταίνειν just
above (533), is an epic word.

543. ἰδίᾳ: gives the right sense,
but the metre requires a cretic.
Probably ἰδίᾳ has replaced μουνάδι,
as a gloss. Cp. ἰδιογνώμων and μονο-
γνώμων, also μονόφρων *Ag.* 757; *Pers.*
734 μονάδα δὲ Ξέρξην ἐρημόν φασιν ...
μολεῖν, Eur. *Andr.* 855 μονάδ' ἔρημον
οὖσαν, *Bacch.* 609 μονάδ' ἐρημίαν, *Phoen.*
1520 μονάδ' αἰῶνα. The tragic poets
use the Ionic form μοῦνος for metrical
convenience. Cp. 804 and note on 345.

544 f. φέρ' ὅπως: pregnant, look
how. δεῦρο δὴ καὶ σκόπησον, Schol. —
ἄχαρις χάρις: ἡ χάρις ἣν ἐχαρίσω τοῖς
ἀνθρώποις ἄχαρις ἦν καὶ ἀμείψασθαί σε
μὴ δυναμένη, Schol. Cp. *Ag.* 1545
ἄχαριν χάριν ἀντ' ἔργων μεγάλων ἀδίκως
ἐπικρᾶναι, *Cho.* 42 τοιάνδε χάριν ἀχάρι-
τον ἀπότροπον κακῶν, Eur. *Iph. T.* 566,
Phoen. 1757, and the Homeric Ἶρος
Ἄϊρος (*Od.* xviii. 73); also note on
904. — ποῦ τίς: see on τῇ πότε, 99.

τίς ἐφαμερίων ἄρηξις; οὐδ' ἐδέρχθης
ὀλιγοδρανίαν ἄκικυν
ἰσόνειρον, ᾷ τὸ φωτῶν
550 ἀλαὸν ⟨δέδεται⟩ γένος ἐμπεποδισμένον; οὔπως
τὰν Διὸς ἁρμονίαν θνατῶν παρεξίασι βουλαί.

ἀντιστροφὴ β'.

ἔμαθον τάδε σὰς προσιδοῦσ' ὀλοὰς τύχας, Προμηθεῦ.
555 τὸ διαμφίδιον δέ μοι μέλος προσέπτα
τόδ' ἐκεῖνό θ' ὅτ' ἀμφὶ λουτρὰ
καὶ λέχος σὸν ὑμεναίουν

546 f. **ἐφαμερίων**: see on 83. With
this description of human helplessness, cp. Αг. Δυ. 685 ἄγε δὴ φύσιν
ἄνδρες ἀμαυρόβιοι, φύλλων γενεᾷ προσό-
μοιοι, ὀλιγοδρανέες, πλάσματα πηλοῦ,
σκιοειδέα φῦλ' ἀμενηνά, ἀπτῆνες ἐφη-
μέριοι, ταλαοὶ βροτοί, ἀνέρες εἰκελόνειροι.
— ὀλιγοδρανίαν: with epic quantity
before δρ. Homer uses the participle ὀλιγοδρανέων as equivalent to
ὀλιγηπελέων. Cp. Orph. *Argon.* 432
ἀνθρώπων ὀλιγοδρανέων πολυευθνέα φύτ-
λην ἤειδον. — ἄκικυς: ἀσθενής, ἀδύνατος,
Hesych. Cp. Aesch. Frg. 230 σοὶ δ'
οὐκ ἔνεστι κίκυς οὐδ' αἱμόρρυτοι φλέβες,
Od. xi. 393 ἀλλ' οὐ γάρ οἱ ἔτ' ἦν ἲς
ἔμπεδος οὐδέ τι κίκυς.
548 f. **ἰσόνειρον**: ι long, following
epic usage, as in ἰσόθεος *Pers.* 80,
ἰσοδαίμων Pind. *Nem.* iv. 136. For the
sense, see on 448, and cp. Pind. *Pyth.*
viii. 135 ἐπάμεροι· τί δέ τις; τί δ' οὔ
τις; σκιᾶς ὄναρ ἄνθρωπος, Eur. *Med.*
1224 τὰ θνητὰ οὐ νῦν πρῶτον ἡγοῦμαι
σκιάν. — **φωτῶν**: = ἀνδρῶν. Cp. Soph.
Ai. 300 ὥστε φῶτας, in distinction to
animals. — **ᾷ δέδεται**: cp. Anth. Pal.
vi. 206 ἐκ γήρως ἀδρανίῃ δέδεται.
550 f. **οὔπως... παρεξίασι βουλαί**:

cp. *Suppl.* 1048 Διὸς οὐ παρβατός ἐστιν
μεγάλα φρὴν ἀπέραντος, *Od.* v. 103 ἀλλὰ
μάλ' οὔπως ἔστι Διὸς νόον αἰγιόχοιο
οὔτε παρεξελθεῖν ἄλλον θεὸν οὔθ' ἁλιῶ-
σαι, Hesiod *Theog.* 613 ὣς οὐκ ἔστι Διὸς
κλέψαι νόον οὐδὲ παρελθεῖν, and see
on 906. For παρεξίασι cp. also *Il.* i.
132 οὐ παρελεύσεαι οὐδέ με πείσεις,
Soph. *Ant.* 60, εἰ νόμου βίᾳ ψῆφον
τυράννων ἢ κράτη παρέξιμεν. — **τὰν Διὸς
ἁρμονίαν**: ὑψηλῶς καὶ τραγικῶς τὸ τῆς
εἱμαρμένης ὄνομα Διὸς ἁρμονίαν εἶπεν,
Schol., but this is inconsistent with
514 ff. By ἁρμονία Διός is meant
rather the compact system of Zeus's
realm. Cp. 230 διεστοιχίζετο ἀρχήν.
555. **διαμφίδιον μέλος**: ἀλλοῖον, δια-
παντὸς κεχωρισμένον· ἀμφὶς γὰρ χωρίς·
Αἰσχύλος Προμηθεῖ δεσμώτῃ, Hesych.
556. **τόδ' ἐκεῖνό τε**: for this use of
τέ, cp. Eur. *Cycl.* 37 μῶν κρότος σικι-
νίδων ὅμοιος ὑμῖν νῦν τε χὤτε
Βακχίῳ κώμοις συνασπίζοντες 'Αλθαίας
δόμους προσῆτε;—**λουτρά**: ἔθος ἦν τοῖς
παλαιοῖς ὅτε ἐγημέ τις ἐπὶ τοῖς ἐγχω-
ρίοις ποταμοῖς ἀπολούεσθαι, Schol. on
Eur. *Phoen.* 349.
558. **ὑμεναιοῦν**: τὸ ᾄδειν τὸν ὑμέ-
ναιον καὶ συνάπτειν τὸν γάμον, Photius.

ἰότατι γάμων, ὅτε τὰν ὁμοπάτριον ἕδνοις
560 ἄγαγες Ἡσιόναν πείθων δάμαρτα κοινόλεκτρον.

ΙΩ.

τίς γῆ; τί γένος; τίνα φῶ λεύσσειν
τόνδε χαλινοῖς ἐν πετρίνοισιν

559. Ἰότατι: an Homeric word. In *Od.* xi. 384 *ἐν νόστῳ δ' ἀπόλοντο κακῆς ἰότητι γυναικός*, it means *by the design of*, but here it means *on the occasion of*. Cp. *ἕκατι.* — **τὰν ὁμοπάτριον**: Hesione is daughter of Oceanus, according to Acusilaus (quoted Schol. *Od.* x. 2, *ὡς δὲ Ἀκουσίλαος, Ἡσιόνης τῆς Ὠκεανοῦ καὶ τοῦ Προμηθέως, sc. Δευκαλίων ἦν υἱός*). The expression *ὁμοπάτριον* implies that she is not a daughter of Tethys, the mother of the Oceanids.

560. The scholiast interprets, *ἕδνοις πείθων τὴν ἐσομένην σοι δάμαρτα κοινόλεκτρον*. The action of *πείθων* is synchronous with *ἄγαγες*, but continued, so that *πείθων ἕδνοις* nearly = *πειθοῖ ἕδνων*. See Krüger I. § 53, 1, 7. Cp. *Suppl.* 918 *τἄμ' ὀλωλόθ' εὑρίσκων ἐγώ.*

561-886. Third Episode. Io and Prometheus. The myth of Io is connected with that of Prometheus by the person of Heracles, the liberator of Prometheus, who is descended from Epaphus, the son of Zeus and Io (see on 774). The appearance of Io therefore prepares the way for the introduction of Heracles in the Προμηθεὺς λυόμενος. But the immediate significance of this scene consists in the present relation of Zeus and Io. Io appears as innocent and yet persecuted; her sufferings, superficially considered, put Zeus in the worst possible light. Accordingly the in-dignation of Prometheus rises more and more, till at last, carried away by passion, he vaunts his secret in such terms that the interposition of Zeus becomes inevitable. So the transition to the catastrophe is prepared. — The geographical part of this episode, with its description of marvels, like the scene of Heracles in the Προμηθεὺς λυόμενος (see below, Frg. VII. and VIII.), doubtless had a peculiar charm for the Athenians of the period.

On the origin of the myth of Io, see Introd. p. 9, footnote. Io appears as a horned maiden (588, 674; so indicated by her mask). In early Greek art, especially in vase-paintings, she has the figure of a cow outright. On the throne of the Amyclaean Apollo, a work of the sculptor Bathycles (about Ol. 60), Hera was represented as glaring at Io, 'who is already a cow' (Paus. iii. 18. 7). On an archaic black-figured vase of the Munich collection (No. 573; see Panofka, *Argos Panoptes*, plate 5), Argus is seen, seated on the ground, a ferocious figure with long hair and beard, and a huge eye in his shaggy breast; he holds in his hand a long cord, attached to the horns of a cow. Near by stands Hermes, grasping the cord near the horns with his left hand, and about to draw his sword with his right. Argus's dog

χειμαζόμενον·
τίνος ἀμπλακίας ποινὰς ὀλέκει;
σήμηνον ὅποι
565 γῆς ἡ μογερὰ πεπλάνημαι.

ἆ ἆ,
χρίει τις αὖ με τὰν τάλαιναν οἶστρος,
εἴδωλον Ἄργου γηγενοῦς,
ἄλευ’ ἆ δᾶ,

stands at bay in front of his master. Through the influence of this tragedy, Io came later to be depicted in art as a maiden with horns. So, for instance, on a red-figured vase of the Berlin Museum (Panofka, *l.c.*, plate 3). The 'stinging gadfly' of the legend (cp. *Suppl.* 306 ΒΑ. τί οὖν ἔτευξεν ἄλλο δυσπότμῳ Βοΐ; ΧΟ. βοηλάτην μύωπα κινητήριον, Verg. *Georg.* iii. 147 cui nomen asilo Romanum est, oestrum Graii vertere vocantes), which is mentioned in Io's narrative, 675 below, had also to be omitted in the scenic representation. The difficulty was met by a figurative conception of οἶστρος; the maddening sting was interpreted as the reminiscence of the crafty eye of Argos (567). — On account of the unusual manner of Io's entrance and exit, the anapaests which commonly accompany the arrival and departure of a personage are here and at 877 given to the actor, not to the chorus. So above, at the entrance of the chorus (120 ff.).

563. χειμαζόμενον : here in its proper sense, *exposed to wind and weather.* Cp. 15. Other commentators take the word figuratively, vexatum, cruciatum, as in Soph. *Phil.* 1459 Ἑρμαῖον ὄρος παρέ-

πεμψεν ἐμοὶ στόνον ἀντίτυπον χειμαζομένῳ, Eur. *Hipp.* 315 ἄλλῳ δ’ ἐν τύχῃ χειμάζομαι, *Suppl.* 269 πόλις χειμασθεῖσα, cp. below 838, 643, 1015.

564. ποινάς : in apposition to ὀλέκει. Destruction is the penalty of the crime. Cp. *Ag.* 224 ἔτλα δ’ οὖν θυτὴρ γενέσθαι θυγατρός, γυναικοποίνων πολέμων ἀρωγὰν καὶ προτέλεια ναῶν. It is rare for an appositive of this sort to precede the verb (Krüger II. § 57, 10, 6), but here this is brought about by the question. Others regard ποινάς as accusative of the inner object; see on 591 below. — ὀλέκει : ὀλέκω (or ὀλέκομαι) is an epic word. Other occurrences of it in tragedy are Soph. *Ant.* 1285 (ὀλέκεις), *Trach.* 1013 (ἀλεκόμαν).

567 f. 'Quod dicit αὖ, id scite et convenienter spectatoris cogitationem ad ea quae extra scenam gesta sunt, traducit' (Schütz). — εἴδωλον : acc. depending on εἰσορῶσα. — γηγενοῦς : cp. *Suppl.* 305 Ἄργον παῖδα γῆς. — ἄλευ’ ἆ δᾶ : in a frenzy of fear, Io interrupts her sentence with this cry. Cp. *Suppl.* 528 and *Sept.* 141 ἄλευσον, *Sept.* 86 ἰὼ ἰὼ θεοὶ θεαί τ’ ὀρόμενον κακὸν ἀλεύσατε. δᾶ is vocative of Δᾶς = Ζᾶς = Ζεύς (cp. ἆ Ζήν, *Suppl.* 162), but it is a mere interjection, not an invocation of the particular god. Cp. *Eum.* 874 οἰοῖ δᾶ, φεῦ.

τὸν μυριωπὸν εἰσορῶσα βούταν.
570 ὃ δὲ πορεύεται δόλιον ὄμμ' ἔχων,
ὃν οὐδὲ κατθανόντα γαῖα κεύθει·
ἀλλά με τὰν τάλαιναν
ἐξ ἐνέρων περῶν κυναγεῖ πλανᾷ
τε νῆστιν ἀνὰ τὰν παραλίαν ψάμμαν.

στροφή.

ὑπὸ δὲ κηρόπακτος ὀτοβεῖ δόναξ
575 ἀχέτας ὑπνοδόταν νόμον.
ἰὼ ἰώ, πόποι, ποῖ μ' ἄγουσιν ⟨πλάναι⟩,
τηλέπλανοι πλάναι;

---

569. τὸν μυριωπὸν εἰσορῶσα βούταν: as if οἰστροῦμαι and Ἄργον γηγενῆ had preceded the intermediate
exclamation. With εἰσορῶσα cp. Eur.
Hec. 970 αἰδώς μ' ἔχει ἐν τῷδε πότμῳ
τυγχάνουσ' ἵν' εἰμὶ νῦν, Iph. T. 947 ἐλθὼν δ' ἐκεῖσε, πρῶτα μέν μ' οὐδεὶς ξένων
ἑκὼν ἐδέξατο, Cycl. 330 δοραῖσι θηρῶν
σῶμα περιβαλὼν ἐμὸν καὶ πῦρ ἀναίθων
χιόνος οὐδέν μοι μέλει, Ion 927 ὑπεξαν-
τλῶν... ὄρθει με, Hipp. 22 τὰ πολλὰ
δὲ πάλαι προκόψασ', οὐ πόνου πολλοῦ με
δεῖ. See Krüger I. § 56, 9, 4, and note
on 201 above. — With μυριωπὸν βούταν
cp. Suppl. 304 πανόπτην οἰοβούκολον,
also 677 below.
570. δόλιον ὄμμα: aptly characterizes the crafty glance of the pur-
suing spectre. — Dochmii are the
proper rhythm for monodies of tragedy which express passionate agita-
tion.
571. κατθανόντα: cp. Suppl. 305
Ἄργον, τὸν Ἑρμῆς παῖδα γῆς κατέκτανε.
572. ἀλλά με: the relative clause
is continued, as usual, by an independent sentence.
573. ψάμμαν: the form ψάμμη (for

ψάμμος) recurs Ar. Lys. 1260 (τᾶς
ψάμμας) and Hdt. iv. 181.
574 f. ὑπὸ... ὀτοβεῖ: see on 126.
On the interposition of important
(not of short) words between preposition and verb, see Krüger II. § 68,
48, 4, and below on 878. — κηρόπακτος: wax-joined. Cp. Eur. Iph. T.
1125 συρίζων ὁ κηροδέτας κάλαμος οὐ-
ρείου Πανός, Theocr. Id. i. 128 ἐνθ'
ὄναξ καὶ τάνδε φέρ' εὐπάκτοιο μελί-
πνουν ἐκ κηρῷ σύριγγα καλάν, Ep. xiii.
4 κηροδέτῳ πνεύματι μελπόμενος, Ovid.
Metam. i. 711 disparibus cala-
mis compagine cerae inter
se iunctis, Verg. Ecl. ii. 32 Pan
primus calamos cera con-
iungere pluris instituit. The
flute of the αὐλητής was here actually
heard, accompanying the strophic
portion of Io's song. The foregoing
portion was recitative (παρακαταλογή).
— ὑπνοδόταν νόμον; the "slumberous
lay" depicts the exhaustion of Io.
576. πλάναι, τηλέπλανοι πλάναι:
for the repetition, cp. Sept. 134 ἐπίλυσιν πόνων, ἐπίλυσιν δίδου, 171 κλύετε
παρθένων κλύετε πανδίκως χειροτόνους

τί ποτέ μ', ὦ Κρόνιε παῖ, τί ποτε
ταῖσδ' ἐνέζευξας εὑρὼν ἁμαρτοῦσαν ἐν
πημοσύναις, ἐή,
580　οἰστρηλάτῳ δὲ δείματι δειλαίαν
παράκοπον ὧδε τείρεις;
πυρί με φλέξον ἢ χθονὶ κάλυψον ἢ ποντίοις
δάκεσι δὸς βοράν,
μηδέ μοι φθονήσῃς
εὐγμάτων, ἄναξ.
585　ᾅδην με πολύπλανοι πλάναι
γεγυμνάκασιν, οὐδ' ἔχω μαθεῖν ὅπα
πημονὰς ἀλύξω.
κλύεις φθέγμα τᾶς βούκερω παρθένου;

ΠΡΟΜΗΘΕΥΣ.

πῶς δ' οὐ κλύω τῆς οἰστροδινήτου κόρης,
590　τῆς Ἰναχείας; ἣ Διὸς θάλπει κέαρ

λιτάς, *Ag.* 1456 τὰς πολλὰς τὰς πάνυ
πολλάς. The formation of a compound adjective from the substantive
which it accompanies, occurs in three
other passages of Aeschylus: 585
below, *Cho.* 315 πάτερ αἰνόπατερ, *Eum.*
690 πόλιν νεόπτολιν. In Sophocles it
is nowhere found, but often in Euri-
ides (τυφλόπους πούς, τρίπους χαλκό-
πους, πόρον εὔπορον, κάματον εὐκάματον,
etc.).

577 f. ταῖσδ' ἐνέζευξας ἐν πημοσύναις: see on 108, and cp. *Il.* ii. 111 Ζεύς
με μέγα Κρονίδης ἄτῃ ἐνέδησε βαρείῃ,
Soph. *O. C.* 526 γάμων ἐνέδησεν ἄτᾳ.

580 f. οἰστρηλάτῳ δείματι: see on
147. — παράκοπον: cp. παράκοποι φρενῶν Eur. *Bacch.* 33. Properly of
coins, *false-struck, counterfeit.*

582. Cp. Soph. *O. T.* 1410 ἔξω μέ
που καλύψατ' ἢ φονεύσατ' ἢ θαλάσσιον

ἐκρίψατε, Eur. *Suppl.* 829 κατά με
πέδον γᾶς ἕλοι, διὰ δὲ θύελλα σπάσαι,
πυρός τε φλογμὸς ὁ Διὸς ἐν κάρᾳ πέσοι.

584. μοι φθονήσῃς εὐγμάτων: cp.
626, 859; Eur. *H. F.* 333 οὐ φθονῶ
τέκνων, 1309 λέκτρων φθονοῦσα Ζηνί.

586. γεγυμνάκασιν: cp. 592; Eur.
Hel. 533 οὐδ' ἀγύμναστον πλάνοις ἥξειν.

588. τᾶς βούκερω παρθένου: equivalent to the announcement of the
speaker's name. See on 296.

589. οἰστροδινήτου: cp. *Suppl.* 573
πολύπλαγκτον ἀθλίαν οἰστροδόνητον Ἰώ,
17 τῆς οἰστροδόνου βοός, *Od.* xxii. 299
βόες ὣς ἀγελαῖαι, τὰς μέν τ' αἰόλος
οἶστρος ἐφορμηθεὶς ἐδόνησεν.

590. τῆς Ἰναχείας: see on 164.
Διὰ τοῦ τὸν πατέρα αὐτῆς ὀνομάσαι ἐνέφηνε τὸν μάντιν, ὡς καὶ παρ' Ὁμήρῳ
(*Od.* xi. 100) ὁ Τειρεσίας 'νόστον δίζηαι
μελιηδέα, φαίδιμ' Ὀδυσσεῦ,' Schol.

ἔρωτι, καὶ νῦν τοὺς ὑπερμήκεις δρόμους
Ἥρᾳ στυγητὸς πρὸς βίαν γυμνάζεται.

ΙΩ.

ἀντιστροφή.

πόθεν ἐμοῦ σὺ πατρὸς ὄνομ' ἀπύεις,
εἰπέ μοι　τᾷ μογερᾷ, τίς ὤν,
595　τίς ἄρα μ', ὦ τάλας, τὰν ταλαίπωρον ὧδ'
ἔτυμα προσθροεῖς,
θεόσυτόν τε νόσον ὠνόμασας,
ἃ μαραίνει με χρίουσα κέντροις, ἰώ,
φοιταλέοις, ἐή.
600　σκιρτημάτων δὲ νήστισιν αἰκίαις
λαβρόσυτος ἦλθον, ⟨ἄλλων⟩
ἐπικότοισι μήδεσι δαμεῖσα.　δυσδαιμόνων
δὲ τίνες οἷ, ἐή,
οἳ ἐγὼ μογοῦσιν;
ἀλλά μοι τορῶς
605　τέκμηρον ὅ τι μ' ἐπαμμένει
παθεῖν, τί μῆχαρ, ἢ τί φάρμακον νόσου·

591 f. δρόμους γυμνάζεται: an ex-
tension of the accusative of the inner
object (= γυμνάζειν τινὰ γυμνασίαν
ὑπερμήκων δρόμων). Cp. Soph. *Ai.*
1107 τὰ σέμν' ἔπη κόλαζ' ἐκείνους, *O. T.*
340 ἔκη, ἃ νῦν σὺ τήνδ' ἀτιμάζεις πόλιν.
Krüger II. § 46, 7, 1; H. 716 a.
597. θεόσυτον: cp. λαβρόσυτος 601,
and see on 116.
599. φοιταλέοις: transferred from
the *person* affected to the *thing* affect-
ing, as in Goethe's expression 'von
durstiger Jagd.' Cp. *Ag.* 193 τυναὶ
κακόσχολοι νήστιδες δύσορμοι, βροτῶν
ἄλαι, and see on ἀφεγγής, 115 above.
601. Ἄλλων: τοῖς τῆς Ἥρας, Schol.
Io shrinks from speaking the name

of her persecutor. Cp. Eur. *Hec.* 640
κοινὸν δ' ἐξ ἰδίας ἀνοίας κακὸν τᾷ Σι-
μουντίδι γᾷ ὀλέθριον ἔμολε συμφορά τ'
ἀπ' ἄλλων (the three contending god-
desses). See also on 673 below.
604. τορῶς: cp. *Pers.* 479 σημῆναι
τορῶς.
605. ὅ τι... τί: cp. Soph. *O. T.* 71
πύθοιθ' ὅ τι δρῶν ἢ τί φωνῶν ῥυσαίμην,
Eur. *Ion* 785 τῶι ἐκπεραίνεται φράζε
χ' ὅστις ἐσθ' ὁ παῖς, *Iph. A.* 606 γένους
δὲ ποίου χ' ὁπόθεν μαθεῖν θέλω, Plat.
Gorg. 448 e οὐδεὶς ἠρώτα ποία τις εἴη ἡ
Γοργίου τέχνη, ἀλλὰ τίς, καὶ ὄντινα δέοι
καλεῖν τὸν Γοργίαν. — ἐπαμμένει: cp.
Pers. 807 οὔ σφιν κακῶν ὕψιστ' ἐπαμμένει παθεῖν.

δεῖξον εἴπερ οἶσθα·
θρόει φράζε τᾷ δυσπλάνῳ παρθένῳ.

ΠΡΟΜΗΘΕΥΣ.

λέξω τορῶς σοι πᾶν ὅπερ χρήζεις μαθεῖν,
610 οὐκ ἐμπλέκων αἰνίγματ', ἀλλ' ἁπλῷ λόγῳ,
ὥσπερ δίκαιον πρὸς φίλους οἴγειν στόμα.
πυρὸς βροτοῖς δοτῆρ' ὁρᾷς Προμηθέα.

ΙΩ.

ὦ κοινὸν ὠφέλημα θνητοῖσιν φανείς,
τλῆμον Προμηθεῦ, τοῦ δίκην πάσχεις τάδε;

ΠΡΟΜΗΘΕΥΣ.

615 ἁρμοῖ πέπαυμαι τοὺς ἐμοὺς θρηνῶν πόνους.

ΙΩ.

οὔκουν πόροις ἂν τήνδε δωρεὰν ἐμοί;

ΠΡΟΜΗΘΕΥΣ.

λέγ' ἥντιν' αἰτεῖ· πᾶν δ' ἂν οὐ πύθοιό μου.

ΙΩ.

σήμηνον ὅστις ἐν φάραγγί σ' ὤχμασε.

608. **θρόει, φράζε**: asyndeton of urgent entreaty; see on 56. — τᾷ **παρθένῳ**: cp. 588. Aeschylus often puts like words in corresponding positions of strophe and antistrophe.

610. Cp. *Suppl.* 464 αἰνιγματῶδες τοῦπος· ἀλλ' ἁπλῶς φράσον, and 949 below.

612. **πυρὸς βροτοῖς δοτῆρα**: on the dative with personal verbal substantives see Krüger I. § 48, 12, 5, and on 501. — This verse, though lacking the regular caesura, is not divided in the middle, because δοτῆρ' and ὁρᾷς are closely connected by elision. Cp. 710 and see note on 640.

613. The stichomythy is introduced by a speech of two verses (see on 38), and at 622 below the transition to a new topic is similarly marked.

615. **ἁρμοῖ**: ἀρτίως, Hesych. According to Heraclides (Eustath. on *Iliad* p. 140, 13), a Syracusan word. Cp. Soph. *Ai.* 787 τί μ' αὖ τάλαιναν ἀρτίως πεπαυμένην κακῶν ἀτρύτων ἐξ ἕδρας ἀνίστατε; Eur. Frg. 337 τί μ', ὦ ξέν', ἄρτι πημάτων λελησμένην ὀρθοῖς;

ΠΡΟΜΗΘΕΥΣ.

βούλευμα μὲν τὸ Δῖον, Ἡφαίστου δὲ χείρ.

ΙΩ.

620 ποινὰς δὲ ποίων ἀμπλακημάτων τίνεις;

ΠΡΟΜΗΘΕΥΣ.

τοσοῦτον ἀρκῶ σοι σαφηνίσας μόνον.

ΙΩ.

καὶ πρός γε τούτοις τέρμα τῆς ἐμῆς πλάνης
δεῖξον τίς ἔσται τῇ ταλαιπώρῳ χρόνος.

ΠΡΟΜΗΘΕΥΣ.

τὸ μὴ μαθεῖν σοι κρεῖσσον ἢ μαθεῖν τάδε.

ΙΩ.

625 μή τοί με κρύψῃς τοῦθ' ὅπερ μέλλω παθεῖν.

ΠΡΟΜΗΘΕΥΣ.

ἀλλ' οὐ μεγαίρω τοῦδέ σοι δωρήματος.

ΙΩ.

τί δῆτα μέλλεις μὴ οὐ γεγωνίσκειν τὸ πᾶν;

ΠΡΟΜΗΘΕΥΣ.

φθόνος μὲν οὐδείς, σὰς δ' ὀκνῶ θρᾶξαι φρένας.

621. τοσοῦτον κτλ.: διὰ τὸ μὴ ταυτολογῆσαι, Schol. — ἀρκῶ σαφηνίσας: for the supplementary participle with ἀρκῶ, see GMT. 899.

625 f. μή τοι: 'τοι non concludendae rationi, sed asseverando hortandoque inservit' (Hermann). Cp. 436 above, Soph. Ant. 544 μή τοι κασιγνήτην μ' ἀτιμήσῃς τὸ μὴ οὐ θανεῖν, O. C. 1407 μή τοι με πρὸς θεῶν σφώ γε ... μή μ' ἀτιμήσητέ γε, 1430 μή τοι μ' ὀδύρου. — μεγαίρω: an epic word.

627. μὴ οὐ: cp. Soph. Ai. 540 τί δῆτα μέλλει μὴ οὐ παρουσίαν ἔχειν; and

1056 below. Krüger II. § 67, 12, 4; GMT. 817. — γεγωνίσκειν: poetic present to γέγωνα, recurs Thuc. vii. 76.

628. θρᾶξαι: ταράξαι, λυπῆσαι, Εὐριπίδης Πειρίθῳ, Hesych. Cp. Bekker's Anecd. 352, 16 ἄθρακτος, ἀτάραχος. καὶ τὸ συνεχύθη ἐθράχθη Σοφοκλῆς λέγει. Eur. Rhes. 863 δέδοικα δ' αὐτὸν καί τί μου θράσσει φρένας. The tenuis, in the shortened form, changes to aspirate from the influence of the following liquid, as in φροίμιον (προ-οίμιον), φροῦδος (πρό-οδος), φρουρός (πρό-ορος), etc. See Curtius Etymol.⁵ p. 501.

ΙΩ.

μή μου προκήδου μᾶσσον ὡς ἐμοὶ γλυκύ.

ΠΡΟΜΗΘΕΥΣ.

630 ἐπεὶ προθυμεῖ, χρὴ λέγειν· ἄκουε δή.

ΧΟΡΟΣ.

μήπω γε· μοῖραν δ' ἡδονῆς κἀμοὶ πόρε.
τὴν τῆσδε πρῶτον ἱστορήσωμεν νόσον
αὐτῆς λεγούσης τὰς πολυφθόρους τύχας·
τὰ λοιπὰ δ' ἄθλων σοῦ διδαχθήτω πάρα.

ΠΡΟΜΗΘΕΥΣ.

635 σὸν ἔργον, Ἰοῖ, ταῖσδ' ὑπουργῆσαι χάριν,
ἄλλως τε πάντως καὶ κασιγνήταις πατρός.

629. μᾶσσον ὡς : = μᾶσσον ἤ. So in German *wie* instead of *als* after comparatives. Cp. *Il.* iv. 277 μελάντερον ἠΰτε πίσσα, Xenophanes in Athen. xii. 526 b οὐ μείους ὥσπερ χίλιοι εἰς ἐπίπαν, Dios in Stob. *Flor.* 65, 16 τούτως γάρ, ὡς ἐνί, μασσότερον οἱ πλεῦνες ὡς θεὼς ἤ θεῶν ἱδρύματα ὑποτρέχοντι καὶ θεραπεύοντι, *Lys.* VII. 12 ἡγούμενος μᾶλλον λέγεσθαι ὣς μοι προσῆκε, VII. 31 ἅπαντα προθυμότερον πεποίηκα ὡς ὑπὸ τῆς πόλεως ἠναγκαζόμην, Dem. xxv. 53 τοῦτον οὐ τιμωρήσεσθε ἀλλὰ καὶ μειζόνων ἀξιώσαντες δωρεῶν ἀφήσετε ὡς τοὺς εὐεργέτας. — προκήδου : contains an allusion to the name Προμηθεύς.

630. ἐπεὶ προθυμεῖ: cp. 786.

631. μήπω γε: the relation of Io's adventures, beginning at this point, is in three parts. First comes Io's own narrative, given at request of the chorus; secondly, Prometheus, at Io's request, foretells her future destiny; and thirdly, he describes her previous wanderings, in order to convince her of his knowledge of the future. The second part is further divided into two distinct portions — wanderings in Europe (700–741), and wanderings in Asia and Africa (786–818). These are separated by a digression, but interest in the continuance of the narrative is ensured by 740 f. Thus by variety of motive, and by frequent hints of what is to come, the poet keeps the spectators' attention (see on 283) and gives his material an effective dramatic form.

632 f. νόσον: cp. 596 and see note on 249. νόσον and τὰς πολυφθόρους τύχας stand in connexion; "let us hear what fatal misfortunes have brought her to this distressful state."

634. τὰ λοιπὰ ἄθλων: cp. 780, 684; Soph. *Phil.* 24 τἀπίλοιπα τῶν λόγων.

635. ὑπουργῆσαι χάριν: like χαρίζεσθαι χάριν. Cp. Eur. *Alc.* 842 Ἀδμήτῳ ὑπουργῆσαι χάριν, Soph. Frg. 313 ἀνθυπουργῆσαι χάριν.

636. ἄλλως τε πάντως καί: cp. *Pers.* 688 ἔστι δ' οὐκ εὐέξοδον, ἄλλως τε πάντως χοἰ κατὰ χθονὸς θεοὶ λαβεῖν ἀμεί-

ὡς τἀποκλαῦσαι κἀποδύρασθαι τύχας
ἐνταῦθ᾽, ὅπου μέλλοι τις οἴσεσθαι δάκρυ
πρὸς τῶν κλυόντων, ἀξίαν τριβὴν ἔχει.

ΙΩ.

640 οὐκ οἶδ᾽ ὅπως ὑμῖν ἀπιστῆσαί με χρή,
σαφεῖ δὲ μύθῳ πᾶν ὅπερ προσχρῄζετε
πεύσεσθε· καίτοι καὶ λέγουσ᾽ ὀδύρομαι
θεόσσυτον χειμῶνα καὶ διαφθορὰν
μορφῆς ὅθεν μοι σχετλίᾳ προσέπτατο.

645 αἰεὶ γὰρ ὄψεις ἔννυχοι πωλεύμεναι
ἐς παρθενῶνας τοὺς ἐμοὺς παρηγόρουν
λείοισι μύθοις· ὦ μέγ᾽ εὔδαιμον κόρη,

τοὺς εἰσὶν ἢ μεθιέναι (here an independent clause follows), *Eum.* 726 ἄλλως τε πάντως χώτε δεόμενος τύχοι. A temporal or conditional clause, or a participle, is the usual construction after ἄλλως τε καί. — κασιγνήταις πατρός: cp. Hesiod *Theog.* 337 Τηθὺς δ᾽ Ὠκεανῷ Ποταμοὺς τέκε δινήεντας.

637. Cp. Eur. Frg. 567 σχολὴ μὲν οὐχί, τῷ δὲ δυστυχοῦντί πως τερπνὸν τὸ λέξαι κἀποκλαύσασθαι πάλιν.

638. μέλλοι: optative of a purely imaginary case. Cp. Soph. *Ant.* 666 ὃν πόλις στήσειε, τοῦδε χρὴ κλύειν, O. T. 314 ἄνδρα δ᾽ ὠφελεῖν, ἀφ᾽ ὧν ἔχοι τε καὶ δύναιτο, κάλλιστος πόνος, 979 εἰκῇ κράτιστον ζῆν ὅπως δύναιτό τις, Thuc. i. 120 ἀνδρῶν γὰρ σωφρόνων μέν ἐστιν, εἰ μὴ ἀδικοῖντο, ἡσυχάζειν. Krüger I. § 54, 14, 4.

639. ἀξίαν τριβὴν ἔχει: = ἀξίαν (substantive) τῆς τριβῆς ἔχει. Cp. Eur. *Med.* 1124 τί δ᾽ ἀξιόν μοι τῆσδε τυγχάνει φυγῆς;

640. Verses lacking the usual caesura, and dividing themselves into two halves, are not frequent in Aeschylus. The greatest number (seven) occurs in the *Persians*. In this place the ill effect is somewhat relieved by a pause after οὐκ οἶδ᾽. — ἀπιστῆσαι: disobey. Cp. *Sept.* 1030 ἔχουσ᾽ ἄπιστον τήνδ᾽ ἀναρχίαν πόλει, Soph. *Ant.* 381 οὐ δή που σέ γ᾽ ἀπιστοῦσαν τοῖς βασιλείοισιν ἄγουσι νόμοις, Eur. *Suppl.* 389 ἦν δ᾽ ἀπιστῶ᾽, οἵδε δεύτεροι λόγοι.

642. καὶ λέγουσ᾽ ὀδύρομαι: "the bare recital costs me tears." Cp. 197; Eur. *Hec.* 519 νῦν τε γὰρ λέγων κακὰ τέγξω τόδ᾽ ὄμμα, πρὸς τάφῳ θ᾽ ὅτ᾽ ἐλλύετο, Verg. *Aen.* ii. 6 quis talia fando ... temperet a lacrimis?

644. Cp. Soph. *Ai.* 282 τίς γάρ ποτ᾽ ἀρχὴ τοῦ κακοῦ προσέπτατο; Eur. *Alc.* 420 οὐκ ἄφνω κακὸν τόδε προσέπτατο.

647. μέγ᾽ εὔδαιμον: cp. Xen. *Cyr.* v. 1, 28 μέγα εὐδαίμονας γενέσθαι, *Suppl.* 141 σεμνᾶς μέγα ματρός, Eur. *Or.* 1691 ὦ μέγα σεμνὴ Νίκη, and 1004 below. Also μέγ᾽ ἔξοχος, μέγα νήπιος in Homer and Hesiod. Krüger II. § 46, 6, 7.

τί παρθενεύει δαρὸν ἐξόν σοι γάμου
τυχεῖν μεγίστου; Ζεὺς γὰρ ἱμέρου βέλει
650 πρὸς σοῦ τέθαλπται καὶ συναίρεσθαι Κύπριν
θέλει· σὺ δ', ὦ παῖ, μἀπολακτίσῃς λέχος
τὸ Ζηνός, ἀλλ' ἔξελθε πρὸς Λέρνης βαθὺν
λειμῶνα, ποίμνας βουστάσεις τε πρὸς πατρός,
ὡς ἂν τὸ Δῖον ὄμμα λωφήσῃ πόθου.

655 τοιοῖσδε πάσας εὐφρόνας ὀνείρασι
συνειχόμην δύστηνος, ἔς τε δὴ πατρὶ
ἔτλην γεγωνεῖν νυκτίφοιτα δείματα.
ὃ δ' ἔς τε Πυθὼ κἀπὶ Δωδώνης πυκνοὺς
θεοπρόπους ἴαλλεν, ὡς μάθοι τί χρὴ
660 δρῶντ' ἢ λέγοντα δαίμοσιν πράσσειν φίλα.

648. Enclitics form, as it were, one word with the preceding; the long thesis of the fifth foot is therefore not a blemish, especially after the hephthemimeral caesura. See on 107.

649 f. ἱμέρου βέλει: = ἔρωτι (591). In an inverse relation τόξευμα is used in *Suppl.* 1003 καὶ παρθένων χλιδαῖσιν εὐμόρφοις ἔπι πᾶς τις παρελθὼν ὄμματος θελκτήριον τόξευμ' ἔπεμψεν ἱμέρου νικώμενος. — τέθαλπται: cp. Soph. *Ant.* 1085 ἀφῆκα καρδίας τοξεύματα βέβαια τῶν σὺ θάλπος οὐκ ὑπεκδραμεῖ. θάλπος is said both of the smart of wounds and the fire of love (590). — συναίρεσθαι Κύπριν: συνουσιάσαι, Schol.

651. Crasis of μὴ ἀ- is frequent. *Cho.* 918, *Eum.* 85 f., 694, 749, *Suppl.* 200. — ἀπολακτίσῃς: ὡς ἀπὸ τῶν ἀλόγων (ζῷων), Schol. The coarse expression is purposely chosen, for intimidation.

652. βαθὺν λειμῶνα: *grassy meadow*, i.e. with thick, deep herbage. Cp. *Od.*

ix. 134 μάλα κὲν βαθὺ λήιον αἰεὶ εἰς ὥρας ἀμῷεν, ἐπεὶ μάλα πῖαρ ὑπ' οὖδας, *Il.* ii. 147 ὡς δ' ὅτε κινήσῃ Ζέφυρος βαθὺ λήιον ἐλθών, ix. 151 Ἄνθειαν βαθύλειμον, Eur. *Hipp.* 1138 βαθεῖαν ἀνὰ χλόαν.

654. ὄμμα λωφήσῃ: cp. 376. Desire betrays itself in the look. Cp. Soph. *Ai.* 140 πεφόβημαι πτηνῆς ὡς ὄμμα πελείας.

657. Cp. *Cho.* 523 ἐκ τ' ὀνειράτων καὶ νυκτιπλάγκτων δειμάτων πεπαλμένη.

658 f. ἐπὶ Δωδώνης: *towards Dodona*. ἐπί with gen. of general direction or end in view, frequent in Homer (cp. *Il.* iii. 5) and Herodotus (cp. i. 1). With our passage cp. Eur. *El.* 1343 στεῖχ' ἐπ' Ἀθηνῶν, Thuc. i. 63 ὁποτέρωσε διακινδυνεύσει χωρῆσαι ἢ ἐπὶ τῆς Ὀλύνθου ἢ ἐς τὴν Ποτίδαιαν. G. 191, VI. 2, 1 a; H. 799, 1, 6. — ἴαλλεν: an epic word.

660. τί δρῶντ' ἢ λέγοντα: this particularization is a favorite one in Greek. Cp. the Homeric ἢ ἔπει ἢ ἔργῳ, *Il.* i. 504. Especially appro-

ἧκον δ' ἀναγγέλλοντες αἰολοστόμους
χρησμοὺς ἀσήμους δυσκρίτως τ' εἰρημένους.
τέλος δ' ἐναργὴς βάξις ἦλθεν Ἰνάχῳ
σαφῶς ἐπισκήπτουσα καὶ μυθουμένη
665 ἔξω δόμων τε καὶ πάτρας ὠθεῖν ἐμὲ
ἄφετον ἀλᾶσθαι γῆς ἐπ' ἐσχάτοις ὅροις,
εἰ μὴ θέλοι πυρωπὸν ἐκ Διὸς μολεῖν
κεραυνὸν ὃς πᾶν ἐξαϊστώσοι γένος.

τοιοῖσδε πεισθεὶς Λοξίου μαντεύμασιν
670 ἐξήλασέν με κἀπέκλῃσε δωμάτων
ἄκουσαν ἄκων· ἀλλ' ἐπηνάγκαζέ νιν
Διὸς χαλινὸς πρὸς βίαν πράσσειν τάδε.
εὐθὺς δὲ μορφὴ καὶ φρένες διάστροφοι

priate in anxious inquiry of an oracle; cp. Soph. *O. T.* 70 *ἐς τὰ Πυθικὰ
ἔπεμψα Φοίβου δώμαθ', ὡς πύθοιθ', ὅ τι
δρῶν ἢ τί φωνῶν τήνδε ῥυσαίμην πόλιν.*
Cp. also *Cho.* 316 *τί σοι φάμενος ἢ τί
ῥέξας*, *Pers.* 174 *μήτ' ἔπος μήτ' ἔργον*,
Eur. *Hec.* 372 *μηδὲν ἐμποδὼν γένη
λέγουσα μηδὲ δρῶσα, Phoen.* 878 *τί οὐ
δρῶν, ποῖα δ' οὐ λέγων ἔπη.* — *πράσσειν φΩα:* = *ἦρα φέρειν, χαρίζεσθαι.
πράσσειν* covers both *δρᾶν* and *λέγειν.*

662. 'Synonymorum coacervatio
non modo rem ipsam, scilicet ambigui-
tatem oraculorum, auget atque exag-
gerat, sed etiam commotum Ius
animum ostendit' (Schütz). So
below *ἐναργὴς … σαφῶς ἐπισκήπτουσα
καὶ μυθουμένη.*

666. **ἄφετον**: for the resolution see
on 116. *ἄφετος, at large*, as said of
sacred animals ranging the enclosure
of a temple. Cp. Plat. *Critias* 119 d
*ἀφέτων ὄντων ταύρων ἐν τῷ τοῦ Ποσει-
δῶνος ἱερῷ, Prot.* 320 a *αὐτοὶ περιόντες*

νέμονται ὥσπερ ἄφετοι, Eur. *Ion* 821 ἤ
*δ' ἐν θεοῦ δόμοισιν ἄφετος, ὡς λάθοι,
παιδεύεται.* — **ἀλᾶσθαι**: consecutive
infinitive. Krüger I. § 55, 3, 20. Cp.
Cho. 489 *ἄνες μοι πατέρ' ἐποπτεῦσαι
μάχην.*

667 f. **μολεῖν κεραυνόν**: see on
358 (ἦλθεν). — **ἐξαϊστώσοι**: see on
151.

671. **ἄκουσαν ἄκων**: see on 19. —
ἀλλ' ἐπηνάγκαζε: refers to the notion
contained in ἄκων. Cp. *Eum.* 458
*ἔφθιθ' οὗτος οὐ καλῶς, μολὼν ἐς οἶκον·
ἀλλά νιν κελαινόφρων ἐμὴ μήτηρ κα-
τέκτα*, Eur. *Bacch.* 1127 *ἀπεσπάραξεν
ὦμον οὐχ ὑπὸ σθένους, ἀλλ' ὁ θεὸς εὐμά-
ρειαν ἐπεδίδου χεροῖν.*

672. **Διὸς χαλινός**: cp. *Ag.* 133
στόμιον μέγα Τροίας, 218 *ἀνάγκης λέπαδνον.* — **πρὸς βίαν**: nearly like *βίᾳ
φρενῶν* (*Sept.* 612), *with inner reluc-
tance.*

673. The poet here omits certain
details, which are related *Suppl.* 291 ff.
The maid Io touches on external

ἦσαν, κεραστὶς δ', ὡς ὁρᾶτ', ὀξυστόμῳ
675 μύωπι χρισθεῖσ' ἐμμανεῖ σκιρτήματι
ἦσσον πρὸς εὐποτόν τε Κερχνείας ῥέος
Λέρνης τε κρήνην· βουκόλος δὲ γηγενὴς
ἄκρατος ὀργὴν Ἄργος ὡμάρτει, πυκνοῖς
ὄσσοις δεδορκὼς τοὺς ἐμοὺς κατὰ στίβους.
680 ἀπροσδόκητος δ' αὐτὸν ἀφνίδιος μόρος

facts only; she passes over the reasons of her persecution. A hint of these has been given by Prometheus at 592. — φρένες διάστροφοι: cp. Soph. Ai. 447 ὄμμα καὶ φρένες διάστροφοι.

674 f. ὀξυστόμῳ μύωπι: see on 561, and cp. Schol. Apollon. Rhod. *Arg.* i. 1265 μύωψ εἶδος μυίας κατὰ τὸ θέαρ γινόμενον, ἥτις ταῖς λαγόσι τῶν βοῶν ἐπικαθεζομένη δάκνει αὐτὰς καὶ εἰς μανίαν ἄγει· ἀφ' οὗ καὶ οἶστρος λέγεται. Σώστρατος δὲ ἐν τῇ τετάρτῃ περὶ ζῴων διαστέλλει τὸν μύωπα τοῦ οἴστρου· ὁ μὲν γὰρ μύωψ ἐκ τῶν ξύλων ἀπογεννᾶται, ὁ δὲ οἶστρος ἐκ τῶν ἐν τοῖς ποταμοῖς ἐπιπλεόντων σκωρίων. But *Suppl.* 307 βοηλάτην μύωπα κινητήριον· οἶστρον καλοῦσιν αὐτὸν οἱ Νείλου πέλας. Cp. Plin. *H. N.* xi. 28, 34, 100 pinnae insectis omnibus sine scissura, nulli cauda nisi scorpioni; ...reliquorum quibusdam aculeus in ore ut asilo, sive tabanum dici placet.

676. εὔποτον: cp. 812. 'The Greeks in general were so little prone to descriptive poetry that we cannot but wonder at the inexhaustible wealth of expression with which their poets describe the blessings of flowing water. It is surprising how carefully they inquired into its properties, and how they compared the waters of distant regions, distinguishing their temperature, taste, color, weight, and

their effect on the human body in drinking and bathing' (Ernst Curtius in *Griechische Quell- und Brunneninschriften*). — Κερχνείας βέος: Κίρχνη κρήνη Ἄργους, Schol. According to Pausanias ii. 24, 7, the small town Κεγχρεαί (the later form of the name) lay on the route from Argos to Tegea. Not far away, near the coast, was the marshy lake of Lerna, renowned in the myth of Heracles. Cp. Pausan. ii. 36, 6. 'The mountain-ridge Pontinus pushes out so close to the sea that the waters welling up at its base have not space to form a river-bed. It is these springs which produce the Lernaean swamp.... Lerna itself was never a town; the name designates either the chief fountain, or the lake, or the whole coast-region' (E. Curtius, *Peloponnesos* II. pp. 340, 371).

678. ἄκρατος: intemperatus, unmitigated, unsoftened, like unmixed wine.

680. Here, too, the poet skilfully passes over details (see on 571). — ἀπροσδόκητος, ἀφνίδιος: joined as in Thuc. ii. 61 δουλοῖ γὰρ φρόνημα τὸ αἰφνίδιον καὶ ἀπροσδόκητον καὶ τὸ πλείστῳ παραλόγῳ συμβαῖνον. The form ἀφνίδιος is from ἄφνω. For the resolution, see on 2. The caesura is to be made after αὐτόν, not after ἀπροσδόκητος δ'.

τοῦ ζῆν ἀπεστέρησεν. οἰστροπλὴξ δ' ἐγὼ
μάστιγι θείᾳ γῆν πρὸ γῆς ἐλαύνομαι.

κλύεις τὰ πραχθέντ' · εἰ δ' ἔχεις εἰπεῖν ὅ τι
λοιπὸν πόνων, σήμαινε · μηδέ μ' οἰκτίσας
685 ξύνθαλπε μύθοις ψευδέσιν · νόσημα γὰρ
αἴσχιστον εἶναί φημι συνθέτους λόγους.

ΧΟΡΟΣ.

ἔα ἔα, ἄπεχε, φεῦ ·
οὔποτ' ⟨ὧδ'⟩, οὔποτ' ηὔχουν ξένους
μολεῖσθαι λόγους ἐς ἀκοὰν ἐμάν,
690 οὐδ' ὧδε δυσθέατα καὶ δύσοιστα
πήματα λύματα δείματα κέντρῳ ψύχειν ψυχὰν ἀμφάκει.

681. οἰστροπλήξ: cp. Soph. *El.* 5 τῆς οἰστροπλῆγος ἄλσος Ἰνάχου κόρης. Whips were sometimes armed with sharp points, to serve as goads (cp. on 691); so the expression οἰστροπλὴξ μάστιγι is especially fitting.

682. γῆν πρὸ γῆς: cp. Ar. *Ach.* 235 διώκειν γῆν πρὸ γῆς. Also the phrases γῆν πρὸ γῆς ἀπιέναι, ἴτω χαιρέτω γῆν πρὸ γῆς ὅτοι βούλοιτο, φεύγω γῆν πρὸ γῆς, quoted by Suidas (*s.vv.* διακαίνειν, ἴτω, and πρὸ γῆς), Lucian *Alex.* 46 γῆν πρὸ γῆς ἐλαύνεσθαι ὡς ἀσεβῆ, Cic. *Att.* xiv. 10 haec et alia ferre non possum; itaque γῆν πρὸ γῆς cogito. The expression (πρὸ = ἀντί) is analogous to ἀμείβεσθαι τόπον.

684. The scholiast compares Telemachus's words, *Od.* iii. 96 μηδέ τί μ' αἰδόμενος μειλίσσεο μηδ' ἐλεαίρων, ἀλλ' εὖ μοι κατάλεξον.

685. νόσημα αἴσχιστον: cp. 1069; Eur. *Or.* 10 ἀκόλαστον ἔσχε γλῶσσαν, αἰσχίστην νόσον.

686. Cp. *Il.* ix. 312 ἐχθρὸς γάρ μοι κεῖνος ὁμῶς Ἀΐδαο πύλῃσιν, ὅς χ' ἕτερον μὲν κεύθῃ ἐνὶ φρεσίν, ἄλλο δὲ εἴπῃ. — συνθέτους λόγους : = composita dicta, in Attius (v. 47, Ribbeck).

688. ηὔχουν: cp. 338, and *Ag.* 506 οὐ γάρ ποτ' ηὔχουν τῇδ' ἐν Ἀργείᾳ χθονὶ θανὼν μεθέξειν φιλτάτου τάφου μέρος, *Suppl.* 329 τίς ηὔχει τήνδ' ἀνέλπιστον φυγὴν κέλσειν ἐς Ἄργος, Eur. *Hel.* 1619 οὐκ ἄν ποτ' ηὔχουν οὔτε σ' οὔθ' ἡμᾶς λαθεῖν Μενέλαον, *Heracl.* 931 οὐ γάρ ποτ' ηὔχει χεῖρας ἵξεσθαι σέθεν.

691 f. πήματα, λύματα, δείματα: the assonance is intentional, as is the alliteration in ψύχειν ψυχάν. Cp. 480, 959; Eur. *Or.* 1302 φονεύετε, καίνετε, ὄλλυτε. — ἀμφάκει κέντρῳ: cp. *Ag.* 642 διπλῇ μάστιγι τὴν Ἄρης φιλεῖ. The goad (see on 323) had two κέντρα. Cp. Soph. *O. T.* 809 διπλοῖς κέντροισι, Frg. 137 μάσθλητα δίγονον. — ψύχειν: chill. So πέφρικα below. Cp. Plaut. *Pseud.* 1215 mihi...ille...cor

ἰὼ ἰὼ μοῖρα μοῖρα,
695 πέφρικ' εἰσιδοῦσα πρᾶξιν Ἰοῦς.

ΠΡΟΜΗΘΕΥΣ.

πρῴ γε στενάζεις καὶ φόβου πλέα τις εἶ·
ἐπίσχες ἔς τ' ἂν καὶ τὰ λοιπὰ προσμάθῃς.

ΧΟΡΟΣ.

λέγ', ἐκδίδασκε· τοῖς νοσοῦσί τοι γλυκὺ
τὸ λοιπὸν ἄλγος προυξεπίστασθαι τορῶς.

ΠΡΟΜΗΘΕΥΣ.

700 τὴν πρίν γε χρείαν ἠνύσασθ' ἐμοῦ πάρα
κούφως· μαθεῖν γὰρ τῆσδε πρῶτ' ἐχρῄζετε
τὸν ἀμφ' ἑαυτῆς ἆθλον ἐξηγουμένης·
τὰ λοιπὰ νῦν ἀκούσαθ', οἷα χρὴ πάθη

perfrigefacit. For the idea cp.
Eum. 155 ἐμοὶ δ' ὄνειδος ἐξ ὀνειράτων
μολὼν ἔτυψεν δίκαν διφρηλάτου
μεσολαβεῖ κέντρῳ ὑπὸ φρένας, ὑπὸ
λοβόν. πάρεστι μαστίκτορος δαμίου βαρὺ
τὸ περίβαρυ κρύος ἔχειν.—The present ψύχειν, after the future μολεῖσθαι,
because the mind of the speaker
reverts to the present moment.

695. πρᾶξιν: *plight*, τὸ πεπραγέναι.
Cp. Soph. *Trach.* 151 τὴν αὐτοῦ σκοπῶν
πρᾶξιν, 293 ἀνδρὸς εὐτυχῆ κλύουσα πρᾶξιν τήνδε, *Ai.* 790 ἥκει φέρων Αἴαντος
ἡμῖν πρᾶξιν ἣν ἤλγησ' ἐγώ.

696. πρῴ: mature, *too soon.* Cp.
Soph. *Trach.* 630 δέδοικα γὰρ μὴ πρῲ
λέγοις ἂν τὸν πόθον τὸν ἐξ ἐμοῦ, πρὶν
εἰδέναι τἀκεῖθεν εἰ ποθούμεθα, Plat. *Par-
men.* 135 c πρῲ γάρ, πρὶν γυμνασθῆναι,
ὁρίζεσθαι ἐπιχειρεῖς καλόν τε τί καὶ
δίκαιον καὶ ἀγαθόν. — πλέα τις: for τις
with an adjective, see H. 702 a.

698. λέγ', ἐκδίδασκε: cp. 608, and
see note on 56.

701. κούφως: *with light labor* (sc.
"on my part"), since it fell to Io
(635) to meet their desire. — ἐχρῄζετε:
cp. 632 f.

702. τὸν ἀμφ' ἑαυτῆς ἆθλον: = ἀμφ'
ἑαυτῆς τὸν ἑαυτῆς ἆθλον ἐξηγουμένης.
An attributive of the subject or object is often modified by the intrusion
of a preposition which would naturally accompany the predicate. This
is most frequent with the prepositions
ἐξ, ἀπό, παρά. Cp. *Cho.* 507 τὸν ἐκ
βυθοῦ κλωστῆρα σῴζοντες λίνου = τὸν
ἐν βυθῷ κλωστῆρα λίνου (i.e. net) σῴζοντες ἐκ βυθοῦ, also *Ag.* 538 κῆρυξ
Ἀχαιῶν χαῖρε τῶν ἀπὸ στρατοῦ. Krüger I. § 50, 8, 10 (cp. H. 788 a). But
it occurs also with other prepositions;
thus εὐσεβεῖν τὰ πρὸς θεούς, Soph. *Phil.*
1441

τλῆναι πρὸς Ἥρας τήνδε τὴν νεάνιδα.
705 σύ τ', Ἰνάχειον σπέρμα, τοὺς ἐμοὺς λόγους
θυμῷ βάλ', ὡς ἂν τέρματ' ἐκμάθῃς ὁδοῦ.

πρῶτον μὲν ἐνθένδ' ἡλίου πρὸς ἀντολὰς
στρέψασα σαυτὴν στεῖχ' ἀνηρότους γύας·
Σκύθας δ' ἀφίξει νομάδας, οἳ πλεκτὰς στέγας
710 πεδάρσιοι ναίουσ' ἐπ' εὐκύκλοις ὄχοις,
ἑκηβόλοις τόξοισιν ἐξηρτυμένοι·

706. θυμῷ βάλε: cp. the Homeric phrase σὺ δ' ἐνὶ φρεσὶ βάλλεο σῇσι (differently Od. i. 200 ὡς ἐνὶ θυμῷ ἀθάνατοι βάλλουσι). For the dative, cp. Sept. 1048 χώραν τήνδε κινδύνῳ βαλεῖν, Soph. Phil. 67 λύπην τᾶσιν Ἀργείοις βαλεῖς, Eur. Phoen. 1535 σκότον ὄμματι σοῖσι βαλών.

708. στρέψασα: not τρέψασα, because Io is to turn aside from Prometheus in beginning her journey.—στεῖχε γύας: cp. 837; Sept. 466 κλίμακος προσαμβάσεις στείχει, in prose πορεύεσθαι πεδίον, etc. G. 159, N. 5; H. 712 b. — The geographical description which follows — a mixture of truth and fable — is based on the vague reports of the merchants who were engaged in the traffic between the Hellenic colonies on the Black Sea and the regions to the northward. Herodotus was the first to bring to the Greeks a more accurate knowledge of the country and peoples north of the Pontus.

709. Cp. Od. xii. 39 Σειρῆνας μὲν πρῶτον ἀφίξεαι. — Σκύθας νομάδας: Hippocr. de Aëre 93 νομάδες δὲ καλεῦνται, ὅτι οὐκ ἔστι σφι οἰκήματα, ἀλλ' ἐν ἁμάξῃσι οἰκεῦσι· αἱ δὲ ἅμαξαί εἰσι αἱ μὲν ἐλάχισται τετράκυκλοι, αἱ δὲ ἑξάκυκλοι· αὗται δὲ πίλοισι περιπεφραγμέναι· εἰσὶ δὲ καὶ τετεχνασμέναι ὥσπερ οἰκήματα, τὰ μὲν διπλᾶ, τὰ δὲ τριπλᾶ· ταῦτα δὲ καὶ στεγνὰ πρὸς ὕδωρ καὶ πρὸς χιόνα καὶ πρὸς τὰ πνεύματα, Hesiod in Strabo p. 302 γλακτοφάγων εἰς γαῖαν ἀπήναις οἰκί' ἐχόντων, Hdt. iv. 46 τοῖσι γὰρ μήτε ἄστεα μήτε τείχεα ᾖ ἐκτισμένα, ἀλλὰ φερέοικοι ἐόντες πάντες ἔωσι ἱπποτοξόται, ζώοντες μὴ ἀπ' ἀρότου, ἀλλ' ἀπὸ κτηνέων, οἰκήματά τέ σφι ᾖ ἐπὶ ζευγέων, κῶς οὐκ ἂν εἴησαν οὗτοι ἄμαχοί τε καὶ ἄποροι προσμίσγειν. According to Hdt. iv. 19, these Scythians lived on the Carcinite gulf, west of the Crimean isthmus: τὸ δὲ πρὸς ἠῶ τῶν γεωργῶν τούτων Σκυθέων (on the Borysthenes), διαβάντι τὸν Παντικάπην ποταμόν, νομάδες ἤδη Σκύθαι νέμονται, οὔτε τι σπείροντες οὐδὲν οὔτε ἀροῦντες. But before Herodotus their residence had not been thus determined, and Aeschylus thinks of them as dwelling far in the north near the Ocean. Cp. Strab. p. 402 τὸ πρῶτον μέρος ἐκ τῶν πρὸς ἄρκτον μερῶν καὶ τὸν Ὠκεανὸν Σκυθῶν τινες νομάδες καὶ ἁμάξοικοι, Plin. H. N. vi. 20, 53 inhabitabilis prima pars a Scythico promuntorio ob nives, proxima inculta saevitia gentium. Anthropophagi Scythae insident humanis corporibus vescentes; ideo iuxta vastae solitudines.

οἷς μὴ πελάζειν, ἀλλὰ γυῖ ἀλιστόνοις
χρίμπτουσα ῥαχίαισιν ἐκπερᾶν χθόνα.
λαιᾶς δὲ χειρὸς οἱ σιδηροτέκτονες
715 οἰκοῦσι Χάλυβες, οὓς φυλάξασθαί σε χρή·
ἀνήμεροι γὰρ οὐδὲ πρόσπλατοι ξένοις.
ἥξεις δ' Ὑβρίστην ποταμὸν οὐ ψευδώνυμον,
ὃν μὴ περάσῃς, οὐ γὰρ εὔβατος περᾶν,
πρὶν ἂν πρὸς αὐτὸν Καύκασον μόλῃς, ὁρῶν
720 ὕψιστον, ἔνθα ποταμὸς ἐκφυσᾷ μένος

712. πελάζειν ... ἐκπερᾶν: jussive infinitive. Cp. *Eum.* 1007 τὸ μὲν ἀτηρὸν χώρας κατέχειν, τὸ δὲ κερδαλέον πέμπειν. GMT. 784.
713. χρίμπτουσά: before ῥ-. See on 1023. — ῥαχίαισιν: κυρίως δὲ τᾶς ὁ πετρώδης αἰγιαλὸς ῥαχία καλεῖται, Etym. Mag. p. 702, 51. — Cp. Choeril. Frg. 2 (p. 719 Nauck) γῆς ὀστοῖσιν (*i.e.* stones) ἐγχριμφθεὶς πόδα.
714. Either verses have fallen out between 713 and 714, in which some other region, to be visited by Io after leaving the Ocean, was mentioned (cp. Frg. IX. of the Προμηθεὺς λυόμενος), or the poet means that Io, having passed the Nomad Scythians in her course along the shore of Ocean, is to leave the Chalybes at her left, that is, wander inland and southward between the Scythians and Chalybes, until she reaches the river Hybristes. This she must follow upwards to its source in the Caucasus (720). — λαιᾶς χειρός: on the genitive, see Krüger II. § 46, 1, 3; G. 179, 2; H. 760; and Schneidewin-Nauck on Soph. *El.* 900.
715. A tribrach in the second foot; the only occurrence in this play. See on 2. Resolutions are more frequent in this description than in other portions of the *Prometheus.* This is due

to the exceptional subject-matter and the number of proper names. See 717, 720, 721, 722, 729, 730, 735, 788, 793, 790, 805, 809, 811, 840, 847, 849, 851, 869. — Χάλυβες: these are elsewhere (Hdt. i. 28; Strab. p. 678) said to live south of the Black Sea. Aeschylus places them in Northern Scythia, because he regards them as Scythians (*Sept.* 728 χάλυβος Σκυθῶν ἄποικος), and identifies their land with the region which produced the Scythian steel (cp. 301). This region was in reality the Ural Mountains.
717. Ὑβρίστην ποταμόν: the scholiast remarks, τὸν Ἀράξην, παρὰ τὸ ἀράσσειν καὶ ἠχεῖν τὰ κύματα αὐτοῦ. The ancient expounders, we see, read ὑβριστήν, and supposed that by the designation "boisterous stream" the poet meant the Araxes, referring its name to ἀράσσειν. Cp. Eustath. on Dionys. Perieget. 739 τοῦ δὲ Μασσαγετικοῦ τούτου Ἀράξου μέμνηται καὶ Αἰσχύλος, καὶ ἀράσσεται καὶ ἐκεῖνος ἀπὸ τοῦ ἀράσσειν καλεῖσθαι αὐτόν. As to Aeschylus's actual notion, see on 714.
718. εὔβατος περᾶν: see on 766.
719 f. πρὸς αὐτὸν Καύκασον ἔνθα κτλ.: = πρὸς αὐτὸν τὸν τοῦ Καυκάσου τόπον ἔνθα ποταμὸς ἐκφυσᾷ μένος, *till thou hast come to its very source on the*

κροτάφων ἀπ' αὐτῶν. ἀστρογείτονας δὲ χρὴ
κορυφὰς ὑπερβάλλουσαν ἐς μεσημβρινὴν
βῆναι κέλευθον, ἔνθ' Ἀμαζόνων στρατὸν
ἥξεις στυγάνορ', αἱ Θεμίσκυράν ποτε
725 κατοικιοῦσιν ἀμφὶ Θερμώδονθ', ἵνα
τραχεῖα πόντου Σαλμυδησσία γνάθος
ἐχθρόξενος ναύταισι, μητρυιὰ νεῶν·
αὐταί σ' ὁδηγήσουσι καὶ μάλ' ἀσμένως.
ἰσθμὸν δ' ἐπ' αὐταῖς στενοπόροις λίμνης πύλαις

heights of Caucasus. αὐτόν belongs in
sense to ἔνθα ποταμός, *etc.*, and contrasts the source with the lower course
of the river. The poet, it would
seem, imagines the Caucasus range to
lie southeast of the scene of the play,
and (as appears from the following)
north of the Black and Azov seas.

722. ὑπερβάλλουσαν: not ὑπερβα-
λοῦσαν, because the southerly course
is to be entered on *during* the passage
of the mountain.

723 f. Ἀμαζόνων: cp. 416. — στυγάνορα: cp. *Suppl.* 287 καὶ τὰς ἀνάνδρους
κρεοβόρους τ' Ἀμαζόνας. — Θεμίσκυραν
... ἀμφὶ Θερμώδοντα: the fabulous race
of the Amazons was sometimes assigned to the river Thermodon and the
city Themiscyra (Strabo p. 505 τὴν δὲ
Θεμίσκυραν καὶ τὰ περὶ τὸν Θερμώδοντα
πεδία καὶ τὰ ὑπερκείμενα ὄρη ἅπαντα
Ἀμαζόνων καλοῦσι καί φασιν ἐξελαθῆναι
αὐτὰς ἐντεῦθεν), sometimes to the part
of Scythia bordering on the sea of
Azov and the Tanais. The first-
named view, in post-Homeric times,
became the more generally accepted.
Aeschylus avoids conflict with it by
assuming a later migration of the
Amazons from Scythia to the Thermodon. Migration in the contrary
direction is assumed by Hdt. iv. 110.

725 f. ἵνα ... Σαλμυδησσία γνάθος:
not a definition of Θερμώδοντα, but of
the whole country of the Amazons,
which is thereby given a greater ex-
tension: *round about the Thermodon to
where, etc.* There is perhaps a reference to *Il.* iii. 187 οἴ ῥα τότ' ἐστρα-
τόωντο παρ' ὄχθας Σαγγαρίοιο ... ἤματι
τῷ ὅτε τ' ἦλθον Ἀμαζόνες ἀντιάνειραι,
in ignorance or neglect of the great
actual distance. Salmydessus, according to Strab. p. 319, is an ἔρημος
αἰγιαλὸς καὶ λιθώδης, ἀλίμενος, ἀνα-
πεπταμένος πολὺς πρὸς τοὺς βορέας,
σταδίων ὅσον ἑπτακοσίων μέχρι Κυανέων τὸ μῆκος (that is, from the cape
Thynias to the Thracian Bosporus).
Cp. Soph. *Ant.* 966 παρὰ δὲ κυανέων
σπιλάδων διδύμας ἁλὸς ἀκταὶ Βοσπόριαι
ἴδ' ὁ Θρηκῶν Σαλμυδησσός, Xen. *Anab.*
vii. 5. 12 Σαλμυδησσόν, ἔνθα τῶν εἰς τὸν
Πόντον πλεουσῶν νεῶν πολλαὶ ὀκέλλουσι
καὶ ἐκπίπτουσι· τέναγος γάρ ἐστιν ἐπὶ
πάμπολυ τῆς θαλάττης.

727. μητρυιά: cp. Hesiod *O. D.* 825
ἄλλοτε μητρυιὴ πέλει ἡμέρη, ἄλλοτε
μήτηρ.

728. μάλ' ἀσμένως: as στυγάνορες
(724), the Amazons will cheerfully
aid Io, who is ἀστεργάνωρ (898).

729. λίμνης: Μαιώτιδος, defined by
what follows. Cp. 364.

730 Κιμμερικὸν ἥξεις, ὃν θρασυσπλάγχνως σε χρὴ
     λιποῦσαν αὐλῶν' ἐκπερᾶν Μαιωτικόν·
     ἔσται δὲ θνητοῖς εἰσαεὶ λόγος μέγας
     τῆς σῆς πορείας, Βόσπορος δ' ἐπώνυμος
     κεκλήσεται. λιποῦσα δ' Εὐρώπης πέδον
735 ἤπειρον ἥξεις 'Ασιάδ'. ἆρ' ὑμῖν δοκεῖ
     ὁ τῶν θεῶν τύραννος ἐς τὰ πάνθ' ὁμῶς
     βίαιος εἶναι; τῇδε γὰρ θνητῇ θεὸς
     χρῄζων μιγῆναι τάσδ' ἐπέρριψεν πλάνας.
     πικροῦ δ' ἔκυρσας, ὦ κόρη, τῶν σῶν γάμων
740 μνηστῆρος. οὓς γὰρ νῦν ἀκήκοας λόγους,
     εἶναι δόκει σοι μηδέπω 'ν προοιμίοις.

                                        ΙΩ.
     ἰώ μοί μοι.
                    ΧΟΡΟΣ.
          ἐὴ ἐή.

730. The only case in our play of a dactyl in the first foot. See on 18. —Join ὃν λιποῦσαν χρή σε ἐκπερᾶν αὐλῶνα Μαιωτικόν.

731. αὐλῶνα: properly *valley*; said of a strait of the sea here and Soph. *Trach.* 100 ποντίας αὐλῶνας. The channel of the Bosporus is meant, not the sea of Azov itself.

732. λόγος μέγας: cp. Soph. *Ai.* 226 ἀγγελίαν ... τὰν ὁ μέγας μῦθος (rumor late serpens) ἀέξει.

733. Βόσπορος: the understanding of this name as βοὸς πόρος (cp. τῆς σῆς πορείας) helped to fix the direction of Io's legendary wandering. The derivation, however, is wrong. At any rate the Thracian Bosporus, which, even more universally than the Cimmerian, was believed to owe its name to Io's passage, really received its name from the goddess 'Εκάτη Φωσφό-

ρος (dialectic Βοσπόρος), who was there worshipped.

734. λιποῦσα δ' Εὐρώπης πέδον: the Cimmerian Bosporus was considered the boundary of Europe and Asia. Cp. 790. All the places hitherto mentioned Aeschylus regards as belonging to Europe. See on 631.

735. ἆρ' ὑμῖν δοκεῖ: ἆρα confidently spoken for ἆρ' οὐ (as -ne for nonne). Cp. Soph. *O. T.* 822 ἆρ' ἔφυν κακός, ἆρ' οὐχὶ πᾶς ἄναγνος; *O. C.* 753 ἆρ' ἄθλιον τοὔνειδος ὀνειδισ' εἰς σὲ κἀμὲ καὶ τὸ πᾶν γένος; 790 ἆρ' ἂν ματαίου τῆσδ' ἂν ἡδονῆς τύχοις; Krüger I. § 69, 9.

736. ὁμῶς: = ὁμοίως. Cp. *Eum.* 387 δυσοδοπαίπαλα δερκομένοισι καὶ δυσομμάτοις ὁμῶς, 695 τό τ' ἦμαρ καὶ κατ' εὐφρόνην ὁμῶς, *Il.* i. 209 ἄμφω ὁμῶς θυμῷ φιλέουσά τε κηδομένη τε.

741. εἶναι ἐν προοιμίοις: like ἐν τισιν ἀριθμεῖσθαι; *belong to the* προοίμια,

ΠΡΟΜΗΘΕΤΣ.

σὺ δ᾽ αὖ κέκραγας κἀναμυχθίζει· τί που
δράσεις, ὅταν τὰ λοιπὰ πυνθάνῃ κακά;

ΧΟΡΟΣ.

745 ἦ γάρ τι λοιπὸν τῇδε πημάτων ἐρεῖς;

ΠΡΟΜΗΘΕΤΣ.

δυσχείμερόν γε πέλαγος ἀτηρᾶς δύης.

ΙΩ.

τί δῆτ᾽ ἐμοὶ ζῆν κέρδος, ἀλλ᾽ οὐκ ἐν τάχει
ἔρριψ᾽ ἐμαυτὴν τῆσδ᾽ ἀπὸ στύφλου πέτρας,
ὅπως πέδοι σκήψασα τῶν πάντων πόνων
750 ἀπηλλάγην; κρεῖσσον γὰρ εἰσάπαξ θανεῖν
ἢ τὰς ἁπάσας ἡμέρας πάσχειν κακῶς.

ΠΡΟΜΗΘΕΤΣ.

ἦ δυσπετῶς ἂν τοὺς ἐμοὺς ἄθλους φέροις,
ὅτῳ θανεῖν μέν ἐστιν οὐ πεπρωμένον·
αὕτη γὰρ ἦν ἂν πημάτων ἀπαλλαγή·
755 νῦν δ᾽ οὐδέν ἐστι τέρμα μοι προκείμενον
μόχθων, πρὶν ἂν Ζεὺς ἐκπέσῃ τυραννίδος.

count as such. Cp. Pers. 435 εὖ νῦν
τόδ᾽ ἴσθι, μηδέπω μεσοῦν κακόν, Eur.
Med. 60 ἐν ἀρχῇ πῆμα κοὐδέπω μεσοῖ.
On the aphaeresis see Krüger II. § 14,
9, 5; H. 83.
742. αὖ: see 696.
745. τῇδε: belongs to λοιπόν.
746. Cp. Sept. 758 κακῶν δ᾽ ὥσπερ
θάλασσα κῦμ᾽ ἄγει· τὸ μὲν πίτνον, ἄλλο
δ᾽ ἀείρει τρίχαλον κτλ., Suppl. 470 ἄτης
ἄβυσσον πέλαγος ... ἐσβέβηκα κοὐδα-
μοῦ λιμὴν κακῶν.
747. Cp. Eur. Med. 145 τί δέ μοι
ζῆν ἔτι κέρδος; 798 ἴτω· τί μοι ζῆν
κέρδος;
748. στύφλου: Hesych. στύφλον ἢ

στυφελόν· τραχύ, σκληρόν. Cp. Pers.
303 στύφλους περ᾽ ἀκτάς, 964 στυφελοῦ
ἐπ᾽ ἀκτᾶς.
749 f. ὅπως ἀπηλλάγην: see on 157.
753. θανεῖν μέν: as if τέρμα δὲ μόχθων οὐδέν ἐστι προκείμενον followed.
754. For the thought cp. Soph.
Trach. 1173 τοῖς γὰρ θανοῦσι μόχθος οὐ
προσγίγνεται, El. 1170 τοὺς γὰρ θανόν-
τας οὐχ ὁρῶ λυπουμένους.
755. νῦν δέ: nunc vero; following the thought εἰ θανεῖν πεπρωμένον
ἦν, αὕτη ἦν ἂν πημάτων ἀπαλλαγή.—
Cp. 257.
756. πρὶν ἂν ἐκπέσῃ τυραννίδος:
unlike the statement made in 258.

ΙΩ.

ἦ γάρ ποτ᾽ ἔστιν ἐκπεσεῖν ἀρχῆς Δία;

ΠΡΟΜΗΘΕΥΣ.

ἥδοι᾽ ἄν, οἶμαι, τήνδ᾽ ἰδοῦσα συμφοράν. .

ΙΩ.

πῶς δ᾽ οὐκ ἄν, ἥτις ἐκ Διὸς πάσχω κακῶς;

ΠΡΟΜΗΘΕΥΣ.

760 ὡς τοίνυν ὄντων σοι γεγηθέναι πάρα.

ΙΩ.

πρὸς τοῦ τύραννα σκῆπτρα συληθήσεται;

ΠΡΟΜΗΘΕΥΣ.

πρὸς αὐτὸς αὑτοῦ κενοφρόνων βουλευμάτων.

Prometheus at last lifts slightly the veil of the secret so often hinted at, and defines somewhat the danger threatening Zeus. But the former statement, πλὴν ὅταν κείνῳ δοκῇ, is really more exact. For ἐκπεσεῖν τυραννίδος is only a possibility, which in the end is not fulfilled.

760. ὄντων: sc. τῶνδε, as Soph. *Ai.* 981 ὡς ὧδ᾽ ἐχόντων ... τάρα στενάζειν, *Ant.* 1179 ὡς ὧδ᾽ ἐχόντων τἆλλα βουλεύειν πάρα. GMT. 848 and 917.

761. τύραννα σκῆπτρα: cp. Soph. *Ant.* 1169 τύραννον σχῆμα, Eur. *Andr.* 3 τύραννον ἑστίαν, *Hipp.* 843 τύραννον δῶμα. Like δοῦλος, κασίγνητος, γέρων, and gentile nouns, τύραννος is a word which hovers between substantive and adjective. Cp. *Ag.* 750 γέρων λόγος, Frg. 317 γέρον γράμμα (Catull. lxviii. 46 charta loquatur anus), Frg. 338 κάπηλα τεχνήματα. σκῆπτρα is accusative. G. 197, N. 2; H. 724 a.

762. πρὸς αὐτὸς αὑτοῦ: the metre would permit αὐτὸς πρὸς αὑτοῦ, but the juxtaposition of αὐτὸς αὑτοῦ adds point to the expression and sharpens its irony. See on 19; and cp. *Ag.* 836 τοῖς τ᾽ αὐτὸς αὑτοῦ πήμασιν βαρύνεται, Soph. *Ai.* 1132 τοὺς γ᾽ αὐτὸς αὑτοῦ πολεμίους, *O. C.* 929 σὺ δ᾽ ἀξίαν οὐκ οὖσαν αἰσχύνεις πόλιν τὴν αὐτὸς αὑτοῦ, 1356 τὸν αὐτὸς αὑτοῦ πατέρα τόνδ᾽ ἀπήλασας, Timocles, Meineke Com. III. p. 593 τὰς αὐτὸς αὑτοῦ συμφορὰς ῥᾷον φέρει, Philemon, Meineke Com. IV. p. 50 τοὺς αὐτὸς αὑτοῦ βούλεθ᾽ ὑγιαίνειν φίλους; also the verse quoted by Macarius VIII. 18 (*Paroemiogr. Graec.* II. p. 216 ed. Leutsch) τὴν αὐτὸς αὑτοῦ (νῦν) θύραν κρούεις λίθῳ, Babr. 56, 9 τά γ᾽ αὐτὸς αὑτοῦ πᾶς τις εὐπρεπῆ κρίνει. In prose, Aeschin. III. 233 καταλέλυκεν τὴν αὐτὸς αὑτοῦ δυναστείαν (where some mss. have the usual order αὐτὸς τὴν), [Plat.] *Alc.* II. 144 c οὐδὲ τὴν ὁτουοῦν μητέρα διενοεῖτο ἀποκτεῖναι, ἀλλὰ τὴν αὐτὸς

ΙΩ.

ποίῳ τρόπῳ; σήμηνον, εἰ μή τις βλάβη.

ΠΡΟΜΗΘΕΥΣ.

γαμεῖ γάμον τοιοῦτον ᾧ ποτ' ἀσχαλᾷ.

ΙΩ.

765 θέορτον ἢ βρότειον; εἰ ῥητόν, φράσον.

ΠΡΟΜΗΘΕΥΣ.

τί δ' ὄντω'; οὐ γὰρ ῥητὸν αὐδᾶσθαι τόδε.

ΙΩ.

ἢ πρὸς δάμαρτος ἐξανίσταται θρόνων;

ΠΡΟΜΗΘΕΥΣ.

ἢ τέξεταί γε παῖδα φέρτερον πατρός.

ΙΩ.

οὐδ' ἔστιν αὐτῷ τῆσδ' ἀποστροφὴ τύχης;

ΠΡΟΜΗΘΕΥΣ.

770 οὐ δῆτα, πλὴν ἔγωγ' ἂν ἐκ δεσμῶν λυθείς.

αὐτοῦ, Nicostrat. in Stob. *Flor.* 70, 12 εἰ γε μέλλει τις ... ἡδέως ... εἰς τὴν οἰκίαν τὴν αὐτὸς αὐτοῦ εἰσελεύσεσθαι, Parthen. 3 πρὸς τῆς αὐτὸς αὐτοῦ γενεᾶς τρωθείς, Aristid. i. p. 128 σαγηνεύων τὴν ἀρχὴν τὴν αὐτὸς αὐτοῦ, ii. p. 148 ὃ δ' ἀφ' ἑστίας ἀρξάμενος τῆς αὐτὸς αὐτοῦ τὸ σύμμετρον ᾑρεῖτο πρὸ τοῦ πλέονος. Also Ovid. *Am.* i. 7, 26 valui poenam fortis in ipse meam, *Ars Amat.* iii. 668 indicio prodor ab ipse meo.

763. εἰ μή τις βλάβη: cp. 196.

764. ἀσχαλᾷ: for the tense see on 171. Krüger II. § 53, 1, 1. Cp. Eur. *Phoen.* 633 οὐ γὰρ οἶδ' εἴ μοι προσειπεῖν αὖθις ἔσθ' ὑμᾶς ποτε.

765. θέορτον: cp. 116.

766. τί δ' ὄντινα: cp. Soph. *O. T.*

1056 τί δ' ὄντιν' εἴπε; ὄντινα refers to the question θέορτον ἢ βρότειον: in full τί δ' ("why ask") ὄντινα γάμον γαμεῖ;—γάρ: because τί δ' ὄντιν' implies a refusal.—ῥητὸν αὐδᾶσθαι: cp. Ar. *Av.* 1713 οὐ φατὸν λέγειν, Orph. *Arg.* 931 οὐ φατὸν εἰπεῖν, also Eur. *Bacch.* 472 ἄρρητ' ἀβακχεύτοισιν εἰδέναι βροτῶν.

767. ἐξανίσταται: for the present tense see note on 513.

768. See Introd. p. 17. The word φέρτερον recalls the passage of Pindar in question (quoted in note to 924).

770. ἂν: peradventure. The uncertainty implied in ἂν refers solely to the possible alternative that Zeus, unwarned by Prometheus, shall enter into the fatal union.

114 ΑΙΣΧΥΛΟΥ

ΙΩ.

τίς οὖν ὁ λύσων ἐστὶν ἄκοντος Διός;

ΠΡΟΜΗΘΕΤΣ.

τῶν σῶν τιν' αὐτὸν ἐκγόνων εἶναι χρεών.

ΙΩ.

πῶς εἶπας; ἢ 'μὸς παῖς σ' ἀπαλλάξει κακῶν;

ΠΡΟΜΗΘΕΤΣ.

τρίτος γε γένναν πρὸς δέκ' ἄλλαισιν γοναῖς.

ΙΩ.

775 ἥδ' οὐκέτ' εὐξύμβλητος ἡ χρησμῳδία.

ΠΡΟΜΗΘΕΤΣ.

καὶ μηδὲ σαυτῆς ἐκμαθεῖν ζήτει πόνους.

ΙΩ.

μή μοι προτείνων κέρδος εἶτ' ἀποστέρει.

ΠΡΟΜΗΘΕΤΣ.

δυοῖν λόγοιν σε θατέρῳ δωρήσομαι.

771 f. ὁ λύσων: see on 27. The object is easily supplied; cp. 27, 176, 337, 721, 783, 785. — Io's words, "who shall free thee against Zeus's will?" imply "no one can free thee." Accordingly Prometheus, without regard to ἄκοντος Διός, answers, to Io's astonishment, "from thy offspring my deliverer shall come." In point of fact the deliverance, in the following drama, does not come about ἄκοντος Διός, but rather, as in Hesiod Theog. 529, οὐκ ἀέκητι Ζηνὸς 'Ολυμπίου ὑψιμέδοντος.

774. ἀπὸ 'Ιοῦς Ἔπαφος, οὗ Λιβύη, ἧς Βῆλος, οὗ Δαναός, οὗ 'Υπερμνήστρα ἡ μὴ κτείνασα τὸν Λυγκία τὸν ὁμόζυγον, ἧς 'Άβας, οὗ Προῖτος, οὗ 'Ακρίσιος, οὗ Δα-

νάη, ἧς Περσεύς, οὗ 'Ηλεκτρυών, οὗ 'Αλκμήνη, ἧς 'Ηρακλῆς, Schol.

775. οὐκέτι: no longer, in contrast to the foregoing revelations. — εὐξύμβλητος: cp. Soph. Trach. 694 ἀξύμβλητον ἀνθρώπῳ μαθεῖν, Cho. 170 εὐξύμβολον τόδ' ἐστὶ παντὶ δοξάσαι.

776 f. καὶ μηδὲ σαυτῆς: and thine own sufferings, too, seek not to learn; that is, "thou understandest not my prophecy; shouldst thou ask to know it, thine own sufferings also would be revealed to thee; the explanation of the prophecy involves the prediction of thy woes." — προτείνων: not προτείνας; "do not hold it forth and at the same moment deprive me of it."

778. On this construction of δωρεῖ-

ΙΩ.

ποίοιν; πρόδειξον αἵρεσίν τ᾽ ἐμοὶ δίδου.

ΠΡΟΜΗΘΕΥΣ.

780 δίδωμ᾽· ἑλοῦ γὰρ ἢ πόνων τὰ λοιπά σοι
φράσω σαφηνῶς ἢ τὸν ἐκλύσοντ᾽ ἐμέ.

ΧΟΡΟΣ.

τούτοιν σὺ τὴν μὲν τῇδε, τὴν δ᾽ ἐμοὶ χάριν
θέσθαι θέλησον, μηδ᾽ ἀτιμάσῃς λόγου·
καὶ τῇδε μὲν γέγωνε τὴν λοιπὴν πλάνην,
785 ἐμοὶ δὲ τὸν λύσοντα· τοῦτο γὰρ ποθῶ.

ΠΡΟΜΗΘΕΥΣ.

ἐπεὶ προθυμεῖσθ᾽, οὐκ ἐναντιώσομαι
τὸ μὴ οὐ γεγωνεῖν πᾶν ὅσον προσχρῄζετε.
σοὶ πρῶτον, Ἰοῖ, πολύδονον πλάνην φράσω,
ἣν ἐγγράφου σὺ μνήμοσιν δέλτοις φρενῶν.

σθαι (accus. of person and dat. of thing) see Krüger II. § 48, 7, 4.

780. Cp. Eur. Phoen. 951 τοῖνδ᾽ ἑλοῦ δυοῖν πότμοιν τὸν ἕτερον· ἢ γὰρ παῖδα σῶσον ἢ πόλιν. — ἑλοῦ γὰρ ἤ: ἤ ... ἤ in indirect question, as in Homer, for the common εἰ ... ἤ, to express sharp contrast of the alternatives (δυοῖν θατέρῳ). Cp. Cho. 890 εἴδωμεν ἢ νικῶμεν ἢ νικώμεθα, Soph. O. C. 80 οἶδε γὰρ κρινοῦσί σοι ἢ χρή σε μίμνειν ἢ πορεύεσθαι πάλιν, Eur. Med. 492 οὐδ᾽ ἔχω μαθεῖν ἢ θεοὺς νομίζεις τοὺς τότ᾽ οὐκ ἄρχειν ἔτι ἢ καινὰ κεῖσθαι θέσμι᾽ ἀνθρώποις τὰ νῦν. See Krüger II. § 65, 1, 3. — πόνων τὰ λοιπά: cp. 634. — The stichomythy ends with a speech of two verses.

782. τούτοιν: sc. τοῖν χαρίτοιν. The dual of ὁ, οὗτος, ὅδε, αὐτός, ὅς, ὅστις has one form for all genders in the older Attic.

783. ἀτιμάσῃς λόγου: sc. με (see on 771). For the expression, cp. Suppl. 378 τάσδ᾽ ἀτιμάσαι λιτάς, Soph. O. C. 49 μή μ᾽ ἀτιμάσῃς, ... ὧν σε προστρέπω φράσαι, 1273 οὐδ᾽ ἀνταμείβει μ᾽ οὐδέν, ἀλλ᾽ ἀτιμάσας πέμψεις ἄναυδος, Ant. 21 οὐ γὰρ τάφου ... τὸν δ᾽ ἀτιμάσας ἔχει; O. C. 1278 ὡς μή μ᾽ ἄτιμον ... οὕτως ἀφῇ με μηδὲν ἀντειπὼν ἔπος, O. T. 788 καὶ μ᾽ ὁ Φοῖβος ὧν μὲν ἱκόμην ἄτιμον ἐξέπεμψεν.

788. πολύδονον: see on 589.

789. ἐγγράφου κτέ.: cp. Suppl. 179 αἰνῶ φυλάξαι τἄμ᾽ ἔπη δελτουμένας, Eum. 274 δελτογράφῳ δὲ πάντ᾽ ἐπωπᾷ φρενί, Soph. Frg. 535 θὲς δ᾽ ἐν φρενὸς δέλτοισι τοὺς ἐμοὺς λόγους, Cho. 450 τοιαῦτ᾽ ἀκούων ἐν φρεσὶν γράφου, Soph. Phil. 1325 καὶ ταῦτ᾽ ἐπίστω καὶ γράφου φρενῶν ἔσω, Pind. Ol. xi. 2 πόθι φρενὸς ἐμᾶς γέγραπται, Paul. Ep. Cor. II. iii. 3 ἐπιστολὴ Χριστοῦ ἐγγεγραμμένη οὐκ ἐν πλαξὶ λιθίναις, ἀλλ᾽ ἐν πλαξὶ καρδίας.

790   ὅταν περάσῃς ῥεῖθρον ἠπείροιν ὅρον,
      πρὸς ἀντολὰς φλογῶπας ἡλιοστιβεῖς

              *   *   *   *   *

      πόντου περῶσα φλοῖσβον, ἔς τ' ἂν ἐξίκῃ
      πρὸς Γοργόνεια πεδία Κισθήνης, ἵνα
      αἱ Φορκίδες ναίουσι δηναιαὶ κόραι
795   τρεῖς κυκνόμορφοι, κοινὸν ὄμμ' ἐκτημέναι,
      μονόδοντες, ἃς οὔθ' ἥλιος προσδέρκεται
      ἀκτῖσιν οὔθ' ἡ νύκτερος μήνη ποτέ.
      πέλας δ' ἀδελφαὶ τῶνδε τρεῖς κατάπτεροι,
      δρακοντόμαλλοι Γοργόνες βροτοστυγεῖς,

790. ῥεῖθρον: i.e. the strait. — ἠπείροιν ὅρον: see on 734.
    791. ἀντολὰς ἡλιοστιβεῖς: peri-
phrasis for ἀντολὰς ἡλίου. With ἡλιο-
στιβής cp. Sept. 859 τὰν ἀστιβῆ 'πόλ-
λωνι. — The following places must
therefore lie in the east.   Thence Io
is to reach Egypt by following the
course of the river Aethiops (809 ff.).
— After 791 some verses have fallen
out.
    792. πόντου: probably the Cas-
pian is meant, with which, however,
the ancients confounded the sea of
Aral.
    793. Γοργόνεια: explained by 798 f.
The home of the Gorgons, although
placed in the west by Hesiod (Theog.
274 f.), was sometimes thought of as
in the east. Cp. Schol. Pind. Pyth. x.
72 αἱ δὲ Γοργόνες κατὰ μέν τινας ἐν τοῖς
Ἐρυθραίοις μέρεσι καὶ τοῖς Αἰθιωπικοῖς,
ἅ ἐστι πρὸς ἀνατολὴν καὶ μεσημβρίαν,
κατὰ δέ τινας ἐπὶ τῶν περάτων τῆς
Λιβύης ἅ ἐστι πρὸς δύσιν. Cisthene
we must accordingly understand to
be in the far east, at the end of the
world. The verse of the comic poet
Cratinus (quoted by Harpocration

under Κισθήνη), κἀνθένδ' ἐπὶ τέρματα
γῆς ἥξεις καὶ Κισθήνης ὅρος ὄψει, is
probably a parody of this passage.
    794. αἱ Φορκίδες ... δηναιαὶ κόραι:
cp. Hesiod Theog. 270 Φόρκυι δ' αὖ
Κητὼ Γραίας τέκε καλλιπαρήους ἐκ
γενετῆς πολιάς, τὰς δὴ Γραίας καλέου-
σιν ... Γοργούς θ' αἳ ναίουσι πέρην κλυ-
τοῦ Ὠκεανοῖο.
    795. τρεῖς κυκνόμορφοι: three is
the number commonly given, but
Hesiod seems to mention only two
Graeae, Pephredo and Enyo. 'Swan-
form — perhaps a swan's body with
a human head — belongs to them because they are sea-divinities, and swim
in the sea like water-fowl. For a like
reason other sea-gods were given the
form of fishes' (Schoemann, Die Hesiodische Theogonie, p. 156). — ἐκτημέναι: the perfect ἐκτῆσθαι, for κεκτῆσθαι,
recurs Il. ix. 402, and in Herodotus.
    796 f. Cp. Frg. 169 ἃς οὔτε πέμφιξ
ἡλίου προσδέρκεται οὔτ' ἀστερωτὸν ὄμμα
Λητῷας κόρης. — The scholiast notes
κατῴκουν δὲ ὑπὸ γῆν καὶ οὔτε ἡλίῳ οὔτε
σελήνῃ ἦσαν θεαταί.
    798 f. ἀδελφαί: cp. Hesiod l.c.
Their names are Σθεινώ, Εὐρυάλη, and

800　ἃς θνητὸς οὐδεὶς εἰσιδὼν ἕξει πνοάς·
　　τοιοῦτο μέν σοι τοῦτο φρούριον λέγω.
　　ἄλλην δ' ἄκουσον δυσχερῆ θεωρίαν·
　　ὀξυστόμους γὰρ Ζηνὸς ἀκραγεῖς κύνας
　　γρῦπας φύλαξαι, τόν τε μουνῶπα στρατὸν

Μέδουσα. — δρακοντόμαλλοι: cp. *Cho.* 1048 γυναῖκες αἵδε (the Erinyes) Γοργόνων δίκην ... πεπλεκτανημέναι πυκνοῖς δράκουσιν. For μαλλός said of hair, cp. Eurip. *Bacch.* 112 πλοκάμων μαλλοῖς.

801. φρούριον: here cautio, οἷον φρουρήσασθαι. The scholiast explains καταγωγὴν ἣν ὀφείλεις φυλάξασθαι. Cp. φρούριον· προφύλαγμα, Hesych. See 715, 804; also 712, 718, 807.

803. See on 804; also Ctesias *Exc. Ind.* 12 ἔστι δὲ καὶ χρυσὸς ἐν τῇ Ἰνδικῇ χώρᾳ, οὐκ ἐν τοῖς ποταμοῖς εὑρισκόμενος καὶ πλυνόμενος, ὥσπερ ἐν τῷ Πακτωλῷ ποταμῷ· ἀλλ' ὄρη πολλὰ καὶ μεγάλα, ἐν οἷς οἰκοῦσι γρῦπες, ὄρνεα τετράποδα, μέγεθος ὅσον λύκος· σκέλη καὶ ὄνυχες οἷάπερ λέων· τὰ ἐν τῷ ἄλλῳ σώματι πτερὰ μέλανα, ἐρυθρὰ δὲ τὰ ἐν τῷ στήθει· δι' αὐτοὺς δὲ ὁ ἐν τοῖς ὄρεσι χρυσὸς πολὺς ἐν γίνεται δυσπόριστος. Cp. Solin. 13 in Asiatica Scythia tervae sunt locupletes, inhabitabiles tamen, nam cum auro et gemmas affluant, Grypes tenent universa, alites ferocissimae et ultra omnem rabiem saevientes, quarum immanitate obsistente ad venas divites accessus difficilis ac rarus est; quippe visos discerpunt veluti geniti ad plectendam avaritiae temeritatem. — Ζηνὸς κύνας: as servants of Zeus; cp. 1021 below. Said of the eagles *Ag.* 136 πτανοῖσιν κυσὶ πατρός, and of the

Harpies Apoll. Rh. *Arg.* ii. 289 μεγάλοιο Διὸς κύνας. — ἀκραγεῖς: Hesych. ἀκραγές· δυσχερές, σκληρόν, ὀξύχολον (Bekk. *Anecd.* p. 369, 17 ἀκρόχολον). From ἄκρος and ἄγη (= ζῆλος), exceedingly violent.

804. μουνῶπα: see on 543. — στρατὸν Ἀριμασπόν: see on 761. On the name, Hdt. iv. 27 οὐνομάζομεν αὐτοὺς σκυθιστὶ Ἀριμασπούς· ἄριμα γὰρ ἓν καλέουσι Σκύθαι, σποῦ δὲ τὸν ὀφθαλμόν, Eustath. on Dion. Perieg. 31 ἀρὶ μὲν γὰρ τὸ ἓν σκυθιστί, μασπὸς δὲ ὁ ὀφθαλμός. This etymology, obviously connected with the belief in a one-eyed race, came probably from the Ἀριμάσπεια, an epic poem by Aristeas, of which Hdt. says (iv. 13) ἔφη δὲ Ἀριστέης ὁ Καϋστροβίου ἀνὴρ Προκοννήσιος ποιέων ἔπεα, ἐπικέσθαι ἐς Ἰσσηδόνας φοιβόλαμπτος γενόμενος, Ἰσσηδόνων δ' ὑπεροικέειν Ἀριμασπούς ἄνδρας μουνοφθάλμους, ὑπὲρ δὲ τούτων τοὺς χρυσοφύλακας γρῦπας, τούτων δὲ τοὺς Ὑπερβορέους κατήκοντας ἐπὶ θάλασσαν. Cp. Paus. i. 24. 6 τούτους τοὺς γρῦπας ἐν τοῖς ἔπεσιν Ἀριστέας ὁ Προκοννήσιος μάχεσθαι περὶ τοῦ χρυσοῦ φησιν Ἀριμασποῖς τοῖς ὑπὲρ Ἰσσηδόνων· τὸν δὲ χρυσὸν ὃν φυλάσσουσιν οἱ γρῦπες ἀνιέναι τὴν γῆν· εἶναι δὲ Ἀριμασποὺς μὲν ἄνδρας μονοφθάλμους πάντας ἐκ γενετῆς, γρῦπας δὲ θηρία λέουσι εἰκασμένα, πτερὰ δὲ ἔχειν καὶ στόμα ἀετοῦ. These stories about griffins and Arimaspi had their origin in the Persian-Indian fable of gold-digging ants (which in Ctesias's account, quoted above, appear as

805 Ἀριμασπὸν ἱπποβάμον', οἳ χρυσόρρυτον
οἰκοῦσιν ἀμφὶ νᾶμα Πλούτωνος πόρου·
τούτοις σὺ μὴ πέλαζε. τηλουρὸν δὲ γῆν
ἥξεις κελαινὸν φῦλον, οἳ πρὸς ἡλίου
ναίουσι πηγαῖς, ἔνθα ποταμὸς Αἰθίοψ.

griffins) and Indian gold-hunters (Hdt. iii. 102). The gold-mining ants have been recognized in the marmots of the sandy plains of Thibet (Lassen *Indische Alterthumskunde* I. p. 1021).

805 f. χρυσόρρυτον: cp. Hdt. iii. 116 πρὸς δὲ ἄρκτου τῆς Εὐρώπης πολλῷ τι πλεῖστος χρυσὸς φαίνεται ἐών· ὅκως μὲν γινόμενος οὐκ ἔχω οὐδὲ τοῦτο ἀτρεκέως εἶπαι, λέγεται δὲ ὑπὲκ τῶν γρυπῶν ἁρπάζειν Ἀριμασποὺς ἄνδρας μουνοφθάλμους. The river Pluton is nowhere else mentioned. Probably it is a fiction, like the Hybristes 717. The name (from πλοῦτος) corresponds to the idea of the region.— πόρου: see on 532.

807 ff. σύ: expresses affectionate interest. — τηλουρὸν γῆν, κελαινὸν φῦλον: personal accusative as appositive to the name of the country. Cp. Krüger II. § 46, 3, 1 and 2. κελαινὸν φῦλον is further defined by ποταμὸς Αἰθίοψ in the next verse. — ἡλίου πηγαῖς: this cannot be the Fount of the Sun, sacred to Ammon, which is described by Hdt. iv. 181 ἐπίκλησιν δὲ αὕτη ἡ κρήνη καλέεται ἡλίου; cp. Quint. Curt. iv. 7, 22 a q u a m s o l i s v o c a n t, Lucret. vi. 848 e s s e a p u d H a m m o n i s f a n u m f o n s l u c e d i u r n a f r i g i d u s, a t c a l i d u s n o c t u r n o t e m p o r e f e r t u r. Rather it appears from Eur. Frg. 771, Μέροπι τῆσδ' ἄνακτι γῆς, ἣν ἐκ τεθρίππων ἁρμάτων πρώτην χθόνα Ἥλιος ἀνίσχων χρυσέᾳ βάλλει φλογί· καλοῦσι δ' αὐτὴν γείτονες μελάμβροτοι Ἔω φαεννὰς

Ἡλίου θ' ἱπποστάσεις, that the ταντοτρόφος λίμνη, described in Frg. II. of the Προμ. λυόμενος below, is meant. Its waters give life and happiness. Originally it was thought to be in the heavens, afterwards on the earth; cp. the Homeric verse (Od. iii. 1) Ἥλιος δ' ἀνόρουσε λιπὼν περικαλλέα λίμνην οὐρανὸν ἐς πολύχαλκον.—Strabo p. 33, quoting the Frg. of the Προμηθεὺς λυόμενος just mentioned, shows that the early Greeks regarded all the south as belonging to Aethiopia, as the whole north to Scythia; he adds μηνύει δὲ καὶ Ἔφορος τὴν παλαιὰν περὶ τῆς Αἰθιοπίας δόξαν . . . προστίθησι δ' ὅτι μείζων ἡ Αἰθιοπία καὶ ἡ Σκυθία· δοκεῖ γάρ, φησί, τὸ τῶν Αἰθιόπων ἔθνος παρατείνειν ἀπ' ἀνατολῶν χειμερινῶν μέχρι δυσμῶν, ἡ Σκυθία δ' ἀντίκειται τούτῳ.

809. ποταμὸς Αἰθίοψ: the scholiast rightly explains ὁ Νεῖλος. The name Nile, it was said, properly belonged only to the lower course of the river, below the last cataract (see note on 811). Cp. Solin. 32 d e m u m q u e a C a t a r a c t e u l t i m o t u t u s e s t, i t a e n i m q u a e d a m c l a u s t r a e i u s A e g y p t i i n u n c u p a n t; r e l i c t o t a m e n h o c p o s t s e n o m i n e q u o N i g r i s v o c a t u r, Vitruv. viii. 2, 6 p e r v e n i t p e r m o n t e s a d c a t a r r h a c t a m a b e a q u e s e p r a e c i p i t a n s N i l u s a p p e l l a t u r. Aeschylus, like others of his time, conceives of the Nile, under the name Αἰθίοψ (N i g r i s) as

810 τούτου παρ' ὄχθας ἔρφ', ἕως ἂν ἐξίκῃ
καταβασμὸν ἔνθα Βυβλίνων ὀρῶν ἄπο
ἵησι σεπτὸν Νεῖλος εὔποτον ῥέος.
οὗτός σ' ὁδώσει τὴν τρίγωνον ἐς χθόνα
Νειλῶτιν, οὗ δὴ τὴν μακρὰν ἀποικίαν,
815 Ἰοῖ, πέπρωται σοί τε καὶ τέκνοις κτίσαι.

τῶν δ' εἴ τί σοι ψελλόν τε καὶ δυσεύρετον,

rising in the east (*i.e.* southeast).
Cp. the Schol. on *Suppl.* 559 χιονό-
βοσκον (said of the Nile)· φασὶ γὰρ
λυομένης χιόνος παρὰ 'Ινδοῖς πληροῦ-
σθαι αὐτόν. Alexander and his com-
panions thought the Indian river Hy-
daspes to be the beginning of the
Nile. Cp. also Frg. 304, γένος μὲν
αἰνεῖν ἐκμαθὼν ἐπίσταμαι Αἰθιοπίδος γῆς,
ἔνθα Νεῖλος ἑπτάρους γαῖαν κυλίνδει
πνευμάτων ἐπομβρίᾳ, ἐν δ' ἥλιος πυρω-
πὸς ἐκλάμψας χθονὶ τήκει πετραίαν
χιόνα· πᾶσα δ' εὐθαλὴς Αἴγυπτος ἀγνοῦ
νάματος πληρουμένη φερέσβιον Δήμη-
τρος ἀντέλλει στάχυν.

811. καταβασμόν: the so-called
Little Cataract, the tenth and last in
descending, is meant. It is now
called *Shellāl* = *Cataract;* its ancient
name was Κατάδουπα. Cp. Hdt. ii.
17 Αἴγυπτον πᾶσαν ἀρξαμένην ἀπὸ Κα-
ταδούπων τε καὶ 'Ελεφαντίνης πόλιος,
Strabo p. 817 μικρὸν δ' ὑπὲρ 'Ελεφαντίνης ἐστὶν καταράκτης . . ., πετρώδης τις
ὀφρύς, ἐπίπεδος μὲν ἄνωθεν ὥστε δέχεσθαι τὸν ποταμόν, τελευτῶσα δ' εἰς κρημ-
νόν, καθ' οὗ καταρρήγνυται τὸ ὕδωρ, Cic.
Somn. Scip. 18 sicut ubi Nilus
ad ea quae Catadupa nomi-
nantur praecipitat ex alti-
simis montibus.—βυβλίνων ὀρῶν:
ἀπὸ τῆς γινομένης παρ' αὐτοῖς βύβλου
ἔκλασεν τὰ βύβλινα ὄρη, Schol. On
·this Stanley remarks, 'non absimile
vero, namque et Niger perinde ac

Nilus papyro viget et calamo
praetexitur, Solin. 30.'

812. σεπτόν: said as in the above-
quoted Frg. ἀγνοῦ νάματος, 434 above
ἀγνορύτων ποταμῶν, *Pers.* 497 ῥέε-
θρον ἀγνοῦ Στρυμόνος, Eur. *Iph. T.*
401 ῥεύματα σεμνὰ Δίρκας. — Νεῖλος:
nearly = Νεῖλος γενόμενος, as the *Nile.*
— εὔποτον ῥέος: *Suppl.* 561 ὕδωρ τὸ
Νείλου νόσοις ἄθικτον, Achill. Tatius
iv. 18 (of the Nile-water) γλυκὺ δὲ
πινόμενον ἦν καὶ ψυχρὸν ἐν μέτρῳ τῆς
ἡδονῆς. Pescennius Niger, when his
soldiers demanded wine, exclaimed,
'Nilum habetis et vinum
quaeritis?' to which Aelius Spar-
tianus (*Pesc. Nig.* 7) adds tanta
illius fluminis dulcitudo ut
accolae vina non quaerant.
For ῥέος cp. 070.

813. τρίγωνον χθόνα: τὸ καλεόμενον
Δέλτα, Hdt. ii. 13.

814. μακράν: dis**t**ant. Not temporal ("lasting till the return of the
Danaides to Argos").

816. τῶν δέ: see on 234. — ψελλόν:
Ar. *Frg.* 536 ψελλόν ἐστι καὶ καλεῖ τὴν
ἄρκτον ἄρτον. Cp. Hesych. ψελλός· ὁ
τὸ σίγμα ταχύτερον λέγων. ψελλίζειν·
ἀσήμως λαλεῖν. Bekk. *Anecd.* p. 116,
18, ψελλός· Αἰσχύλος Προμηθεῖ. τέ-
θεικε δὲ τὴν λέξιν ἐπὶ τοῦ σαφῶς μὴ
εἰρημένου. "Lisping" = "indistinct."
Cp. the use of τυφλός (see note on
499).

ἐπαναδίπλαζε καὶ σαφῶς ἐκμάνθανε·
σχολὴ δὲ πλείων ἢ θέλω πάρεστί μοι.

ΧΟΡΟΣ.

εἰ μέν τι τῇδε λοιπὸν ἢ παρειμένον
820 ἔχεις γεγωνεῖν τῆς πολυφθόρου πλάνης,
λέγ'· εἰ δὲ πάντ' εἴρηκας, ἡμῖν αὖ χάριν
δὸς ἥνπερ αἰτούμεσθα, μέμνησαι δέ που.

ΠΡΟΜΗΘΕΥΣ.

τὸ πᾶν πορείας ἥδε τέρμ' ἀκήκοεν.
ὅπως δ' ἂν εἰδῇ μὴ μάτην κλύουσά μου,
825 ἃ πρὶν μολεῖν δεῦρ' ἐκμεμόχθηκεν φράσω,
τεκμήριον τοῦτ' αὐτὸ δοὺς μύθων ἐμῶν.
ὄχλον μὲν οὖν τὸν πλεῖστον ἐκλείψω λόγων,
πρὸς αὐτὸ δ' εἶμι τέρμα σῶν πλανημάτων.
ἐπεὶ γὰρ ἦλθες πρὸς Μολοσσὰ γῆς πέδα
830 τὴν αἰπύνωτόν τ' ἀμφὶ Δωδώνην, ἵνα
μαντεῖα θᾶκός τ' ἐστὶ Θεσπρωτοῦ Διὸς
τέρας τ' ἄπιστον, αἱ προσήγοροι δρύες,

817. For the resolution in the first foot, see on 116.

821. See on 107 respecting the long thesis in the fifth foot.

822. μέμνησαι δέ που· joined loosely to ἥνπερ αἰτούμεσθα. Cp. Soph. *Ant.* 531 σὺ δ', ἣ κατ' οἴκους ... λήθουσά μ' ἐξέπινες, οὐδ' ἐμάνθανον τρέφων δύ' ἄτα, κτέ.

823. τὸ πᾶν πορείας τέρμα: see on 1. "The whole journey-goal" = "the goal of the whole journey."

827 f. ὄχλον ... τέρμα: the route from Argos to Dodona is omitted. Aeschylus probably thought of it as passing over the Aegean to Asia Minor (cp. *Suppl.* 547 ff.) and thence

back by the Thracian Bosporus to Dodona.

829. Μολοσσὰ γῆς πέδα: see on 1.

830 ff. αἰπύνωτον: Dodona lay on the flank of the Tomaros or Tmaros range. At the foot of the mountain stood the temple. — ἀμφί: cp. 1029, Soph. *Ai.* 1064 ἀμφὶ χλωρὰν ψάμαθον ἐκβεβλημένος. — Δωδώνην: Hdt. ii. 52 τὸ γὰρ δὴ μαντήιον τοῦτο νενόμισται ἀρχαιότατον τῶν ἐν Ἑλλησι χρηστηρίων εἶναι. It was a sign-oracle; the rustling of a sacred oak (φηγός) was interpreted, originally by the Σελλοί, afterwards by three priestesses (πελιαί, i.e. πολιαί). Cp. *Od.* xiv. 327 τὸν δ' ἐς Δωδώνην φάτο βήμεναι, ὄφρα

ὑφ' ὧν σὺ λαμπρῶς κοὐδὲν αἰνικτηρίως
προσηγορεύθης ἡ Διὸς κλεινὴ δάμαρ, —
835 [μέλλουσ' ἔσεσθαι] τῶνδε προσσαίνει σέ τι; —
ἐντεῦθεν οἰστρήσασα τὴν παρακτίαν
κέλευθον ᾖξας πρὸς μέγαν κόλπον Ῥέας,
ἀφ' οὗ παλιμπλάγκτοισι χειμάζει δρόμοις·
χρόνον δὲ τὸν μέλλοντα πόντιος μυχός,

θεοῖο ἐκ δρυὸς ὑψικόμοιο Διὸς βουλὴν
ἐπακούσαι, Il. xvi. 233 Ζεῦ ἄνα Δωδω-
ναῖε Πελασγικέ, τηλόθι ναίων, Δωδώνης
μεδέων δυσχειμέρου· ἀμφὶ δὲ Σελλοί σοὶ
ναίουσ' ὑποφῆται ἀνιπτόποδες χαμαιεῦ-
ναι. — Θεσπρωτοῦ: cp. Eur. Phoen. 982
Θεσπρωτὸν οὖδας . . . σεμνὰ Δωδώνης βά-
θρα, Strabo p. 328 Δωδώνη τοίνυν τὸ
μὲν παλαιὸν ὑπὸ Θεσπρωτοῖς ἦν . . . καὶ
οἱ τραγικοὶ δὲ καὶ Πίνδαρος Θεσπρωτίδα
εἰρήκασι τὴν Δωδώνην· ὕστερον δὲ ὑπὸ
Μολοττοῖς ἐλέγετο. — αἱ προσήγοροι
δρύες: cp. Soph. Trach. 171, 1166 ἃ
τῶν ὀρείων καὶ χαμαικοιτῶν ἐγὼ Σελλῶν
ἐσελθὼν ἄλσος εἰσεγραψάμην πρὸς τῆς
πατρῴας καὶ πολυγλώσσου δρυός, Sen.
Herc. Oet. 1475 quercus fatidica.
833. λαμπρῶς: cp. Eum. 797 λαμ-
πρὰ μαρτύρια παρῆν.
834. ἡ: the article with the predicate noun, because the words of the
oracle are directly quoted. Cp. Eur.
H. F. 581 Ἡρακλῆς ὁ καλλίνικος ὣς
πάροιθε λέξομαι, Or. 1140 ὁ μητροφόντης
δ' οὐ καλεῖ ταύτην κτανών. — κλεινή:
noble; an epithet of princely and high-
born personages.
835. μέλλουσ' ἔσεσθαι: in place of
these interpolated words we expect
something like κλύεις μάται' (= ἆρα
μάτην λέγω; cp. 824) ἢ τῶνδε προσσαίνει σέ τι; Prometheus would then
mean that his exact knowledge of
the words of the oracle is the best
τεκμήριον (826). Cp. Ag. 1194, where

Casandra, after showing her acquaint-
ance with the grewsome history of the
Atridae, asks the chorus ἥμαρτον, ἢ
θηρῶ τι τοξότης τις ὥς; ἢ ψευδόμαντίς
εἰμι θυροκόπος φλέδων, Soph. O. T.
1140 λέγω τι τούτων ἢ οὐ λέγω πε-
πραγμένον; — προσσαίνει: ὑπομιμνή-
σκει σε, Schol., touches thee caressingly
= "awakens in thee a pleasant memory." Cp. Soph. Ant. 1214 παιδός με
σαίνει φθόγγος, Eur. Hipp. 862 καὶ μὴν
τύποι γε σφενδόνης χρυσηλάτου τῆς οὐκέτ' οὔσης τῆσδε προσσαίνουσί με. Observe that the sentence is parenthetic.
836. οἰστρήσασα: cp. Eur. Iph. A.
77 ἢ δὲ καθ' Ἑλλάδ' οἰστρήσας δρόμῳ
ὅρκους παλαιοὺς Τυνδάρεω μαρτύρεται.
837. κόλπον Ῥέας: καὶ Ἀπολλώνιος
Κρονίην ἅλα τὸν Ἰόνιόν φησι, οὕτω γὰρ
ἐκαλεῖτο, Schol. The passage is Argon.
iv. 327 δή ῥα τότε Κρονίην Κόλχοι ἅλα
δ' ἐκπρομολόντες. — μέγαν: cp. Verg.
Aen. iii. 211 insulae Ionio in
magno, and Servius's note scien-
dum Ionium sinum esse im-
mensum ab Ionia usque ad
Siciliam, et huius partes
esse Adriaticum, Achaicum,
Epiroticum.
838. παλιμπλάγκτοισι: πάλιν means
back from the sea, into the interior.
Cp. Od. xiii. 5 παλιμπλαγχθέντα. —
χειμάζει: see on 563. The present
signifies that this last stage of her
journey brings her to Prometheus.

840　σαφῶς ἐπίστασ', Ἰόνιος κεκλήσεται,
　　　τῆς σῆς πορείας μνῆμα τοῖς πᾶσιν βροτοῖς.
　　　σημεῖά σοι τάδ' ἐστὶ τῆς ἐμῆς φρενὸς
　　　ὡς δέρκεται πλέον τι τοῦ πεφασμένου.

　　　τὰ λοιπὰ δ' ὑμῖν τῇδέ τ' ἐς κοινὸν φράσω,
845　ἐς ταὐτὸν ἐλθὼν τῶν πάλαι λόγων ἴχνος.
　　　ἔστιν πόλις Κάνωβος ἐσχάτη χθονὸς
　　　Νείλου πρὸς αὐτῷ στόματι καὶ προσχώματι·
　　　ἐνταῦθα δή σε Ζεὺς τίθησιν ἔμφρονα
　　　ἐπαφῶν ἀταρβεῖ χειρὶ καὶ θιγὼν μόνον.

840. Ἰόνιος: a false etymology. The first syllable of the name is short, both here and Eur. *Phoen.* 208, when Ἰόνιον κατά responds to Ἴσα δ' ἀγάλμασι. (Yet Ovid *Her.* xiv. 103 makes the first syllable of Io short.)

841. τῆς σῆς πορείας: 'itineris tui, aditus tui' (Schütz). Differently 733 (traiectionis tuae).

843. τοῦ πεφασμένου: τοῦ φανεροῦ, Schol.

845. τῶν πάλαι λόγων: the reference is to 815. πάλαι of the recent past, as *Ag.* 587 ἀνωλόλυξα μὲν πάλαι χαρᾶς ὕπο, ὅτ' ἦλθ' ὁ πρῶτος νύχιος ἄγγελος πυρός.

846. ἔστιν πόλις Κάνωβος: the narrative begins, in epic fashion, with a description of the locality. Cp. *Od.* iii. 293 ἔστι δέ τις λισσὴ αἰπεῖά τε εἰς ἅλα πέτρη, *Il.* ii. 811 ἔστι δέ τις προπάροιθε πόλιος αἰπεῖα κολώνη (in Latin poets est locus), Soph. *Trach.* 237 ἀκτή τις ἔστ' Εὐβοῖίς, 752 ἀκτή τις ἀμφίκλυστος ἔστιν, *Ant.* 966 παρὰ δὲ κυανέων σπιλάδων ἀκταὶ Βοσπόριαι ἴδ' ὁ Θρηκῶν Σαλμυδησσὸς ἵνα κτέ., Eur. *Hipp.* 1199 ἀκτή τις ἔστι τοὐπέκεινα τῆσδε γῆς, *Iph. T.* 262 ἦν τις διαρρὼξ κυμάτων πολλῷ σάλῳ κοιλωπὸς ἀγμός, 1450 χῶ-

ρός τις ἔστιν Ἀτθίδος πρὸς ἐσχάτοις ὅροισι, also Aesch. *Pers.* 447.: of its region. Cp. *Suppl.* 717 οἴακος ἰθυντῆρος ὑστάτου νεώς. For the story cp. *Suppl.* 311 καὶ μὴν Κάνωβον κἀπὶ Μέμφιν ἵκετο (sc. Ἰώ).

847. προσχώματι: τῷ ὑπὸ τοῦ ποταμοῦ ἐτησίῳ προσθήματι τοῦ χώματος, Schol. Cp. Solon Frg. 28 Νείλου ἐπὶ προχοῆσι Κανωβίδος ἐγγύθεν ἀκτῆς.

848. τίθησιν: to Prometheus's prophetic vision the future is like the present. See on 109 and 211. — ἔμφρονα: Aeschylus has changed the story. The prevailing account (see on 561) was, according to the scholiast on Eur. *Phoen.* 678, ὁ Ζεὺς ἐπαφησάμενος τῆς Ἰοῦς πάλιν εἰς γυναῖκα μετεμόρφωσε. Cp. Ovid *Met.* i. 738 vultus capit illa priores, fitque quod ante fuit.

849. ἐπαφῶν: the word is chosen with reference to the name Ἔπαφος and its supposed etymology. Cp. *Suppl.* 46 ἐπωνυμίᾳ δ' ἐπεκραίνετο μόρσιμος αἰὼν εὐλόγως, Ἔπαφόν τ' ἐγέννασεν. The ease and painlessness of the transformation, expressed by ἐπαφῶν ἀταρβεῖ χειρί, is further emphasized by καὶ θιγὼν μόνον. Cp. *Suppl.*

850 ἐπώνυμον δὲ τῶν Διὸς γεννημάτων
τέξεις κελαινὸν Ἔπαφον· ὃς καρπώσεται
ὅσην πλατύρρους Νεῖλος ἀρδεύει χθόνα·
πέμπτη δ' ἀπ' αὐτοῦ γέννα πεντηκοντάπαις
πάλιν πρὸς Ἄργος οὐχ' ἑκοῦσ' ἐλεύσεται
855 θηλύσπορος, φεύγουσα συγγενῆ γάμον
ἀνεψιῶν· οἱ δ' ἐπτοημένοι φρένας,
κίρκοι πελειῶν οὐ μακρὰν λελειμμένοι,
ἥξουσι θηρεύοντες οὐ θηρασίμους
γάμους, φθόνον δὲ σωμάτων ἕξει θεός·
860 Πελασγία δὲ δέξεται θηλυκτόνῳ

676 δίψ δ' ἀτημάντῳ σθένει καὶ θείαις
ἐπιπνοίαις ταύεται, 1005 Ἰὼ πημονᾶς
ἐλύσατ' εὖ χειρὶ παιωνίᾳ κατασχεθών,
εὐμενεῖ βίᾳ κτίσας, 45 ἐξ ἐπιπνοίας
Ζηνὸς ἔψαψιν.

850. Prometheus, in saying τῶν
Διὸς γεννημάτων instead of τῆς Διὸς
ἐπαφῆς, hints at what is expressly
stated Suppl. 312 καὶ Ζεύς γ' ἐφάπτωρ
χειρὶ φιτύει γόνον. To this 834 above
also alludes. — ἐπώνυμον τῶν Διὸς
γεννημάτων: means "called after the
manner of his begetting" (by ἐπαφή).
Similarly Suppl. 314 Ἔπαφος ἀληθῶς
ῥυσίων ἐπώνυμος, where ῥύσια = "re-
storation by ἐπαφή."

851. τέξεις: the same form 809,
the middle form 768.

852. πλατύρρους: cp. Frg. 304
ἔνθα Νεῖλος ἑπτάρους. The uncon-
tracted -ροος appears in Frg. 280
πλεκτάνην χειμάρροον.

853. πέμπτη: see on 774.

854. οὐχ ἑκοῦσα: explained by
φεύγουσα . . . ἀνεψιῶν below. — ἐλεύσεται: ἐλεύσομαι recurs Suppl. 522.
Elsewhere the Attic poets use only
εἶμι.

855 f. συγγενῆ: gives the motive

for φεύγουσα. — ἀνεψιῶν: cp. Suppl.
320 Δαναὸς· ἀδελφὸς δ' ἐστὶ πεντακον-
τάπαις . . . Αἴγυπτος. — ἐπτοημένοι: cp.
Eur. Iph. A. 586 ἔρωτι δ' αὐτὸς ἐπ-
τοήθης, Sappho Frg. 2, 5 καὶ γελαίσας
ἱμερόεν, τό μοι μὰν καρδίαν ἐν στήθεσιν
ἐπτόασεν, Apoll. Rhod. Arg. i. 1232 τῆς
δὲ φρένας ἐπτοίησεν Κύπρις.

857. κίρκοι: the simile is added
without comparative conjunction, in
poetic fashion. For the comparison
cp. Suppl. 223 ἐν ἁγνῷ δ' ἐσμὸς ὡς
πελειάδων ἵζεσθε κίρκων τῶν ὁμοπτέρων
φόβῳ, Il. xxii. 130 ἠύτε κίρκος ὄρεσφιν
ἐλαφρότατος πετεεινῶν ῥηιδίως οἴμησε
μετὰ τρήρωνα πέλειαν.

859. φθόνον ἕξει: = φθονήσει. Cp.
χρείαν ἔχειν 109, and Cho. 481. The
sense: "God will begrudge them
their desire," σωμάτων τῶν παρθένων
φθονήσει αὐτοῖς (cp. 584), 'puella-
rum fructum deus maritis invidebit'
(Heyne). The marriage will be celebrated, but will be dissolved in blood.

860 f. Πελασγία: cp. Eur. Suppl.
367 καὶ μεγαλᾷ Πελασγίᾳ καὶ κατ' Ἄργος, Strabo p. 221 Αἰσχύλος ἐκ τοῦ περὶ
Μυκήνας Ἄργους φησὶν ἐν Ἱκέτισι καὶ
Δαναΐσι τὸ γένος αὐτῶν (i.e. τῶν Πελασ-

Ἄρει δαμέντων νυκτιφρουρήτῳ θράσει·
γυνὴ γὰρ ἄνδρ' ἕκαστον αἰῶνος στερεῖ,
δίθηκτον ἐν σφαγαῖσι βάψασα ξίφος·
τοιάδ' ἐπ' ἐχθροὺς τοὺς ἐμοὺς ἔλθοι Κύπρις.
865 μίαν δὲ παίδων ἵμερος θέλξει τὸ μὴ
κτεῖναι σύνευνον, ἀλλ' ἀπαμβλυνθήσεται
γνώμην· δυοῖν δὲ θάτερον βουλήσεται,
κλύειν ἄναλκις μᾶλλον ἢ μιαιφόνος·
αὕτη κατ' Ἄργος βασιλικὸν τέξει γένος.
870 μακροῦ λόγου δεῖ ταῦτ' ἐπεξελθεῖν τορῶς.

γῶν) καὶ τὴν Πελοπόννησον δὲ Πελασγίαν φησὶν Ἔφορος κληθῆναι. Argos (*Suppl.* 634), the land of Pelasgus (*Suppl.* 250), is meant.—δάξεται: both sense and syntax demand αἱμάξεται (= αἱμαχθήσεται, as Soph. *Phil.* 48 φυλάξεται = φυλαχθήσεται). Cp. *Ag.* 1589 θανὼν πατρῷον αἱμάξαι πέδον, *Pers.* 595 αἱμαχθεῖσα δ' ἄρουρα, Eur. *H. F.* 573 Δίρκης νᾶμα αἱμαχθήσεται. The verse would thus lack the usual caesura; but see on 640, and Introd. p. 26, footnote. —Ἄρει := φόνῳ. — δαμέντων: sc. αὐτῶν. GMT. 848; H. 972 a. —νυκτιφρουρήτῳ: τῷ νυκτὸς ἐπιτηρήσαντι, Schol. More exactly *night-waking, awake at night.* See on 599.

. 862. ἕκαστον: goes in sense with γυνή as well as ἄνδρα. —αἰῶνος στερεῖ: cp. *Il.* xxii. 58 αὐτὸς δὲ φίλης αἰῶνος ἀμερθῇς, xvi. 453 ἐπὴν δὴ τόν γε λίπῃ ψυχή τε καὶ αἰών.

863. ἐν σφαγαῖσι βάψασα ξίφος: cp. Soph. *Ai.* 95 ἔβαψας ἔγχος εὖ πρὸς Ἀργείων στρατῷ. The phrase ἐν σφαγαῖσι = ἐν φόνῳ, *in the blood of the slaughtered men.* Blomfield, after Ruhnken, explains ἐν σφαγαῖσι as 'in iugulo,' comparing Eur. *Or.* 291 μήποτε τεκούσης εἰς σφαγὰς ὦσαι ξίφος, Aristot. *Hist. An.* i. 14 κοινὸν δὲ μέρος

αὐχένος καὶ στήθους σφαγή (in animals), Polyaen. viii. 48 τὸ ξίφος καθεῖσα διὰ τῆς σφαγῆς, Antonin. Liberal. 25 ἐπάταξαν ἑαυτὰς τῇ περκίδι παρὰ τὴν κλεῖδα καὶ ἀνέρρηξαν τὴν σφαγήν.

864. With this wish cp. *Suppl.* 1032 μηδ' ὑπ' ἀνάγκας γάμος ἔλθοι Κυθερείας· στυγερῶν πέλοι τόδ' ἄθλον, Xen. *Anab.* iii. 2. 3 οἶμαι γὰρ ἂν ὑμᾶς τοιαῦτα παθεῖν, οἷα τοὺς ἐχθροὺς οἱ θεοὶ ποιήσειαν.

865. μίαν: Hypermnestra; see on 774. —θέλξει τὸ μή: see on 236.

866. ἀπαμβλυνθήσεται: 'ἀπαμβλύνειν ut ἀμβλύνειν de impetu animi retardato ponitur. Comparatio a retusa ferri acie ducta est. Sic *Sept.* 715 τεθηγμένον τοί μ' οὐκ ἀπαμβλυνεῖς λόγῳ' (Schütz). Cp. the words of Hypermnestra in Ovid. *Her.* xiv. 7 esse ream praestat quam sic placuisse parenti; non piget immunes caedis habere manus.

869 f. Prometheus begins as if about to tell the whole story, but suddenly breaks off. Hence the asyndeton μακροῦ λόγου δεῖ. With μακροῦ λόγου cp. *Pers.* 713, πάντα γὰρ ἀκούσει μῦθον ἐν βραχεῖ λόγῳ.

σπορᾶς γε μὴν ἐκ τῆσδε φύσεται θρασὺς
τόξοισι κλεινὸς ὃς πόνων ἐκ τῶνδ' ἐμὲ
λύσει. τοιόνδε χρησμὸν ἡ παλαιγενὴς
μήτηρ ἐμοὶ διῆλθε Τιτανὶς Θέμις·
875 ὅπως δὲ χὦπῃ, ταῦτα δεῖ μακροῦ λόγου
εἰπεῖν, σύ τ' οὐδὲν ἐκμαθοῦσα κερδανεῖς.

ιω.

ἐλελεῦ, ἐλελεῦ,
ὑπό μ' αὖ σφάκελος καὶ φρενοπλῆγες
μανίαι θάλπουσ', οἴστρου δ' ἄρδις
880 χρίει μ' ἄπυρος·

874. διῆλθε: like διεῖπε, set forth
fully. — Τιτανὶς Θέμις: see on 210.
875. ὅπως, ὅπῃ: these are joined,
to include every possible circumstance. For the ellipsis cp. 915.
What Prometheus here passes over,
the spectator learns in the Προμηθεὺς
λυόμενος.
877 ff. As a motive for Io's departure, the poet employs a fresh accession of madness (οἴστρος). 'Io
primos tantum furoris impetus verbis
describit, reliquos vero scena egressa
spectatoris imaginationi coniciendos
relinquit' (Schütz). — ἐλελεῦ: θρηνῶ-
δες ἐπίφθεγμα, Schol. ἐλελεῦ· ἐπιφώ-
νημα πολεμικόν· οἱ δὲ, προαναφώνησις
παιανισμοῦ· τίθησι δὲ αὐτὸ Αἰσχύλος
ἐπὶ σχετλιασμοῦ ἐν Προμηθεῖ δεσμώτῃ,
Hesych. The battle-cry serves to
depict the fury of madness. — ὑπό...
θάλπουσι: see on 574. In trimeter,
Aeschylus nowhere interposes important words, or several words, between
preposition and verb, except in Ag.
1215 and the doubtful passage Sept.
1028. ὑπό here implies inception,
"begins to burn." For θάλπειν cp.
Ag. 1256 παπαῖ, οἷον τὸ πῦρ· ἐπέρ-
χεται δέ μοι, spoken by Casandra,

seized with prophetic mania. — σφάκελος: σπασμὸς τοῦ ἐγκεφάλου, Schol.
Cp. Eur. Hipp. 1351 διά μου κεφαλᾶς
ᾄσσουσ' ὀδύναι, κατὰ δ' ἐγκέφαλον πηδᾷ
σφάκελος. — ἄρδις: ἀκίς, Αἰσχύλος Προμηθεῖ δεσμώτῃ, Hesych.
880. ἄπυρος: the scholiast explains, ἡ πολύπυρος διὰ τὸ σφοδρὸν πά-
θος (assuming 'alpha intensivum')
ἢ πῦρ μὴ ἔχουσα. The latter interpretation, in the sense of 'telum igni
non admotum, sine igne factum,' was
shown to be right by Schütz and
Hermann. 'Adiectivo ἄπυρος telum
metaphorice dictum a proprie sic ap-
pellato discrevit Aeschylus' (Schütz).
Cp. Cho. 493 πέδαις ἀχαλκεύτοις (of
Clytaemnestra's entangling noose),
Frg. 298, 4 ἄπτεροι πελειάδες (of the
Pleiades), Ag. 1258 δίπους λέαινα (of
Clytaemnestra), Sept. 64 κῦμα χερσαῖον
στρατοῦ, ibid. 942 ὁ πόντιος ξεῖνος ἐκ
πυρὸς συθείς (the sword), Soph. Trach.
874 βέβηκε Δηιάνειρα τὴν πανυστάτην
ὁδῶν ἁπασῶν ἐξ ἀκινήτου ποδός, O. T.
190 Ἄρεα ... ὃς νῦν ἄχαλκος ἀσπίδων
(the pest), Eur. Frg. 698 αἰδοῦς ἀχαλ-
κεύτοισιν ἔζευκται πέδαις, Iph. T. 1095
ἄπτερος ὄρνις, Or. 621 ὑφῆψε δῶμ' ἀνη-
φαίστῳ πυρί.

κραδία δὲ φόβῳ φρένα λακτίζει·
τροχοδινεῖται δ' ὄμμαθ' ἑλίγδην,
ἔξω δὲ δρόμου φέρομαι λύσσης
πνεύματι μάργῳ, γλώσσης ἀκρατής·
885 θολεροὶ δὲ λόγοι παίουσ' εἰκῇ
στυγνῆς πρὸς κύμασιν ἄτης.

ΧΟΡΟΣ.
στροφή.

ἦ σοφὸς ἦ σοφὸς ὃς

881. **φρένα**: see on 361. — For the conception cp. *Cho.* 165 ὀρχεῖται δὲ καρδία φόβῳ, 1025 πρὸς δὲ καρδία φόβος ᾄδειν ἕτοιμος, ἡ δ' ὑπορχεῖσθαι κρότῳ, *Ag.* 996 πρὸς ἐνδίκοις φρεσὶν τελεσφόραις δίναις κυκλούμενον κέαρ, *Il.* vii. 216 Ἕκτορί τ' αὐτῷ θυμὸς ἐνὶ στήθεσσι πάτασσεν.

882. **τροχοδινεῖται**: cp. στροφοδινοῦνται, *Ag.* 51.

883. **ἔξω δρόμου φέρομαι**: (δρόμος = track) cp. *Cho.* 1022 ὥσπερ ξὺν ἵπποις ἡνιοστροφῶ δρόμου ἐξωτέρω· φέρουσι γὰρ νικώμενον φρένες δύσαρκτοι, *Ag.* 1245 ἐκ δρόμου πεσὼν τρέχω. Also Engl. 'be deranged.'

884. **γλώσσης ἀκρατής**: cp. Theogn. 503 οἰνοβαρέω κεφαλήν ... γλώσσης οὐκέτ' ἐγὼ ταμίης ἡμετέρης, τὸ δὲ δῶμα περιτρέχει, Lucret. iii. 453, claudicat ingenium, delirat lingua.

885 f. **θολεροί**: Hesych. θολερόν· ταραχῶδες, ἀκάθαρτον, βορβορῶδες, τεταραγμένον. Cp. Schol. *Ai.* 206 (θολερῷ χειμῶνι νοσήσας). The adjective suggests the mud (κελαινὰν θῖνα, Soph. *Ant.* 589) stirred up from the bottom of the sea by the waves. Io's words are like this; they beat against the billows of madness and are tossed by

them at random (εἰκῇ, corresponding to foregoing ἀκρατὴς γλώσσης), so as to be planless and incoherent. — **παίουσι πρὸς κύμασιν**: cp. Eur. *Hec.* 116 πολλῆς δ' ἔριδος συνέπαισε κλύδων.

887–906. **Third Stasimon.** For the dactylo-epitritic rhythms, see on 526. The tranquil reflexions of the chorus contrast agreeably with the turmoil of the preceding scene.

887. **ἦ σοφός**: the scholiast explains that Pittacus is meant, who, when consulted by a man in doubt whether to marry a rich woman, or a poorer one whose rank was the same as his own, directed his questioner to listen to a group of boys who were playing at tops close by. These were heard to cry τὴν καθ' ἑαυτὸν ἔλαυνε. An epigram of Callimachus, in Diog. Laert. i. 80, gives τὴν κατὰ σαυτὸν ἔλα. Another scholiast compares Pind. *Pyth.* ii. 64 χρὴ δὲ καθ' αὑτὸν αἰεὶ παντὸς ὁρᾶν μέτρον, εὐναὶ δὲ παράτροποι ἐς κακότατ' ἀθρόαν ἔβαλον ποτὶ κοῖτον ἰόντα. — In like manner a proverb is introduced in Soph. *Ant.* 620 σοφίᾳ γὰρ ἔκ του κλεινὸν ἔπος πέφανται. Cp. *Ag.* 369 οὐκ ἔφα τις θεοὺς βροτῶν ἀξιοῦσθαι μέλειν κτέ., 750 παλαίφατος δ' ἐν βροτοῖς γέρων

πρῶτος ἐν γνώμᾳ τόδ' ἐβάστασε καὶ γλώσσᾳ δια-
μυθολόγησεν,
890 ὡς τὸ κηδεῦσαι καθ' ἑαυτὸν ἀριστεύει μακρῷ,
. καὶ μήτε τῶν πλούτῳ διαθρυπτομένων
μήτε τῶν γέννᾳ μεγαλυνομένων
ὄντα χερνήταν ἐραστεῦσαι γάμων.

ἀντιστροφή.

μήποτε μήποτέ μ', ὦ
895 ⟨πότνιαι⟩ Μοῖραι, λεχέων Διὸς εὐνάτειραν ἴδοισθε
πέλουσαν·
μηδὲ πλαθείην γαμέτᾳ τινὶ τῶν ἐξ οὐρανοῦ.
ταρβῶ γὰρ ἀστεργάνορα παρθενίαν
εἰσορῶσ' Ἰοῦς ἀμαλαπτομέναν
900 δυσπλάνοις Ἥρας ἀλατείαις πόνων.

λόγος τέτυκται, Cho. 313 δράσαντι παθεῖν τριγέρων μῦθος τάδε φωνεῖ.—On the
omission of ἣν see Krüger I. § 62, 1, 6.

888. ἐβάστασε: *weighed* (by lifting).
The scholiast explains by ἐδοκίμασεν,
and quotes *Od.* xxi. 405 ἐπεὶ μέγα τόξον
ἐβάστασε καὶ ἴδε πάντῃ. Cp. Ar. *Thesm.*
438 πάσας δ' ἰδέας ἐξήτασεν, πάντα δ'
ἐβάστασεν φρενί, Polyb. viii. 18 τῶν
ἐβάστασε πρᾶγμα καὶ πᾶσαν ἐπίνοιαν
ἐψηλάφα.

891 f. διαθρυπτομένων, μεγαλυνομένων: the assonance is significant;
wealth and birth are equally valueless.

895 f. εὐνάτειραν ... πλαθείην: cp.
Soph. *O. T.* 1099 τίς σ' ἔτικτε τᾶν
μακραιώνων ἄρα Πανὸς ὀρεσσιβάτα πατρὸς πελασθεῖσ', ἢ σέ γ' εὐνάτειρα Λοξίου; — τῶν ἐξ οὐρανοῦ: as
902 κρεισσόνων θεῶν. The preposition
ἐξ conveys the notion "descending to
me from heaven." See on 702.

898. ἀστεργάνορα παρθενίαν: '"vir-
ginitatem viri sive proci non aman-

tem" ut φυξανορίᾳ *Suppl.* v. 9 "proco-
rum fuga." Odium erga Iovem Io
ipsa prodiderat v. 759' (Schütz). Cp.
στυγάνορα 724, γάμον δυσάνορα *Suppl.*
1064.

899. ἀμαλαπτομέναν: cp. Lycophr.
34 ἡμάλαψε κάρχαρος κύων, Hesych.
ἡμαλάψαι· κρύψαι, ἀφανίσαι (read ἡμά-
λαψε· ἔκρυψε, ἠφάνισε)· Σοφοκλῆς
'Ὀδυσσεῖ μαινομένῳ. Also Photius p.
68, 3 ἡμάλαπτεν· ἔκρυπτεν, ἠφάνιζεν,
Hesych. ἀμαλόν· ἀπαλόν, ἀσθενῆ (Eur.
Heracl. 75).

900. δυσπλάνοις ἀλατείαις: cp. *Ag.*
1136 κακόποτμοι τύχαι, *Pers.* 711 βίοτον εὐαίωνα, Soph. *O. C.* 716 εὐήρετ-
μος πλάτα, *Ai.* 138 λόγος κακόθρους,
Eur. *Hipp.* 200 εὐήχεις χεῖρας.—
ἀλατείαις πόνων: for the qualitative
force of the attributive genitive see
Krüger II. § 47, 5, 2; and cp. Eur.
Iph. A. 1230 πόνων τιθηνοὺς ἀποδιδοῦσά
σοι τροφάς, *Bacch.* 1218 μόχθων (usually read μοχθῶν) μυρίοις ζητήμασι,
Soph. *Ai.* 888 τὸν μακρῶν ἀλάταν πόνων.

ἰπῳδός.

ἐμοὶ δὲ τιόμενος ὁμαλὸς ὁ γάμος ἄφοβος
[οὐ δέδια] μηδὲ κρεισσόνων θεῶν
ἔρως ἄφυκτον ὄμμα προσδράκοι με.
ἀπόλεμος ὅδε γ᾽ ὁ πόλεμος, ἄπορα πόριμος·
905   οὐδ᾽ ἔχω τίς ἂν γενοίμαν·
τὰν Διὸς γὰρ οὐχ ὁρῶ
μῆτιν ὅπα φύγοιμ᾽ ἄν.

ΠΡΟΜΗΘΕΥΣ.

ἦ μὴν ἔτι Ζεὺς καίπερ αὐθάδης φρενῶν
ἔσται ταπεινός, οἷον ἐξαρτύεται

901. ἐμοὶ τιόμενος: sc. ἐστί. Cp. *Pers.* 1000 ἔταφον, οὐκ ἀμφὶ σκηναῖς τροχηλάτοισιν ὕπιθεν ἑπόμενοι (sc. εἰσίν), Eur. *Ion* 517 ἦ γὰρ ἀρχὴ τοῦ λόγου πρέπουσά μοι, also *Eum.* 546 ξενοτίμους ἐπιστροφὰς δωμάτων αἰδόμενός τις ἔστω.—ὁμαλὸς ὁ γάμος: = ὁμαλὸς ἂν ὁ γάμος, "when the union is equal (between equals)."

902 f. θεῶν ἔρως: poetical for θεοὶ ἐρῶντες. —ἄφυκτον ὄμμα κτέ.: free cognate accus. In place of δέργμα προσδέρκεσθαι is said ὄμμα (= ὄψιν) προσδέρκεσθαι. Cp. *Pers.* 81 λεύσσων δέργμα, 305 πήδημ᾽ ἀφήλατο. For the whole construction (direct object and cognate accusative), cp. Eur. *Phoen.* 293 γονυπετεῖς ἕδρας προσπίτνω σ᾽ ἄναξ, *Or.* 1020 ὥς σ᾽ ἰδοῦσ᾽ ἐν ὄμμασι πανυστάτην πρόσοψιν ἐξέστην φρενῶν. Krüger. II. § 46, 12, 1.

904. ἀπόλεμος ὁ πόλεμος: cp. *Ag.* 1142 νόμον ἄνομον, *Eum.* 1033 παῖδες ἄπαιδες, *Pers.* 680 νᾶες ἄναες, Eur. *H. F.* 1133 ἀπόλεμον πόλεμον, Soph. *Ai.* 665 ἄδωρα δῶρα, *El.* 1154 μήτηρ ἀμήτωρ, *O. T.* 1214 ἄγαμος γάμος.— ἄπορα πόριμος: the verbal noun πόριμος takes the regimen of its verb, as

Cho. 23 χοὰς προπομπός, *Pers.* 981 μυρία πεμπαστάν, *Suppl.* 594 τὸ πᾶν μῆχαρ οὔριος Ζεύς, *Ag.* 1090 πολλὰ συνίστορα (στέγην) αὐτόφονα κακά, also *Suppl.* 149 ἀδμῆτας ἀδμῆτα ῥύσιος γενέσθω (= ῥυσάσθω), Soph. *Ant.* 787 καί σε φύξιμος (= φεύγειν δύναται), Eur. *Iph. A.* 1255 ἐγὼ τά τ᾽ οἰκτρὰ συνετός εἰμι καὶ τὰ μή, Lys. III. 27 ταῦτα ἐξαρνός ἐστι, [Plat.] *Alc.* II. 141 d ἀνήκοον εἶναι χθιζά τε καὶ πρωΐζα γεγενημένα, Plat. *Charm.* 158 c ἐξάρνῳ εἶναι τὰ ἐρωτώμενα. G. 158, Ν. 3; H. 713.

905. τίς ἂν γενοίμαν: equivalent to the more usual τί ἂν γενοίμαν.

906. Cp. 551, and *Il.* viii. 143 ἀνὴρ δέ κεν οὔτι Διὸς νόον εἰρύσσαιτο οὐδὲ μάλ᾽ ἴφθιμος, ἐπεὶ ἦ πολὺ φέρτερός ἐστιν, Hesiod *O. D.* 105 οὕτως οὔτι πῃ ἔστι Διὸς νόον ἐξαλέασθαι.

907-943. First Scene of the Exodos. Prometheus and the Coryphaeus. Preparation of the catastrophe.

907. ἦ μὴν ἔτι: cp. 167. — αὐθάδης φρενῶν: genitive of relation. Krüger I. § 47, 26, 9; II. § 47, 26, 7.

908. οἷον: = ὅτι τοιοῦτον. Cp. *Od.* ii. 239 νῦν δ᾽ ἄλλῳ δήμῳ νεμεσίζομαι,

γάμον γαμεῖν· ὃς αὐτὸν ἐκ τυραννίδος
910 θρόνων τ᾽ ἄιστον ἐκβαλεῖ· πατρὸς δ᾽ ἀρὰ
Κρόνου τότ᾽ ἤδη παντελῶς κρανθήσεται,
ἣν ἐκπίτνων ἠρᾶτο δηναιῶν θρόνων.

τοιῶνδε μόχθων ἐκτροπὴν οὐδεὶς θεῶν
δύναιτ᾽ ἂν αὐτῷ πλὴν ἐμοῦ δεῖξαι σαφῶς.
915 ἐγὼ τάδ᾽ οἶδα χᾠ̂ τρόπῳ. πρὸς ταῦτα νῦν
θαρσῶν καθήσθω τοῖς πεδαρσίοις κτύποις
πιστὸς τινάσσων τ᾽ ἐν χεροῖν πύρπνουν βέλος.
οὐδὲν γὰρ αὐτῷ ταῦτ᾽ ἐπαρκέσει τὸ μὴ οὐ
πεσεῖν ἀτίμως πτώματ᾽ οὐκ ἀνασχετά·
920 τοῖον παλαιστὴν νῦν παρασκευάζεται
ἐπ᾽ αὐτὸς αὑτῷ, δυσμαχώτατον τέρας·
ὃς δὴ κεραυνοῦ κρεῖσσον᾽ εὑρήσει φλόγα
βροντῆς θ᾽ ὑπερβάλλοντα καρτερὸν κτύπον·

οἷον ἔπαντες ἦσθ᾽ ἄνεῳ, Il. xxii. 346
αἱ γάρ τοι αὐτόν με μένος καὶ θυμὸς
ἀνοίη ὅμ᾽ ἀποταμνόμενον κρέα ἔδμεναι,
οἷά μ᾽ ἔοργας, Eur. H. F. 816 ἆρ᾽ εἰς
τὸν αὐτὸν πίτυλον ἥκομεν φόβου, οἷον
φάσμ᾽ ὑπὲρ δόμων ὁρῶ; Ion 796 ἂν᾽
ὑγρὸν ἀμπετάην αἰθέρα . . ., οἷον οἷον
ἄλγος ἔπαθον, Ar. Nub. 1157 οὐδὲν
γάρ ἂν με φλαῦρον ἐργάσαισθ᾽ ἔτι, οἷος
ἐμοὶ τρέφεται, Hdt. i. 31 αἱ δὲ Ἀργεῖαι
τὴν μητέρα αὐτῶν (ἐμακάριζον), οἵων
τέκνων ἐκύρησε, viii. 12 ἐς φόβον κατι-
στέατο ἐλπίζοντες πάγχυ ἀπολέεσθαι, ἐς
οἷα κακὰ ἧκον.

910. ἄιστον ἐκβαλεῖ: i.e. ἐκβαλεῖ
ὥστε ἄιστον εἶναι. For ἄιστος see on
151.

911. Κρόνου . . . κρανθήσεται: alliteration of κρ-.

915 f. πρὸς ταῦτα: see on 902.—
πεδαρσίοις: see on 269.

917. πύρπνουν βέλος: see on 359.
For the contracted form πύρπνουν see

on 852, and Soph. Ant. 224 δύσπνους
ἰσάνω. In melic passages only -πνοσς
is used.

920. τοῖον: demonstratives at the
beginning of a sentence often state
the cause or reason of what goes
before, in Greek as in Latin. Cp.
Soph. Ai. 560 οὗτοι σ᾽ Ἀχαιῶν, οἶδα,
μή τις ὑβρίσῃ . . . τοῖον πυλωρὸν φύλακα
Τεῦκρον ἀμφί σοι λείψω.

921. ἐπ᾽ αὐτὸς αὑτῷ: see on 762.

922. κεραυνοῦ: κεραυνός, ignea
coruscatio; βροντή, fragor
caeli tonantis.

923. βροντῆς ὑπερβάλλοντα: ὑπερ-
βάλλειν takes the genitive, as a verb
of surpassing, here and Plat. Gorg.
475 c ἆρα λύπῃ ὑπερβάλλει τὸ ἀδικεῖν
τοῦ ἀδικεῖσθαι; also Aristot. Hist. An.
ii. 11 πολὺ ὑπερβάλλοντες τῶν περὶ τὰ
λοιπὰ ὑπαρχόντων. Cp. the use of
ὑπερφέρω (Soph. O. T. 380 τέχνη
τέχνης ὑπερφέρουσα) and ὑπερέχειν

θαλασσίαν τε, γῆς τινάκτειραν νόσον,
925 τρίαιναν, αἰχμὴν τὴν Ποσειδῶνος, σκεδᾷ.
πταίσας δὲ τῷδε πρὸς κακῷ μαθήσεται
ὅσον τό τ᾽ ἄρχειν καὶ τὸ δουλεύειν δίχα.

ΧΟΡΟΣ.

σύ θην ἃ χρήζεις, ταῦτ᾽ ἐπιγλωσσᾷ Διός.

ΠΡΟΜΗΘΕΥΣ.

ἅπερ τελεῖται, πρὸς δ᾽ ἃ βούλομαι λέγω.

ΧΟΡΟΣ.

930 καὶ προσδοκᾶν χρὴ δεσπόσειν Ζηνός τινα;

ΠΡΟΜΗΘΕΥΣ.

καὶ τῶνδέ γ᾽ ἕξει δυσλοφωτέρους πόνους.

(Plat. *Gorg.* 475 c οὐκ ἄρα λύπῃ γε ὑπερέχει, following the words quoted above).

924 f. **θαλασσίαν τρίαιναν**: cp. Eur. *Ion* 282 πληγαὶ τριαίνης ποντίου.— **νόσον**: 'ubi Latinis pestis, noxa aut calamitas, ibi Graecis νόσος in usu est' (Schütz). Cp. Soph. *Ant.* 418 καὶ τότ᾽ ἐξαίφνης χθονὸς τυφὼς ἀείρας σκηπτόν, οὐράνιον ἄχος, πίμπλησι πεδίον· ... μύσαντες δ᾽ εἴχομεν θείαν νόσον.— According to Pindar *Isthm.* vii. 60 ff., the sagacious Themis, when Zeus and Poseidon sought the hand of Thetis, announced to the gods, εἵνεκεν πεπρωμένον ἦν φέρτερον γόνον ἄνακτα πατρὸς τεκεῖν ποντίαν θεόν, ὃς κεραυνοῦ τε κρίσσον ἄλλο βέλος διώξει χερὶ τριόδοντός τ᾽ ἀμαιμακέτου, Δἰ γε μισγομέναν ἢ Διὸς παρ᾽ ἀδελφεοῖσιν. Aeschylus, for the sake of effect, has retained the part of the prophecy relating to Poseidon, although its occasion — the competition of Poseidon for Thetis's hand — is absent from his account. One may understand him to mean that Poseidon's dominion would perish along with Zeus's.

926. **πταίσας τῷδε πρὸς κακῷ**: cp. *Sept.* 210 νεὼς καμούσης ποντίῳ πρὸς κύματι.

927. For **τέ ... καί** with a word meaning 'differ' or 'different,' cp. Soph. *O. C.* 808 χωρὶς τό τ᾽ εἰπεῖν πολλὰ καὶ τὰ καίρια, Eur. *Alc.* 528 χωρὶς τό τ᾽ εἶναι καὶ τὸ μὴ νομίζεται, Xen. *Hier.* i. 2 πῇ διαφέρει ὁ τυραννικός τε καὶ ὁ ἰδιωτικὸς βίος. See Elmsley on Soph. *l.c.*

928. **θήν**: this particle is chiefly epic. Krüg. II. § 69, 38.— **ἐπιγλωσσᾷ**: *prophesy ill, utter ominous words;* ἐποιωνίζῃ κατὰ τοῦ Διὸς ἃ βούλει γενέσθαι αὐτῷ, Schol. So Hesych. ἐπιγλωσσᾶ· ἐποιωνίζου διὰ γλώττης, Αἰσχύλος Ἡρακλείδαις. Cp. *Cho.* 1044 μηδ᾽ ἐπιζευχθῇς στόμα φήμῃ πονηρᾷ μηδ᾽ ἐπιγλωσσῶ κακά, Ar. *Lys.* 37 περὶ τῶν Ἀθηνῶν δ᾽ οὐκ ἐπιγλωττήσομαι τοιοῦτον οὐδέν.

929. **τελεῖται**: may be either future or present (see on 211). — **πρὸς δ᾽**: see on 73.

931. **τῶνδε**: τῶν ἐμῶν.

ΧΟΡΟΣ.

πῶς δ' οὐχὶ ταρβεῖς τοιάδ' ἐκρίπτων ἔπη;

ΠΡΟΜΗΘΕΥΣ.

τί δ' ἂν φοβοίμην ᾧ θανεῖν οὐ μόρσιμον;

ΧΟΡΟΣ.

ἀλλ' ἆθλον ἄν σοι τοῦδ' ἔτ' ἀλγίω πόροι.

ΠΡΟΜΗΘΕΥΣ.

935 ὁ δ' οὖν ποιείτω· πάντα προσδοκητά μοι.

ΧΟΡΟΣ.

οἱ προσκυνοῦντες τὴν Ἀδράστειαν σοφοί.

ΠΡΟΜΗΘΕΥΣ.

σέβου, προσεύχου, θῶπτε τὸν κρατοῦντ' ἀεί.
ἐμοὶ δ' ἔλασσον Ζηνὸς ἢ μηδὲν μέλει.
δράτω, κρατείτω τόνδε τὸν βραχὺν χρόνον
940 ὅπως θέλει· δαρὸν γὰρ οὐκ ἄρξει θεοῖς.

932. ἐκρίπτων: see on 312.

933. ᾧ θανεῖν οὐ μόρσιμον: the thought recurs 1053; in a different relation 753 and Frg. III. of the Προμηθεὺς λυόμενος 23 f.

934. Cp. 313.

936. οἱ προσκυνοῦντες τὴν Ἀδράστειαν: Hesych. Ἀδράστια· ἡ Νέμεσις. 'Ad vitandam invidiam Graeci solebant dicere προσκυνῶ τὴν Νέμεσιν. Dem. adv. Aristogit. I. p. 496 [xxv. 37] καὶ Ἀδράστειαν μὲν ἄνθρωπος ὢν ἔγωγε προσκυνῶ, Plat. Rep. v. 451 a προσκυνῶ δὲ Ἀδράστειαν, ὦ Γλαύκων, χάριν οὗ μέλλω λέγειν' (Giacomelli). Cp. also Eur. Rhes. 342 Ἀδράστεια μὲν ἁ Διὸς παῖς εἴργοι στομάτων φθόνον, 408 σὺν δ' Ἀδραστείᾳ λέγω, ... ξὺν σοὶ στρατεύσειν γῆν ἐπ' Ἀργείων θέλω καὶ πᾶσαν ἐλθὼν Ἑλλάδ' ἐκπέρσαι δορί, Alciphr. Ep. i. 33 προσκυνῶ δὲ τὴν Νέμεσιν, Soph. Phil. 776 τὸν φθόνον δὲ πρόσκυσον.

937. σέβου, προσεύχου, θῶπτε: cp. 302. — τὸν κρατοῦντ' ἀεί := τὸν ἀεί (for the time being) κρατοῦντα. Cp. Eur. Or. 889 ὑπὸ τοῖς δυναμένοισιν ὢν ἀεί, Ar. Vesp. 1318 κωμῳδολοιχῶν περὶ τὸν εὖ πράττοντ' ἀεί, Plut. 1020 φάσκων βοηθεῖν τοῖς ἀδικουμένοις ἀεί, Xen. Cyr. viii. 5. 16.

938. ἔλασσον ἢ μηδέν: cp. Plat. Theaet. 179 e ἧττον αὐτοῖς ἔνι ἢ τὸ μηδέν. The abstract idea of nothingness is expressed by μηδέν (not οὐδέν) or τὸ μηδέν. Cp. Soph. Ai. 1275 ἤδη τὸ μηδὲν ὄντας, El. 1166 δέξαι με τὴν μηδὲν εἰς τὸ μηδέν, Eur. Cycl. 355 ἄλλως νομίζει Ζεὺς τὸ μηδὲν ὢν θεός, Soph. Ai. 1231 ὅτ' οὐδὲν ὢν τοῦ μηδὲν ἀντίστης ὕπερ.

939. δράτω, κρατείτω: cp. Ag. 1609 πράσσε, πιαίνου μιαίνων τὴν δίκην, ἐπεὶ πάρα, Soph. Ant. 768 δράτω, φρονείτω μεῖζον ἢ κατ' ἄνδρ' ἰών.

940. ἄρξει θεοῖς: see on 40.

ἀλλ' εἰσορῶ γὰρ τόνδε τὸν Διὸς τρόχιν,
τὸν τοῦ τυράννου τοῦ νέου διάκονον,
πάντως τι καινὸν ἀγγελῶν ἐλήλυθε.

ΕΡΜΗΣ.

σὲ τὸν σοφιστήν, τὸν πικρῶς ὑπέρπικρον,
945 τὸν ἐξαμαρτόντ' εἰς θεοὺς ἐφημέροις
πορόντα τιμάς, τὸν πυρὸς κλέπτην λέγω·
πατὴρ ἄνωγέ σ' οὕστινας κομπεῖς γάμους
αὐδᾶν, πρὸς ὧν ἐκεῖνος ἐκπίπτει κράτους·
καὶ ταῦτα μέντοι μηδὲν αἰνικτηρίως,
950 ἀλλ' αὖθ' ἕκαστ' ἔκφραζε· μηδέ μοι διπλᾶς
ὁδούς, Προμηθεῦ, προσβάλῃς· ὁρᾷς δ' ὅτι
Ζεὺς τοῖς τοιούτοις οὐχὶ μαλθακίζεται.

ΠΡΟΜΗΘΕΥΣ.

σεμνόστομός γε καὶ φρονήματος πλέως
ὁ μῦθός ἐστιν, ὡς θεῶν ὑπηρέτου.

941. ἀλλ' εἰσορῶ γάρ: cp. Eur. Hec. 724 ἀλλ' εἰσορῶ γὰρ τοῦδε δεσπότου δόμας Ἀγαμέμνονος, τοὐνθένδε σιγῶμεν, φίλαι.—τρόχιν: Hesych., τρόχις· ἄγγελος, ἀκόλουθος. Here, however, a contemptuous designation of the divine messenger, as διάκονος τοῦ νέου τυράννου. So throughout the following scene Hermes is treated with lofty disdain by Prometheus. The phrase Διὸς τρόχις suffices for the spectators, without mention of the name. τρόχις furthermore alludes to Hermes's winged shoes, and it is probable that he is swung from above upon the stage, by means of the αἰώρημα (see on 284).

944–1039. Second Scene of the Exodos. Prometheus and Hermes. Development of the catastrophe.

944. σοφιστήν: see on 62. — τὸν πικρῶς ὑπέρπικρον: see on 328.

945. Cp. 82.

948. ἐκπίπτει: see on 171.

949. μηδὲν αἰνικτηρίως: cp. 610.

950. αὖθ' ἕκαστα: everything as it really is, = "explicitly." Cp. Eur. Phoen. 404 ταῦτ' αὖθ' ἕκαστα, μῆτερ, οὐχὶ περιπλοκὰς λόγων ἀθροίσας, εἶπον, Or. 1393 σαφῶς λέγ' ἡμῖν αὖθ' ἕκαστα τὰν δόμοις.

952. τοῖς τοιούτοις : the Schol. wrongly interprets τοῖς μὴ πειθομένοις αὐτῷ. The words are neuter, and refer to the shifts and evasions just mentioned. For τοιούτοις see on 237.

954. Cp. Eur. Tro. 424 ἦ δεινὸς ὁ λάτρις· τί ποτ' ἔχουσι τοὔνομα κήρυκες; ἓν ἀπέχθημα πάγκοινον βροτοῖς οἱ περὶ τυράννους καὶ πόλεις ὑπηρέται.

955 νέον νέοι κρατεῖτε καὶ δοκεῖτε δὴ
ναίειν ἀπενθῆ πέργαμ'· οὐκ ἐκ τῶνδ' ἐγὼ
δισσοὺς τυράννους ἐκπεσόντας ᾐσθόμην;
τρίτον δὲ τὸν νῦν κοιρανοῦντ' ἐπόψομαι
αἴσχιστα καὶ τάχιστα. μή τί σοι δοκῶ
960 ταρβεῖν ὑποπτήσσειν τε τοὺς νέους θεούς;
πολλοῦ γε καὶ τοῦ παντὸς ἐλλείπω. σὺ δὲ
κέλευθον ἥνπερ ἦλθες ἐγκόνει πάλιν·
πεύσει γὰρ οὐδὲν ὧν ἀνιστορεῖς ἐμέ.

ΕΡΜΗΣ.

τοιοῖσδε μέντοι καὶ πρὶν αὐθαδίσμασιν
965 ἐς τάσδε σαυτὸν πημονὰς καθώρμισας.

ΠΡΟΜΗΘΕΥΣ.

τῆς σῆς λατρείας τὴν ἐμὴν δυσπραξίαν,
σαφῶς ἐπίστασ', οὐκ ἂν ἀλλάξαιμ' ἐγώ.

ΕΡΜΗΣ.

κρεῖσσον γὰρ οἶμαι τῇδε λατρεύειν πέτρᾳ
ἢ πατρὶ φῦναι Ζηνὶ πιστὸν ἄγγελον.

955. **νέον κρατεῖτε**: sce on 35.

956. **πέργαμα**: Servius on Verg. *Aen.* i. 96 propter Pergama quae altissima fuerunt: ex quibus omnia alta aedificia pergama vocantur, sicut Aeschylus dicit.

957. **δισσοὺς τυράννους**: Uranus and Cronus.

959. **αἴσχιστα καὶ τάχιστα**: sc. ἐκπίπτοντα. — The assonance is effective; cp. 480,601,891 f.,Soph.*Ant.*1327 βράχιστα γὰρ κράτιστα τὰν ποσὶν κακά.

961. **πολλοῦ γε καὶ τοῦ παντὸς ἐλλείπω**: cp. 1006. πολλοῦ γε δεῖ or πολλοῦ γε καὶ δεῖ (*il s'en faut bien*) is a common expression.

962. **ἐγκόνει πάλιν**: a contemptu-ous expression (cp. τρόχις) for simple ἀναστρέφου.

963. Cp. Soph. *O. C.* 991 ἐν γὰρ μ' ἀμείψαι μοῦνον ἄν σ' ἀνιστορῶ. The attraction οὐδὲν ὧν, very common in Soph. and Eur., occurs in Aeschylus only here and 984 below.

965. **καθώρμισας**: cp. Eur. *H. F.* 1004 δεσμοῖς ναῦς ὅπως ὡρμισμένον πρὸς ἡμιθραύστῳ λαΐνῳ τυπίσματι ἧμαι, Ar. *Thesm.* 1105 τίν' ὄχθον τόνδ' ὁρῶ καὶ παρθένον θεαῖς ὁμοίαν ναῦν ὅπως ὡρμισμένην; The metaphor is further carried out in Frg. III. of Προμηθεὺς λυόμενος, 3 navem ut horri-sono freto noctem paventes timidi adnectunt navitae.

968 f. **οἶμαι**: ironical. — τῇδε λα-

ΠΡΟΜΗΘΕΥΣ.

* * * * * *

970　οὕτως ὑβρίζειν τοὺς ὑβρίζοντας χρεών.

ΕΡΜΗΣ.

χλιδᾶν ἔοικας τοῖς παροῦσι πράγμασι.

ΠΡΟΜΗΘΕΥΣ.

χλιδῶ; χλιδῶντας ὧδε τοὺς ἐμοὺς ἐγὼ
ἐχθροὺς ἴδοιμι· καὶ σὲ δ' ἐν τούτοις λέγω.

ΕΡΜΗΣ.

ἦ κἀμὲ γάρ τι συμφοραῖς ἐπαιτιᾷ;

ΠΡΟΜΗΘΕΥΣ.

975　ἁπλῷ λόγῳ τοὺς πάντας ἐχθαίρω θεοὺς
ὅσοι παθόντες εὖ κακοῦσί μ' ἐκδίκως.

ΕΡΜΗΣ.

κλύω σ' ἐγὼ μεμηνότ' οὐ σμικρὰν νόσον.

ΠΡΟΜΗΘΕΥΣ.

νοσοῖμ' ἄν, εἰ νόσημα τοὺς ἐχθροὺς στυγεῖν.

τρείειν πέτρᾳ : see on 463. The expression is here chosen with reference to the next verse (φῦναι Ζηνὶ ἄγγελον). — πέτρᾳ ἦ πατρί : the assonance emphasizes the contrast.

970. This verse was preceded by some telling retort to Hermes's taunt λατρεύειν πέτρᾳ.

972. Cp. 804, Soph. Trach. 819 τὴν δὲ τέρψιν ἣν τὠμῷ δίδωσι πατρί, τήνδ' αὐτὴ λάβοι, Phil. 794 Ἀγάμεμνον, ὦ Μενέλας, πῶς ἂν ἀντ' ἐμοῦ τὸν ἴσον χρόνον τρέφοιτε τήνδε τὴν νόσον ;

973. καὶ ... δέ: and ... too. H. 1042 end; Krüger II. § 69, 41, 2. Cp. Eur. El. 1117 τρόποι τοιοῦτοι· καὶ σὺ δ' αὐθάδης ἔφυς.

974. συμφοραῖς: ob calamita-tes tuas. For this use of the causal dative, cp. Cho. 81 δακρύω ματαίοισι δεσπόταν τύχαις, Eum. 717 ἦ καὶ πατήρ τι σφάλλεται βουλευμάτων πρωτοκτόνοισι προστροπαῖς Ἰξίονος ; Eur. Med. 1286 πίτνει δ' ἁ τλαίν' ἐς ἅλμαν φόνῳ τέκνων δυσσεβεῖ, Heracl. 474 θράσος μοι μηδὲν ἐξόδοις ἐμαῖς προσθῆτε.

975. ἁπλῷ λόγῳ: cp. 46. In Ar. Av. 1547 Prometheus expresses the same sentiment, μισῶ δ' ἅπαντας τοὺς θεούς, ὡς οἶσθα σύ.

977. The dialogue becomes stichomythic as the heat of the speakers increases. — κλύω: the sense is, "from your speech I perceive that, etc." — μεμηνότα νόσον: like μεμηνότα μανίαν. Krüger II. § 46, 6.

ΕΡΜΗΣ.

εἴης φορητὸς οὐκ ἄν, εἰ πράσσοις καλῶς.

ΠΡΟΜΗΘΕΥΣ.

ὤμοι.

ΕΡΜΗΣ.

980 ὤμοι, τόδε Ζεὺς τοὔπος οὐκ ἐπίσταται.

ΠΡΟΜΗΘΕΥΣ.

ἀλλ' ἐκδιδάσκει πάνθ' ὁ γηράσκων χρόνος.

ΕΡΜΗΣ.

καὶ μὴν σύ γ' οὔπω σωφρονεῖν ἐπίστασαι.

ΠΡΟΜΗΘΕΥΣ.

σὲ γὰρ προσηύδων οὐκ ἂν ὄνθ' ὑπηρέτην.

ΕΡΜΗΣ.

ἐρεῖν ἔοικας οὐδὲν ὧν χρῄζει πατήρ.

ΠΡΟΜΗΘΕΥΣ.

985 καὶ μὴν ὀφείλων γ' ἂν τίνοιμ' αὐτῷ χάριν.

ΕΡΜΗΣ.

ἐκερτόμησας δῆθεν ὡς παῖδ' ὄντα με.

979. Cp. Frg. 294 κακοὶ γὰρ εὖ πράσσοντες οὐκ ἀνασχετοί.

980. ὤμοι, τόδε τοὔπος : = "this word ὤμοι." Cp. Pers. 124 ὀᾶ, τοῦτ' ἔπος γυναικοπληθὴς ὅμιλος ἀπύων, Ag. 1334 'μηκέτ' ἐσέλθῃς' τάδε φωνῶν, Eum. 510 τοῦτ' ἔπος θροούμενος, ἰὼ δίκα. — Hermes means that Zeus is not moved by lamentations (cp. 952), but Prometheus, in the next verse, takes the statement in a different sense : κἀκεῖνος οὖν τῷ χρόνῳ μαθήσεται τὸ στενάζειν, Schol.

982. καὶ μήν: see on 246. — οὔπω:

said with reference to the preceding sentiment (ἐκδιδάσκει πάνθ' ὁ χρόνος).

983. ὄνθ' ὑπηρέτην: cp. 942, 954.

985. ὀφείλων γε:= εἰ ὀφείλόν γε. 'Ich dich ehren? Wofür?' says Goethe's Prometheus. For the optative with ἄν after εἰ ὀφείλον cp. Isocr. Paneg. 102 εἰ μὲν ἄλλοι τινὲς τῶν αὐτῶν πραγμάτων πρότερον ἐπεμελήθησαν, εἰκότως ἂν ἡμῖν ἐπιτιμῷεν. Krüger I. § 54, 12, 7; GMT. 443 b.

986. δῆθεν: see on 202. — ὡς παῖδ' ὄντα με: cp. Ag. 277 παιδὸς νέας ὡς κάρτ' ἐμωμήσω φρένας, 479 τίς ὧδε παιδ-

ΠΡΟΜΗΘΕΥΣ.

οὐ γὰρ σὺ παῖς τε κἄτι τοῦδ' ἀνούστερος,
εἰ προσδοκᾷς ἐμοῦ τι πεύσεσθαι πάρα;
οὐκ ἔστιν αἴκισμ' οὐδὲ μηχάνημ' ὅτῳ
990　προτρέψεταί με Ζεὺς γεγωνῆσαι τάδε,
πρὶν ἂν χαλασθῇ δεσμὰ λυμαντήρια.

πρὸς ταῦτα ῥιπτέσθω μὲν αἰθαλοῦσσα φλόξ,
λευκοπτέρῳ δὲ νιφάδι καὶ βροντήμασι
χθονίοις κυκάτω πάντα καὶ ταρασσέτω·
995　γνάμψει γὰρ οὐδὲν τῶνδέ μ' ὥστε καὶ φράσαι
πρὸς οὗ χρεών νιν ἐκπεσεῖν τυραννίδος.

νὸς ἢ φρενῶν κεκομμένος; Il. xx. 200
Πηλείδη, μὴ δή μ' ἐπέεσσί γε νηπύτιον
ὣς ἔλπεο δειδίξεσθαι.
987. τοῦδε: i.e. παιδός. Cp. Soph.
Ant. 910 καὶ ταῖς ἀπ' ἄλλου φωτός, εἰ
τοῦδ' ἡμπλακον, Eur. Hipp. 914 οὐ μὴν
φίλους γε κἄτι μᾶλλον ἢ φίλους κρύπτειν
δίκαιον.
992. πρὸς ταῦτα: often used with
the imperative to express unalterable
resolution or conviction. "I have
spoken; do what you will," or "let
what will happen." Cp. 915, 1030,
1043, Soph. Ant. 658, Eur. Med. 1358,
Hipp. 304, Heracl. 978 etc. — αἰθαλοῦσσα: cp. Hesiod Theog. 707, αἰ-
θαλόεντα κεραυνόν, Eur. Phoen. 183
κεραυνῶν τε φῶς αἰθαλόεν. — For the
thought cp. 1043, Il. xv. 115 μὴ νῦν
μοι νεμεσήσετ', 'Ολύμπια δώματ' ἔχοντες, τίσασθαι φόνον υἱὸς ἰόντ' ἐπὶ νῆας
'Αχαιῶν, εἴπερ μοι καὶ μοῖρα Διὸς πληη-
γέντι κεραυνῷ κεῖσθαι ὁμοῦ νεκύεσσι
μεθ' αἵματι καὶ κονίησιν, Soph. Phil.
1107 οὐδέποτ' οὐδέπον',... οὐδ' εἰ πυρφόρος ἀστεροπητὴς βροντᾶς αὐγαῖς μ'
εἶσι φλογίζων, Eur. Phoen. 521 πρὸς
ταῦτ' ἴτω μὲν πῦρ, ἴτω δὲ φάσγανα,
ζεύγνυσθε δ' ἵππους, πεδία πίμπλαθ'

ἁρμάτων, ὡς οὐ παρήσω τῷδ' ἐμὴν τυραννίδα, Frg. 688 πίμπρη, κάταιθε σάρκας,
ἐμπλήσθητί μου πίνων κελαινὸν αἷμα·
πρόσθε γὰρ κάτω γῆς εἶσιν ἄστρα, γῆ δ'
ἄνεισ' εἰς αἰθέρα, πρὶν ἐξ ἐμοῦ σοι θῶπτ'
ἀπαντῆσαι λόγον.
993. λευκοπτέρῳ: cp. Hdt. iv. 31
οἶκε γὰρ ἡ χιὼν πτεροῖσι, ibid. 7 ὑπὸ
πτερῶν κεχυμένων.
994. Cp. Ar. Pax 320 ὣς κυκάτω
καὶ πατείτω πάντα καὶ ταραττέτω. —
χθονίοις: see 1082 f. Cp. Frg. 55 τι-
πάνου δ' εἰκὼν ἔσθ' ὑπογαίου βροντῆς
φέρεται βαρυταρβής, Soph. O. C. 1606
κτύπησε μὲν Ζεὺς χθόνιος, Eur. Hipp.
1201 ἔνθεν τις ἠχώ, χθόνιος ὡς βροντὴ
Διός, βαρὺν βρόμον μεθῆκε. — κυκάτω:
the subject is he (Zeus); so in 1051
below, after πνεῦμα and κῦμα.
995. ὥστε καί: (= οὕτως ὥστε καί)
implies that the result corresponds in
nature with the action which causes
it. Cp. Plat. Phaed. 66 b ἀνάγκη ἐκ
πάντων τούτων παρίστασθαι δόξαν τοιάνδε τινὰ τοῖς γνησίως φιλοσόφοις ὥστε
καὶ πρὸς ἀλλήλους τοιαῦτ' ἄττα λέγειν,
Soph. Ai. 1325 τί γάρ σ' ἔδρασεν ὥστε
καὶ βλάβην ἔχειν, Eur. Phoen. 1328
οὐκ εἰς τόδ' ἦλθον ὥστε καὶ τάδ'

ΕΡΜΗΣ.

ὅρα νυν εἴ σοι ταῦτ᾽ ἀρωγὰ φαίνεται.

ΠΡΟΜΗΘΕΥΣ.

ὦπται πάλαι δὴ καὶ βεβούλευται τάδε.

ΕΡΜΗΣ.

τόλμησον, ὦ μάταιε, τόλμησόν ποτε
1000 πρὸς τὰς παρούσας πημονὰς ὀρθῶς φρονεῖν.

ΠΡΟΜΗΘΕΥΣ.

ὀχλεῖς μάτην με κῦμ᾽ ὅπως παρηγορῶν.

εἰσελθέτω σε μήποθ᾽ ὡς ἐγὼ Διὸς
γνώμην φοβηθεὶς θηλύνους γενήσομαι
καὶ λιπαρήσω τὸν μέγα στυγούμενον
1005 γυναικομίμοις ὑπτιάσμασιν χερῶν
λῦσαί με δεσμῶν τῶνδε· τοῦ παντὸς δέω.

εἰδέναι, Pel. 841 πῶς οὖν θανούμεθ᾽ ὥστε
καὶ δόξαν λαβεῖν; For the thought
cp. Hor. *Carm.* iii. 3, 1 iustum et
tenacem propositi virum, *etc.*
998. Cp. Schiller *Wallenstein's Tod*
IV. 11 'Bedenken Sie doch ja wohl
was Sie thun.' 'Bedacht ist schon,
was zu bedenken ist.'
999 f. τόλμησον, τόλμησον ὀρθῶς
φρονεῖν: cp. Horace's sapere aude
(*Epist.* i. 2, 40). For the repetition
see on 266.
1001. ὀχλεῖς: absolute, as in Soph.
O. T. 446 παρὸν σύ γ᾽ ἐμποδὼν ὀχλεῖς.
— κῦμ᾽ ὅπως: λαλῶν ὡς πρὸς κῦμα ἀναίσθητον, Schol. Cp. Eur. *Med.* 28 ὡς
δὲ πέτρος ἢ θαλάσσιος κλύδων ἀκούει
νουθετουμένη φίλων, *Hipp.* 304 πρὸς
τάδ᾽ αὐθαδεστέρα γίγνου θαλάσσης,
Andr. 537 τί με προσπίτνεις ἁλίαν πέτραν ἢ κῦμα λιταῖς ὡς ἱκετεύων, Lycophr. 1452 εἰς κῦμα κωφὸν βάζω, Philo-

dem. *Anthol. Pal.* v. 107 τοῦτ᾽ ἐβόων ἀεὶ
καὶ προύλεγον, ἀλλ᾽ ἴσα πόντῳ Ἰονίῳ
μύθων ἔκλυες ἡμετέρων, Ovid. *Met.* xiii.
804 surdior aequoribus.
1005. γυναικομίμοις: cp. Soph. Frg.
706 γυναικομίμοις ἐμπρέπεις ἐσθήμασιν,
Eur. *Bacch.* 980 ἐν γυναικομίμῳ στολᾷ,
Frg. 185 γυναικομίμῳ διαπρέπεις μορφώματι. — ὑπτιάσμασιν: in entreaty the
ancients raised the hands with palms
upwards. Cp. the quotation (*s.v.*
ὕετιος) in Suidas προθυμίᾳ τῇ πάσῃ
ἀνεπετάσαντες τὰς πύλας ἐδέξαντο ὑπτίαις χερσὶ τοὺς πολεμίους, Verg. *Aen.*
iii. 176 tendoque supinas ad
caelum cum voce manus, Hor.
Carm. iii. 23, 1 caelo supinas si
tuleris manus. This attitude is
seen in the fine statue of the 'praying
boy' in the Berlin Museum (Baumeister, *Denkmäler*, p. 591, n. 635).
1006. τοῦ παντὸς δέω: cp. 961.

ΕΡΜΗΣ.

λέγων ἔοικα πολλὰ καὶ μάτην ἐρεῖν·
τέγγει γὰρ οὐδὲν οὐδὲ μαλθάσσει κέαρ
λιταῖς· δακὼν δὲ στόμιον ὡς νεοζυγὴς
1010 πῶλος βιάζει καὶ πρὸς ἡνίας μάχει.
ἀτὰρ σφοδρύνει γ᾽ ἀσθενεῖ σοφίσματι.
αὐθαδία γὰρ τῷ φρονοῦντι μὴ καλῶς
αὐτὴ καθ᾽ αὑτὴν οὐδενὸς μεῖζον σθένει.
σκέψαι δ᾽, ἐὰν μὴ τοῖς ἐμοῖς πεισθῇς λόγοις,
1015 οἷός σε χειμὼν καὶ κακῶν τρικυμία
ἔπεισ᾽ ἄφυκτος· πρῶτα μὲν γὰρ ὀκρίδα
φάραγγα βροντῇ καὶ κεραυνίᾳ φλογὶ

1007. πολλὰ καὶ μάτην: cp. *Eum.*
144 ἢ πολλὰ δὴ παθοῦσα καὶ μάτην
ἐγώ.
1010. βιάζει: = βίᾳ φέρεις. Cp. Eur.
Hipp. 1223 αἱ δ᾽ ἐνδακοῦσαι στόμια πυρι-
γενῆ γναθμοῖς βίᾳ φέρουσιν, οὔτι ναυ-
κλήρου χερὸς μεταστρίφουσαι, *Med.*
242 μὴ βίᾳ φέρων ζυγόν, Soph. *El.*
725.
1011. σφοδρύνει, ἀσθενεῖ: outward
turbulence, but inner powerlessness.
1013. αὐτὴ καθ᾽ αὑτήν: that is,
χωρὶς τοῦ καλῶς φρονεῖν. — οὐδενὸς μεῖζον σθένει: 'nulla re est validior, *i.e.*
quavis re est infirmior' (Halm). Explanation and confirmation of the
foregoing ἀσθενεῖ. Cp. Theogn. 411
οὐδενὸς ἀνθρώπων κακίων δοκεῖ εἶναι
ἑταῖρος, ᾧ γνώμη θ᾽ ἕπεται, Κύρνε, καὶ ᾧ
δύναμις, Thuc. vii. 71 οὐδεμιᾶς δὴ τῶν
ξυμπασῶν ἐλάσσων ἔκπληξις, 85 πλεῖστος γὰρ δὴ φόνος οὗτος καὶ οὐδενὸς
ἐλάσσων τῶν ἐν τῷ Σικελικῷ πολέμῳ
τούτῳ, Dem. I. 27 ἡ τῶν πραγμάτων
αἰσχύνη, οὐδεμιᾶς ἐλάττων ζημίας τοῖς
γε σώφροσι, Plat. *Prot.* 335 a εἰ τοῦτο
ἐποίουν, οὐδενὸς ἂν βελτίων ἐφαινόμην,

Eur. *Andr.* 726 τἄλλ᾽ ὄντες ἴστε μηδενὸς βελτίονες. — For the thought cp.
Soph. *O. T.* 549 εἴ τοι νομίζεις κτῆμα
τὴν αὐθαδίαν εἶναί τι τοῦ νοῦ χωρίς, οὐκ
ὀρθῶς φρονεῖς.
1014. σκέψαι δέ: the same formula
introduces an argument Soph. *O. T.*
584 σκέψαι δὲ τοῦτο πρῶτον, Eur.
Suppl. 476 σκέψαι δὲ καὶ μὴ τοῖς ἐμοῖς
θυμούμενος λόγοισιν ... σφρίγωντ᾽ ἀμεί-
ψῃ μῦθον. Cp. Soph. *Trach.* 1077 σκέψαι δ᾽ ὁποίας ταῦτα συμφορᾶς ὕπο πί-
πονθα.
1015. χειμών: cp. 643. For the position of κακῶν see on 458. — τρικυμία:
cp. the Latin *decima unda, de-
cumanus fluctus*, *Sept.* 760 κακῶν δ᾽ ὥσπερ θάλασσα κῦμ᾽ ἄγει, τὸ μὲν
πίτνον, ἄλλο δ᾽ ἀείρει τρίχαλον, Eur.
Hipp. 1213 σὺν κλύδωνι καὶ τρικυμίᾳ,
Plat. *Rep.* 472 a τὸ δύω κύματε ἐκ-
φυγόντι τὸ μέγιστον καὶ χαλεπώτατον
τῆς τρικυμίας ἐπάγεις.
1016. ἔπεισ᾽: elision of ι in the
verb-ending -σι is rare. — πρῶτα μέν:
answered by simple δέ 1020. Cp. 447.
— ὀκρίδα: cp. ὀκριοέσσῃ, 281.

πατὴρ σπαράξει τήνδε, καὶ κρύψει δέμας
τὸ σόν, πετραία δ' ἀγκάλη σε βαστάσει.
1020 μακρὸν δὲ μῆκος ἐκτελευτήσας χρόνου
ἄψορρον ἥξεις ἐς φάος· Διὸς δέ τοι
πτηνὸς κύων δαφοινὸς αἰετὸς λάβρως
διαρταμήσει σώματος μέγα ῥάκος,
ἄκλητος ἕρπων δαιταλεὺς πανήμερος,
1025 κελαινόβρωτον δ' ἧπαρ ἐκθοινάσεται.

τοιοῦδε μόχθου τέρμα μή τι προσδόκα,
πρὶν ἂν θεῶν τις διάδοχος τῶν σῶν πόνων

1019. πετραία ἀγκάλη: cp. Cho.
680 πόντιαι ἀγκάλαι, Ar. Ran. 704 τὴν
πόλιν ἔχοντες κυμάτων ἐν ἀγκάλαις, in
imitation of Archilochus's verse ψυ-
χὰς ἔχοντες κυμάτων ἐν ἀγκάλαις. —
πετραία ... βαστάσει: states what is
properly only a circumstance (= ἐν
πετραίᾳ ἀγκάλη βασταζόμενον). Prometheus is to sink, fetters and all,
into the bowels of the earth, encir-
cled by the cliff to which he is bound.
By this device the poet avoids, at the
opening of the Προμηθεὺς λυόμενος, the
uninteresting repetition of the bind-
ing of Prometheus.
1020. μακρὸν μῆκος: cp. Eur. Or.
72 μακρὸν δὴ μῆκος χρόνου. μῆκος =
spatium, stretch.
1021. τοι: confirmative, mark well.
1022. κύων: see on 803.
1023. διαρταμήσει ... μέγα ῥάκος:
cp. below, Frg. III. of Προμηθεὺς λυόμενος 10 iam tertio me quoque
funesto die tristi advolatu
aduncis lacerans unguibus
Iovis satelles pastu dilaniat
fero. — μέγα ῥάκος: gives the result
of διαρταμήσει, tear into great shreds.
So κελαινόβρωτον below. Observe

μέγα before ῥ-. ῥ is the only liquid
which maintains in post-Homeric
poetry both the internal doubling
(-ρρ-) and the force of two conso-
nants at the beginning of a word
(the after-effect of a dropped initial
consonant; ῥάκος = ϝράκος, Aeol. βρά-
κος). The preceding vowel may also
(in the thesis) be short; see 713,
902.
1024. πανήμερος: not daily (for
according to the passage just quoted
on 1023, the eagle comes tertio
quoque die), but διὰ πάσης τῆς
ἡμέρας. Cp. the use of πανῆμαρ, πανη-
μέριος in Homer. So Hesiod Theog.
523 καὶ οἱ ἐπ' αἰετὸν ὦρσε τανύπτε-
ρον· αὐτὰρ ὅγ' ἧπαρ ἤσθιεν ἀθάνατον·
τὸ δ' ἀέξετο ἶσον ἀπάντη νυκτὸς, ὅσον
πρόπαν ἦμαρ ἔδοι τανυσίπτερος
ὄρνις.
1025. κελαινόβρωτον: τὸ μελαινό-
μενον ἐκ τῆς βρώσεως, Schol. Proleptic. — ἐκθοινάσεται: see on 61.
1027. θεῶν τις διάδοχος κτέ.: this
is really fulfilled, for Heracles offers
to Zeus the centaur Chiron (θεὸν
Χείρωνα, Soph. Trach. 714) as a voluntary (θελήσῃ) substitute for Pro-

φανῇ θελήσῃ τ' εἰς ἀναύγητον μολεῖν
Ἀιδην κνεφαῖά τ' ἀμφὶ Ταρτάρου βάθη.

1030 πρὸς ταῦτα βούλευ'· ὡς ὅδ' οὐ πεπλασμένος
ὁ κόμπος, ἀλλὰ καὶ λίαν ὀρθούμενος·
ψευδηγορεῖν γὰρ οὐκ ἐπίσταται στόμα
τὸ Δῖον, ἀλλὰ πᾶν ἔπος τελεῖ. σὺ δὲ
πάπταινε καὶ φρόντιζε, μηδ' αὐθαδίαν
1035 εὐβουλίας ἄμεινον ἡγήσῃ ποτέ.

ΧΟΡΟΣ.

ἡμῖν μὲν Ἑρμῆς οὐκ ἄκαιρα φαίνεται
λέγειν· ἄνωγε γάρ σε τὴν αὐθαδίαν
μεθέντ' ἐρευνᾶν τὴν σοφὴν εὐβουλίαν.
πιθοῦ· σοφῷ γὰρ αἰσχρὸν ἐξαμαρτάνειν.

metheus. See Introd. p. 12. Here, indeed, Hermes announces the contingency as one inconceivable, or hardly to be expected. See on 27.

1029. ἀμφί: see on 830, and cp. Hom. *Hymn* ii. 157 Τιτῆνές τε θεοὶ τοὶ ὑπὸ χθονὶ ναιετάοντες Τάρταρον ἀμφὶ μέγαν (*somewhere in Tartarus*), Eur. *Andr.* 215 εἰ δ' ἀμφὶ Θρῄκην ... τύραννον ἴσχες ἄνδρα (*in some part of Thrace*). The conception is that of an unknown point inside a given region. This suggests the idea of looking "round about" that region.

1030 f. πεπλασμένος ὁ κόμπος ... ὀρθούμενος: cp. Hdt. vii. 103 οὕτω μὲν ὀρθοῖτ' ἂν ὁ λόγος ... εἰ δὲ ... ὅρα μὴ μάτην κόμπος ὁ λόγος οὗτος εἰρημένος ᾖ, Thuc. ii. 41 ὡς οὐ λόγων ἐν τῷ παρόντι κόμπος τάδε μᾶλλον ἢ ἔργων ἐστὶν ἀλήθεια, αὐτὴ ἡ δύναμις τῆς πόλεως σημαίνει, Soph. *O. T.* 828 ἆρ' οὐκ ἀπ' ὠμοῦ ταῦτα δαίμονός τις ἂν κρίνων ἐπ' ἀνδρὶ

τῷδ' ἂν ὀρθοίη λόγον; *Ai.* 354 οἴμ', ὡς ἔοικας ὀρθὰ μαρτυρεῖν ἄγαν. — καὶ λίαν: this frequent combination occurs even in Homer. *Od.* i. 46 καὶ λίην κεῖνός γε ἐοικότι κεῖται ὀλέθρῳ, also xiii. 393, xv. 155.

1032. ψευδηγορεῖν: Zeus says, *Il.* i. 526, οὐ γὰρ ἐμὸν παλινάγρετον οὐδ' ἀπατηλὸν οὐδ' ἀτελεύτητον ὅ τι κεν κεφαλῇ κατανεύσω.

1035. ἄμεινον: for the neuter cp. *Suppl.* 190 κρεῖσσον δὲ πύργου βωμός. G. 138, N. 2 c; H. 617. — ἡγήσῃ ποτέ: *be at length convinced* (cp. ποτέ in 999). The negation belongs properly only to αὐθαδίαν εὐβουλίας ἄμεινον, although μηδέ has influenced the mood of ἡγήσῃ (for ἡγήσαι). — For the form of expression, cp. Eur. *Cycl.* 310 τὸ δ' εὐσεβὲς τῆς δυσσεβείας ἀνθελοῦ.

1037. The leader of the chorus reiterates the foregoing sentiment. See on 472.

ΠΡΟΜΗΘΕΥΣ.

1040 εἰδότι τοί μοι τάσδ' ἀγγελίας
ὅδ' ἐθώϋξεν, πάσχειν δὲ κακῶς
ἐχθρὸν ὑπ' ἐχθρῶν οὐδὲν ἀεικές.
πρὸς ταῦτ' ἐπ' ἐμοὶ ῥιπτέσθω μὲν
πυρὸς ἀμφήκης βόστρυχος, αἰθὴρ δ'
1045 ἐρεθιζέσθω βροντῇ σφακέλῳ τ'
ἀγρίων ἀνέμων· χθόνα δ' ἐκ πυθμένων
αὐταῖς ῥίζαις πνεῦμα κραδαίνοι,
κῦμα δὲ πόντου τραχεῖ ῥοθίῳ
συγχώσειεν τῶν οὐρανίων
1050 ἄστρων διόδους, εἴς τε κελαινὸν
Τάρταρον ἄρδην ῥίψειε δέμας
τοὐμὸν ἀνάγκης στερραῖς δίναις·
πάντως ἐμέ γ' οὐ θανατώσει.

ΕΡΜΗΣ.

τοιάδε μέντοι τῶν φρενοπλήκτων

1040-1093. The catastrophe. Five anapaestic systems, of which the pair spoken by Prometheus (14 = 14) and the pair spoken by Hermes (9 = 9) correspond in length, while the system of the Coryphaeus forms the mesode.

1040. εἰδότι μοι: see on 441.

1042. ἀεικές: refers to the reproach in 1039 (αἰσχρόν).

1043. Cp. 902, Eur. Frg. 910 πρὸς ταῦθ' ὅ τι χρὴ καὶ παλαμάσθω καὶ πᾶν ἐπ' ἐμοὶ τεκταινέσθω· τὸ γὰρ εὖ μετ' ἐμοῦ καὶ τὸ δίκαιον σύμμαχον ἔσται κοὐ μή ποθ' ἁλῶ κακὰ πράσσων.

1044. πυρὸς ἀμφήκης βόστρυχος: ἡ ἑλικοειδὴς (cp. 1083) τοῦ πυρὸς καταφορά, Schol. Cp. Cleanth. Hymn to Zeus 10 ἀμφήκη πυρόεντα ἀεὶ ζώοντα κεραυνόν, Eur. Hipp. 559 βροντᾷ ἀμφι-

πύρῳ, Hesych. ἀμφήκες δέ, ἐξ ἑκατέρου μέρους ἠκονημένον βέλος, ἢ κεραυνὸς ἢ ξίφος. Cp. also Ag. 306 φλογὸς μέγαν πώγωνα, Catull. lxi. 77 viden ut faces splendidas quatiunt comas. ἀμφήκης is an Homeric word.

1045. σφακέλῳ: σπασμῷ, συντόνῳ κινήσει, Schol. Cp. 878.

1047. αὐταῖς ῥίζαις: cp. 221 and note.

1049. συγχώσειεν: συγκαλύψειεν, Schol.

1051. ῥίψειε: the subject is he (Zeus); so also of θανατώσει below. See on 994.

1052. Cp. Eur. Hec. 1295 στερρὰ γὰρ ἀνάγκη.

1053. πάντως ... οὐ: as in 333. For the thought cp. 933.

1055 βουλεύματ' ἔπη τ' ἐστὶν ἀκοῦσαι.
τί γὰρ ἐλλείπει μὴ οὐ παραπαίειν
ἡ τοῦδ' εὐχή; τί χαλᾷ μανιῶν;
ἀλλ' οὖν ὑμεῖς γ' αἱ πημοσύναις
συγκάμνουσαι ταῖς τοῦδε τόπων
1060 μετά ποι χωρεῖτ' ἐκ τῶνδε θοῶς,
μὴ φρένας ὑμῶν ἡλιθιώσῃ
βροντῆς μύκημ' ἀτέραμνον.

ΧΟΡΟΣ.

ἄλλο τι φώνει καὶ παραμυθοῦ μ'
ὅ τι καὶ πείσεις· οὐ γὰρ δή που
1065 τοῦτό γε τλητὸν παρέσυρας ἔπος.
πῶς με κελεύεις κακότητ' ἀσκεῖν;
μετὰ τοῦδ' ὅ τι χρὴ πάσχειν ἐθέλω·
τοὺς προδότας γὰρ μισεῖν ἔμαθον,
κοὐκ ἔστι νόσος
1070 τῆσδ' ἥντιν' ἀπέπτυσα μᾶλλον.

ΕΡΜΗΣ.

ἀλλ' οὖν μέμνησθ' ἁγὼ προλέγω·

1056 f. τί ἐλλείπει μὴ οὐ παραπαίειν: what lacks it of wild delusion?
ἐλλείπειν contains a negative notion.
Cp. 627, Eur. Iph. A. 41 τῶν ἀπόρων
οὐδενὸς ἐνδεῖς μὴ οὐ μαίνεσθαι, Tro. 797
τίνος ἐνδέομεν μὴ οὐ πανσυδίᾳ χωρεῖν
ὀλέθρου διὰ παντός, Soph. O. T. 1232
λείπει μὲν οὐδ' ἃ πρόσθεν ᾔδεμεν τὸ μὴ
οὐ βαρύστον' εἶναι. GMT. 815, 2;
G. 283, 7 N.; H. 1034 b. — For παραπαίειν cp. 581, and Frg. 320 εἴτ' οὖν
σοφιστὴς κᾶλα παραπαίων χέλυν, Ar.
Plut. 508 ξυνθιασώτα τοῦ ληρεῖν καὶ
παραπαίειν. — εὐχή: the passage 1043–
1052 is meant.
1059. συγκάμνουσαι: cp. 414.
1062. ἀτέραμνον: cp. 190.

1065. παρέσυρας: the proper meaning of παρασύρω may be seen from the
figure in Ar. Eq. 526 Κρατίνου μεμνη-
μένος δὲ πολλῷ ῥεύσας ποτ' ἐπαίνῳ διὰ
τῶν ἀφελῶν πεδίων ἔρρει καὶ τῆς στά-
σεως παρασύρων ἐφόρει τὰς δρῦς καὶ τὰς
πλατάνους καὶ τοὺς ἐχθροὺς π,οθελόμ-
νους. The expression παρασύρειν ἔπος
is therefore like αἴσσειν αὐδήν. The
verb imparts to ἔπος a strong notion
of reproach, "utter an outrageous
speech."
1069 f. Cp. 685. — ἀπέπτυσα: on
this use of the aorist see Krüger II.
§ 53, 6, 2; GMT. 60; H. 842.
1071–79. Provision is here made
for removing the chorus from the

μηδὲ πρὸς ἄτης θηραθεῖσαι
μέμψησθε τύχην, μηδέ ποτ' εἴπηθ'
ὡς Ζεὺς ὑμᾶς εἰς ἀπρόοπτον
1075 πῆμ' εἰσέβαλεν· μὴ δῆτ', αὐταὶ δ'
ὑμᾶς αὐτάς. εἰδυῖαι γὰρ
κοὐκ ἐξαίφνης οὐδὲ λαθραίως
εἰς ἀπέραντον δίκτυον ἄτης
ἐμπλεχθήσεσθ' ὑπ' ἀνοίας.

ΠΡΟΜΗΘΕΥΣ.

1080 καὶ μὴν ἔργῳ κοὐκέτι μύθῳ
χθὼν σεσάλευται·
βρυχία δ' ἠχὼ παραμυκᾶται
βροντῆς, ἕλικες δ' ἐκλάμπουσι
στεροπῆς ζάπυροι, στρόμβοι δὲ κόνιν

orchestra. For them to remount their winged car would impair the effect of the last scene. They sink, at the close, through the ἀναπίεσμα (trap-door) of the orchestra, at the moment when Prometheus disappears by the ἀναπίεσμα of the stage.

1078 f. δίκτυον ἄτης: cp. *Ag.* 361 γάγγαμον ἄτης παναλώτου. — ἀπέραντον: impervious. Cp. *Ag.* 1382 ἄπειρον ἀμφίβληστρον ὥσπερ ἰχθύων περιστιχίζω, *Eum.* 634 ἐν ἀτέρμονι δαιδάλῳ πέπλῳ. — At 1079 Hermes soars aloft and disappears.

1080. ἔργῳ κοὐκέτι μύθῳ: cp. 336. Stage thunder and lightning the ancients produced by a thunder-machine (βροντεῖον) and a lightning-tower (κεραυνοσκοπεῖον). Skins filled with heavy stones were rolled on copper plates behind the scene, and a revolving contrivance aloft (περίακτος ὑψηλή) emitted flashes of light. The quaking of the earth may have been indicated by the turning of the two περίακτοι. The ancients in such things demanded only hints and symbols, not illusions.

1081. The monometer (see on 97) takes the place of a dimeter; see on 1040.

1082. βρυχία: Hesych. βρύχιος· ὑποβρύχιος, *i.e.* under the surface. Cp. *Pers.* 397 ἔπαισαν ἅλμην βρύχιον. 'Vocabulum βρύχιος eo hic significatu dictum est, quo etiam ὑποβρύχιος interdum non id quod in aqua demersum est, sed omnino quod aut aliqua re obrutum denotat' (Hermann). Accordingly βρυχία ἠχὼ βροντῆς means the same as χθόνια βροντήματα, 994. With the description cp. Hesiod *Theog.* 705 τόσσος δοῦπος ἔγεντο θεῶν ἔριδι ξυνιόντων· σὺν δ' ἄνεμοί τ' ἐνοσίς τε κονίην ἐσφαράγιζον.

1083 f. ἕλικες: αἱ ἑλικοειδεῖς (zigzag) κατὰ τὰ νέφη τῶν ἀστραπῶν κινήσεις, Schol. Cp. 1044. — ζάπυροι: cp. ζαπληθῆ *Pers.* 316. — στρόμβοι: Hesych. στρόμβος· δῖνος, συστροφὴ ἀνέ-

1085 εἰλίσσουσι· σκιρτᾷ δ᾽ ἀνέμων
πνεύματα πάντων εἰς ἄλληλα
στάσιν ἀντίπνουν ἀποδεικνύμενα·
ξυντετάρακται δ᾽ αἰθὴρ πόντῳ.
τοιάδ᾽ ἐπ᾽ ἐμοὶ ῥιπὴ Διόθεν
1090 τεύχουσα φόβον στείχει φανερῶς.
ὦ μητρὸς ἐμῆς σέβας, ὦ πάντων
αἰθὴρ κοινὸν φάος εἰλίσσων,
ἐσορᾷς μ᾽ ὡς ἔκδικα πάσχω.

μου. — κόνῑν: for the quantity, cp.
Suppl. 180 ὁρῶ κόνιν ἄναυδον, Cho. 928
τόνδ᾽ ὄφιν ἐθρεψάμην, Suppl. 782 κόνις
ἄτερθε, Cho. 544 οὔφις ἐμοῖσι.

1087. ἀντίπνουν: as a rule, only
the mediae (β, γ, δ) before λ, μ, ν
make position in thesis in dramatic
poetry. Lengthenings like this in
anapaests are found Ar. Αυ. 216 ἕδρας,
579 ἀγρῶν. — For the contraction see
on 917.

1090. φανερῶς: belongs with Διόθεν, evidently from Zeus and none other.
τεύχουσα φόβον stands in a causal relation to it.

1091. ὦ μητρὸς ἐμῆς: ὦ Γῆ ἠ ὦ
Θέμις (read ὦ Γῆ Θέμι, see on 210),
Schol. ' In huiusmodi obtestatione

eos appellari deos convenit, quorum
vis et potestas universam rerum na-
turam complectitur, i.e. caelum et
terram, quo quidquid usquam testari
insigne facinus possit, uno complexu
comprehendatur ' (Hermann). Cp.
Soph. El. 86 ὦ φάος ἁγνὸν καὶ γῆς ἰσό-
μοιρ᾽ ἀήρ. — σέβας: cp. Eum. 885 ἀλλ᾽
εἰ μὲν ἁγνόν ἐστί σοι Πειθοῦς σέβας.

1092. φάος εἰλίσσων: cp. Eur.
Phoen. 3 Ἥλιε, θοαῖς ἵπποισιν εἰλίσσων φλόγα, Theodect. Frg. 10 (p. 805
Nauck) ὦ καλλιφεγγὴ λαμπάδ᾽ εἰλίσσων φλογός, Ἥλιε. Here φάος is the
proper light of the φαεννὸς αἰθήρ.

1093. Prometheus sinks into the
depths, with the rock on which he
hangs (1019).

FRAGMENTS

ΠΡΟΜΗΘΕΥΣ ΛΥΟΜΕΝΟΣ.

I.

(201 Herm., 191 Dind., 190 f. Nauck.)

Arrian *Peripl. Pont. Euxin.* p. 19. Αἰσχύλος ἐν Προμηθεῖ λυομένῳ τὸν Φᾶσιν ὅρον τῆς Εὐρώπης καὶ τῆς Ἀσίας ποιεῖ. λέγουσι γοῦν
αὐτῷ οἱ Τιτᾶνες πρὸς τὸν Προμηθέα ὅτι

> Ἥκομεν —
> τοὺς σοὺς ἄθλους τούσδε, Προμηθεῦ,
> δεσμοῦ τε πάθος τόδ' ἐποψόμενοι.

ἔπειτα καταλέγουσιν ὅσην χώραν ἐπῆλθον,

> τῇ μὲν δίδυμον χθονὸς Εὐρώπης
> μέγαν ἠδ' Ἀσίας τέρμονα Φᾶσιν.

I. This fragment belonged to the parodos, with which the play (like the *Persians* and the *Supplices*) began. This appears from Procop. *Hist. Goth.* iv. 6, p. 336, 11 ἀλλὰ καὶ ὁ τραγῳδοποιὸς Αἰσχύλος ἐν Προμηθεῖ τῷ λυομένῳ εὐθὺς ἀρχόμενος τῆς τραγῳδίας τὸν ποταμὸν Φᾶσιν τέρμονα καλεῖ γῆς τῆς τε Ἀσίας καὶ τῆς Εὐρώπης. — The Titans (twelve in number) compose, we see, the chorus of the Προμηθεὺς λυόμενος. They have been released from Tartarus; cp. 219 above, Pind. *Pyth.* iv. 518

λῦσε δὲ Ζεὺς ἄφθιτος Τιτᾶνας· ἐν δὲ χρόνῳ μεταβολαὶ λήξαντος οὔρου, Hesiod *O. D.* 169 τηλοῦ ἀπ' ἀθανάτων τοῖσιν Κρόνος ἐμβασιλεύει. Now they come, like the Oceanida in the Προμηθεὺς δεσμώτης, as sympathizing witnesses of Prometheus's sufferings.

In the first verses the chorus give the motive for their presence (δι' ἣν αἰτίαν πάρεστι, see on 128 above). Then the countries are enumerated which they have traversed on the way from their distant home. The following fragment (II.) is part of

145

II.

(202 H., 192 D., 192 N.)

Strabo I p. 33. φημὶ ... τὰ μεσημβρινὰ πάντα Αἰθιοπίαν καλεῖσθαι τὰ πρὸς Ὠκεανῷ. μαρτυρεῖ δὲ τὰ τοιαῦτα· ὅ τε γὰρ Αἰσχύλος ἐν Προμηθεῖ τῷ λυομένῳ φησὶν οὕτω:

Φοινικόπεδόν τ' ἐρυθρᾶς ἱερὸν
χεῦμα θαλάσσης
χαλκοκέραυνόν τε παρ' Ὠκεανῷ
λίμνην παντοτρόφον Αἰθιόπων,
ἵν' ὁ παντόπτης Ἥλιος αἰεὶ
χρῶτ' ἀθάνατον κάματόν θ' ἵππων
θερμαῖς ὕδατος
μαλακοῦ προχοαῖς ἀναπαύει.

this narration. Finally the Phasis is mentioned, which is near the spot in the Caucasus (see Introd. p. 24 f.) where Prometheus is chained. The Phasis here appears as the boundary of Europe and Asia, whereas above, 734 and 790, the sea of Azov is thus designated. Consequently the poet must have fancied the Phasis as flowing from the north and emptying into the sea of Azov.

II. As late as Herodotus's time the term Ἐρυθρὴ θάλασσα embraced the whole sea lying south of Asia and Africa. This he calls the 'South Sea' (νοτίη θάλασσα) in distinction from the Mediterranean (βορηίη θάλασσα), ii. 158 τῇ δὲ ἐλάχιστόν ἐστι καὶ συντομώτατον ἐκ τῆς βορηίης θαλάσσης ὑπερβῆναι ἐς τὴν νοτίην καὶ Ἐρυθρὴν τὴν αὐτὴν ταύτην καλεομένην. — φοινικόπεδον ἐρυθρᾶς: cp. Stephan. Byz. s.v. Ἐρυθρά: Ἐρυθρὰ ἡ θάλασσα, ἀπὸ Ἐρύθρου τοῦ ἥρωος, Οὐράνιος δ' ἐν Ἀραβικῶν δευτέρᾳ ἀπὸ τῶν παρακειμένων ὀρῶν ἃ ἐρυθρὰ δεινῶς εἰσι καὶ πορφυρᾶ, καὶ ἐπὴν βάλλῃ εἰς αὐτὰ ὁ ἥλιος τὴν αὐγήν, κατατέμπει εἰς τὴν θάλασσαν σκιὰν ἐρυθράν· καὶ ὄμβρῳ δὲ κατακλυσθέντων τῶν ὀρέων κάτω συρρέοντι εἰς θάλασσαν οὕτω γίγνεται ἡ θάλασσα τὴν χρόαν. — χαλκοκέραυνον: bronze-flashing, a bold formation designating metallic gleam of the lake's surface. Cp. Il. xi. 83 χαλκοῦ τε στεροπήν, 922 above κεραυνοῦ κρείσσονα φλόγα, Eur. Tro. 1104 κεραυνοφαὲς πῦρ. — τέ: the enclitic is separated from χαλκοκέραυνον by the caesura, as Cho. 864 ἀρχάς | τε. — λίμνην παντοτρόφον: see note on 808 above. For the lack of caesura see on 173.

III.

(203 H., 193 D., 193 N.)

Cic. *Tusc.* II 10. Affixus ad Caucasum (*sc.* Prometheus apud Aeschylum) dicit haec :

Titanum suboles, socia nostri sanguinis,
generata Caelo, adspicite religatum asperis
vinctumque saxis, navem ut horrisono freto
noctem paventes timidi adnectunt navitae.
5 Saturnius me sic infixit Iuppiter,
Iovisque numen Mulciberi adscivit manus.
hos ille cuneos fabrica crudeli inserens
perrupit artus : qua miser sollertia
transverberatus castrum hoc Furiarum incolo.
10 Iam tertio me quoque funesto die
tristi advolatu aduncis lacerans unguibus
Iovis satelles pastu dilaniat fero ;
tum iecure opimo farta et satiata affatim
clangorem fundit vastum, et sublime avolans

III. These verses are in Cicero's own translation (*ibid.* c. 11). — In the Προμηθεὺς δεσμότης the hero is chained before the eyes of the spectators; here narrative takes the place of action. — 1 f. Cp. 164 above. — **asperis saxis**: cp. φάραγγι πρὸς δυσχειμέρῳ, 15. — 3 f. **navem ... adnectunt**: see on 1015. — 6. Cp. 619 Βούλευμα μὲν τὸ Δῖον, Ἡφαίστου δὲ χείρ. — 7. **cuneos**: cp. σφηνὸς αὐθάδη γνάθον στέρνων διαμπάξ, 64. — 8. **sollertia**: cp. τέχνης, 87. — 9. **castrum Furiarum**: perhaps Ἐρινύων φρουράν, after 143. In that case Ἐρινύων would be

metonymic, " camp of revenge." Cp. *Ag.* 645 παιᾶνα τόνδ' Ἐρινύων. — 10. See on 1024. Perhaps the gloss in Photius and Suidas, τρίτῳ φάει · τρίτῃ ἡμέρᾳ, relates to the original of tertio die. — 11. **lacerans unguibus**: the original was εἰσαφάσματα (from εἰσαφάσσω). Cp. Hesych. εἰσαφάσματα · εἰσπτήματα, ἀπὸ τοῦ εἰσαφίεναι, ἢ σπαράγματα · Αἰσχύλος Προμηθεῖ λυομένῳ. The derivation from εἰσαφίεναι is erroneous, but was doubtless suggested by the expression which Cicero translates by tristi advolatu. — 12. **Iovis satelles**: cp. 1021 Διὸς

15 pinnata cauda nostrum adulat sanguinem;
quom vero adesum inflatu renovatum est iecur,
tum rursum taetros avida se ad pastus refert.
Sic hanc custodem maesti cruciatus alo,
quae me perenni vivom foedat miseria;

20 namque, ut videtis, vinclis constrictus Iovis
arcere nequeo diram volucrem a pectore.
Sic me ipse viduus pestes excipio anxias,
amore mortis terminum anquirens mali;
sed longe a leto numine aspellor Iovis,

25 atque haec vetusta saeclis glomerata horridis
luctifica clades nostro infixa est corpori,
e quo liquatae solis ardore excidunt
guttae, quae saxa assidue instillant Caucasi.

IV.

(205 H., 194 D., 194 N.)

Plut. *Moral.* p. 98 c (cp. p. 964 f.). νῦν δὲ οὐκ ἀπὸ τύχης οὐδὲ αὐτομάτως περίεσμεν αὐτῶν (sc. τῶν θηρίων) καὶ κρατοῦμεν, ἀλλ' ὁ Προμηθεὺς τουτέστιν ὁ λογισμὸς αἴτιος

> ἵππων ὄνων τ' ὀχεῖα καὶ ταύρων γονὰς
> δοὺς ἀντίδουλα καὶ πόνων ἐκδέκτορα.

δέ τοι πτηνὸς κύων. — 15. **adulat:** προσσαίνει, "wags at." The eagle's tail gloats, as it were, over Prometheus's mangled flesh. Cp. *Eum.* 254 ὀσμὴ βροτείων αἱμάτων με προσγελᾷ. — 22. **sic me ipse viduus:** αὐτὸς δ' ἐμαυτοῦ χῆρος. — 24. **a leto numine aspellor Iovis:** = ἐμοὶ θανεῖν οὐ τετρωμένον, οὐ μόρσιμον (753, 933). For the thought, see on 933. The prediction of 512, μυρίαις δὲ πημοναῖς δύαις τε

καμφθείς, is now fulfilled. — 27 f. From Prometheus's blood, according to the fable, came the Colchian poison used by Medea in her sorcery.

IV. Cp. 462 ff. above. As Prometheus there sets forth in detail his services to mankind, it is likely that here only a summary account is given, for the information of the new chorus. — πόνων ἐκδέκτορα: cp. διάδοχοι μοχθημάτων, 404.

V.

(212 H., 205 D., 200 N.)

Plut. *Moral.* p. 757 d. ὁ δὲ Ἡρακλῆς ἕτερον θεὸν παρακαλεῖ μέλλων ἐπὶ ὄρνιν αἴρεσθαι τὸ τόξον, ὡς Αἰσχύλος φησίν:

ἀγρεὺς δ' Ἀπόλλων ὀρθὸν ἰθύνοι βέλος.

VI.

(213 H., 201 D., 201 N.)

Plut. *Vit. Pomp.* c. 1. πρὸς δὲ Πομπήιον ἔοικε τοῦτο παθεῖν ὁ Ῥωμαίων δῆμος εὐθὺς ἐξ ἀρχῆς, ὅπερ ὁ Αἰσχύλου Προμηθεὺς πρὸς τὸν Ἡρακλέα σωθεὶς ὑπ' αὐτοῦ λέγων:

ἐχθροῦ πατρός μοι τοῦτο φίλτατον τέκνον.

VII.

(206 H., 198 D., 196 N.)

Stephanus Byzant. *s. v.* Ἄβιοι p. 7, 5. Αἰσχύλος τε Γαβίους διὰ τοῦ γ ἐν λυομένῳ Προμηθεῖ:

ἔπειτα δ' ἥξεις δῆμον ἐνδικώτατον
(βροτῶν) ἁπάντων καὶ φιλοξενώτατον,

V. and VI. ἀγρεύς: Apollo is so called as hunter and archer. It appears that Heracles, when he shoots the eagle, is upon the stage, standing somewhat at the side. The result of his shot may have been indicated by a heavy fall behind one of the periaktoi. Prometheus then joyfully exclaims, looking at Heracles, ἐχθροῦ πατρός μοι τοῦτο φίλτατον τέκνον.

VII. and VIII. Corresponding to the scene with Io in the Προμηθεὺς δεσμότης, with its geographical description, was the account given to Heracles, in the Προμηθεὺς λυόμενος, of his future expedition to the Hesperides (cp. the words of Strabo preceding Frg. X.). The goal of Io's wanderings lay in the east, that of Heracles's in the west. Thus the

Γαβίους, ἵν' οὔτ' ἄροτρον οὔτε γατόμος
τέμνει δίκελλ' ἄρουραν, ἀλλ' αὐτόσποροι
γύαι φέρουσι βίοτον ἄφθονον βροτοῖς.

VIII.

(208 H., 203 D., 108 N.)

Strabo VII p. 300. καὶ Αἰσχύλος δ' ἐμφαίνει συνηγορῶν τῷ ποιητῇ, φήσας περὶ τῶν Σκυθῶν:

ἀλλ' ἱππάκης βρωτῆρες εὔνομοι Σκύθαι.

IX.

(209 H., 195 D., 195 and 208 N.)

Galenus vol. IX p. 385 ed. Charter. δοκεῖ μὲν γὰρ αὐτὴν (sc. πέμφιγα) ἐπὶ τῆς πνοῆς Σοφοκλῆς ἐν Κολχίσι λέγειν ... Αἰσχύλος δὲ ἐν Προμηθεῖ δεσμώτῃ (probably a mistake for λυομένῳ, but see note on 714 above):

two plays afforded the Athenians, who at that epoch were enormously interested in such accounts (see on 501 above), a description of all the wonders of the world.

According to the scholiast on Apoll. Rhod. iv. 284 (τὸν Ἴστρον φησὶν ἐκ τῶν Ὑπερβορέων καταφέρεσθαι καὶ τὸν Ῥιπαίων ὀρῶν, οὕτω δὲ εἶπεν ἀκολουθῶν Αἰσχύλῳ ἐν λυομένῳ Προμηθεῖ λέγοντι τοῦτο) Heracles proceeds from the Caucasus to the Rhipaean mountains. Aeschylus makes these the source of the Ister; he must therefore suppose them to lie in the north-west of Europe. On this route Heracles meets with Scythian tribes, the

Gabii, or Abii, and the Hippemolgi, known to us from *Il.* xiii. 4

νόσφιν ἐφ' ἱπποπόλων Θρηκῶν καθορώμενος αἶαν
Μυσῶν τ' ἀγχεμάχων καὶ ἀγαυῶν Ἱππημολγῶν
γλακτοφάγων Ἀβίων τε, δικαιοτάτων ἀνθρώπων.

— ἵν' οὔτ' ἄροτρον ... βροτοῖς: cp. the passage about the land of the Cyclopes, *Od.* ix. 107 οἵ ῥα θεοῖσι πεποιθότες ἀθανάτοισιν οὔτε φυτεύουσιν χερσὶν φυτὸν οὔτ' ἀρόωσιν, ἀλλὰ τά γ' ἄσπαρτα καὶ ἀνήροτα πάντα φύονται κτλ. — ἱππάκης: cp. the passage of Hippocrates quoted on Frg. IX.

εὐθεῖαν ἕρπε τήνδε· καὶ πρώτιστα μὲν
Βορεάδας ἥξεις πρὸς πνοάς, ἵν' εὐλαβοῦ
στρόμβον καταιγίζοντα, μή σ' ἀναρπάσῃ
δυσχειμέρῳ πέμφιγι συστρέψας ἄφνω.

ἐπὶ δὲ τῆς ρανίδος ὁ αὐτός φησιν ἐν Προμηθεῖ:

ἐξευλαβοῦ δὲ μή σε προσβάλῃ στόμα
πέμφιξ. πικροὶ γὰρ κοὐ διὰ ζόης ἀτμοί.

X.

(210 II., 196 D., 109 N.)

Strabo IV p. 182. μεταξὺ τῆς Μασσαλίας καὶ τῶν ἐκβο-
λῶν τοῦ Ῥοδανοῦ πεδίον ἐστὶ τῆς θαλάττης διέχον εἰς ἑκατὸν σταδίους,
τοσοῦτον δὲ καὶ τὴν διάμετρον, κυκλοτερὲς τὸ σχῆμα. καλεῖται δὲ
Λιθῶδες ἀπὸ τοῦ συμβεβηκότος. μεστὸν γάρ ἐστι λίθων χειροπληθῶν,
ὑποπεφυκυῖαν ἐχόντων αὐτοῖς ἄγρωστιν· ἀφ' ἧς ἄφθονοι νομαὶ βοσκή-
μασίν εἰσιν, ἐν μέσῳ δ' ὕδατα καὶ ἁλυκίδες ἐνίστανται καὶ ἅλες. . . . τὸ
μέντοι δυσαπολόγητον Αἰσχύλος καταμαθὼν ἢ παρ' ἄλλου λαβὼν εἰς μῦθον

IX. εὐθεῖαν ἕρπε τήνδε: perhaps
up the Ister, towards the Rhipaean
mountains, ὅθεν ὁ Βορέης πνέει, according to Hippocrates de Aer., Aq.
et Loc., p. 291, 49, who says of the
Scythian region κεῖται ὑπ' αὐταῖς ταῖς
ἄρκτοις καὶ τοῖς ὄρεσι τοῖς Ῥιπαίοισιν,
and of the Scythians themselves
ἐσθίουσιν κρέα ἐφθὰ καὶ πίνουσι γάλα
ἵππων καὶ ἱππάκην τρώγουσι· τοῦτο
δ' ἐστὶ τυρὸς ἵππων.—Βορεάδας: for
the tribrach in the first foot see on
116.—εὐλαβοῦ: similar warnings are
given Io. See on 801.—στρόμβον:
cp. 1084 above.
ἐξευλαβοῦ κτέ.: this passage per-
tains to the description of another
monster, which, as it seems, exhales
blood.—πέμφιξ: cannot stand outright for ῥανίς, as Galen says; nor
is this the case in the verse from
Aeschylus's Pentheus, which Galen
quotes as another example, μηδ' αἵμα-
τος πέμφιγα πρὸς πέδῳ βάλῃς. The
word means breath (cp. Curtius, Gr.
Etymol.⁵ p. 718), and stands in both
passages much as πνοὴ φοινίου σταλάγ-
ματος, Soph. Ant. 1238. — σε . . . στόμα: cp. Eum. 88 σε νικάτω φρένας, 875
τίς μ' ὑποδύεται πλευρὰς ὀδύνα, Sept. 834
κακόν με καρδίαν τι περιπίτνει κρύος,
Pers. 161 καί με καρδίαν ἀμύσσει φρον-
τίς. Krüger II. § 46, 16, 3; H. 625 c.
— κοὐ διὰ ζόης: cp. 800 above.

ἐξετόπισε. φησὶ γοῦν Προμηθεὺς παρ' αὐτῷ καθηγούμενος Ἡρακλεῖ
τῶν ὁδῶν τῶν ἀπὸ Καυκάσου πρὸς τὰς Ἑσπερίδας:

ἥξεις δὲ Λιγύων εἰς ἀτάρβητον στρατόν,
ἔνθ' οὐ μάχης, σάφ' οἶδα, καὶ θοῦρός περ ὢν
μέμψει· πέπρωται γάρ σε καὶ βέλη λιπεῖν
ἐνταῦθ'· ἑλέσθαι δ' οὔτιν' ἐκ γαίας λίθον
5   ἕξεις, ἐπεὶ πᾶς χῶρός ἐστι μαλθακός.
ἰδὼν δ' ἀμηχανοῦντά σ' ὁ Ζεὺς οἰκτερεῖ,
νεφέλην δ' ὑπερσχὼν νιφάδι γογγύλων πέτρων
ὑπόσκιον θήσει χθόν', οἷς ἔπειτα σὺ
βαλὼν διώσει ῥαδίως Λίγυν στρατόν.

X. From the northern region Heracles turns southward. His next destination is the realm of the monster Geryones. On the way he comes into conflict with the Ligyes, and is saved by the miracle of a shower of stones. Cp. Dionys. Hal. *Antiq.* i. 41 δηλοῖ δὲ τὸν πόλεμον τόνδε (that of the Hellenes against the Ligyes) τῶν ἀρχαίων ποιητῶν Αἰσχύλος ἐν Προμηθεῖ λυομένῳ· πεποίηται γὰρ αὐτῷ ὁ Προμηθεὺς Ἡρακλεῖ τά τε ἄλλα προλέγων, ὡς ἕκαστον αὐτῷ τι συμβήσεσθαι ἔμελλε κατὰ τὴν ἐπὶ Γηρυόνην στρατείαν, καὶ δὴ καὶ περὶ τοῦ Λιγυστικοῦ πολέμου ὡς οὐ ῥᾴδιος ὁ ἀγὼν ἔσται διηγούμενος. This adventure Aeschylus described in a choral passage of his *Heraclidae*, from which these words are preserved: ἐκεῖθεν ὁρμενος ὀρθόκερως βοῦς ἤλασ' ἐπ' ἐσχάτων γαίας ὠκεανὸν περάσας ἐν δέπαι χρυσηλάτῳ βοτῆρά[ς] τ' ἀδίκους ἔκτεινε δεσπότην τε τρίζυγα τὸν τρία δόρη πάλλοντα χερσί τρία δὲ λαιαῖς σάκη προτείνων τρεῖς τ' ἐπισσείων λόφους ἔστειχεν ἴσος Ἄρει βίαν.

1. On the tribrach in the second foot, in a proper name, see on 715 and 2 above. — 2. καὶ ... περ: this occurs in Homer, though καίπερ does not. Krüger II. § 56, 13, 1. — 7. Frequent resolutions occur in these descriptions (cp. on 715) owing to the novelty of the subject. Here two resolutions in one verse. For the anapaest see on 6 above; for the dactyl, on 18. — 9. διώσει: cp. Hdt. iv. 102 τὸν Δαρείου στρατὸν ἰθυμαχίῃ διώσασθαι. — Λίγυν: see on 2 above. On Heracles's visit to Atlas see Introd. p. 13, footnote 1.

LYRIC VERSES IN THE PROLOGUE.

115. Bacchic tetrameter.

∪ ⫶ _ _ ∪ | _ _ ∪ | _ _ ∪ | _ _

117. Dochmius and cretic.

> ⫶ ∪∪ ⩗ ∪ | ∪∪ ∪∪ ∪ | _

PARODOS.

FIRST STROPHE, 128–135 = 144–151.

Ionic.

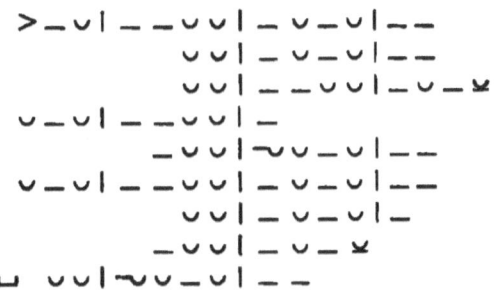

NOTE. — For the acephalous phrase which begins lines 1, 4, and 6 (the common dipody ∪∪ ⩗ ᷓ _ ∪ ⩗ _, lacking the first three syllables), see Christ, *Metrik*², p. 608. In lines 5 and 9 occurs a peculiar form of measure, in which ⌣∪ ∪ replaces _ ∪.

159

SECOND STROPHE, 159–166 = 178–185.

Iambic and Logaoedic.

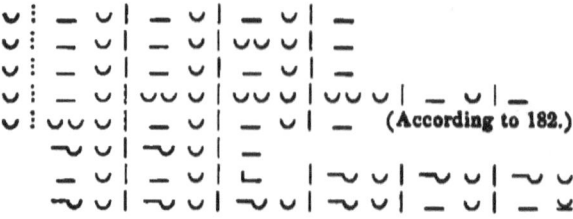

(According to 182.)

FIRST STASIMON.

FIRST STROPHE, 397–405 = 406–414.

Ionic.

SECOND STROPHE, 415–419 = 420–424.

Trochaic and Logaoedic.

THIRD STROPHE, 425–430 = 431–435.

Iambic and Logaoedic.

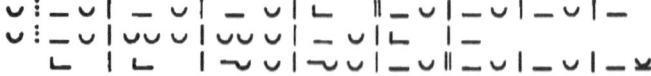

NOTE. — This scheme follows the antistrophe. See on 425–430.

SECOND STASIMON.

FIRST STROPHE, 526–535 = 536–544.

Dactylo-Epitritic.

```
‒ ∪∪ | ‒ ∪∪ | ‒
‗ ∪ | ‒ ‒ ‖ ‒ ∪∪ | ‒ ∪∪ | ‒ ‒
‗ ∪ | ‒ ‒ ‖ ‒ ∪∪ | ‒ ∪∪ | ‒ ‒ ‖ ‒ ∪∪ | ‒ ∪∪ | ‒
‗ ∪ | ‗ ⌣ ‖ ‒ ∪∪ | ‒ ∪∪ | ‒ ‒ ‖ ‗ ∪ | ‒
‒ ∪∪ | ‒ ∪∪ | ‒
‗ ∪ | ‗ ⌣ | ‗ ∪ | ‒ ‒ ‖ ‗ ∪ | ‗ ∪ | ‒ ‒
```

SECOND STROPHE, 545–552 = 553–560.

Logaoedic.

```
∪∪ ⋮ ⌣∪ | ⌣∪ | ⌣∪ ‖ ‒ ∪ | ‒ ∪ | ‒ ⌣
∪∪ ⋮ ⌣∪ | ‒ ∪ | ‒ ∪ ‖ ‒ ∪ | ‒ ⌣
∪∪ ⋮ ⌣∪ | ‒ ∪ | ‒ ∪
        ‒ ∪ | ‒ ∪ | ‒ ∪ | ‒ ⌣
∪∪ ⋮ ⌣∪ | ⌣∪ | ⌣∪ | ⌣∪ | ‒ ⌣
        ⌣∪ | ⌣∪ | ‒ > ‖ ‒ ∪ | ‒ ∪ | ‒ ∪ | ‒ ⌣
```

MONODY OF IO.

PROÖDE, 566–573.

Iambic, with Dochmii.

```
> ⋮ ‒
> ⋮ ‒ ∪ | ‒ ∪ | ‒ ∪ | ‒ ∪ | ‒ ∪
> ⋮ ‒ ∪ | ‒ > | ‒ ∪ | ‒
∪ ⋮ ‒ > | ‒
> ⋮ ‒ ∪ | ‒ ∪ | ‒ ∪ | ‒ ∪ | ‒ ⌣
∪ ⋮ ∪∪ ∠ ∪ | ‒ , ∪ | ∪∪ ∠ ∪ | ‒   Two dochmii.
∪ ⋮ ‒ ∪ | ‒ ∪ | ‒ ∪ | ‒ ∪ | ‒ ⌣
> ⋮ ∪∪ ∠ ∪ | ‒ ⌣   Lengthened dochmius. Christ², p. 431.
> ⋮ ∪∪ ∠ ∪ | ‒ , ∪ | ‒ ∠ ∪ | ‒   Two dochmii.
∪ ⋮ ‒ ∪́∪ ∪ | ‒ , ∪ | ∪∪ ∠ > | ‒   Two dochmii.
```

STROPHE, 574–588 = 593–600.

Dochmii, with other Rhythms.

∪ ⋮ ∪∪∠∪ | _ ∪ | ∪∪∠∪ | _	Two dochmii.
_ ∪ | _ , ∪ | ∪∪∠∪ | ⋎	Cretic and dochmius.
∪ ⋮ ∪∪∠∪ | _ _∪ | _ _∪ | _	Dochmius and two cretics.
> ⋮ ∪∪∠∪ | _	Dochmius.
∪ ⋮ ∪∪∠∪ | ∪∪∠∪ | ∪∪	Dochmius and cretic.
_ ∪ | _ _∪ | _ _∪ | _ _∪ | _	Four cretics.
> ⋮ ∪∪∠∪ | _	Dochmius.
> ⋮ _ ∪ | _ ∪ | _∪∪ | _ > | _	Logaoedic.
∪ ⋮ ∪∪∪ | _ ∪ | _ ⋎	Trochaic.
∪ ⋮ ∪∪∠∪ | _ ∪ | ∪∪∠∪ | _ _ ∪ | _	Two dochmii and cretic.
∪ ⋮ ∪∪∠∪ | _	Dochmius.
_ ∪ | _ ∪ | _ ⋎	
_ ∪ | _ ∪ | _	
♂ ⋮ _ ∪ | ∪∪∪ | _ ∪ | _	Trochaic-iambic.
∪ ⋮ _ ∪ | _ ∪ | _ ∪ | _ ∪ | _ ∪ | _	
_ ∪ | _ ∪ | _ ⋎	
∪ ⋮ _ ∠∪ | _ _ ∪ | _ _ ∪ | _	Dochmius and two cretics.

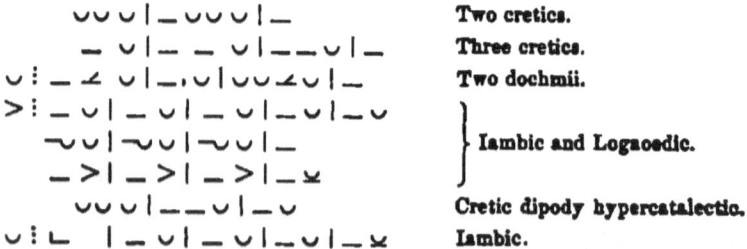

CHORICUM.

687–695.

Cretics and Dochmii, with other Rhythms.

∪∪∪ | _ ∪∪∪ | _	Two cretics.
_ ∪ | _ _ ∪ | _ _∪ | _	Three cretics.
∪ ⋮ _ ∠ ∪ | _ , ∪ | ∪∪∠∪ | _	Two dochmii.
> ⋮ _ ∪ | _ ∪ | _ ∪ | _∪ | _ ∪	
∪∪ | _∪∪ | _∪∪ | _	Iambic and Logaoedic.
_ > | _ > | _ > | _ ⋎	
∪∪∪ | _ _ ∪ | _ ∪	Cretic dipody hypercatalectic.
∪ ⋮ ∟ | _ ∪ | _ ∪ | _∪ | _ ⋎	Iambic.

THIRD STASIMON.

Strophe, 887–893 = 894–900.

Dactylo-Epitritic.

```
_ ∪∪ | _ ∪∪ | _
∟ ∪ | _ _ ‖ _ ∪∪ | _ ∪∪ | _ _ ‖ _ ∪∪ | _ ∪∪ | _ ×
∟ ∪ | _ _ ‖ _ ∪∪ | _ ∪∪ | _ _ ‖ ∟ ∪ | _
_ ⋮ ∟ ∪ | _ _ ‖ _ ∪∪ | _ ∪∪ | _
∟ ∪ | _ _ ‖ _ ∪∪ | _ ∪∪ | _
∟ ∪ | _ _ ‖ ∟ ∪ | _ _ ‖ ∟ ∪ | _
```

Epode, 901–906.

Iambo-Trochaic.

```
∪ ⋮ _ ∪ | ∪∪ ∪ | ∪∪ ∪ | ∪∪ ∪ | ∪∪ ∪ | _
      _ ∪ | _ ∪ | _ ∪ | _
∪ ⋮ _ ∪ | _ ∪ | _ ∪ | _ ∪ | _ ∪
∪ ⋮ ∪∪ ∪ | ∪∪ ∪ | ∪∪ ∪ | ∪∪ ∪ | ∪∪ ∪
      _ ∪ | _ ∪ | _ ∪ | _ ×
      _ ∪ | _ ∪ | _ ∪ | _
    ⌣ ∪ | _ ∪ | ∟   | _        Logaoedic close.
```

APPENDIX

A. LITERATURE.

1. Editions: Schutz 1809 (2d ed.), Blomfield 1810 (7th ed. 1837). Bothe 1831, W. Dindorf 1841, Fix 1843, Schoemann 1844, G. Hermann 1852, Hartung 1852, Meineke 1853, Weil (Giessen) 1864, W. Dindorf *Poetae scenici* 1869 (5th ed.), L. Schmidt 1870, Paley 1879 (4th ed.), Weil (Paris) 1884, Wecklein (Berlin, critical edition) 1885.

2. Treatises on the text: C. Reisigii *emendationes in Aeschyli Prometheum*, reprinted in Ritschl's *Opuscula*, I, pp. 378-393. Fr. Wieseler. *adversaria in Aeschyli Prometheum vinctum et Aristophanis Aves philologica et archaeologica*, Göttingen 1843. Schoemann, *Mantissa animadversionum ad Aeschyli Prometheum* (1845), reprinted in his *Opuscula*, III, pp. 81-94. E. J. Kiehl, *Aeschylea, Spec. I*, Leyden 1850. Wieseler, *zu Aeschylos' Prometheus*, in *Philologus* IX, p. 710 ff.; *schedae criticae in Aeschyli Prometheum vinctum* in *Index lectionum Gotting. aestiv.* 1860. F. V. Fritzsche, *de Aeschylo G. Hermanni, accedunt emendationes*, Rostock 1880; *Miscellanea*, Rostock 1882. Ad. Reuter, *de Promethei, Septem, Persarum fabularum codicibus recentioribus*, Rostock 1883. A. Nauck, *Kritische Bemerkungen*, St. Petersburg 1885. F. W. Schmidt, *Kritische Studien zu den griech. Dramatikern; I. Aeschylos und Sophokles*, Berlin 1886. C. G. Cobet, *de locis quibusdam in Aeschyli Prometheo et scholiis antiquis ad hanc tragoediam*, in *Mnemosyne N. S. XIV*, p. 121 ff. Hans Flach, *zum Prometheus des Aeschylos*, in *Jahrbücher für Philologie*, vol. 129, p. 827 ff.

3. On the Myth of Prometheus: Weiske, *Prometheus und sein Mythenkreis*, Leipzig 1842. E. von Lausaulx, *Prometheus, der Mythus und seine Bedeutung*, in Würzburg lecture-list, 1843. Preller, *Griechische Mythologie* (4th ed.), I, pp. 91-102. Zinsow, *die Prometheussage*, in *Paedagog. Archiv*, 1866, pp. 641-683.

4. On the Composition of the Trilogy: A. W. von Schlegel, *Vorlesungen über dramatische Kunst*, I, p. 164. Blümner, *die Idee des Schicksals in den Tragödien des Aeschylos*, Leipzig 1814. Other material cited in Schoemann's edition, p. 90 ff. Welcker, *die Aeschyleische Trilogie Prometheus*, etc., Darmstadt 1824; *Nachtrag* to the same, Frankfort 1826. G. Hermann, *de Aeschyli Prometheo soluto*, 1828, reprinted in his *Opuscula*, Vol. IV. Dissen (letter to Welcker) printed in Welcker's *Trilogie*, pp. 92-94. J. H. Theoph. Schmidt, *de Prometheo vincto*, Augsburg 1831.

Anselm Feurbach, *de Promethei Aeschyli consilio atque indole* (in his *Nach-gelassene Schriften* edited by Hettner, Brunswick 1853, Vol. IV, p. 129). J. Caesar, review of Schoemann's edition in the *Zeitschrift für das Alter-thum*, 1845, n. 41. G. Hermann, *de Prometheo Aeschyleo*, Leipz. 1845 (*Opuscula*, Vol. VIII, pp. 144-158). Schoemann, *Vindiciae Iovis Aeschylei*, Greifswald 1846 (*Opuscula*, III, p. 95), and *über den Prometheus des Aeschylos* in *Zeitschrift für d. Alterthum*, 1846, n. 111 (*Opuscula*, III, p. 120). Caesar, reply to Schoemann, in same periodical, n. 113, p. 899. H. Keck, *der theologische Charakter des Zeus in Aesch. Prometheus*, Glück-stadt 1851. Moriz Carriere, *Prometheus*, in the *Deutsches Museum*, 1855, n. 14. Doellinger, *Heidenthum und Judenthum*, Ratisbon 1857, p. 269. Welcker, *Griechische Götterlehre*, Göttingen 1859-60, II, p. 246. Her-mann Koechly, *Akademische Vorträge und Reden*, I, Zürich 1857, p. 1 (reviewed by Karl Lehrs in the *Jahrbücher für Philologie*, 1859, p. 555). Schoemann, *Noch ein Wort über Aeschylos' Prometheus*, Greifswald 1859. Caesar, *der Prometheus des Aeschylos; zur Revision der Frage über seine theologische Bedeutung*, Marburg 1859. W. Vischer, *über die Prometheus-tragödien des Aeschylos*, Basle 1859. H. Keck, *die neueste Literatur über Aeschylos' Prometheus* in *Jahrbücher für Philologie*, 1860, p. 459. W. Teuf-fel, *über des Aeschylos Prometheus und Orestie*, Tübingen 1861. W. Mar-cowitz, *de Aeschyli Prometheo*, Düsseldorf 1865. B. Steussloff, *Zeus und die Gottheit bei Aeschylos*, Lissa 1867. Th. Henri Martin, *la Prométhéide, étude sur la pensée et la structure de cette trilogie d'Eschyle*, Paris 1875. Paul Schwarz, *die Darstellung des Zeus im Prometheus des Aeschylus*, Salz-wedel 1875. Karl Frey, *Aeschylus-Studien*, Schaffhausen 1875. F. Seel-mann, *de Prometheo Aeschyleo*, Dessau 1876. Alexander Kolisch, *der Prometheus des Aeschylos nur zu verstehen aus der Eigenthümlichkeit seiner Entstehung*, Berlin 1876. Patin, *Études sur les tragiques Grecs* (5th ed.), 1877, I, pp. 250-305. Alceste Lenzi, *il mito del Prometeo di Eschilo*, pro-gram of the Liceo Pontano in Spoleto, 1877. Lewis Campbell, *the inten-tion of Aeschylus in the Prometheus-Trilogy*, in *Academy*, 1877, n. 271, p. 43. Christian Muff, *zwei Titanen, Prometheus und Faust*, Halle 1883. Alexan-der Kolisch, *über den Prometheus des Aeschylos*, in *Philologus*, XLI, p. 227 ff.; *Wer löst die Fesseln des Prometheus?* in *Zeitschrift für das Gymna-sialwesen*, XXXIII, p. 65 ff.

5. On Place and Scenery: Pet. Jos. Meyer, *Aeschyli Prometheus vinc-tus quo in loco agi videatur*, Bonn 1861. Bernhard Foss, *de loco in quo Prometheus apud Aeschylum vinctus sit*, Bonn 1862. C. Fr. Müller, *die scenische Darstellung des aeschyleischen Prometheus*, Stade 1871.

6. On the symmetry of the dialogue: O. Ribbeck, *qua Aeschylus arte in Prometheo fabula diverbia composuerit*, Berne 1859.

B. Variations from the Medicean Manuscript.

[See G. Hermann, *Aeschyli Tragoediae*, ed. II. (1859), vol. II.; R. Merkel, *Aeschyli quae supersunt in codice Laurentiano veterrimo*, Oxonii, 1871; N. Wecklein, *Aeschyli Tragoediae*, Berolini, 1885, vol. I. The reading of the text precedes the colon; that of the manuscript follows it. W. = Wecklein.]

2. ἄβροτον Schol. on *Il.* xiv. 78 and on Ar. *Ran.* 827: ἀβατόν τ' (other mss. ἄβατον).—6. ἀδαμαντίνων δεσμῶν ἐν ἀρρήκτοις πέδαις Schol. on Ar. *Ran.* 827: ἀδαμαντίναις πέδησιν ἐν ἀρρήκτοις πέτραις.—15. πρὸς: τῆι with προς written above.—16. σχεθεῖν Elmsley on Eur. *Med.* 108: σχέθειν.—17. εὐωριάζειν Blomfield after glosses of Hesych. and Photius: ἐξωριάζειν.—20. τάγῳ other mss.: τόπῳ.—28. ἰπηύρου Elmsley: ἰπηύρω.—42. γε other mss.: τε.—49. ἰταχθῆ Stanley: ἐπράχθη.—54. ψάλια other mss.: ψάλια.—55. βαλών Stanley: λαβών.—65. διαμπάξ: διαμπάξ.—66. ὑπὸ στένω W.: ὑποστένω first hand, ὑπεροστένω second.—77. γε other mss.: σε (τ for σ by later hand).—80. τραχυτῆτα Dindorf (cp. Arcad. p. 28, 8): τραχύτητα.—90. παμμῆτορ other mss.: παμμήτωρ.—96. ἐξηῦρ' (cp. 400): ἐξεῦρ'.—99. τῆ Turnebus: τοί.—πότε W.: ποτε (see on 544).

112. τοιῶνδε other mss.: τοιάσδε.—113. ὑπαιθρίοις Blomfield: ὑπαίθριος.—προυσελούμενος W.: πασσαλεύμενος.—114. ἇ ἇ Dindorf: ἀ ἀ ἴα ἴα (cp. 500).—116. θεόσυτος another ms.: θεόσσυτος (cp. 279).—118. ἐμῶν other mss.: ἡμῶν.—128. ἅδε Hermann: ἧδε.—134. θερμερῶπιν first hand, θερμερῶπιν second hand.—136. αἰαῖ αἰαῖ Dindorf after other mss.: αἰ αἰ al.—142. προσπορπατός other mss.: πρὸς πατρός.—144. δνοφερά Hirschig: φοβερά.—145. ὁμίχλα other mss.: ὁμίχλη.—146. εἰσιδούσαν Hermann: εἰσίδουσα (α by later hand).—147. τῷδ' Elmsley: ταῖσδ'.—ἀδαμαντοδέτοισι Turnebus: ἀμαντοδέτοις (δα over ἀμ and το by later hand).—150. ἀθέτως Bentley from Hesych.: ἀθέσμως.—152. θ' Ἀίδου Turnebus: τ' ἀίδου.—155. ἀγρίοις other mss.: ἀγρίοις ('ἀγρίοις Aeschylus si scripsisset, posuisset ἀλύτοις δεσμοῖς ἀγρίοις' Hermann).—156. See under C.—161. ξυνασχαλᾷ (after 243): ξυνασχαλᾷ.—167. ἐν' ἐμοῦ other mss.: ἐτ' ἀπ' ἐμοῦ (cp. Heimsoeth *Krit. Stud.* p. 315).—170. ἀφ' ὅτου first hand, ὑφ' ὅτου second hand.—172. οὔτε Porson: οὔτοι.—176. τε τίνειν Turnebus: τέ μοι τίνειν.—177. τῆσδ' other mss.: τῆς.—181. ἐρέθισε Turnebus: ἠρέθισε.—183. τᾶ Turnebus: ὅτα.—πότα W.: ποτα (see on 99).—185. ἀπαράμυθον other mss.: οὐ παράμυθον.—186. τραχὺς καὶ other mss.: τραχύς τε καί.—187. See under C.—189. ῥαισθῆ other mss.: ῥωσθῆ (ω in an erasure, apparently of αι).—198. παντάχη W.: παντάχη.

201. ἵδρας other mss.: ἵδρης.—204. πιθεῖν: πείθειν first hand.—213. χρείη, δόλῳ δὲ τοὺς: χρή. ἢ δόλῳ τοὺς first hand.—ὑπερσχόντας Porson: ὑπερέχοντας.—226. αἰτίαν other mss.: αἰτίην.—235. δ' ἐτόλμησ' other mss.: δὲ τόλμησ'.—237. τῷ τοι other mss. and Schol.: τῷ ταῖς (τοι over ταῖς by another hand).—240. ἀλλὰ νηλεῶς Elmsley: ἀλλ' ἀνηλεῶς.—246. ἐλπίνός Porson: ἐλεεινός.

—247. μή πού τι other mss.: μή ποί τι. —248. θνητούς other mss.: θνητούς τ'. —256. See under C. —κούδαμή W.: κούδαμῆ. —264 f. τὸν κακῶς πράσσοντ' Stanley: τοὺς κακῶς πράσσοντας. —269. κατισχναινέσθαι other mss.: κατισχανείσθαι. —πιδαρσίοις later hand, πιδαρσίαις first hand. —274. πίθεσθε Blomfield: πείθεσθε (see on 204 and 333). —279. κραιπνόσυτον other mss.: κραιπνόσσυτον. —293 f. γνώσει ... χαριτογλωσσείν Athen. iv. p. 165 c: γνώσῃ ... σὺ τὸ χαριτογλωσσείν. —295. συμπράσσειν Brunck: συμπράττειν.

313 f. τὸν νῦν χόλον παρόντα μόχθον Lowinski: τὸν νῦν χόλον παρόντα μόχθων (μόχθον other mss.). —331. μετασχείν Weil (see under C): μετασχόν. —332. μηδί other mss.: μηδίν. —333. πείσεις other mss.: πείθεις. —334. σημανθῇς: σημανθῇς later hand, σημαθῇς first hand. —340. κούδαμή other mss.: κούδὲ μή. —343. θέλοις other mss.: θέλεις. —347. See under C. —χαι Porson: καί. —348. πρός other mss.: ἐς. —353. ἑκατογκάρανον Pauw and Blomfield: ἑκατονταικάρηνον (with a over ῆ). —354. πᾶσι δ' ἀντέστη Hermann: πᾶσιν δὲ ἀντέστη —371. θερμοῖς ... βέλεσι other mss., ἀπλάτου Schütz: θερμῆς ἀπλήστου βέλεσσι (cp. 716, Eum. 53). —378. ὀργῆς σφριγῶσης: ὀργῆς νοσούσης (see under C). —380. σφυδῶντα: σφριγῶντα (see under C). —ἰσχναίνῃ other mss.: ἰσχναίει (with ν over ει). —392. σφίς (as 374 in the Med.) W.: σῶζε. —395. ἐὶ τὸν Blomfield: δ' ἐν' ἐν. —398 f. δακρυσίστακτα W.: δακρυσίστακτον. —ῥαδινὸν other mss.: ῥαδινῶν.

401. παγαῖς other mss.: πηγαῖς. —405. ἐνδείκνυσιν αἰχμάν other mss.: ἐνδεικνύειν αἰχμήν. —407. See under C. —420. Ἀρίας Hartung: Ἀραβίας. —421. ἱψίκρημνον Bothe and Elmsley: ὑψίκρημνον Γ. —428. Ἄτλανθ' ὃς other mss.: Ἄτλανθ' ὡς. See further under C. —432. βυθὸς other mss.: βαθύς. 433. κελαινὸς Hermann: κελαινὸς δ'. —438. προσείλούμενον Askew (after Etym. M. p. 690, 11 and Ar. Ran. 730): προσήλούμενον (ε over ῆ by early hand). —450. εἰκῇ W.: εἰκῆ. —451. προσείλους other mss. and Schol.: προσήλους (with ει over η). —452. ἀήσυροι first hand, ἀείσυροι later hand. —459. σοφισμάτων other mss. and Stobaeus Ecl. Phys. i. 1: νοσφισμάτων (σοφισμάτων very late hand in margin). —460. ἐξηύρον Stobaeus: ἐξεύρον (so 468 εὕρε; cp. W. Curae Epigr. p. 33). —461. ἐργάνην Stobaeus Floril. 81, 1: ἐργάτιν (ἀτιν by later hand over ἐργαν ... by first hand). —463. σάγμασιν Pauw: σόμασιν. —464. διάδοχοι: διάδοχον first hand. —465. γένοιθ' Dawes Misc. Crit. p. 272: γένωνθ'. —ἅρμα τ' Turnebus: ἅρματ'. —468. ναυτίλων other mss.: ναυτιλόχων (i.e. ναυτίλων and ναυλόχων). —470. σόφισμ' ὅτῳ other mss.: σοφισμάτων (ὅτῳ written above by very late hand). —472. αἰκὶς Porson: ἀεικές. —479. οὔτε other mss.: οὐδέ. —480. οὔτε Blomfield: οὐδέ. —494 f. See under C.

502. σίδηρον ... τε other mss.: σίδαρον ... δὲ. —505. πάντα other mss.: ταῦτα. —507. μή νυν Scaliger: μὴ νῦν. —510. ἰσχύσειν: ἰσχύσει first hand. —519. πλὴν other mss.: πρίν. —520. οὐκ ἂν ἰκπύθοιο another ms.: οὐκ ἂν οὖν πύθοιο. —524. σώζων (see 392): σώζων. —530. ποτινισσομένα other mss.: ποτινισομένα. —536. ἁδύ Hermann: ἡδύ. —537. τείνειν other mss.: τίνειν. —544 f. ἄχαρις χάρις Turnebus: χάρις ἄχαρις. —τοῦ τίς another ms.: τοῦ τις. —

}:

550. δίδεται added by Meineke (*Zeitschr. für Alterth.* 1845 p. 1063). — οὗτος Paley (οὕτω Hermann): οὕποτε. — **554.** προσιδοῦσ' other mss.: προιδοῦσ'. — **556.** ἐκεῖνό θ' ὅτ' Brunck: ἐκεῖν' ὅτε τότ' (other mss. ἐκεῖνό τε θτ'). — **562.** χαλινοῖς other mss.: χαλινοῖσιν. — **566.** ἃ ἅ Dindorf: ἃ ἃ θ ἴ. — **567.** με τὰν τάλαιναν other mss.: με τάλαιναν. — οἶστρος: οἴστροις first hand. — **569.** τὸν Triclinius: φοβοῦμαι τὸν. — **572.** κυναγεῖ Hermann: κυνηγετεῖ. — **574.** κηρόπακτος Meineke (*Philol.* XX. 52): κηρόπλαστος. — **575.** ἰὼ ἰὼ πόποι Seidler (*de vers. dochm.* p. 84 and 141): ἰὼ ἰὼ ποῖ ποῖ 'πότοι 'πότοι. — ποι μ' other mss.: πῇ μ'. — πλάναι added by Meineke (*Philol.* XX. 231). — τηλέπλανοι Seidler: τηλέπλαγκτοι. — πλάναι other mss.: πλάνοι. — **579.** σημοσύναις Hermann: σημοναῖσιν. — ἰή Dindorf: ἰ ἴ. — **582.** με added by Elmsley. — **586.** ὅτα: ὅτη. — **588.** Given by Hermann and Elmsley to Io; formerly to the chorus. — **592.** Ἥρᾳ ... γυμνάζεται: Ἥρα ... γυμνάζεται. — **597.** θεόσυτον Hermann: θεόσσυτον. — **598.** κίντροις, ἴ(ω) W.: κίντροισι. — **599.** φοιταλέοις Hermann: φοιταλέοισιν.

601. λαβρόσυτος Hermann: λαβρόσσυτος. — ⟨Ἑλλων⟩: see under C. — **602.** ἰή Dindorf: ἰ ἴ. — **606.** τί μῆχαρ ἢ τί φάρμακον Fr. Martin (τί μῆχαρ; τί φάρμακον Elmsley): τί μὴ χρὴ φάρμακον. — **608.** φράζε τῷ other mss.: φράζετε. — **609.** ὅπερ *Et. M.* p. 762, 30: ὅτι. — χρῄζεις: χρήζεις. — **617.** πᾶν δ' ἂν οὐ F. V. Fritzsche: πᾶν γὰρ οὖν (πᾶν γὰρ ἂν other mss.). — **621.** σαφηνίσας Linwood, Keck (*Jahrb. für Philol.* 81, p. 478): σαφηνῆσαι. — **626.** τοῦδέ σοι Turnebus: τοῦδε τοῦ (Lips. Aug. τοῦδε). — **627.** οὐ added by later hand. — **628.** θρᾶξαι Buttmann *Lexil.* I. p. 212: θρᾷξαι. — **633.** λεγούσης: λεγούσας first hand. — **637.** ᾗ τ' other mss.: ὡς κ'. — **647.** εὔδαιμον: εὐδαίμων first hand (ο written above by later hand). — **657.** νυκτίφοιτα δείματα Nauck (*Bulletin de l'Acad. de St. Petersb.* 1860 p. 381), after Lycophr. 225 χρησμῶν ἀπῶσαι νυκτίφοιτα δείματα: νυκτίφαντ' (νυκτίφοιτ' other mss.) ὀνείρατα. — **660.** φίλα other mss.: φίλωι (α over ωι by later hand). — **667.** εἰ Naber: κεἰ. — πυρωπὸν other mss.: πυρωτὸν (cp. *Cho.* 600). — **668.** ἐξαϊστώσοι Blomfield: ἐξαϊστώσει. — **670.** κάπέκλησι (cp. W. *Curae Epigr.* p. 63): κάπέκλεισεν. — **677.** See under C. — **680.** ἀφνίδιος Elmsley: αἰφνίδιος. — **683.** ὅ τι Turnebus: ἔτι. — **684.** πόνων other mss.: πόνον. — **688.** See under C. — **690.** δυσθέατα καὶ other mss.: δυσθέατα. — **691 f.** δείματα κέντρῳ ψύχειν ψυχὰν ἀμφάκει Weil: δείματ' ἀμφήκει κέντρῳ ψύχειν ψυχὰν ἐμάν. — **695.** εἰσιδοῦσα other mss.: ἐσιδοῦσα. — **696.** πρῴ γε Brunck: πρῶγε corrected to πρῶιγε (ὁ over ω by later hand).

700. χρείαν other mss.: χρείαν τ'. — **706.** βάλ' other mss.: μάθ'. — **710.** ναίουσ' other mss.: νέουσ'. — **711.** ἐξηρτυμένοι another ms.: ἐξηρτημένοι. — **712 f.** See under C. — **716.** πρόσπλατοι Elmsley (cp. 371): πρόσπλαστοι. — **727.** ναύταισι Eustath. p. 500, 19 and Tzetzes on Lycophr. 1286: ναύτησι (cp. W. *Curae Epigr.* p. 5). — **741.** μηδάτω 'ν Turnebus: μηδ' ἐπῶν. — **742.** XO. ἰή ἰή W.: ἰ ἰ. — **749.** πίδοι Dindorf: πέδῳ. — **752.** ἢ δυσπετῶς other mss.: ἠδὺ πετᾶσ. — **758.** ἥδοι' ἄν: ἥδοιμ' ἄν (ἥδοιο ἄν another ms.). — **760.** See under C. — **767.** δάμαρτος other mss.: δάμωρτος. — **770.** See under C. — **772.** αὐτὸν ἐκγόνων other mss.: αὐτῶν ἐγγόνων. — **776.** σαυτῆς other mss.: σαυτῆς τ'. — **782.** τούτοιν

W.: τούτων. — 783. λόγου Elmsley: λόγουι. — 787. τὸ μὴ οὐ γεγωνεῖν: τὸ μὴ γεγωνεῖν with οὐ over the first γ. — 790. ἤπειρον Herwerden (*Exerc. Crit.* p. 93): ἤπειρων. — 791. The lacuna after this verse was observed by Brunck. — 792. πόντος other mss.: πόντον. — 796. μονόδοντες other mss.: μονόδοντες.

806. πόρου other mss. and Schol.: πόρον. — 807. τηλουργὸν later hand: τηλουργὸν. — 811. Βυβλίνων other mss. and Schol.: βιβλίνων. — 822. ἤντιρ Hermann (cp. 609): ἤντιν'. — 829. γῆς πέδα Weil (the Schol. on *Sept.* 304 τοῖον δ' ἀμείψεσθε γαίας πέδον remarks ἀντὶ τοῦ τοῖον οἰκήσετε δάπεδον): δάπεδα (the first syllable of which is short). — 831. θᾶκος Brunck: θῶκος. — 835. See under C. — 838. παλιμπλάγκτοισι: παλιπλάκτοισι first hand, παλιμπλάκτοισι second hand. — 840. κεκλήσεται other mss.: κληθήσεται. — 848. τίθησιν: τίθεισιν first hand. — 853. πεντηκοντάταις other mss. (acc. to *Et. M.* p. 346, 14 the Attic language does not alter the endings of the numerals in composition): πεντηκοντάταις. — 858. See under C. — 860. See under C. — 864. ἱν' other mss.: ἱς. — 866 f. ἀπαμβλυνθήσεται and δυοῖν other mss.: ἀπαμβλυθήσεται and δυεῖν. — 872. κλεινὸς other mss.: κλεινοῖς. But see under C. — 877. ἰλελεύ ἰλελεύ Pauw after Hesych.: ἰλελελελελεῦ. — 878. φρενοπλῆγες Cobet: φρενοπληγεῖς. — 881. κραδία other mss.: καρδία. — 885. παίουσ' other mss. and Schol.: πταίουσ'. — 887. ὃς Monk: ἣν ὅς. — 895. πόντιαι added by Paley. — 896. πλαθείην γαμέτᾳ Canter: πλαθείη ἐν γαμέτᾳ (with σ over θ and ν after η by later hand). — 899. ἀμαλαπτομέναν Weil (see his edition of the *Persians*, p. 132, and Heimsoeth *Krit. Stud.* p. 322): γ́δμω δαπτομέναν.

900. δυσπλάνοις ... ἀλατείαις other mss.: δυσπλάγχνοις ... ἀλατείαισι. — 901 f. See under C. — 903. προσδράκοι Salvinius: προσδάρκοι (other mss. προσδέρκοι). — 910. θρόνων τ' other mss.: θρόνων. — δ' Turnebus: τ'. — 911. τότ' later hand: τόδ'. — 912. δηναιὸν corrected from δηναιδν. — 917. πιστὸς corrected from πίστως. — 922. εὑρήσει other mss.: εὑρήσοι. — 926. κακῷ other mss.: κακῶν (with ῷ over ῶν by later hand). — 927. ὅσον other mss.: ὅσσον. — 932 f. πῶς δ' and τί δ' ἂν other mss.: πῶς and τί δαί. — 934. τοῦδ' ἵν' Elmsley and Wellauer: τοῦδέ γ'. — 945. ἐφημέροις other mss.: τὸν ἡμέροις. — 948. See under C. — 950. ἐκφράζε other mss.: φράζε. — 956. ναίειν second hand, ναί first hand. — 961. γε other mss.: δέ. — 965. See under C. — 968 ff. See under C. — 969. φῦναι other mss.: φῆναι. — 977. σμικρὰν Brunck: μικρὰν. — 980. See under C. — 986. παῖδ' ὄντα με other mss.: παῖδά με. — 987. κάτι Valckenaer: καὶ ἔτι. — 988. πεύσεσθαι other mss.: πευσεῖσθαι (cp. 1043). — 992. αἰθαλοῦσσα Canter: αἰθάλουσα. — 995. γνάμψει ... φράσαι other mss.: γνάψει first hand (μ over α second hand) ... φράσειν. — 998. ὦται other mss. and Schol.: ὦ παῖ.

1002. μήπω θ' other mss.: μηπάθ'. — 1008 f. κέαρ | λιταῖς Porson (κέαρ λιταῖς ἐμαῖς Robortelli's edition): λιταῖς | ἐμαῖς. — 1016. ἄφυκτος other mss.: ἀφύκτοις (with ος over ως by very late hand). — 1021. ἐς Turnebus: εἰς. — 1025. ἐκθοινάσεται Nauck, *Eurip. Stud.* II. p. 175 (cp. Eur. *Cycl.* 377 τεθοίναται, 550 θοινάσομαι, *El.* 830 θοινασόμεσθα): ἐκθοινήσεται. — 1026. τι other mss.: τοι. — 1031. See under C. — 1035. ἄμεινον first hand (cp. Meineke

Philol. XIX. 233) : usually written ἀμείνον'. — 1039. πιθοῦ other mss.: πείθου. — 1043. ἐπ' ἐμοὶ ῥιπτέσθω other mss.: ἐπὶ μοι ῥιπτείσθω. — 1049. τῶν Weil: τῶν τ'. — 1050. εἴς τε W.: ἴς τε (conjunction). — 1056. See under C. — 1057. ἡ τοῦθ' εὐχή Koechly (*Akad. Vorträge und Reden* I. p. 404), Weil, Madvig (*Advers. Crit.* p. 193): ἢ τοῦθ' εὐτυχῇ (this arose from εὐχή with superscribed τυ, i.e. τύχη; cp. ναυτιλόχων 408). — 1058. γ' αἱ Turnebus: γε. — 1060. τοι another ms.: τοῦ. — 1071. ἐγώ Porson: ἔτ' ἐγώ. — 1077. κοὐκ Turnebus: καὶ οὐκ. — 1078. ἀτέραντον: ἀτέρατον (ν over τ by later hand). — 1085 and 1092. εἱλίσσουσι ... εἱλίσσων Turnebus: ἑλίσσουσι ... ἑλίσσων.

C. Remarks on Particular Passages.

[Cp. the works named in App. A.]

2. A. Nauck (*Kritische Bemerkungen* VII. *Bulletin de l'Académie imp. de St. Pétersbourg,* Tome XXII. p. 75 sq.) Σκυθῶν ἐς αἶαν. F. W. Schmidt *Krit. Stud.* I. Σκύθην ἀκύμον'. — On resolutions in tragic trimeter cp. R. Enger *Rhein. Mus.* XI. 444; C. Fr. Müller, *de pedibus solutis in dialog. sen. Aesch. Soph. Eur.,* Berol. 1866 ; Rumpel *Philol.* XXV. 54.

12–15. M. Schmidt *Zeitschr. für öst. Gymn.* XVI. 585 τ' ἐκ σφῶν and φάραγγι τῆδε δυσχίμῳ. Cp. Heimsoeth *Wiederherstellung* p. 286, *Krit. Stud.* p. 281. Hermann ἐμποδὼν ἄρῃ, Hartung ἐμποδὼν ματᾶν, Heimsoeth *Krit. Stud.* p. 28 ἐμπεδᾷ μ' ἔτι.

37. Kiehl p. 50 requires θεός for θεόν, but thinks the verse spurious because it disturbs the stichomythic arrangement. For the same reason Ludwig, *zur Kritik des Aesch.* p. 26, strikes out the following verse. Cp. Kvičala *Zeitschr. für öst. Gymn.* 1858 p. 609 ff.

38. Nauck (*Bulletin de l'Acad. de St. Pét.* 1868 p. 404) στάσιν γέρας.

41. The question-point, standing in most recent editions after πῶς, we have again put after οἷόν τε. Hartung's objection, that disobedience to Zeus is possible, leaves out of account the peculiar attitude of the menial's mind; cp. 36, 44. The conjecture of R. Meister (*Comment. Sem. Phil. Lips.* 1874 p. 280), ὀκνοῦντα for οἷόν τε, is attractive.

49. If ἐπράχθη is to be retained, it must be defended by *Eum.* 125 τί σοι πέπρακται πρᾶγμα πλὴν τεύχειν κακά, Eur. *Med.* 1064 πάντως πέπρακται ταῦτα κοὐκ ἐκφεύξεται (Schol. ἀντὶ τοῦ 'κέκριται, εἵμαρται, πέπρωται'), Hdt. ix. 110 οὕτω δή τοι, Μάσιστα, πέπρηκται, and explained "all else was subject to allotment (assignment), save only dominion over the gods"; that is, "chieftainship of the gods was impossible for thee, and another office would have been equally a position of dependence." But how this interpretation of ἐπράχθη can be reconciled with the known uses of πράττειν, is hard to see. The connexion gains greatly by Stanley's emendation. The conjectures ἐπρώθη (Abresch), ἐτάχθη (C. G. Haupt), ἐκράνθη (Reisig), ἐφράχθη (Caesar), ἐπρίθη and ἐπρακτεῖ

(Wieseler), τέραντα τρᾶσσι (Lowinski), ἐτράχθη Ζηνὶ θεοῖσι κοιρανεῖν (Weil), ἐτάχθη (Merkel *Aesch. cod. Laur. praefationis lineamenta*, Quedlinburg 1871 p. 8), are valueless (cp. Schoemann *Mantissa Anim.*, at beginning). That ἐταχθής occurs nowhere else in tragedy is not a valid objection. The same is true of ἀτεχθής (Soph. *Ant.* 50). The more usual word ἀχθεινός would here be less appropriate than ἐταχθής.

51. Reisig τοῖσδ' ἐτ' οὐδέν, Blomfield καὶ τοῖσδ' οὐδέν, Hartung τοῖσδέ γ', Meineke *Philol.* XIX. 230 τοῖσδέ τ', Koechly p. 401 ἔγνωκα κἀγώ, Nauck ἔγνωκα κἀγώ or καὐτός, Heinze τοῖς δ' ἐγ' οὐδέν, M. Schmidt τοῖσδ' ἐγὼ οὐδέν. O. Ribbeck understands τοῖσδε of the fetters in Hephaestus's hand.

64. Cp. Hermann and Bergk *Jahrb. für Philol.* 81, 293.

66 f. The common reading is ὑπὲρ στένω (Schütz, Bothe); but the correction ὑπερστένω is due solely to the following ἐχθρῶν ὑπερ στένεις. Heimsoeth *de diversa div. mend. emend. comm. altera*, Bonn 1867 p. VIII. σῶν ὅσον στένω (cp. Eur. *Phoen.* 1430).—On the position of the preposition cp. Lehrs *Jahrb. für Philol.* 85 p. 312, Wecklein *Studien zu Aesch.* p. 79, Tycho Mommsen *Gebrauch von σύν und μετά c. Gen. bei Euripides*, Frankfurt a. M. 1876 p. 13 ff.

77. Helmsoeth *Wiederh.* p. 35 τοῦδ' ἔργου, on ground that the words εἰ κακὸν γένοιτο, written in cod. Guelph. above the line, indicate the singular.

83. Blomfield conjectures προστίθη after *Et. M.* 478, 10 οὕτω καὶ οἱ Ἀττικοὶ ... χρῶνται τοῖς τρίτοις προσώποις τῶν παρατατικῶν ἐν τοῖς προστακτικοῖς· οἷον ἐτίθην, ἐτίθης, ἐτίθη, τίθη.

86 f. Elmsley προμηθίας.—The reading τύχης in other mss. is a correction for τέχνης misunderstood.

89 f. Nauck τηγαί τε ποταμῶν ποντίων τε κυμάτων νήριθμον ἀγκάλισμα.

94. Oberdick *Zeitschr. für öst. G.* XXII. p. 328 τρισμυριετῇ for τὸν μυριετῇ following the Schol. (see above).

99. On the spellings πῇ, οὐδαμῇ, εἰκῇ, σῴζω etc. cp. La Roche *Zeitschr. für öst. G.* XVI. 89, W. *Curae Epigr.* p. 45.

100. Coenen (*de comparationibus et metaphoris apud Atticos praesertim poetas*, Utrecht 1875) τέρματι τῶνδ' ἐτικίλσαι.

107. On the form of the fifth foot see Wecklein *Studien zu Aeschylos*, p. 130.

112. The analogy of *Cho.* 42 (Wunderlich *Obs. Crit. in Aesch. trag.* p. 113 and Hermann on Soph. *Ai.* 448) and of the Latin hic dolor (Schoemann) does not justify τοιάσδε. This reading would be correct only on the supposition that ποινὰς ἀμπλακημάτων expressed a single idea, like χθονὸς πέδον. But here ἀμπλακημάτων is logically distinct, and should be also syntactically distinct; else the thought loses its proper point. Cp. 563, 620. Similarly in *Ag.* 1626 the Med. has αἰσχύνους' for αἰσχύνων.

113. The reading πασσαλευτός (Turnebus wrote πασσαλευτὸς ὤν) of other mss. is only a correction of the reading of Med. πασσαλεύμενος (sic!). Dindorf regards πασσαλευμένος as a gloss upon προσπεπαρμένος. But ὑπαιθρίοις demands an idea like αἰκιζόμενος; accordingly πασσαλεύμενος should be changed to προυσελεύμενος. Cp. Wecklein *Studien zu Aesch.* p. 34. The explanation of προυσελεῖν

mentioned in the notes is that of Buttmann *Lexil.* II. 159; another (προ-εσ-ειλεῖν) has been proposed by W. Clemm in *Acta Soc. Philol. Lips.* ed. F. Ritschl, I. 1 p. 77. — Meanwhile the emendation προυσελούμενος has been proposed independently by M. Schmidt, *Rhein. Mus.* 26, p. 223. This is also accepted by F. V. Fritzsche (*Miscellanea*, Rostock 1882), who lays down four forms, προσε-λεῖν, προυσελεῖν, προτελεῖν, προυτελεῖν, and derives thence Lat. protelare.

117. Dindorf τίς ἵκετ' αἴας τόνδε τέρμιον πάγον; against this see Heimsoeth *Wiederh.* p. 307. C. Fr. Müller makes two dochmii, ἵκετο τόνδε τερμόνιον ἐπὶ πάγον.

139. Weil thinks παῖδες and Ὠκεανοῦ glosses; but this system corresponds with 152 ff. if the interjection αἰαῖ αἰαῖ 136 is not counted (cp. *Sept.* 870). Or an interjection like φεῦ φεῦ may have fallen out before 152.

142. προσπορπατός might easily pass into πρὸς πατρός, through the omission of πορ after προ. The variant of the cod. Lips. προσπαρτός, received by Dindorf, is objectionable because ἐγώ has to be added.

156 f. The cod. Med. has ὡς μήποτε θεὸς μήτε τις ἄλλος (not ἀνος). Dindorf, in the belief that ἄλλος in the ms. had been altered from ἀνος (= ἄνθρωπος), which stands in the lemma of the Schol., wrote ὡς μήτε θεῶν μήτε τις ἀνδρῶν; for this, in the first edition, the editor gave ὡς μήτε θεὸς μήτε τις ἀνδρῶν, nearer the tradition, and with a poetical shift of construction (cp. *Ag.* 358, *Eum.* 70, Soph. *El.* 109, *Ai.* 243, Eur. *El.* 1234). Now, however, it appears from Merkel's collation and R. Schöll's statement in *Hermes* xi. p. 219 ff. that ἄλλος was the original reading of the ms. From this we have no reason for departing. We must suppose that ἀνος (= ἄνθρωπος) in the lemma of the schol. arose from a gloss written over ἄλλος. — Elmsley and Cobet write ἐγεγήθει, following Hesych. ἐγεγήθει· ἔχαιρεν. Dindorf (who thinks ἐπήγηθεν possible) says rightly that ἐπιγηθεῖν is here specially appropriate. *Cho.* 772 (γηθοούσῃ φρενί) proves the complete use of the verb γηθεῖν for Aeschylus.

161. L. Dindorf (*Thesaurus* I. 2 p. 2320) considers ἀσχαλᾶν un-Attic for ἀσχάλλειν (see 303), so that ἀσχαλεῖ would have to be written here, 243, and 704 for ἀσχαλᾷ. See also Herwerden *Exerc. Crit.* p. 63. But as the epic language employs both verbs, there is no good ground for denying either of them to the lofty tragic diction of Aeschylus. Besides, ἀσχαλᾶν is proved for tragedy by Eur. *Iph. A.* 920. In none of the three passages does the sense demand the future; this Dindorf acknowledges. Even συνασχαλᾶν 303 can be taken as present.

163. Hermann ἀστραφῆ, Dindorf ἄκναφον and 182 δέδια δ' with Porson for δέδια γάρ. The double change, of strophe and antistrophe, is inadmissible. Ahrens (*Philol.* XXIII. 6), after Hermann, refers the gloss of Hesych. ἀκαν-θόν· ἄγναμπτον to our passage, and corrects it to ἀκνάμπτον νόον· ἄγναμπτον with much probability.

170. The original reading of the Med. ἀφ' ὅτου was restored by Weil.

187. The Med. has ἔχων Ζεύς· ἀλλ' ἔμπας ὀΐω (o in an erasure) with a superfluous anapaest. Brunck omitted ὀΐω. Hermann changes ὀΐω to οἴῳ and

assumes, with Scholefield, a lacuna after it, to make this anapaestic system equal to the foregoing. Bothe and Heimsoeth (*Wiederh.* p. 248) rightly think Ζεύς and ἀλλ' to be glosses.

203. This verse, attacked by Nauck *Zeitschr. für Alterth.* 1855 p. 110, who compares Eur. *Hec.* 789, is rightly defended by Weil.

210. "Itaque potius Γαῖα mater Themidis intelligenda, nisi forte totum hunc versiculum ab interpolatore adiectum esse placeat" (Schütz). Jacobs *Att. Mus.* III. p. 405, Schoemann, and Caesar also think Gaea and Themis different persons. The contrary view is maintained by Hermann, Welcker (*Tril.* p. 39), Ahrens (*über die Göttin Themis.* I. Hannover 1862 p. 9), K. Keil, (*Philol.* XXIII. p. 708), Weil and others. Reisig assumes a gap between 209 and 210.

211. Elmsley and Dindorf κρανοῖτο.

213. Wunder (*Advers. in Soph. Phil.* p. 37) ὑπεφόχους, Hermann ὑπερτέρους, F. V. Fritzsche (*Miscellanea*, 1882) προέξοντας.

217. The Schol. also read προσλαβόντι. Most editors adopt the reading προσλαβόντα of other mss. See commentary.

223. Hermann τιμαῖς, with a few lesser mss. — The reading ἀντημείψατο (two lesser mss.), generally adopted since Blomfield, is only a substitution of the commoner for the less common word.

234. Elmsley τοιῶιδ'.

239. Nauck (*Bulletin de l'Acad. de St. Pét.* 1860 p. 317) ἐν οἴκτῳ θέμενος εἶτ' οἴκτου τυχεῖν. Passow's explanation "sich jemand in seinem Mitleid zur Aufgabe machen" cannot be right.

246. Hermann φίλοισιν οἰκτρός, because φίλοισιν stands in some mss. (Hesych. οἰκτρά· ἐλεεινά, οἰκτρός· ἐλεεινός). But cp. Ar. *Ran.* 1063, where all mss. have ἐλεεινοὶ for ἐλεινοί. Probably φίλοις γ' is necessary (cp. Blomfield *Gloss.* on 1018). Mitschenko (*Revue de Philol.*, nouv. sér. 1877, p. 268) καὶ μὴ φίλοις ("even to those who are not my friends").

248. The τ' after θνητούς in the Med. is due, as in 700, 776, 948, to a whim of the copyists; cp. W. *Ars Soph. emend.* p. 27. On θνητούς γ', which some mss. have, see Meineke *Philol.* XIX. 231. Hermann γε παύσας, to which Hartung added κατοικίσας in 250. — As the Med. has προσδέρκεσθαι with σ scratched out (cp. *Cho.* 647 προσχαλκεύει for προχαλκεύει), Keck *Jahrb. für Phil.* 81, 479, conjectures προσόσσεσθαι, thinking it incredible that men leading a dull, dreamlike life should have had foreknowledge of death. Cp. Weil's note.

253. Meineke, *l.c.*, φλογωπὸν φῶς (as *Sept.* 25 πυρὸς has crept into the text for φάους). But the epithet φλογωπόν and the emphasis which lies on ἐφήμεροι, makes a change of this sort needless.

255-257. In the mss. all these verses are given to the chorus-leader. The stichomythy was restored by Welcker *Tril.* p. 62 (*Nachtrag* p. 69); the addition οὐδαμῇ χαλᾷ is a confirmation. So just below the change of person (ΠΡ.) is not indicated at 263, but at 266. O. Ribbeck αἰκίζεταί γ'.

260. On the interpretation of ἥμαρτες, see Moller *Philol.* VIII. 735, Caesar *Philol.* XIII. 608, Welcker *Götterlehre* II. p. 259.

264. Reisig τοὺς κακῶς πράσσοντας· αὐτὸς ταῦ́, Elmsley τοὺς κακῶς πράσσοντας· ἐὸ δὲ ταῦ́. Cp. *Eum.* 313.

268. Elmsley τοιαυτίδε and τυχόν. Probably τοιαῦσδέ με ought to be written. Aeschylus appears to use τοῖος only where τοιόσδε is metrically inconvenient (*Prom.* 920, *Sept.* 580, *Suppl.* 400, *Pers.* 606, *Eum.* 378).

271. The change of καί μοι to καί τοι (Blomfield, Hermann) is unsuitable. See commentary.

272. Schol. γρ. βλάβας, a clumsy explanation.

275. Weil τυκνά τοι or ταρταχοῖ.

291. Madvig (*Advers. Crit.* p. 189) οὐκ ἔστ' ἐν ὅτῳ; but νείμαιμ' ἄν (without ἢ σοί) would be better, supposing that ἄν were really necessary.

298. Dindorf ἕα, | τί χρῆμα λεύσσω, after *Cho.* 10.

313. Schoemann interprets χόλον μόχθων "the wrath of chastisement," that is, "the wrath that manifests itself in the sufferings inflicted on thee"; he compares ἐν δέδωκ' εὔνοιαν 446. A better parallel would be ἐλατείαις τόπων 900. But both are different; to make the relation of the words identical, μόχθων would have to be referred to Zeus. Caesar (*Philol.* XIII. 609) joins μόχθων and παιδίαν, but this again is improbable. The order of words, τὸν νῦν χόλον παρόντα, for τὸν νῦν παρόντα χόλον, is much more endurable, if the following word also belongs to χόλον. Against Haupt (*Ind. lect. Berol.* 1860 p. 6), who pronounced this order defensible neither on metrical nor stilistic grounds, Dindorf (*Jahrb. für. Philol.* 87, p. 75) cited Thuc. i. 11 (cp. Classen's note), iii. 54, Xen. *Anab.* v. 3, 4. Döderlein's emendation (*Reden u. Aufsätze*, p. 393), ὄχλον for χόλον, as 'multitude' (cp. μυρίοις 541), has received much approval. Meineke (*Philol.* XV. 130) proposed ὕλον; afterward (Soph. *Oed. Col.* p. 227) he preferred Haupt's conjecture, τὸν νῦν πολὺν παρόντα μόχθον. But the sense demands χόλος as a connecting link between the ideas of κλύοι and μόχθων. Accordingly the editor has written τὸν νῦν χόλου παρόντα μόχθον, an emendation proposed by Lowinski (*Zeitschr. für Gymnasialw.* XX. p. 638). χόλου passed into χόλον after τὸν νῦν, as 792 πόντου became πόντον, 806 πόρου became πόρον.

328. On the relation of ἀκριβῶς to περισσόφρων, see Meineke *Philol.* XX. 638.

331. The infin. μετασχεῖν (restored by Weil) passed into μετασχόν, because καί was assumed to be 'and.' Schütz wished to supply μετά with τετολμηκώς (Welcker's *Rhein. Mus.* XI. p. 315), but his citations, Soph. *Ant.* 537, *O. T.* 347, are not pertinent. Kiehl (p. 55) changes αἰτίας to αἰκίας and omits 331–333, because participation of Oceanus in Prometheus's deeds is not known to the legend, nor consistent with Oceanus's character in this play. In fact v. 234 excludes the supposition that Prometheus was aided by any god. Nevertheless there is no interpolation. See commentary above. For the change of πάντων to τούτων, cp. the reading of the Med. ταῦτα for πάντα in 505.

334. Fr. W. Schmidt *Anal. Soph. et Eur.* 1864 p. 86 σημανθῆς μολών.

340. Nauck *Krit. Bemerk.* 1885 writes κούδὲ μὴ λήξω.

345. Hirschig οὐ κεἰ. — Brunck changes εἴνεκα to οὕνεκα everywhere; but οὕνεκα (οὗ ἕνεκα, cp. ὀθούνεκα) is a conjunction, not a preposition. Cp. W. *Curae Epigr.* p. 36.

347–372 are given to Oceanus in the mss. Elmsley rightly added them to Prometheus's speech. Wieseler and Bergk *Zeitschr. für Alterth.* 1851 p. 533 propose to leave to Oceanus 347–369 or 347–365. Hartung aptly remarks, 'This recital of Zeus's deeds is so magnificent, that it is almost too evident that the poet is speaking through Prometheus's mouth.' Cp. also Weil's note.

348. Valckenaer (on Eur. *Hipp.* p. 277) remarked that πρός must here have the dative, because there is no idea of motion or direction. Accordingly Hartung and others have edited πρὸς ἑσπέροις τόποις (Bergk *Jahrb. für Philol.* 1860 p. 417 προσεσπέροις τόποις). It would be more probable to regard πρὸς as metrical correction for ἐς, and ἐς as a repetition of the first syllable of ἑσπέρους, and to write καθ᾽ ἑσπέρους τόπους. But see the commentary.

349 f. Blomfield ἕστηκε κίων ... ἐρείδων ἄχθος. — Schoemann erroneously thinks κίον' dual. The plural in Homer is different.

354. Gaisford and Porson ὅστις (without τᾶσιν) ἀντέστη, Wunderlich (*Observ. Crit. in Aesch. trag.* Gott. 1809 p. 27) τᾶσιν δ᾽ ἀντέστη (against this Bergk. *Zeitschr. für Alterth.* 1835 p. 946, Dindorf *ibid.* 1836 p. 5); Naeke *Opusc.* I. 175 assumes a lacuna between τᾶσιν δ᾽ and ἀντέστη; Weil εἶς δ᾽ ἀντέστη, Heimsoeth (*de diversa div. mend. emend.* Bonn 1866) τᾶσιν δὲ προύστη, which Lobeck had before proposed, but afterwards recalled (on Soph. *Ai.* 803 p. 355 ²). Hermann's emendation is right.

359. Heimsoeth *Wiederh.* p. 98 ἐκφυσῶν φλόγα.

378 ff. The mss. have ὀργῆς νοσούσης, Stobaeus *Flor.* xx. 13 ὀργῆς ματαίας (and αἴτιοι for ἰατροί), Plut. *Consol. ad Apoll.* p. 102 b ψυχῆς γὰρ νοσούσης εἰσὶν ἰατροὶ λόγοι, ὅταν τις ἐν καιρῷ γε μαλθάσσῃ κέαρ, Themist. *Or.* vii. p. 98 φάρμακον δὲ ὀργῆς οἰδαινούσης τὸ μὲν αὐτίκα λόγος ἐστίν, ᾧ σὺ τηνικαῦτα ἐπράθνας σφαδάζουσαν καὶ ζέουσαν ἔτι. Hermann remarks, 'νοσοῦσα non erit nimia et modum excedens ira intelligenda, sed quae non impleat modum nec possit recte censeri ira esse,' and writes ψυχῆς νοσούσης after Plutarch; at the same time, guided by schol. A οἱ λόγοι οἱ παρακλητικοὶ θεραπεύουσι τὴν ὀργὴν ἀργιαίνουσαν καὶ ἐπαιρομένην, he suggests ὀργῆς σφριγώσης, which Heimsoeth, *Wiederherst.* p. 130, proves to be right. Reisig conjectures ὀργῆς νοσούσιν, Dindorf ὀργῆς ζεούσης, Weil φρενὸς νοσούσης. It is certain that the reading ὀργῆς νοσούσης arose from a gloss, ψυχῆς νοσούσης. Plutarch has preserved the whole of this gloss, whereas in our mss. half the original (ὀργῆς) is retained. Now that we know that in 380 the Med. has σφριγῶντα, with the other mss., and not σφυδῶντα, it is still clearer that the original σφριγώσης in 378 was confused with σφυδῶντα in 380. For in 380 σφυδῶντα is required by the sense (see commentary) and by Cicero's translation, in which g r a v e s c e n s corresponds to σφυδῶντα, and the words preceding the quotation, e r a t i n t u m o r e a n i m u s, to σφριγώσης. So in Themistius ὀργῆς οἰδαινούσης is the paraphrase of ὀργῆς σφριγώσης, and σφαδάζουσαν καὶ ζέουσαν ἔτι that of σφυδῶντα θυμόν.

384. Turnebus τήνδε τὴν νόσον.

386. Hermann δόκει σύ, Weil μεῖζον δοκήσει.

398 ff. To restore the responsion Heath omitted δὲ and λειβομένα, and in the next verse wrote ἔτεγξε after Par. A. 'Sed particula abesse non potest neque λειβομένα delendum est, sed excidit aliquid in antistropha' Hermann, who writes δακρυσίστακτον ἀπ' ... ῥαδινῶν δ' εἰβομένα, and remarks on the reading ῥαδινόν, 'potest videri verum esse, ut Aeschylus expresserit τέρεν δάκρυον.' On the questionable position of δέ, see commentary on 321, Burgard Quaestt. gramm. Aesch. p. 71. Weil δακρυσίστακτον ἀπ' ... δ' ἀδινόν, G. Wolff Rhein. Mus. 19, 464 (and before, Hermann El. doctr. Metr. p. 494) δακρυσιστακτὶ δ'. The word ἀστακτί, formed with a privative, is not a proof of this. The right reading is δακρυσίστακτα δ'.

408. Hermann ⟨δακρυχέει⟩ στένουσα (so minor mss. for στένουσι). Dindorf supplies πενθομέναν, Weil τ' ἐσχατιαί. The needed sense is given by θ' ἑσπέριοι. See commentary.

420. Ἀραβίας of the mss. is metrically wrong, and it is inconceivable that a well-known country could be so atrociously misplaced. Boissonade Ἀβαρίας, Schütz Χαλυβίας, Wieseler after Plin. H. N. vi. 17. 19 Ἀραμίας; Hermann Σαρματᾶν, Heimsoeth (Wiederh. p. 488 and de interpol. comm. alt. p. X) Χαλκίδος (i.e. the Scythian Chalcis; see Steph. Byz. s.v. Χαλκίς), B. Foss Ἀερίων. Hartung Ἀρίας τ' or Κάρίας after Cho. 423. The latter is open to grave objections; see W. Studien, p. 12. The poet might treat the quantity of such a word arbitrarily; thus in Pers. 318 he has Μᾶγος, and in Pers. 20, 302, 31, 957, he makes the penult of Ἀρτεμβάρης and Φαρανδάκης now long, now short.

422. Hermann Καυκάσου πύλας, Wieseler Καυκάσου λέπας. — The lemma of the Schol. and several mss. have νέμονται. The reading of the Med. νέμουσιν has been retained for the sake of variety after νέμονται 412.

425-430. Hermann restored the responsion, rejecting ἄλλον and assuming a gap after 431. Cp. O. Ribbeck Rhein. Mus. XIV. p. 627, who writes δαμέντ' ἀκαμάτοις εἰσιδόμαν θεόν, and Heimsoeth de parodi in Aesch. fab. Theb. conform. p. 8, who proves similar interpolations for Sept. 885, 912, 952, 906. Heimsoeth conjectures εἰδόμαν θεῶν (so other mss. for θεὸν) δαμέντ'. That ἀκαμαντοδέτοις (ἀδαμαντοδέτοις) λύμαις comes from 148 is shown in the commentary. Τιτᾶνα is a gloss on θεόν. Even Ἄτλαν or Ἄτλανθ' is recognizable as an interpolation. — Before οὐράνιόν τε πόλον we expect the idea 'Earth.' Hermann Ἄτλαντος ὑπέροχον σθένος κραταιόν, ὃς γᾶν οὐράνιόν τε, Halm (Lectt. Aeschyl. Monach. 1835) Ἄτλανθ' ὃς αἰὲν ὑπερέχων χθονὸς (χθονὸς was given by Schütz) κραταιόν, Ludwig and Pleitner (Beiträge zur Kritik u. Erkl. von Aesch. Agam. u. Soph. Antig. p. 23) ὃς αἶαν for ὃς αἰὲν (but αἶα means 'land,' not 'earth'). — For ὑποστενάζει Hermann, to get the idea of carrying, writes ὑποστεγάζει after Hesych. στέγει · βαστάζει, ὑπομένει, Suidas (s.v. στέγει) στεγόντων · ἀνεχόντων, βασταζόντων, Aesch. Frg. 298 πατρὸς (sc. Ἄτλαντος) μέγιστον ἄθλον οὐρανοστεγῆ.

Dindorf ὀχῶν στενάζει. The notion of στενάζειν is to be retained, on account of what follows (see commentary). The sense of *carrying* is probable only for στέγειν. Responsion may be produced by writing, for instance, μόνον δὲ πρόσθεν ἐν πόνοισιν δαμέντ᾽ ἐσειδόμαν | θεῶν, ὃς ὑπέροχον σθένος κραταιὸν | γαίας οὐράνιόν τε πόλον στέγων ὑποστενάζει.

433 f. Dindorf transposes δ᾽ after Ἄϊδος. Heimsoeth conjectures ἐμβρέμει for ὑποβρέμει and θρηνοῦσιν for στένουσιν.

442. Koechly (p. 402) βροτοῖς δ᾽ εὑρήματα, Meineke δὲ πράγματα, Fr. W. Schmidt (*Satura Critica*, Neu-Strelitz 1874) τὰ δὲ βροτοῖς δωρήματα. The ms. reading is right; see commentary.

446. Meineke εὔσοιαν.

450 ff. Porson κοὔτι. — On ἄῃσυρος, see G. Curtius *Studien z. Gr. u. Lat. Gramm.* I. p. 297.

458. Dobree ὁδούς, from Stob. *Ecl. Phys.* i. 1; Hermann φίσεις. That δυσκρίτους belongs also to ἀντολὰς is noted by Heimsoeth *Wiederh.* p. 43.

461. Hemsterhuis (on Lucian I. p. 88) μνήμης (and γραμμάτων τε σύνθεσιν). Hermann's remark, 'multo aptius et commodius cum aperto genitivo coniungitur ἐργάνην, quam si Μουσῶν ex μουσομήτορα esset intelligendum,' cannot outweigh the consensus of the mss. and Stobaeus. Nor is it quite true that Μουσῶν is to be supplied for ἐργάνην from μουσομήτορα.

463. Hermann understands σώμασιν of the mss. as the bodies of the riders he compares σωματηγός, σωματηγεῖν. But this does not comport with ζεύγλαισι, nor with the thought ὅπως ... μοχθημάτων γένοιντο.

472. Brunck πέπονθας αἰκὲς πῆμ᾽ ἀποσφαλεὶς φρενῶν πλάνῃ, Hermann πέπονθας αἰκὲς πῆμ᾽ ἀποσφαλεὶς φρενῶν, κακὸς δ᾽ ... πεσὼν κακοῖς ἀθυμεῖς, Hartung πέπονθας εἰκὸς πῆμ᾽, Weil πέπονθας ἀνιθὲς πῆμ᾽, Heimsoeth *Krit. Stud.* 203, αἰκὲς πεπονθὼς πῆμ᾽. See commentary.

475. Hartung ἰατέον, Nauck (*Bulletin de l'Acad. de St. Pét.* 1863 p. 34) and Meineke (*Philol.* XX. 52) ὅτοις εἰ (or οἷσις εἰ), Heimsoeth and Weil ἰάσιμον, Herwerden (*Exerc. Crit.* p. 93) ἰατὸς εἰ. See commentary on 42.

494 f. ἔχουσ᾽ ... ἡδονὴν χολῇ, for ἔχοντ᾽ ἡδονήν, χολῆς, Wieseler. Hermann assumes instead a lacuna between 494 and 495.

496. Reisig χἄμ᾽ ἄκραν, Hartung σύν τ᾽ ἄκραν (better would be συγκαλυπτά τ᾽ ἠδ᾽ ἄκραν). Schoemann interprets "long back-piece," "chine"; but ἡ ῥάχις τρεῖς ἐπωνυμίας ἔχει, καὶ ἡ μὲν πρώτη καλεῖται αὐχήν, ἡ δὲ δευτέρα ἰξύη, ἡ δὲ τρίτη ὀσφύς, *Et. M.* p. 630, 23. Hermann 'μακρὰν ὀσφὺν dicit, quod ea pars etiam caudam comprehendebat.' It is true that the tail of a victim had, acc. to the Schol. on Eur. *Phoen.* 1255 (cp. Ar. *Pax* 1054), special significance in empyromancy, and possibly a verse has fallen out after 496, the scribe's eye having wandered from καὶ μακρὰν | ⟨κίρκον⟩ to ἄκραν ὀσφύν. For the explanation given in the commentary, see Caesar, *ad loc.*

511. Keck μ᾽ αἶσα for μοῖρα.

522. Heimsoeth *Krit. Stud.* p. 142 τοῦτον for τόνδε δ᾽.

535. Hermann and Bergk μᾶλλα μοι τόδ᾽ ἐμμένοι. Weil τοῦτ᾽ for τόδ᾽.

541. 'Excidisse videtur adverbium "crudeliter" significans' (Hermann). Dindorf γυιοφθόροις, Hartung θεῖον δέμας, Heimsoeth μυρίοις δέμας διακναιόμενον μοχθήμασιν.

543 f. For ἰδίᾳ γνώμᾳ, Reisig αὐτογνωμόνως (γν makes position), Dindorf αὐτόνῳ (an unattested word) γνώμᾳ, Meineke αὐτόβουλος ὢν (Sept. 1053), Weil οἰόφρων γνώμαν, Heimsoeth (de interp. comm. alt. p. XI) αὐτοβουλίᾳ (late Greek). See commentary. — Dindorf ῥ᾽ for φέρ᾽.

548. Reisig ἀντόνειρον (just so in Cho. 319 ἰσοτίμοιρον has arisen from ἀντίμοιρον with ἰσο- superscribed). Hermann in 558 λέχος εἰς for καὶ λέχος.

550 ff. Hermann ἁρμονίαν βροτῶν, Dindorf οὔποτε θνατῶν τὰν Διὸς ἁρμονίαν ἀνδρῶν. It seems best to keep θνατῶν and in 560 πείθων (generally πιθών, after other mss., is read).

559. That Hesione here, as elsewhere, is sister of the Oceanids, not, as Hermann thinks, of Prometheus, appears from the statement that the Oceanids sing the bridal song.

561. On Io in art, see R. Engelmann de Ione, Halae 1868, and Archäol. Zeit. III. p. 37.

564. Dindorf after Guelf. and Robortelli τοιναῖς. H. Stephanus τοίνδ σ᾽ ὀλέκει.

568. Dindorf with Schleusner (on Et. M. p. 60, 8) ἀλεῦ δᾶ, Hermann with Monk ἄλευε δᾶ. For the meaning, see Ahrens Philol. XXIII. 206.

570. Wieseler δόλιον ὄμμ᾽, Koechly φόνιον ὄμμ᾽, Thomas (Münch. Gel. Anz. 1859, 49, p. 385) θαλερὸν ὄμμ᾽.

575 f. Hartung ὑπνολέταν. — Hermann ἄγουσιν (μακραὶ or χθονὸς) πλάναι; Dindorf supplies πάλιν.

598. Hermann κέντροις (φρένας) or κεντήμασιν.

601. Hermann supplies Ἥρας from the Schol. τοῖς τῆς Ἥρας; but the scholiast evidently did not have Ἥρας in his text. A general designation is more suitable; this can scarcely be anything else than ἄλλων.

613. Fr. W. Schmidt ὃ κλεινὸν ὠφέλημα.

623. Herwerden Stud. Crit. in Poet. Scen. Gr. 1872 p. 95, thinks this verse interpolated.

624. Hermann is inclined to suppose that the words ἃ δεῖ γενέσθαι, ταῦτα καὶ γενήσεται, quoted by the Schol., have fallen out after this verse.

628. Cobet Nov. Lect. p. 655, in proof of the long α in θρᾶξαι, adduces the pun in Aristot. Rhet. iii. 11. 2 Θρᾷττης εἶ and θράττει σε.

629. Brunck μᾶσσον ἢ ὥς, following a reading cited by Turnebus. Elmsley suggested μασσόνως ἢ 'μοί, Hermann μᾶσσον ὢν ἐμοί. Dindorf adopted ὤν; but against this Foerster de attractionis usu Aesch. p. 28 ('consentaneum non est modum curandi et rem ipsam ad quam cura spectat inter se comparari'). The ὡς of the mss. is defended, with the examples given in the commentary, by Bekker Homerische Blätter p. 314, Meineke Philol. XIX. 237, Schoemann Lehre von den Redetheilen p. 233. Schoemann comes to the conclusion that ὡς after the comparative has, logically at least, as good warrant as ἤ, or as the German *als* and *wie*, which correspond to ὡς in meaning. See *Gött. Gel. Anz.* 1862 II. p. 729 f.

636. Ribbeck inclines to throw out this verse as an interpolation, so as to obtain the frequently recurring group of four verses. It is more reasonable to make Prometheus's five verses correspond to Io's first five.

642. Med. (and most mss.) ὀδύρομαι, with the addition γρ. αἰσχύνομαι. Most editors have slighted the genuine tradition and adopted a poor conjecture, for αἰσχύνομαι is nothing more. Wieseler ὀρίνομαι.

657. Well prefers νυκτίφοιτα φάσματα (after Soph. *El.* 502).

677. τε κρήνην Canter (cp. Schol. A καὶ πρὸς τὴν Λέρνην τὴν πηγήν) for Λέρνης ἄκρην τε of the Med. Blomfield ἀκτήν τε Λέρνης, Reisig and Hermann Λέρνης τ' ἐς ἀκτήν. Probably the reading ἄκρην is due to a gloss κρήνην written over νᾶμα (Λέρνης τε νᾶμα). Cp. Frg. 399 παρᾶς τε Δίρκης, Eur. *Phoen.* 120 Λερναῖα νάματα.

680. Porson αἰφνίδιος αὐτὸν μόρος, Gaisford (on Hephaest. p. 242) ἐξαίφνης μόρος, Hermann αἰφνίδια, Wieseler αἰφνηδίς (cp. Hermann's note).

686. Koechly (p. 403) ἔχθιστον (cp. *Il.* ix. 312). This would be in place if the sentiment were like that of 1069.

688 ff. Med. οὔποτ' οὔποτ' ηὐχόμην: Schol. and several mss. ηὔχουν. — Hermann οὐπώποτ' οὐπώποτ' with some mss.; Dindorf thinks something lacking, and suggests οὔποτ' οὔποτ' ηὔχουν ἐν ἄντροις ἐμοῖς ὧδε παραξένους μολεῖσθαι λόγους εἰς ἀκοὰν ἐμάν, Schoemann οὔποτ' οὐπώποτ', Heimsoeth *Krit. Stud.* p. 221 ηὐχόμαν τοιούσδε σκυθροὺς μολεῖσθαι. Wecklein οὔποθ' ⟨ὧδ'⟩ οὔποτ'. — Hermann πήματα, λύματ' ἀμφάκει σὺν κέντρῳ, Meineke *Zeitschr. für Alterth.* 1844 p. 11 ψήχειν (cp. Stob. *Flor.* 38, 53 ὥσπερ ὁ ἰὸς σίδηρον, οὕτως ὁ φθόνος τὴν ἔχουσαν ψυχὴν ἀναψήχει), Dindorf δεῖματ' ἐμὰν ἀμφάκει κέντρῳ ψήξειν ψυχάν. Weil's emendation seems the most available; he supports ψύχειν by *Eum.* 101.

706. Hartung θυμῷ ἔμβαλ'.

708. Hermann τρέψασα, after some mss.

712 f. The mss. have ἀλλ' ἀλιστόνοις γύποδας. Turnebus πόδας, Elmsley γ' ὑπό, Hartung ἀλλὰ λισσάσιν πόδα, Hermann ἀλλὰ γυῖ' ἀλιστόνοις. A gloss πόδας, written over γυῖα (Hesych. γυῖα· μέλη, χεῖρές τε καὶ πόδες), gave rise to the word Γύποδας, which was fancied to be the name of a people (Γήπαιδες, Gepidae). — Meineke (*Philol.* XX. 718) supposes a gap between πελάζειν and ἀλλ' (οὐ γὰρ προσήγοροι ξένοις πέλουσιν). Jos. Meyer (p. 10) proposes to insert 729–731 after 713; Foss (p. 24) argues for a lacuna after 713.

717. Hermann, from the passages quoted in the commentary, infers that a verse like σμερδνοῖς 'Αράξην κύμασιν βρυχώμενον has fallen out. See on the other hand Weil's note. Robortelli has ἥξεις δ' 'Αράξην. — Reisig proposes to put 717–728 after 791.

732. Nauck λόγος πολύς.

735. Elmsley 'Ασίδ' for 'Ασιάδ'.

738. Heimsoeth *Wiederh.* p. 97 ἐπίσκηψεν (cp. *Pers.* 102, 514, 740). But ἐπέρριψεν is more characteristic.

741. For μηδέτω 'ν cp. *Ag.* 1200, which Enger has emended to ἀλλόθρῳ 'ν. Ahrens, *de crasi et aphaer.* p. 24, doubts the aphaeresis of ε in ἐν, and requires μηδέτω προοιμίοις. Wieseler μηδ' ἐτῶν ἐν φροιμίοις.

760. Med. ὄντων τῶνδε μαθεῖν σοι (ν σοι in litura) πάρα. Turnebus τῶνδέ σοι μαθεῖν πάρα. Schütz conjectures τῶνδέ σοι γηθεῖν πάρα, Weil τῶνδ' ἰανθῆναι πάρα. The corruption of the passage is due to a superscribed τῶνδε, by which σοι was crowded out, and had to be put in later, so that of γεγηθέναι (or γεγαθέναι, cp. *Cho.* 772 γαθούσῃ) only γαθέν was left.

761 f. Meineke σκῆπτρα δὲ στερήσεται or δ' ἀποσυλήσεται. — On πρὸς αὐτὸς αὐτοῦ cp. Haupt *l. c.* p. 3. — Ludwig κενεόφρων.

766. Brunck θεμιτὸν for ῥητόν.

770. Other mss. have πρὶν for πλὴν and λυθῶ for λυθείς. Dindorf πλὴν ἐὰν ἐγὼ 'κ δεσμῶν λυθῶ, Hartung πλὴν ἐγὼ αὐτὸς ἐκ δεσμῶν λυθείς, Wieseler ἂν' (i.e. ἀναλυθείς) for ἂν.

776. Blomfield μή τι, Hermann σαυτῆς γ'. In the latter case it should be καὶ μὴ σεαυτῆς γ'. See on 248.

780. The change to εἰ πόνων is unwarranted; and γάρ forbids our making ἢ πόνων . . . ἐμέ an independent question.

782. On the change to τούτοιν see Wecklein *Studien* p. 46. Heimsoeth *Krit. Stud.* 247 ἀτιμάσῃς μ' ἔτους.

794 f. Hermann Φορκυνίδες for αἱ Φορκίδες, and 797 οὔτε νύκτερος. — Wieseler κυκνόφορκοι (following Hesych. φορκόν· λευκόν, πολιόν, ῥυσόν, and Eur. *Bacch.* 1302 πολιόχρως κύκνος) or κυκνοκόρυφοι, κυκνόκορσοι.

801. Elmsley τοιοῦτον ἐν σοι, Blomfield τοιόνδε μέν σοι: but see Wecklein *Curae Epigr.* p. 30. — Paley's conjecture φροίμιον (for φρούριον) is valueless.

803. Dindorf ἀκλαγγεῖς.

806 ff. Wieseler Πλουτωνόστοπον. — Elmsley γῆς. Bergk (who treats, in *Jahrb. für Philol.* 81, 409 of the παντοτρόφος λίμνη) Κελαινῶν, Wieseler κελαινόφυλον.

817. Dindorf ἐπανδίπλαζε. Cp. C. Fr. Müller *de pedibus solutis*, p. 15.

822. Hermann thinks ἣν πρὶν ἡτούμεσθα possible, and Koechly (p. 403) commends this reading.

829. Porson γάπεδα, perhaps rightly. Cp. Dindorf *Lex. Aesch. s.v.* γάπεδον. Meineke λάπεδα.

832. Nauck, *Krit. Bemerk.* 1885, proposes ἄπιστον, θεοφατηγόροι.

835. Turnebus ἔσεσθ' εἰ. Dindorf 'hic versus aut delendus est aut ex duobus versibus defectis conflatus.' That only μέλλουσ' ἔσεσθαι is to be struck out as a gloss, was seen by Hartung (ἢ δὴ μάκαιρ' εἰ), Heimsoeth *Wiederh.* p. 177 (κλύουσαν εἴ τι), Weil (εἰ τὴν τάλαιναν). For the thought, see commentary.

838. Weil assumes a gap after this verse. But the required idea, 'donec ad hanc orbis extremam rupem venires,' lies in the present χειμάζει.

839. Probably μέλλονθ' ὁ πόντιος μυχός should be written.

848 ff. Madvig (*Adv. Crit.* p. 192) τίθησ' ἐγκύμονα. Dindorf, with Elmsley, throws out 849, thinking it to have replaced a lost verse. Hermann believes a verse to be lost after 849, such as ταύσας τε μόχθων τῶνδε φιτύει γόνον (after *Suppl.* 312). Heimsoeth *Wiederherst.* p. 459 takes καὶ θιγὼν μόνον as a gloss, and writes ἐπαφῶν τ' ἀταρβεῖ χειρὶ φιτύει γόνον. Wieseler writes γόνημ' ἐφῶν for γεννημάτων; Heimsoeth φιτυμάτων. All are needless changes. (In *Suppl.* 576 βίῳ should be written for βίᾳ.)

858. The Med., with most mss., θηρεύσοντες. Weil defends this, remarking that θηρᾶν and θηρεύειν often mean *seize* in Aeschylus. Dindorf θηρεύοντες, after some mss. The poet would have written θηράσοντες, had he not preferred the present (*Cho.* 493 Dindorf has emended to δ' ἡρέθης). Cp. *Sept.* 406 μαντεύεται by first hand, μαντεύσεται by second.

859 f. σωμάτων must refer to the maidens, not to the youths. Nauck, *Krit. Bemerk.* 1885, requires φθονῶν δὲ σωμάτων εἴρξει θεός. Hermann assumes a lacuna between δέξεται and θηλυκτόνῳ. Others read δαμέντα (so a minor ms.) or δαμέντας. The fault seems to lie in δέξεται: Hartung κλέγξεται, Schoemann (*Philol.* XVII. 228) δ' ἐνέξεται ... ἄγει δαμέντων, W. Hoffmann (*Jahrb. für Phil.* 85, 589) δεύεται ... Ἄρει δαμάρτων. The transition from δ' αἱμάξεται to δὲ δέξεται was probably due to the lack of the usual caesura. According to Merkel's reproduction, the Med. has δί, δέξεται, i.e. δ'. δέξεται.

870. Hermann, with Schütz, δὲ for δεῖ. The scholia which Hermann adduces as confirmation belong to 875.

872. As several of the other mss. waver in the position of ἐκ τῶνδε (τῶνδ' ἐκ πόνων ἐμέ, ἐκ πόνων τῶνδ μέ, ἐκ πόνων τῶν ἐμέ, πόνων τῶν ἐμέ), it is likely that the Med. reading κλεινοῖς is a conflation of κλεινὸς and Ἴνις (i.e. ινος and ινις), and ἐκ τῶνδε a later supplement. So τόξοισι κλεινὸς Ἴνις ὃς πόνων ἐμέ would be the original. Cp. *Philol.* XXXI. p. 727.

874 f. Hermann, from cod. Guelf., Τιτανὶς θεῶν, Heimsoeth Τιτανὶς θεός. — Some mss. have χρόνου for λόγου (cp. *Pers.* 713).

884. For the interpretation, see W. *Studien* p. 8.

894. Weil μήποτέ τοί μ', keeping ἦν in 887.

898. Hermann, rejecting Doederlein's explanation (on Soph. *O. C.* 563), "virginitas mortalium conubium detrectans," interprets "virginitas non amans alicuius mariti i. e. expers conubii."

901 ff. Elmsley and Hermann make strophe and antistrophe. Hermann ἐμοὶ δέ γ' ὅτε (ὅτε for ὅτι Pauw) μὲν ὁμαλὸς ὁ γάμος, ἄφοβος, οὐδὲ δέδια. Schoemann rightly pronounces οὐ δέδια a gloss upon ἄφοβος, and conjectures ἐμοὶ δὲ τίμιος ὁμαλὸς γάμος. Dindorf ἐμοὶ δ' ἔτι μὲν ὁμαλὸς ἄγαμος ὁ βίος ἐν πατρὸς δόμοις, Weil ἐμοὶ δ' εἴη μὲν ὁμαλὸς ὁ γάμος ἄφοβος, εὔδιος. It is better to change δοτιμενομαλὸς of the Med. to δὲ τιδμενος ὁμαλὸς. — In the next verse, Musgrave and Blomfield omit θεῶν, Schütz and Dindorf omit ἔρως (κρεισσόνων ἐμοῦ θεῶν ἄφυκτον). — Dindorf ἀπολέμιστος and γενοίμαν· Διός. — Weil, with Meineke (*Philol.* XIX. 232, revoked *ibid.* 704), writes τί ἂν γενοίμαν. The hiatus τί ἄν occurs only in comedy, though Aeschylus has τί οὖν.

907 f. Against the reading of other mss., αὐθάδη φρονῶν and τοῖον, Hermann rightly holds to the Medicean text.

917. Porson τινάσσων χειρὶ πυρπνόον βέλος, Weil τινάσσων πυρπνόον χειροῖν βέλος. See commentary.

923. Blomfield βροντᾶς, Weil ὑπερφέροντα.

926. L. Schmidt τῶνδε πρὸς κακῶν.

937. Rutherford, *Class. Review* II. p. 261, σὺ μὲν προσεύχου.

941. Nauck (*Bulletin de l'Acad. de St. Pétersb.* 1863 p. 35) τὸν Διὸς λάτριν.

946. For πορόντα, we should perhaps write προδόντα (38).

948. As the Med. has πρὸς . . . τ' (with ὂν written above by another hand), Dindorf's conjecture, πρὸς οὗ τ' (see 906) seems apposite. Hermann understands πρὸς ὂν τ' of the other mss. in the same sense. But on this theory the tense of ἐκτίνει remains unexplained. Hence Elmsley is right in requiring πρὸς ὂν, without τί. See on 248. — For ἐκτίνει the editor formerly conjectured ἐκτίνοι.

965. Med. καθόρισας, with ι altered to ο by the same hand. Hermann κατούρισας, which is not suitable here. The ending -οσας might rather suggest to us καθήρμοσας, and this καθήρμασας, especially as καθηρμόσθαι and καθηρμάσθαι are elsewhere confused. For καθήρμασας, *hast planted* (or *fixed*), cp. Hesych. ἁρμάζει· στηρίζει, and ἥρμασεν· ὠχύρωσεν, *Ag.* 1005 ἔταισεν ἄφαντον ἕρμα.

968–970. In the mss. continued to Prometheus. Erfurdt gave the right assignment. Dindorf keeps the ms. arrangement, but thinks 970 spurious, with Kiehl. Ribbeck throws out 908–970. Flach (*Jahrb. für Philol.* 129, p. 830) conjectures τοὺς ὑπηρέτας χρεών. The right view is Keck's (*Jahrb. für Philol.* 81, 840), who assumes a gap before 970.

974. Valckenaer (on Eur. *Phoen.* 632) adopts from a minor ms. συμφοραῖς (cp. Soph. *O. T.* 645, Thuc. vi. 28). The dative Hermann explains "propter casus tuos," and Weil defends it by *Cho.* 81.

980. For ΠΡ. ὤμοι, ΕΡΜ. τόδε Ζεύς, Lachmann (*de Chor. Syst.* p. 124), Meineke and R. Schneider have put ΠΡ. ὤμοι, ΕΡΜ. ὤμοι; τόδε Ζεύς, because an ἀντιλαβή occurs nowhere else in Aeschylus. This is right, except that ὤμοι, τόδε should be written. Cp. Wecklein *Studien* p. 46. The traditional interpretation of τόδε Ζεὺς τοῦτος οὐκ ἐπίσταται (Bothe: 'Iovem id vocabulum nosse atque uti eo negat, ut qui nunquam doleat, sed perpetua fruatur felicitate') does not suit the context.

986. Hermann ὅστε ταὖδά με (cp. Heimsoeth *Indir. Ueberl.* p. 15).

1001. Cp. Valckenaer on Eur. *Hipp.* 305, Elmsley on Soph. *O. T.* 445, M. Haupt, *l. c.* p. 6.

1009 f. In obedience to a hint of Kvičala, the ms. reading βιάζει is here restored, instead of the editor's former conjecture λιάζει (cp. Hesych. λιαζόμενοι· σκιρτῶντες). Heimsoeth's alteration (*Indir. Ueberl.* p. 35), δάκνων for δακόν (after Schol. A) seems also needless in view of the passage quoted in the commentary, Eur. *Hipp.* 1223. Coenen (see on 100) proposes σφαδάζεις for λιάζει.

1013. Against the commonly adopted conjecture of Stanley, μεῖον, the reading μεῖζον of the mss. is defended by Halm (*Lectt. Aesch.* p. 9). Cp. also Schömann *Mantissa Animad.* (*Opuscul.* III. p. 87). If a change were to be made, μηδενὸς μεῖον or rather μεῖον ἢ μηδέν would be necessary.

1017 f. Nauck πέμφργι βροντῆς ... πατὴρ ἀράξει τήνδε, and 1023 διασπαράξει σώματος.

1021. Reisig δ' ἔτι, Hermann δί σοι.

1022 f. Brunck and Dindorf ἀετός with a lesser ms. Cp. W. *Curae Epigr.* p. 03. — Heimsoeth *Wiederh.* p. 430 σώματος μελάνδρυον, Weil σώματος κύτος μέγα.

1031. Med. εἰριμμένος (ει altered from another letter by first hand). Commonly εἰρημένος is adopted from other mss. Hartung ἐτήτυμος, Wieseler ἐρρωμένος. F. W. Schmidt *Krit. Stud.* I. ἀλλ' ἐκ καρδίας εἰρημένος. Formerly the editor wrote εἰμαρμένος, now ὀρθούμενος (*confirming, maintaining itself*) following Hdt. vii. 103.

1034 f. Heimsoeth *Krit. Stud.* p. 247 φρόντιζε μὴ δυσβουλίαν φρονήσεως ἀμείνον' ἡγήσῃ ποτέ. Weil supposes a gap between ἡγήσῃ and ποτε, thinking ποτέ meaningless. See commentary.

1037 ff. Schütz regards the words ἄνωγε ... πιθοῦ as an interpolation, and Hermann and Bernhardy (*Gr. Lit.* II. 2 p. 271³) are inclined to the same view. See, however, commentary on 196.

1040. That the following anapaestic systems correspond antithetically was remarked by Hermann *Elem. Doct. Metr.* p. 784.

1048 f. Schütz κῦμα δὲ πόντον. It is better, with Weil, to omit τ' after οὐρανίων in the next verse.

1052. Hermann 'praeferenda videtur apud Aeschylum antiquior forma στεραῖς, qua versu quoque 174 usus est.'

1056. For μὴ παραπαίειν of the mss., it seems necessary to write μὴ οὐ παραπαίειν. See the examples in commentary, and 627, 787, where also οὐ was originally omitted in the Med.

1057. Porson εἰ μηδ' ἀτυχῶν τι, Wellauer εἰ τῆδε τύχῃ τί χαλᾷ, Dindorf ἢ τοῦδε τύχη; τί χαλᾷ, Hermann εἰ γ' οὐδ' εὐχῇ τι χαλᾷ, Heimsoeth *Wiederh.* p. 250 εἰ δ' εὖ τὰ τύχῃ, τί χαλᾷ.

1068. Bothe τοὺς γὰρ προδότας.

1081. Hartung believes that two anapaests have fallen out after σεσάλευται; see on 1090. The dipody corresponds to the tetrapody, as *Sept.* 1069, 1075. Cp. Westphal *Griech. Metrik*, 2d edition, p. 177, W. *Studien*, p. 70.

1087. On account of the contracted form and the lengthened middle syllable of ἀντίπνουν, Kiehl (p. 70) proposes πάντων ἀποδεικνύμενα στάσιν ἀντίπνοον. Dindorf would simply throw ἀποδεικνύμενα out, or regard it as a gloss on another word (Weil ἀντίπνοον στασιαζόμενα). Wieseler and Meineke ἀντίπνουν (cp. Hesych. ἀντιόφρων· ἐναντίον φρονῶν, and ἀντιοστατεῖν) or ἀντιόπνουν. See commentary.

1090. To make this system exactly like its corresponding system, Hermann inserts ὦ Θέμις, ὦ Γῆ before ὦ μῆτρός. See on 1081. — Keck *Jahrb. für Philol.* 81, 485 gives a different interpretation; he thinks that Prometheus does not invoke his mother and Aether, but only Aether, "my mother's joy."

ON THE FRAGMENTS OF THE Προμηθεὺς λυόμενος.

II. For χαλκοκέραυνον Hermann conjectures χαλκομάραυγον, Bothe χιλιόκρουνον, Wieseler (*Observ. in Theogon. Hesiod.* p. 10) εἰλικόκρουνόν τε παρ' Ὠκεανοῦ, Weil χαλκοστέροτον (cp. χαλκοῦ στεροπὴν *Il.* xi. 83). But χαλκοκέραυνον is synonymous with χαλκοστέροτον. See commentary. — Lobeck πάντων τροφόν.

VI. Hermann τοῦ τὸ, Heimsoeth (*de interpol. comm. alt.* p. IX) κλῦθι for τοῦτο. See commentary.

VII. ἥξεις for ἥξει Stanley. Meineke ἵξει. — Βροτῶν is Hermann's supplement. — δίκελλ' for δικέλλης Holstein.

IX. ἕρπε τήνδε for ἑρπετὴν δὲ, πνοὰς ἵν' for πνοαῖσιν, ἄφνω for ἄνω Casaubon and Bentley. The further change of βρόμον to στρόμβον seems needful, because βρόμον accords ill with καταιγίζοντα and with ἀναρπάσῃ ... πέμφιγι συστρέψας. — The four verses εὐθεῖαν ... ἄφνω Paley would insert above, after 791, writing περῶσαν in 792. But the following words ἔστ' ἂν ἐξίκῃ make against this. See on 711. — The two verses ἐξευλαβοῦ ... ἀτμοὶ Nauck, with Conington, ascribes to the satyr play Προμηθεύς.

X. 6. Meineke σε for σ' ὁ, Cobet σ' οἰκτερεῖ πατήρ. — 7. ὑπερσχὼν for ὑποσχὼν Casaubon. — 8. σὺ βαλὼν for συμβαλὼν Salmasius. — 9. διώσεις Leopardus, διώσει Dobree, for δρώσει.

ADVERTISEMENTS

COLLEGE SERIES OF GREEK AUTHORS.

EDITED BY

PROFESSOR JOHN WILLIAMS WHITE AND

PROFESSOR THOMAS D. SEYMOUR.

THIS series will include the works either entire or selected of all the Greek authors suitable to be read in American colleges. The volumes contain uniformly an Introduction, Text, Notes, Rhythmical Schemes where necessary, an Appendix including a brief bibliography and critical notes, and a full Index. In accordance with the prevailing desire of teachers, the notes are placed below the text, but to accommodate all, and, in particular, to provide for examinations, the text is printed and bound separately, and sold at the nominal price of forty cents. In form the volumes are a square 12mo. Large Porson type, and clear diacritical marks emphasize distinctions and minimize the strain upon the student's eyes. As the names of the editors are a sufficient guaranty of their work, and as the volumes thus far issued have been received with uniform favor, the Publishers have thought it unnecessary to publish recommendations.

Texts are supplied free to professors for classes using the text and note editions. See also the Announcements.

The Clouds of Aristophanes.

Edited on the basis of Kock's edition. By M. W. HUMPHREYS, Professor in University of Virginia. Square 12mo. 252 pages. Cloth: Mailing Price, $1.50; for introduction, $1.40.
TEXT EDITION. 88 pages. Paper. Mailing price, 45 cents; for introduction, 40 cents.

SINCE the place of Aristophanes in American Colleges is not definitely fixed, the Commentary is adapted to a tolerably wide range of preparation.

The Bacchantes of Euripides.

Edited on the basis of Wecklein's edition. By I. T. BECKWITH, Professor in Trinity College. Square 12mo. 146 pages. Cloth: Mailing Price, $1.35; for introduction, $1.25.
TEXT EDITION. 64 pages. Paper. Mailing price, 45 cents; for introduction, 40 cents.

THE Introduction and Notes aim, first of all, to help the student understand the purport of the drama as a whole, and the place each part occupies in the development of the poet's plan; and in the second place, while explaining the difficulties, to encourage in the learner a habit of broader study.

Introduction to the Language and Verse of Homer.

By THOMAS D. SEYMOUR, Hillhouse Professor of Greek in Yale College. Square 12mo. 104 pages. Cloth: Mailing price, 80 cents; Introduction, 75 cents.

THIS is a practical book of reference designed primarily to accompany the forthcoming edition of Homer in the College Series of Greek Authors, but equally well adapted to any other edition. It clears away many of the student's difficulties by explaining dialectic forms, metrical peculiarities, and difficult points in Homeric style and syntax, with carefully chosen examples.

The Table of Contents occupies one page; the Index ten pages.

Homer's Iliad, Books I.-III. and Books IV.-VI.

Both edited on the basis of the Ameis-Hentze edition, by THOMAS D. SEYMOUR, Hillhouse Professor of Greek in Yale College. Square 12mo. Books I.-III. 235 pages. Cloth: Mailing price, $1.50; for introduction, $1.40.
Books IV.-VI. 213 pages. Cloth: Mailing price, $1.50; for introduction, $1.40.
TEXT EDITION of each. 66 pages. Paper. Mailing price, 45 cents; for introduction, 40 cents.

THE editor has made many additions to the German edition in order to adapt the work more perfectly to the use of American classes. But he has endeavored to aid the teacher in doing scholarly work with his classes, not to usurp the teacher's functions. References have been made to the editor's Homeric Language and Verse for the explanation of Epic forms. Illustrations have been drawn freely from the Old Testament, from Vergil, and from Milton. A critical Appendix and an Index are added.

The second of these volumes contains the only full commentary published in this country on Books IV.-VI.

Homer's Odyssey, Books I.–IV.

Edited on the basis of the Ameis-Hentze edition. By B. PERRIN, Professor of Greek in Yale College. Square 12mo. 229 pages. Cloth. Mailing Price, $1.50; introduction, $1.40.
TEXT EDITION. 75 pages. Paper. Mailing price, 45 cents; for introduction, 40 cents.

Homer's Odyssey, Books V.–VIII.

Edited, with Introduction and Notes, by B. PERRIN, Professor of Greek in Yale University. Square 12mo. Cloth. iv + 136 pages. Mailing price, $1.50, for introduction, $1.40.
TEXT EDITION. 62 pages. Paper. Mailing price, 45 cents; for introduction, 40 cents.

THE German edition has been freely changed to adapt it to the needs of American college classes, but record is made in the appendix of all important deviations from the opinions of the German editors. References are rather liberally given to the leading American grammars, and also to Monro's *Homeric Grammar.* Much attention has been paid to the indication or citation of iterati, conventional phrases, and metrical formulæ. The latest accepted views in Homeric Archæology are presented. The Appendix gives not only strictly critical data, but also material which should enable a student with limited apparatus to understand the historical and literary status of controverted views.

The Apology and Crito of Plato.

Edited on the basis of Cron's edition. By LOUIS DYER, Acting Professor of Greek, Cornell University. Square 12mo. iv + 204 pages. Cloth. Mailing price, $1.50; introduction, $1.40.
TEXT EDITION. 50 pages. Paper. Mailing price, 45 cents; for introduction, 40 cents.

THIS edition gives a sketch of the history of Greek philosophy before Socrates, a Life of Plato and of Socrates, a summarized account of Plato's works, and a presentation of the Athenian law bearing upon the trial of Socrates. Its claims to the attention of teachers rest, first, upon the importance of Schanz's latest critical work, which is here for the first time made accessible — so far as the *Apology* and *Crito* are concerned — to English readers, and second, upon the fulness of its citations from Plato's other works, and from contemporary Greek prose and poetry.

The Protagoras of Plato.

Edited on the basis of Sauppe's edition, with additions. By Professor
J. A. TOWLE, formerly Professor of Greek in Iowa College, Grinnell,
Iowa. Square 12mo. 179 pages. Cloth. Mailing price, $1.35; for intro-
duction, $1.25.
TEXT EDITION. 69 pages. Paper. By mail, 45 cents; for intro-
duction, 40 cents.

THE *Protagoras* is perhaps the liveliest of the dialogues of Plato.
In few dialogues is the dramatic form so skilfully maintained
without being overborne by the philosophical development. By the
changing scenes, the variety in the treatment of the theme, and the
repeated participation of the bystanders, the representation of a
scene from real life is vivaciously sustained.

Noticeable, too, is the number of vividly elaborated characters:
Socrates, ever genial, ready for a contest, and toying with his oppo-
nents. Protagoras, disdainful toward the other sophists, conde-
scending toward Socrates. Prodicus, surcharged with synonymic
wisdom. Hippias, pretentious and imposing. The impetuous
Alcibiades and the tranquil Critias.

Herr Geheim-Rath Sauppe was the Nestor of German philolo-
gists, and his Introduction and Commentary have been accepted
as models by scholars.

The Antigone of Sophocles.

Edited on the basis of Wolff's edition. By MARTIN L. D'OOGE, Ph.D.,
Professor of Greek in the University of Michigan. Square 12mo. 196
pages. Cloth. Mailing price, $1.50; for introduction, $1.40.
TEXT EDITION. 59 pages. Paper. Mailing price, 45 cents; for introduction, 40 cents.

THE Commentary has been adapted to the needs of that large
number of students who begin their study of Greek tragedy
with this play. The Appendix furnishes sufficient material for an
intelligent appreciation of the most important problems in the text-
ual criticism of the play. The rejected readings of Wolff are placed
just under the text.

Thucydides, Book I.

Edited on the basis of Classen's edition. By the late CHARLES D.
MORRIS, M.A. (Oxon.), formerly Professor in the Johns Hopkins University. Square 12mo. 349 pages. Cloth. Mailing price, $1.75; for
introduction, $1.65.
TEXT EDITION. 91 pages. Paper. Mailing price, 45 cents; for introduction, 40 cents.